JK COOPER

Awakening

Copyright © 2017 Kristen Cooper
Cover design by Deranged Doctor Design
Interior design: Mikey Brooks (mikeybrooks.com)

All rights reserved.

Summary: Nightmares are doomed to repeat themselves. Shelby Brooks learned she is a werewolf on the same night she learned that love and betrayal go hand in hand. She was sixteen. Now, going into her senior year in a new town, love is the last thing Shelby is looking for, but she finds herself irresistibly drawn to Kale, the son of an Alpha. As her heart slowly reopens to the possibility of happiness, threats mount and her very presence brings mortal danger to Kale and his entire pack. Is her destiny to be a savior? Or a harbinger of death, as the Summer Omega prophecies foretell? Shelby Brooks must reach deep within and discover what lies there, something she fears to unleash.

Paperback Edition

ISBN: 0-9996797-0-8
ISBN-13: 978-0-9996797-0-8

DEDICATION

This book is dedicated to C. Scott Gill and Elizabeth Gill. Mom,
your love for reading and stories was contagious and I caught it. Bad.
Dad, you made love the most important thing in life
and inspired me and others daily.
I miss you.

THE SUMMER OMEGA SERIES
AWAKENING

PROLOGUE

Mareus, Alpha Prime of the Advent, sent his orders through the mental link to his werewolf pack as they scoured the Hoia Baciu forest in Romania. He sniffed a pile of moss-covered rocks with his long snout then moved on. Already, the pale gray of the pre-dawn morning brightened. The sun would crest the horizon within the hour, and his pack would have to retreat. The world could not know of his movement. Not yet.

We must find it. He allowed these thoughts to be perceived by the pack. *A great reward lies in store for the one who brings me the Isluxua.*

The ancient tome had to be here. Mareus had tracked the legends of it to this forest over the centuries. Unlike other Lycans, he had actually seen the *Isluxua*, handled it. That had been long ago in a place he could barely remember. Just the echoes of memory remained, really. Viersin, his Immortal Wolf, had been dribbling those memories back to him since his awakening. Viersin had slept for centuries.

The cool mist of the morning condensed upon the twisted trees and blackened stumps. It had always been a mystery of this forest, the unexplained erratic growth of the vegetation and randomly charred trees. The Hoia Baciu was considered the most haunted forest in the world, even a gateway to another dimension by some. Mareus smiled, or would have if his wolf form allowed for it. He wondered what the frequent visitors to this forest from across the world would say once they encountered his pack.

They were thousands now, he having united dozens of packs across Europe. Never had his kind seen such a uniting. *The Advent is rising.* Few Alphas had acquiesced to his claim as the Alpha Prime destined to bring about the Advent, but he supposed he would have been disappointed by such weak-spirited leadership. Each Lycan harbored the remnant of an Immortal Wolf from the realms of Alsvoira within them, no matter how miniscule. To simply abdicate rule of a pack to another . . . yes, that would have disappointed him, even if they understood who he really was. Still, the deaths of so many strong werewolves bothered him.

All will be needed as I bring the Advent upon this world, Mareus thought.

But first, he needed the *Isluxua* to discover—no, rediscover—the secrets of the Immortal Wolves of Alsvoira. Even he was not strong enough to see the Advent to fruition without its secrets.

I had known them once . . . the secrets of Alsvoira. But his journey here had changed him, stripped most of his memories. *The price of survival,* he mused. But survival was not enough. He must *rule*.

Athena, his daughter, glanced at him in her wolf, roughly a stone's cast from him, backdropped by a vine covered tree that glistened with a thin sheen of humidity. She was beautiful: a coat of white with slanted black markings across her rib cage, golden eyes rimmed by thick black circles, and a sleek body that bespoke her agility. As an Omega, she brought oneness to his pack. Of course, other Omegas had been assimilated into the pack as it grew, absorbing others from across Europe.

The dew is thinning, Father, she said through the pack link. *The sun rises. We must retreat.*

Mareus hid his agitation from the other wolves, but let his emotions run more freely between him and his daughter.

Twenty minutes more, he said, only to her.

Otto, his lieutenant, a former Alpha from a German pack along the French border and one of the few who had abdicated rule to Mareus, approached him. Mareus did not hide his mental disgust from the weaker-willed creature.

We have found something, Otto said. *In a cave. The mouth is hidden by thick growth. We almost missed it.*

And? Mareus asked. He often masked his desperation as impatience.

It is better for you to see for yourself, Alpha Prime. Otto looked to Athena, and Mareus felt Otto's attraction to his daughter through the pack link. *Both of you.*

Very well, Mareus said.

Behind a curtain of foliage, the cave floor fell away quickly, turning to a steep slope. Beneath his paws, Mareus felt the rough, almost sharp, rocky terrain. His eyes adjusted quickly to the fading light, and he spotted several pairs of glowing amber eyes from other wolves ahead of him.

What is it? Mareus asked.

The wolves parted and let him through. There, between two unnaturally smooth rocks, sat something that appeared to be a glass rectangle, crusted over with time's patina and the forest's detritus. Flashlight beams lit the scene with their sudden harsh light as more of his pack, having switched to their human forms, entered the cave. Their lights focused on the object, revealing the shape to indeed be a rectangle with rounded edges. Insects scurried away from the light.

The object cast reflections of tiny dull rainbows from the flashlight beams, and Mareus could barely see through the translucent glass. A dark object, something that had the shape of a book, came into focus.

Mareus smiled internally. The *Isluxua*. It had to be. After all these centuries, he had found it. He felt Viersin's excitement and relief. Instinctively, he sniffed the book, but only caught the mineral-scent of whatever crusted over the glass capsule.

Otto shifted to his human form, naked. "I will break it open, my Alpha."

Mareus growled. *No,* he said through the pack link, knowing Otto could still hear his thoughts even if the lieutenant could not transmit his own in human form. *The air could damage the book. Retrieve it with its shell. We will proceed cautiously.*

Mareus turned to his daughter. *With these secrets, Athena, you will help us achieve Ascension. I will forge you into that which has been prophesied by our Mystics for ages. The Summer Omega. Then, we will bring about the Advent and Earth will fall to its knees.*

I want to see the world bleed first, Father, for what it has done to you, Athena said.

It will, Mareus answered. *It will bleed like the Five Rivers of Alsvoira.*

Shelby Brooks caught a scent in night air. *Them.* It had to be. She had smelled that acrid sweet scent only once before but could never forget it. Of course, her sense of smell had become superhuman last year after that new, terrifying, part of her had awoken. Her Converse Chucks made no sound on the freshly paved street as she came to a sudden stop.

"Dad."

Chills raced up her spine despite her seemingly ever-present hoodie, rooting themselves between her shoulder blades and at the nape of her neck. She and her dad had taken to walking at night in their new town just outside Odessa, Texas. It had only been a few weeks since they arrived, not-so-patiently yet apprehensively waiting to find some sign of those they sought.

She hissed her words. "Dad, wait. Don't move."

"Shel?" her dad asked, turning back to her. He hadn't shaved today, and his stubble mixed with the soft light of the moon seemed to sharpen his hard facial features. "You okay?"

"Something's following us."

Grant, her dad, looked behind them and then to the too-perfectly manicured shrubs on either side of the street. Shovels and gardening equipment lay at their base, the landscaping crews from earlier obviously not concerned with theft in this new development. Partially finished homes, tractors, and piles of plywood and conduit sat on every corner, abandoned until morning when construction would resume. A few streetlights lined the newly paved roads, but power had not yet been routed to them.

His hand moved slightly closer to his hip. "Are you sure?" he asked. "I can't—"

A breeze carried confirmation to her. She wrinkled her nose at the unmistakable Lycan scent, something like salty citrus.

"Yes."

Shelby's long hair, veins of sandy blonde mixed with a brown base, tickled her back and neck, the skin more sensitive suddenly. A threat hung in the air, a different feeling than she had sensed with Lucas almost a year before. She had not heeded the warnings then.

She didn't hide or try to escape what had happened. Not really. The Night of Scars had seemed magical at first, but had quickly turned to one of terrifying revelations. She had discovered that love and betrayal went hand in hand that night . . . and that she was a werewolf. In only minutes, her world had changed so abruptly. So violently. But she did not fully remember that night with Lucas, other than she had hurt him. Scarred him for life. But hadn't he deserved it? After what he had tried to do to her?

She needed a pack. Though she was still new to this werewolf thing a year later, that much she knew. Her dad had told her of the danger of not finding a pack after she had manifested. Lycans without a pack lost their humanity and identity, shifting to wolf form and one day never being able to shift back, becoming one of the Feral. Perhaps searching for other Lycans was foolish, but it was a promise—an oath—her father had made to her mother. Shelby knew her dad could not shirk a mission, especially one given him by his dead wife. The Special Operations Forces Delta training still ran deep within him, an ethos which would see him succeed or die trying. For her dad, Shelby knew, death was the only excuse for failure.

Grant scanned their environment, but Shelby stood still. Frozen. Anxiety started to burn in her eyes and she fought the urge building within her. He glanced at his daughter, the question on his face. Shelby nodded. She was sure.

She saw the tension in her dad's countenance increase. He became focused, preparing for a fight if needed. She prayed it wouldn't be. His hand checked the pistol at his hip, concealed by his shirt, and then the blade sheathed horizontally on the belt at his back. Extra magazines for the pistol waited in each of his pockets.

"They're close," Shelby whispered.

She pulled her hood over her head, holding the draw stings but not pulling them tight. She spotted a small copse of trees surrounded by shrubs just ahead, to their left. As if knowing her thoughts, her dad said, "It won't matter."

She realized he was right. "If I can smell them—"

"They can smell us," her dad finished. "Can you tell how many?"

Shelby shook her head. "Maybe a few. Not more than half a dozen."

"If you meant that to be comforting, it wasn't."

The chills between her shoulder blades strengthened, and she thought maybe the gooseflesh would become permanent. Grant turned around, facing the direction they had walked from —where *they* were—and took a couple steps past Shelby. She spun as well, staying slightly behind her dad and to his right. Even in the dim moonlight, his rigid muscles showed through his Under Armor t-shirt as a breeze whipped it tight against his body. Despite the breeze's warmth, Shelby shivered.

"We mean you no harm," he said. Not a shout but a full voice nonetheless. "We have sought you out for help."

Shelby took his arm in hers, still just a bit behind him, peering down the vacant street beneath the soft rim of her hood. Though she would probably be more a protection for him, she felt shielded and safer behind him. There was that part of her, even at seventeen, that believed her dad was immortal.

A single figure appeared in the street. She tensed. He took slow, deliberate steps toward them. The man stood at average height, several inches shorter than Grant. Was he wearing a trench coat? It looked like something from a different age, Colonial almost. Buttons that ran from the chin-high collar of the coat to below the waist caught the moon's dull glint. As he strode forward, Shelby's apprehension stoked hotter.

"Dad," she said, tugging on his arm. "This doesn't feel right."

She released his arm as he raised his hands. The man stopped about ten feet from them. His brow bone jutted forward severely, enough to hide his eyes in deep shadow, save for the flecks of amber that almost glowed in the night.

"We have been sent here to seek you out. My daughter," Grant motioned to Shelby, "she—"

The man raised a hand in a dramatic fashion—almost if he were conducting an orchestra—and pointed at Grant with his index finger and letting his other fingers dangle freely. "You . . . you are not one of us." The tone bespoke a warning.

Shelby grabbed her dad's arm again and tugged.

"My daughter is one of you," Grant said.

"You do not remember me," the man said. "But I . . . I remember you. I remember the havoc you brought upon us."

He knows my dad? Shelby wondered. *The havoc?*

Grant did not answer.

"You are her father?" the man asked, raising his chin.

"I am," Grant said. "Moriahna sent us to you."

The man snorted a growl and looked away. "Moriahna. And, pray tell, where is she? It has been quite some time."

"Dead," Grant said. "Sixteen years ago."

The man smiled. Shelby didn't think that was a good thing.

"So," he said, "the deserter has met with justice and sent her half-spawn crawling home." Shelby felt his judging eyes upon her.

Deserter? Shelby thought. She felt her lip sneer slightly at the insult to her mother.

"She followed her heart," Grant said. "I make no apology for her, nor would she want me to. She left your pack with the blessing of Tobias and the promise of welcome at any time. I have the letter with his seal, unbroken."

Grant slowly took out a folded envelope from his left, rear pocket, the rounded corners frayed and paper crinkled with time. A red blot of dried wax sealed the envelope, a signet of a small crest with a crescent moon and a comet.

The man they faced spat. "Tobias has since departed from our ranks. Well, to be truthful, he has simply *departed*."

Grant took a step back, finally obeying Shelby's insistent tug on his arm, and returned the letter to his pocket. His hand found the hilt of the knife at his back and held firm.

"I only wish to find a home for my daughter," he said. Pain laced his words. "The home I . . . cannot provide. She never knew about her mother, but Moriahna made me swear to find her a pack if she shifted. I thought the time had passed, but she shifted last year. Her time is running short. She needs a pack."

The man snorted, quite dramatically, Shelby decided. "You should divert your eyes from me, little one," he said pointedly to Shelby.

She felt the urge to obey, something within responding to his direct words. *He's an Alpha,* she thought, the first time she had ever met one. Yes, there was power in his words, as her dad told her she would feel. But she did not obey. Would not. Why should she? He was not *her* Alpha, for her wolf had not chosen him. That she felt most powerfully.

The man, as if sensing her defiance, stepped forward, shoulders hunched aggressively. Grant and Shelby took another step back. A howl broke through the silence of the night, and Shelby started breathing heavily.

"Please," Grant said, "my wife only wanted—"

"Do you remember, *Grant,* when she chose you instead of me?"

Her dad went completely still. Shelby could almost feel him searching his mind, plowing through memories nearly two decades old.

"Nicholas?" he asked, squinting.

"Tobias was weak," the man—Nicholas—said. "Too careless with our secret. To forgive you, *Grant,* for what you brought upon this pack, to let one of our own outside the pack and mother a half-spawn with *you,* knowing what *you* were . . ."

What he was? Shelby glanced at her dad. *Does he mean a regular human that mom supposedly chose over him?* But no, somehow Shelby didn't think so. She felt the accusation in Nicholas's words run deeper than that.

Nicholas waved a finger back and forth, as if speaking to a child, and made a clicking noise with his tongue. The wind tugged at the hem of his long coat and she heard the golden buttons rustle against each other. "Tobias should have killed you, not forgiven you. I could not tolerate such weakness, nor could our pack. I have rectified that weakness. There are rules, human. I admit you are quite skilled at evading our kind. We had given up trying to track you. Thankfully, you have come here so that we might exact penance for your actions."

They searched for my dad? Because of my mom? Her dad's stories over the past year about Lycans and her mother having been one suddenly felt very abridged.

Grant drew the knife from its sheath at his back. The six inch blade was heavy and thick, meant for only one type of work.

"Run," Grant whispered to Shelby.

Another howl, this one much closer.

"Who's Nicholas?" Shelby whispered. "What's happening?"

"Go, Shel."

"Daddy?"

"I promise, we'll see to her care," Nicholas said. "Moriahna's daughter will pay the penance owed."

"I do not think so," Grant said.

His words carried no bravado or threatening tones, but rather the calm confidence of a father, a warrior, standing between his child and darkness.

Nicholas shrugged off his coat—definitely something from another age—eyeing Grant with a cold stare as he carefully laid it on the pavement. A loose white tunic remained underneath, something Shelby imagined sailors in the 1700s wearing. Then, he shifted, the remnants of his clothing splitting and falling to the road in tatters and ribbons as his body grew and morphed. In seemingly the blink of an eye, a werewolf, black even in the bluish-white moonlight, bore down on them with menacing amber eyes. A wave of fear nearly paralyzed Shelby.

With the practiced efficiency of a Delta Force Operator, Grant drew his sidearm with his right hand and brought his left, still gripping the knife, under his right for support. He fired. Shelby flinched at the sound of the gunshot.

Nicholas dodged to the side just before the bullet struck, chipping the pavement. The ricochet's twang echoed briefly before dying. Shelby's nose wrinkled as the acidic citrus scent grew stronger. Two more werewolves, one gray and the other tan, emerged between two vacant houses to their left, sprinting straight for Grant and Shelby.

Shift! Shelby screamed in her mind. *Shift!*

With danger flanking her on all sides, she pleaded fervently with her body to do whatever it had done on the Night of Scars, to do what she knew it *could*. To change. *Shift.* Though it terrified her, she needed it now. Desperately.

Grant's gun shot two more times before he was violently

knocked to the street, falling into Shelby and toppling her to the ground as well. She heard the scraping sound of metal skidding against pavement. *The gun,* she realized. It had flown from Grant's hand when he hit. She rolled backward, onto her shoulders, and sprang to her feet, muscles tense with adrenaline. Her eyes started to burn.

Jaws snapped only millimeters from Grant's throat, Nicholas on top of him, vying viciously to tear him open. The muscles of Grant's right arm bulged as he grabbed fur and skin at the werewolf's chest and pushed hard. With his left arm, he swung the knife at the wolf's face, but it recoiled too fast. The strike missed.

Shelby charged Nicholas, eyes stinging but still unable to shift. A rumbling in her chest rose, expanded—*yes*—but not to the point she needed it to. Her feet felt lighter, her speed increased. And then the rage grew large enough to rival the well of fear within her.

Almost.

She was close, Shelby could feel it. The burning in her eyes became unbearable and—

The other two werewolves hit her before she even got close to Nicholas, claws raking across her back and legs, shredding her clothes and flesh. She screamed, and the terror eclipsed the rage, forcing it into a small corner of her mind. Pain radiated through her. Her vision blurred. And then her dad was there, suddenly, almost magically, spinning, punching, thrusting. One of the wolves howled in pain, a howl that quickly turned to a whimper. Grant dropped the knife, now coated with dark crimson, and hurled the wolf into the same copse she had spotted earlier.

From the corner of her eye, Shelby saw Nicholas on his side, but coming back to his feet and shaking his head as if to clear it. Shelby's wounds bled only for a few seconds before beginning to close. The tan wolf clawed at her dad, but he evaded and swiped the dropped knife from the pavement. Jaws barely missed Grant's back but caught his shirt, tearing it free from his body. Shelby's eyes seared as she punched the wolf in its side. It yelped, but the strike was not hard enough to make a real difference. It snapped its fangs at her twice and she flinched. It could have easily bit her but didn't. It turned back to Grant.

They're not trying to kill me, she realized.

"Dad!" Shelby screamed her warning too late. Nicholas sprang, his massive black body sailing unnaturally fast. He landed on Grant's back, forcing her dad to the ground face down. Grant rolled quickly, trying to get from under Nicholas, but long claws found his back. Nicholas tore Grant's skin from his shoulder blade to his ribs, ending at the front of his pelvis. Shelby smelled the salty odor of wet iron, and her heart lurched.

Grant elbowed Nicholas savagely in the snout then stood, his left hand covering the portion of the wound near his stomach. Blood poured down his backside, glistening dark. In his right hand, he held the knife outstretched toward Nicholas. The tan wolf held Shelby at bay, cutting her off every time she tried to run past him.

She hated herself. She couldn't shift, couldn't fight, couldn't protect her dad.

"Please stop!" she cried. "I'll do whatever you want, just leave him alone!"

"You remember what I taught you?" Grant said, his voice pained. "About shooting?"

Shelby dropped her eyes. The gun lay four feet from her. She had almost missed it, its black frame blending with the pavement.

"Aim small, miss small," she said, jaw quivering.

Grant nodded, wobbling a bit. Nicholas barked and took a step toward her father, hackles raised, obviously feeling the end was near for his wounded prey. Shelby saw her dad look into Nicholas's eyes, his gaze turning steely.

"You were never worthy of Moriahna," Grant said. "Nor are you worthy of her daughter."

Nicholas sprang toward Grant, lips pulled back, exposing long fangs. Shelby dove into a forward roll, snatching the gun mid-roll, and stood with it in hand. She felt the tan wolf lunging toward her, felt its hot breath almost upon her neck. With an eerie calmness, she lined up Nicholas's body in the sights and emptied the magazine. Nicholas fell to the street, howling and snarling in pain. She knew in that instant that she had not mortally wounded him, silver rounds or not. The tan wolf collided with her a heartbeat later, and they flew then rolled entangled together across the road.

Swivel, thrust hips, elbow jab to the throat or snout—

But before she could attack, she felt the wolf's weight lift from her back. She rolled and heard her dad bellowing. He'd lifted the wolf, no doubt a couple hundred pounds, over his head, then slammed it down on the street. He raised the wolf, and slammed it again. And again. And again, until the beast fell still with blood running from its ears. In only moments, the wolf became human again. A naked, still form of a young man, not more than twenty. His glassy eyes stared blankly at nothing.

Grant collapsed to the street, heaving for breath. Shelby rushed to him. His torn shirt, barely hanging on him, soaked up blood that freely ran from his wounds. Nicholas, after struggling to find his feet, sprawled on the street, the holes in him smoking from silver bullets.

Nevertheless, the Alpha was regaining his strength. More howls, distant but closing fast, cut the night air. Dull clinks sounded on the road as Nicholas expelled the silver slugs from his body.

"Dad," Shelby said, trying to lift him. "We have to go. More are coming."

With quivering but strong arms, Grant pushed himself up. Shelby's hands slid on his red-slicked back as she tried to help him stand. She handed him the Glock, and he ejected the spent magazine then replaced it with a fresh one. He holstered the gun and sheathed the knife.

"I'm sorry, Shel," he said with a wince. "I should have known."

"No time for that. Move it, Grant!"

Her dad grinned despite the pain. "You would make a good soldier."

The wounds across his back looked like shredded ribbons of red beneath his torn shirt. "I couldn't shift," Shelby said. "I wanted to. I tried. I'm sorry."

"You're not hurt?" he asked, huffing.

"Nothing permanent."

"Then it doesn't matter. Let's get out of here."

Shelby ran, doing her best to hold her father up, but he found his gait after only a few strides. She saw him fight through what must be excruciating pain with each bit of movement, but still he ran, though awkwardly, swifter with each step.

"Did he bite you?" she asked.

Grant didn't answer right away.

What if Nicholas *had* bitten him? Wouldn't it be better if he were a Lycan as well? For both of them? Regardless, the thought turned her stomach, her dad becoming like her. A monster. A creature without a soul. Damned. No, she would not wish her condition on anyone. Not even Lucas.

For him she simply wished death. Even that might be kinder than how she had left him, his face maimed grotesquely from her claws.

Finally, Grant said, "No. Just scratches. I'll heal." He grunted as he brought a hand to his stomach wound.

Just scratches?! Talk about the understatement of the decade.

"We won't outrun them," her dad said.

She knew he was right, but still she ran down the lonely road, almost having to pull him along. They passed a pile of PVC and metal conduit. She spied a pipe as long as her arm, she could wield that. But she shouldn't have to. She should be able to shift and fight!

Grant's pace slowed.

"You have to push through the pain!" she said. "Please, Dad. They're closer. I feel them!"

Grant heaved, leaning over with his hands on his knees. He raised his head, sweat glistening as it ran the creases of his forehead. "I know, Shel." He drew the Glock and started to turn toward the pursuing pack. Nicholas had regained his feet. Though they had fought for every step, she and her dad had only made it maybe a hundred yards.

"No," Shelby said, desperate. "No, *please!*" Hot tears stung her eyes. She wiped them away furiously. "They weren't trying to kill me. They want me. I can trade myself for your life. Let me try."

"They're not getting you, Shel. You don't understand. The things they would do to you . . ." Grant shook his head. "Run, baby girl. Daddy's got this." He knelt with one knee upon the street, raising the gun with a shaky arm.

Something broke inside her, a deep sob that she somehow stifled. Perhaps that caused the pain in her chest that made her want to double over, perhaps it was her heart literally bouncing off her rib cage.

"I can't. I won't"

"You need to, Shel."

Two more wolves came into view, each standing taller than Grant's waist.

"You'll be okay, Shel," her dad whispered. "I know you will." He drew the knife again from the sheath with his left hand, taking the familiar position that Shelby knew as he brought it under his right hand for support, the tip of the blade pointed toward the approaching pack.

"No! I won't!" Shelby cried. "I can't do this without you."

"No time, Shelby. Go!" His voice turned hard, that military edge creeping in.

The pain in her chest peaked and warmth spread through her like a blanket being unraveled. Then came the cold, a bitterness crawling through her bones. Her joints ached. The world shook as Shelby locked her gaze on the wolves that had come so close now. They growled, snarled, like predators just before the inevitable kill. Though her vision shook and morphed like a kaleidoscope on the edges, the wolves remained centered in her sight, sharply focused.

Her eyes stung.

Burned.

Hotter. Deeper. She reached within for that warmth that had turned to coldness, a well of indignant strength brewing. She knew what it was. *I need you.* A scream through gritted teeth erupted from her as her grip on that strength faltered. She steeled herself, refusing to let go with her mind. For reasons she could not explain she *knew* she must hold fast despite the caustic cold that ached in her bones and joints. She screamed again, this time savagely, hearing a second—foreign—voice come from her as well as her own. Even as the blackness crept in from the sides of her seizing vision, she did not relent in holding her eyes—blurring with fury—fixed upon the wolves. Something *left* her, shot from her, the feeling like a tendon snapping but in her brain. Nicholas, in the lead, faltered in his stride, almost imperceptibly.

But Shelby saw it.

She glared more fiercely now, sneering, tasting something new in the back of her throat . . . something awakening within her. Again. The cold in her bones turned utterly bitter and her mind's grasp on that coldness brittle. Her control slipped, and the coldness surged, enveloping her. The last thing she heard before blacking out completely was another shot from her dad's gun followed by brutal snarls.

Two Months Later

"I don't know why you think Lansborough will be any different than Odessa," Shelby mumbled into the crook of her arm as she stared out the passenger window of the old Chevy Blazer. *We're going to end up dead if we keep this up,* she thought, but didn't dare say that out loud, as if saying it would make it true. "What if . . ."

She looked at herself in the side view mirror without really focusing on her reflection. Her cheek, lightly dusted with mocha freckles, rested in the crook of her arm on the windowsill. Tall shadows, cast by telephone poles in the mid-morning sun, flickered across her face as the Blazer sped past them.

"What if . . ." Grant prompted.

Shelby sighed, her stomach tingling. "What if there's just another Nicholas waiting?"

"There was . . . history there, Shel."

"You think?"

"Not all packs will be like that," Grant said. "And watch your tone."

"But some will. Be like that."

"I wish I could tell you that's not the case, but you already know that it is. You've been sheltered from this world, Shel, and not just because you manifested late. I . . . . really thought you wouldn't manifest. Your mother said it would happen in the early stages of puberty or it wouldn't. Thirteen at the latest."

"So this is her fault?"

Her dad grimaced.

"I'm sorry," Shelby said. "I didn't mean that. It's been a very . . . odd year."

"Yeah. I know," her dad said softly. "We just have to find the right pack, the one that will accept me and you, one that will trust me with the secret and not abuse you for your unique standing."

Some lame song about being a champion and "roaring" was on the radio. Shelby pivoted more toward the car door in her seat.

"More like 'freak' standing," Shelby mumbled.

"What?"

"Nothing, dad."

"You always get in this mood when a Christina Perry song is on." Her dad reached for the radio. "Want me to change it?"

Shelby actually cracked a small smile, but she tried to hide it from her dad. "It's *Katy* Perry, and no. It's bad but better than that country noise you listen to."

"You still a music snob?"

Shelby shrugged.

"And you're defending Katy Curry with that snobbery?" Grant asked.

"Would you rather I berate James Taylor instead? Go ahead, change it."

Grant pulled his hand away from the radio. "No ma'am, we'll leave Perry on."

"So, you do know her name."

"You're offended over me making fun of her name now?"

Crap. He had her there. And he had gotten her talking when she was so determined to be grumpy! The nerve of her dad to be . . . well, awesome, made her even madder.

"I still can't remember," Shelby mumbled. She knew her dad knew what she meant. Nicholas and his pack . . . her dad avoided questions of that night.

"I know," he said. "It's better that way."

"Can you promise this time will be different?"

Silence. Then, "I wish I could."

She was used to the apprehension of moving from town to town by now, a seemingly constant companion of late. She pulled her shoulder-length, sun-streaked brunette hair up, and the air felt cool as it touched the nape of her neck. The numbing drone of the highway had morphed into bumpier vibrations as they turned off the exit. Funny, that word. Exit. It was, in fact, an entrance to yet another unknown.

"I can still see your scowl," her dad said. "It doesn't matter if you turn away from me."

"I'm not turned away from you," Shelby said into her arm. "And

I'm not scowling. This is just my face."

"You're scowling."

Shelby sighed.

"Shel, look, I know this isn't easy," her dad started, but she didn't want to hear it anymore.

She fully buried her face in the crook of her arm now. "Why do I even have to try out for the team? We'll just be leaving in a few months."

"I thought you still loved gymnastics," her dad said. "At least it's the summer this time. You'll get to start school with everyone else instead of the middle of the year. Less attention, right? Some sort of normalcy?"

Shelby sat up, knowing the scowl she had denied existing plainly showed upon her face. Knowing that made her scowl deepen even further.

"This is the third time in a year. How many more times are we going to have to do this? Why *this* little one-stoplight town in Mexico?"

"Texas."

"That's what I said. Besides, I thought you got out of the army so we wouldn't have to move like this."

Her dad sat silent for a minute. He had withdrawn from active duty when she was barely a year old, just before her mother died, not that Shelby remembered any of that. But, she wished so much that she did, at least a memory of her mother. Just one.

"I know it's not fair, but this is important for you. We have to find them. I didn't want this, either, but I'll do anything for you."

I don't want to do this anymore. I don't want any of . . . this!"

She jerked her hands open in front of her face, palms toward her, trying to encompass as much of herself in the gesture as possible. Grant gave her that look that said, "We have no choice." He didn't have to say the words. She hated that look, even if he was right. Maybe that was the part she hated most.

"I feel good about this place," he said. She could hear the hopeful optimism in his voice.

"You sound like you bought me a birthday present that you're really not sure I'll like."

"It's your birthday?"

"Grant. You know what I mean."

Her dad rubbed his square chin with a scarred hand. She loved his hands, powerful hands that had saved her. That was something else she hated, that she had needed saving. She should have been able to do the saving against Nicholas. Would she always need him to save her? She had saved herself from Lucas, hadn't she?

No. Don't think of him.

Her dad turned his head and gazed out his window briefly before turning his eyes back to the road.

"I'm not sure this place is different. But it might be."

"How could you possibly know that?" Shelby asked.

Her dad switched his grip on the Blazer's steering wheel. "Just some things your mother left us, I guess."

Shelby perked up. "What things?"

"Clues, hints. Nothing concrete, but trial and error, right?"

"Did you forget where trial and error has gotten us so far?"

Grant breathed out a long exhale as they pulled into the parking lot of the high school. Kids swarmed all around, sifting between parked cars and walking across a large field. For a small town, the high school looked surprisingly large. Tryouts were being held for football, track and field, cheerleading, and gymnastics today. A few broad-shouldered jocks dressed in practice jerseys and pads yelled as they passed by, their helmets held in the air like some victory trophy. Shelby shrank in her seat, trying to disappear into the old fabric.

"It's okay," Grant said. "Nothing is going to happen like before. I promise. Lucas is hundreds of miles from here. He can't hurt you again."

The sound of his name sent both anger and shame racing through her veins, competing for dominance. Why did her dad have to mention him? Even if he was far from here, others might not be, others of her kind. She might fear them more. Finally, she nodded and bit her lower lip, surpassing her emotions. "Okay."

"I'll be back in a couple hours after I get things settled with the landlord. Good luck, Shel. I know you'll do great."

The Blazer's door creaked as she opened it and stepped out into the humid Texas air and slung her Nike gym bag over her shoulder.

The heat radiated off the parking lot pavement in waves. Texas heat in all its glory. Some girls passed Shelby, laughing and talking, saying absolutely nothing just like most teenage girls. Shelby hadn't realized how trivial her everyday life had been before Lucas. The girls had mascara plastered on so thick, Shelby didn't know how it wasn't melting into black rivers in this heat. She hadn't needed much makeup, or so her dad always told her. Maybe if her mom had survived cancer, maybe if she had sisters, maybe then she would have been more . . . girly.

The old hoodie she took everywhere suddenly felt like a sweltering sauna. She liked the loose fit. It let her hide, disappear. But this heat! She dropped her gym bag then took off the hoodie and tied it around her waist.

As she picked up her gym bag and took a step, a flash of something came over her, seeming to press down upon her chest in surges. The pressure did not burden her, she realized, but it made her insides flutter with a comforting warmth, not the kind that came from mortal embarrassment. What was this? *Am I having a hot flash?* Seventeen was a little early for menopause. Wait, were the female life cycles the same for werewolves? Apprehension stirred at the edges of sensation, but its hot center grew. A feeling of falling hit Shelby, then something caught her, a forgotten soothing oasis in her soul. A home that memory had long since stricken from recall but could not erase the very etchings of its existence. Wait, when did she start thinking in this way? She had pretty much failed creative writing. She clutched her heart, not because of pain; no, the tender warmth . . . it wrapped around her, all encompassing, failing language arts not withstanding.

The world seemed to tumble with her, and she nearly tripped as she walked, probably looking like an invalid. Awesome. There was the mortal embarrassment. Thanks universe. But no one around her seemed to notice. She did not like crowds, even ones that seemed oblivious to her. The sudden rush of warm pressure left as quickly as it had risen. In its wake, Shelby's mind felt empty and the world seemed quiet, unnaturally sucked free of any noise, like the grand auditorium as the final echoes of the symphony's finale fade to nothing. *Stop it!* she chided herself. What had come over her? She didn't recognize her own thoughts. Slowly, the ambient sounds of her surroundings came back to her.

"Okay . . ." She huffed and collected herself. Hormones were so weird. That had to explain it.

The gymnasium was to her right, across a field that must have been used for soccer. Goals sat at either end. Today, it was devoid of screaming teenagers dressed in bright colors, high socks, and shin guards. Other students strutted across the open field in every direction. More jocks in football jerseys passed by, surrounded by three gawking cheerleaders. The football players pretended not to notice but didn't discourage the hungry stares. Shelby rolled her eyes and started walking toward the gym.

Inside, she found the locker room and changed into her leotard. A few other girls changed as well, but she kept her head down. She felt their stares, obviously knowing she was new, but she didn't feel very social and changed in silence.

Why did every locker room have to be painted in drab colors? The beige-bordering-on-pink paint was so thick it felt almost like a rubber coating. The benches had the typical scratched and chipped appearance but had been lacquered over instead of repaired. Somehow, she knew a fine collection of already-been-chewed gum was plastered on the underside. And, of course, there were the so-typical white cinderblock walls. Sheesh, did every school district use the same contractor?

"Who's she?" one of the girls finally asked with perfect pouty lips and a tone of entitlement. Her blonde hair curled up at her shoulders and bounced a little as she spoke. Sharp cheek bones looked even sharper with the amount of makeup plastered on her face. She casually pointed at Shelby but looked at the other two with her. They shrugged.

What? Like I'm not here or something?

Pouty Lips looked at her and finally addressed her directly, "Who are you?"

Shelby adjusted her shoulder straps and sighed. She knew these kinds of girls, the kind that believed they were worthy of worship and that everyone else wanted to be them. *Here we go.*

"I'm Shelby."

"And, like, why are you here?" Pouty Lips asked with raised eyebrows, looking her up and down.

"Well," Shelby said with a slight smirk, "I thought I'd try out for the football team, but after I dodged every tackle and jumped the defensive line doing a double front twist for a touchdown, they sent me to cheerleading. But, sadly, they were all out of pom-poms, so I got sent here. This is the esthetician class, right? But I honestly had higher hopes now that I see the end result."

Pouty Lips and her two cohorts stood with open mouths, the inevitable high-pitched gasps following.

"Did she just say that to you, Chelsea?" the girl to Pouty Lips's right asked.

"Mmm hmm, I think she did," the one to Chelsea's left said.

Pouty Lips, Chelsea, morphed her open mouth to a wicked smile. "Don't worry ladies, those white chicken legs won't get her far."

The two cohorts snickered. Raising her chin so that she looked her nose at Shelby, Chelsea asked, "What's your event?"

Shelby shrugged. "Uneven bars, floor, vault . . . whatever."

"All around, huh?" Chelsea looked left then right to her minions. "You know what they say about all-arounders, right girls?" Her friends snickered again.

"They really get all around," the one to Chelsea's left said, and they all laughed with that annoying condescending air.

"So, you're just one-trick ponies," Shelby said. "Should have known. Shallow and one-dimensional."

The laughing stopped.

"Listen, *Shelby*," Chelsea said with a warning in her tone, "you won't get anywhere here without us. I'm the captain of the gymnastics team, and Coach Anders and I decide who gets on this team."

"Huh," Shelby said, disinterested.

She shoved her gym bag the locker and shut the metal door. The dull clang sounded louder than she had expected.

"A little jumpy, are we?" Chelsea teased. "Come on girls, greatness is awaiting some of us."

As Shelby watched the threesome walk out, the false front of bravery she had held fell, and she realized how mad she was at her dad for making her tryout.

Normalcy, she thought. *As if there is anything like that anymore.*

K ale Copeland, quarterback for the Lansborough High School football team, leaned over his center defensive lineman, placing his hands just below Bubba's legs. No one would get past Bubba. The black man had to be twice the size of any defensive lineman. The sun beat down on the football field, and Kale was glad they were practicing on real grass instead of turf. The fake stuff could easily add 10-15° to the field. Besides, he loved the smell of fresh cut grass.

Two receivers left, one right. Kale scanned the defense, watching their eyes, trying to ignore the sweat-soaked padding in his helmet. This would be a play-action pass play. Behind him, the running back stood, ready for the fake handoff.

"Six-eight-six pump! F stop on two!" he yelled out. "On two! Hut hut!"

Bubba hiked the ball into Kale's hands. The defense plowed into his offensive line. Kale turned, faked the handoff to the running back, then froze mid-stride. A surge of frantic emotion crashed down upon him, and his environment seemed to morph. He smelled the air change, from the scent of evaporating dew to ashes and smoke. Within him, anticipation pulsed. Anxiety. Danger had come to his people again. *Wait, what people?* The feeling was not related to his pack; but even if it were, would he intuit such danger instead of his father? Kale was not the Alpha. Not yet. No, this feeling related to others that he thought he should know but didn't. He needed to find *her*. Protect her.

Who?

A silhouetted shape formed in the haze of his mind. Feminine. *Her.* His heart leaped. He knew her, didn't he? He *should* know her, the feeling whispered to him. He squinted. *Why can't I remember you?* Yes, this was a memory he was seeing: the smoke, the smell of ashes. The danger. Her.

As the haze grew around her, taking her from him, his eyes burned, and he felt that presence within him—his wolf—rage against her disappearance. His body began to change. *No, not here!* But it wouldn't subside. In the past, he'd always been able to control his shifting, but something was pushing it out from him. His shoulders bulged against his pads and his practice jersey went tight on his chest. This was going to be bad. *What in the—*

A lumbering body crashed into him, breaking Kale's stupor. Anton. He recognized that bad breath as Anton bellowed a victorious cry. The football went sailing from Kale's hand, along with the air from his lungs. As big as Kale was, getting hit by a 210 lb. defensive tackle at full force was never fun. The facemask of his helmet dug in the grass, and that pleasant smell became overpowering as mud and grass flew into his face.

"Fumble!" someone yelled.

Anton sprang up and chased after the loose ball. A whistle blew.

"Are you serious, Copeland?" Coach Hank screamed. "You just stop in the middle of a play? Did you find a nice flower for that girl who follows you around?"

"No, Coach!" Kale grunted and found his feet. "Bubba let Anton by him. Couldn't make the throw."

"Coach, he's on drugs!" Bubba said. "Ain't nobody get past me. Hallucinating."

"You saw me put your boy down, though, right?" Anton said to Bubba, jogging back to the defensive line.

"He ain't my boy, playing like that," Bubba said.

"All right, ladies, line it up and run it again!" Coach called. "Copeland, if I see that kind of lollygagging again, you'll sit the bench the first game. Get your head screwed on right."

What had that been? Was he sick? He shook his head, worked his shoulder, and touched his ribs. Tender. Normally, he might have been sore, but he knew his body would heal unnaturally fast.

"Alright, Coach," he said. "My bad."

"Fo' sho', your bad," Bubba said. "Blamin' me. Wait 'till I tell Momma."

"Shut up and open your legs."

Bubba rolled his eyes and bent over the ball again. Kale came up behind him, hands ready for the ball.

Who was she? he wondered as his mind spun. *The girl in the haze. Was it actually smoke?* He had smelled smoke . . .

"Delay of game!" Coach Hank roared. "Copeland, take a break."

Kale took his helmet off, ran a hand through his hair, and jogged toward the sideline. He accepted a Gatorade bottle from Coach as the second string QB headed onto the field.

"What in tarnation is going on with you?" Coach stammered.

Kale ran a hand through his hair again and looked down at his Nike cleats. "Not sure, Coach. Just some . . . girl."

"Girl?" Coach Hank got in Kale's face. He saw his own reflection in Coach's aviator sunglasses. "You brought thoughts of a girl onto my football field?"

"I, uh—"

"Look, Copeland, I don't care how many sweet little things you have flopping themselves in front of you, stroking that ego of yours."

"Coach, I really don't think—"

"The only thing I expect you to be *think*ing about while on my field is the current play and executing. You got that, Copeland?"

"Yeah."

"What was that?"

"Yes, Coach!"

Coach Hank tore the sunglasses from his face and used them to point, bringing his grizzly grill an inch from Kale's face, his cheek bulging with that bolus of sunflower seeds he always chewed on. "Perhaps you'd like to join the cheerleading squad."

Kale followed Hank's point. Cheerleaders were shouting some incomprehensible cry with blue and white pom-poms. "Sorry, Coach. I'm good."

Coach Hank smiled. "I thought so. Ya know, I heard Coach Anders makes his gymnast girls do push-ups with a smile when they disappoint him. I kinda like the idea. But with pom-poms."

Coach waved a cheerleader over. "I'm going to need to borrow these for a moment, darling," he said to the brunette. "Captain Copeland here needs them to do some push-ups. You don't mind?"

The cheerleader shrugged and handed them over. Coach Hank shoved the pom-poms into Kale's chest. "Now, Copeland, if you please, with a smile."

Kale sighed and dropped down, plastic shimmering pom-poms in his grip.

"With every push-up, I expect you to lift an arm, wave that pom-pom with gusto, and repeat," Coach Hank said. "Fifty should do it." To the cheerleader, he said, "Why don't you girls help him count?"

As Kale pumped out the embarrassment, his mind again turned to what he had felt and seen, and the other side within him—the werewolf side—stirred with apprehension and longing.

"Shelby Brooks!" Coach Anders called. "Vault!"

Shelby arose from the bleachers. She had sat alone, away from the other girls. Most were already on the team, and this was nothing more than a formality for them. The few not on the team seemed to already be "in," either sisters or friends with the other team members. The only one who seemed to have to prove anything was her.

She came to the edge of the long, narrow mat with the vault 82 feet away at the other end. The run up area was just more than a yard wide, slightly elevated from the floor by diamond shaped foam tiles. She raised herself onto the balls of her feet a couple times, feeling the tiles. They were spongier than she was used to.

She glanced at Coach Anders. He held a clipboard in his left hand, the bottom of it against his waist, and a pen in his other hand. Fit physique, kind face. Then Chelsea came up to him and whispered something. He raised his pen to the clipboard, making a note. Chelsea looked smugly at Shelby, the expression of false sympathy across her face.

A growl came from Shelby; nothing audible, just internal—a strength that welled inside her, a strength that seemed to come when she felt threatened. The first time that had happened, unintended consequences came, things she couldn't explain, things she prayed would never come again.

With the strength came agility, however. If she could control it . . .

Coach Anders gave her a nod, encouraging her to proceed. Chelsea still stood beside him, one hand on a very sassy hip.

Fine.

Rising up on the balls of her feet once more, Shelby launched forward, sprinting. The inner growl grew louder in her mind, and her vision singled out the vault, everything else blurring out of focus. Something within her peaked, and her eyes burned, just for a second. With the instincts of a natural gymnast, along with another, more primal, instinct, she pounced on the springboard. It groaned in protest as she launched off it and she hit the vault with a velocity that should have sent her tumbling to the ground with a broken wrist.

Her world spun as she pushed off the vault, propelling herself high. Too high. She closed her eyes and *let both* instincts take over. Legs straight, toes pointed. Rotating the torso with arms crossed over the chest. Curl into a tuck, thrust head weight forward. One rotation, then two. She closed her eyes as she went into the third front-flip.

It was one too many.

She hit the ground. The top of her back struck the mat and sounded like a jet breaking the sound barrier. Its echo lasted for several seconds. Shelby lay still, slowly opening her eyes. Above her, Coach Anders was saying something, but his words were muddled.

"Shelby! Can you hear me? Are you okay?"

"What?" she moaned.

Other figures appeared in her vision standing over her, girls in leotards.

"Don't try to get up," Anders said. He handed his cell phone to one of the girls. "Call an ambulance."

"What? No," Shelby said and started to stand up. "I'm fine."

Anders put a hand on her shoulder to hold her down. "No, you're hurt. You could make it worse."

Shelby's eyes wandered. When they found their focus, she clearly saw Chelsea and her two cohorts staring at her with amazed and . . . envious looks? Then, Chelsea's expression turned conniving.

"Clearly, you can't let her on the team, Coach Anders," Chelsea said. "She can't be trusted and will just, like, hurt herself. And the team."

Anders gave the team captain a withering look. Other murmurs found Shelby's ears.

"Did you see that? How high she got?"

"Crazy, just crazy high."

"Uh, coach?" one girl called out. "Take a look at the springboard."

"Not now, Sadie," Anders said.

"No, really, Coach. It's some crazy bull feces."

Anders sighed. "Just stay here. Please, don't try to move."

He got up and walked around to the other side of the vault where the girl had called to him. Several others left to investigate as well.

"Great," came Chelsea's shrill voice. "She's dangerous *and* fat."

Oh screw this! Shelby kipped up. A few vertebrae did pop as her back arched, but when she landed on her feet, all was right.

Anders knelt beside the springboard. A crack split it down the middle. One of the metal springs underneath was broken. Coach Anders looked shocked, then concerned, then somewhat relieved once he saw her on her feet. He stood up.

"You're okay? I know teenagers think they're indestructible and all. Nothing wrong with taking it easy."

"Yeah, I'm fine," Shelby said, staring at Chelsea. Shelby felt her eyes start to burn again, the way they had when she had run at the vault. Chelsea took a step back. Shelby smelled something in the air, and the growl within her started to return. Fear. She smelled Chelsea's fear. Well, it was more startlement, not quite fear, but still a welcome reaction.

"Call me fat again, powder puff, and we're going to have a serious problem."

"Whatever," Chelsea said dismissively. "You can't be on the team."

"Oh yes she sure as bat feculence can!" another girl said, the one who had discovered the springboard. Her dark red hair was pulled back into a tight bun, accenting ears that stuck out just a little farther than normal. It was a cute quality.

Did the redhead just say . . . "bat feculence?"

"She just tried to do too much," the redhead said, "but even what she did was twice what you've *ever* done on the vault! And, isn't that your main event?"

The scene quickly devolved into a shouting match with increasingly higher pitched voices.

"Ladies!" came the only male voice in the gym. "Ladies, please!"

The argument died down as Coach Anders regained control.

"I think this is enough for today," he said. "Hit the showers." To the redhead, he said, "Swearing Sadie, let Shelby know the practice schedule. You'll be working with her."

"You mean she's on the cussing team?" Sadie asked with a triumphant grin aimed at Chelsea.

"Well," Anders said, "we need to work on her control, obviously." Shelby put her head down, slightly embarrassed. "But," he continued, "that height off the vault we can use."

"But the springboard—" Chelsea started, but Anders cut her off.

"From what I've seen, she doesn't actually need one."

"Yay!" the redhead, "Swearing Sadie," apparently, said as she did a series of quick claps and took Shelby by the arm. "Come on! I'll show you around this dung hole after we shower and change."

"Um, okay . . ." Shelby said. Sadie's enthusiasm made her smile.

As Shelby finished getting changed back into her jeans and Pink Floyd *Dark Side of the Moon* t-shirt, Sadie asked, "So, what year are you?"

"Senior," Shelby said, tying her hoodie around her waist. "You?"

"Junior. But, wow, new school for your senior year? That's gotta suck the big one."

Shelby shrugged. "Just a bit, I guess. Had two different schools for my junior year."

"Whoa. What the copulation? Work or something? What do your parents do? Wait, they're drug runners, right? Are you on the run from the cops? You guys are all like Breaking Bad, right? Is your dad's name Walter?" Sadie winked at her, as if to say, it's okay, you can tell me!

"Uh, no, but that would be exciting at least. Just stuff, I guess. My mom actually died when I was really young, and my dad used to be in the military. Did some superhero stuff or something, but that ended when my mom died."

Sadie stared wide-eyed and sad. "Oh, fecal matter. I'm sorry. I didn't mean to—"

"It's okay. I barely even remember her. Just flashes here and there. Hey, can I ask you something?"

Sadie shrugged. "Only if it'll make me blush."

"I don't think I know you well enough to made you blush."

"Don't be shy."

Yep, redhead all the way. Feisty and bold. "So, what's up with all the 'bat feculence' and 'dung hole' talk?"

Sadie chuckled. "Oh. That. Well, see, I cussed out my ten-year old brother one too many times. He tattled. I got busted. My dad said the words and combos I used would make sailors take notes. Had to promise not to swear any more. Sooo now I'm just very literal. They can't complain about that, right? My vocab really went through the roof. You know how copulating hard it is to come up with literal substitutions?"

"Um, copulating?" Shelby asked.

"Technical term for the act of having sex," Sadie said.

"What does that have to do with—" Shelby stopped. Oh. "So, you're literally Swearing Sadie."

"Endearing, right? Funny thing is, I didn't get that nickname until *after* I stopped swearing."

Shelby pulled her Converse All Stars on and started tying her laces.

"You're blushing, springboard slayer," Sadie said. "So, how'd your mom die?" Then, before Shelby could answer, Sadie covered her mouth. "Condemn it, I'm sorry, I'm not very good at these things. My mom says I have no cussing filter."

Shelby pursed her lips and half shrugged with one shoulder. "Cancer. And it's okay. Like I said, it was a long time ago."

"What does your dad do now?"

"That's a tough one."

"What, you don't know? Cussing really?" Sadie asked with a scrunched up brow.

Shelby realized she might have already said too much and tried to stall while she thought of something, tying already-tied shoelaces. Sadie must have seen it on her face.

"Sorry," Sadie said. "Filter. But maybe he still does superhero stuff, and you don't know it!" Sadie raised her eyebrows several times. "Right? I bet your dad's hot."

"I, uh . . ."

Sadie laughed. "You're turning as red as my hair!"

Shelby laughed as well. It felt good. "I really couldn't say if my dad's hot."

"You wouldn't know hot if it burned a hole in your thick, empty skull," a new voice said.

Chelsea, with her perfect pouty lips, and her two followers rounded the corner of the aisle, arms folded.

"Here comes the daily dose of solid waste from the anal crevice," Sadie whispered to Shelby. "Well, if it isn't the whorey trinity. Tell me, do you practice your snobbery and little diminutive stares? On average, how many hours per day? It's for research so, please, be honest."

Chelsea glared at Sadie.

"Exactly!" Sadie said. "That one, for example, did you stand in front of a mirror until you got it right? Were Amanda and Trish there to assist?"

"My boyfriend is the hottest guy in the school!" Chelsea retorted, nearly squealing.

Oh. Now Shelby understood. Chelsea was one of those girls that validated her standing by whom she dated. How awesome. And shallow.

"Our epic kiss is on YouTube and has over 19,000 views!," Chelsea said. "Who hasn't even gone on a date in over a year?" She raised her eyebrows at Sadie.

"You've hung out with Kale a couple times," Sadie said. "That doesn't exactly make him your boyfriend. Neither does hiding a camera by your front door and tricking him into kissing you."

"Well," Amanda chimed in, the girl seemingly glued to Chelsea's left, "rumor has it that Kale is going to ask Chelsea to homecoming. They're sure to win king and queen. They're so perfect together."

Shelby looked at Sadie. "Does she always caw like that?"

"Kinda hurts the ears, doesn't it?" Sadie answered. "Sort of like those condemned Styrofoam peanuts in a box."

"Ooooh, yeah, hate that noise. Wonder what else she posts on YouTube," Shelby said conspiratorially.

"We're gonna put you both in a box six feet under!" Chelsea said.

"Together or separate?" Sadie asked. "I'm scared of being alone."

Chelsea batted her eyelashes and raised her eyebrows, narrowing her annoyingly perfectly proportioned forehead. "How about in pieces?"

"Can you at least withhold the Styrofoam?" Shelby asked.

"Listen, sister," Chelsea said, "you're new so I'll cut you some slack. It's still the summer, but when school starts, you'll want to be careful about what side you choose. Swearing Sadie," she pointed to Sadie, "is not a side you want to be on."

"So, you're accepting applications for new minions, then?" Sadie asked.

Three high-pitched gasps sounded out, one right after the other.

Chelsea leaned closer to Sadie. "You're small, oh, so small to me, and everyone that matters."

Trish and Amanda nodded in unison, like brainwashed disciples, and the threesome walked away, exiting the locker room.

Shelby giggled. "Daily dose of solid waste from the anal crevice? Really?"

"Yeah, it's the technical description of sh—"

"I know," Shelby said. "It's kinda even more offensive."

Sadie smiled a knowing smile.

"Why not just swear when your parents aren't around?" Shelby asked.

"I *promised* them. I'm all noble like that. Besides, I'd just slip up at home if I'm not consistent all the time."

"So, who's this Kale guy? Some mindless baboon?"

"Captain of the football team, of course," Sadie said.

"You're kidding. Could it be any more cliché?"

"Yeah, actually. Chelsea could be a cheerleader."

Shelby made gagging noises, and they both laughed.

"It gets better," Sadie said. "Chelsea *used* to be a cheerleader and found out Kale had sworn off dating cheerleaders. So, she quit and joined the gymnastics team her sophomore year, just when I got here as a copulating freshman."

Copulating freshman? Oh, right. Technical term. "Huh, so she's had her eye on this Kale guy for some time."

"She follows him around like a lost puppy."

"He doesn't like her?"

Sadie shrugged.

"But," Shelby said, "it sounded like they've gone out before."

"If you ask me," Sadie whispered, "it was more a pity thing from Kale. Otherwise, why hasn't he asked her to be his girlfriend?"

"But . . . Chelsea said she was."

"That's her version of the story. She's full of dung."

"Not feculence?"

"I try to avoid alliteration in my swearing."

"Well, maybe Kale isn't a mindless baboon after all."

"He's a sucker for lost puppies," Sadie said. "But a cussing hot one, at least."

Shelby cocked her head to the side. "Oh?"

Sadie said, "Yeah, if you like that tight chest, broad shoulder, huge biceps-that-you-just-want-to-bite kind of look. I bet he'd give your dad a run for his money."

"Uh . . . right." Shelby laughed, genuinely feeling a smattering of happiness. "Hey, thanks, by the way."

"What the Underworld for?"

"You know, sticking up for me or whatever."

"Anything to stick it to the whorey trinity."

Shelby grinned. Sadie closed her locker and went to the door. As she opened it, a shaft of bright sunlight invaded the dull room. Shelby squinted.

"Holy coitus, that's bright! See you around?" Sadie asked.

"Yeah, for sure, Swearing Sadie."

Sadie smirked and took a step out, then stopped. She looked over her shoulder. The sun made her hair glow like strands of wispy fire as she stood in the threshold. "By the way, I know what you are."

Shelby shot to her feet, a feeling of falling within her stomach. Before she could say anything, the door closed, banishing the sun. The locker room regained its dullness.

Sadie was gone.

S helby stood in the locker room, stunned, for what felt like an hour. Maybe just a few seconds.

By the way, I know what you are.

She couldn't mean that. It's not what you think.

Shelby burst out of the same door Sadie had disappeared through, her gym bag slung over her shoulder. The bright afternoon sun hurt her eyes, and she raised an arm over her brow. The sounds of chatter filled her ears, and a few people bumped into her as they filed past, boys that were large enough to certainly be called men even if their minds weren't quite there. They laughed and carried on as if she were invisible.

Shelby doubted she would ever be the same around men again. The effects of one year ago—of Lucas—still consumed her at times. Any boy larger than her—most her age—sent apprehension through her.

She shrank back against the wall, frantically reaching for the door handle to get back into the locker room, back to safety. No use. It had locked behind her as she exited.

Of course, she thought, the anxiety building within her.

Slumping down to her haunches, the stucco wall scraped her back through her shirt. She pulled her knees tight against her chest, praying she could just disappear.

But the threat—was it really a threat?—passed her by in a couple of seconds.

This is stupid! one side of her brain yelled at her.

She knew that side was right. It was stupid.

"Okay," she said into her folded arms. Even to her ears, her voice sounded tender, hurt, almost like a whine. That did not help her self-esteem.

She breathed in deeply and held it for a second. After letting it go, she tried again. "Okay."

Better.

"Stand up."

Her legs felt like Jell-O and didn't respond. That's when the anger surfaced. She wasn't this timid, not this shy. This person she became around perceived threats—false threats—was definitely not her. Her dad had taught her to fight, to be mentally tough.

But she wasn't. Not in these moments. Her eyes began to burn again, like they had when she focused on the vault, like they had a year ago with Lucas.

"Stand up!" she hissed through gritted teeth, finding the strength and suppressing the anxiety. An accidental jump, that was what happened next. She meant to only come to her feet, but the soles of her Converse Chucks left the grass for an instant.

"Well that was . . . energetic."

Shelby turned toward the smooth tenor voice, a little startled, and saw a boy standing next to her. He stood a few inches taller than her with dusty brown hair that, backlit from the sun, had a slight halo of a golden shine around it. Khaki shorts ended before well-defined calves, supported by white ankle socks and a new pair of Asics running shoes.

"I'm Sean," he said, holding out his hand. "You're new, right?"

"I, uh, think so." Now she sounded like a baboon.

Sean gave her a half-smile and cocked his head a little to the right.

"Yeah, I'm new. Sorry, just trying to figure out where to go."

"What's your name?"

Shelby noticed his hand still waited expectantly. "Oh, sorry. I'm Shelby. Shelby Brooks." She took his hand—a little rough but warm—and then quickly released it, hoping she didn't appear curt. She wasn't "alone" with this guy—other students constantly passed by—but it still made her a little anxious to interact with him one-on-one. Yet, there was something disarming about him; not completely, but enough that she didn't run away like a frightened girl from a big purple dinosaur on TV with a pervert's name that was always trying to hug people. Oh, the nightmares she used to have from "kid" shows.

Different kinds of nightmares plagued her now.

She overheard some students comparing schedules, groaning over their classes or what teachers they got.

Crap, I guess I need to find out my schedule eventually. Tomorrow, she told herself. This was enough for today.

"Junior?" Sean asked.

Whoever said ignoring an annoying guy would make him go away was full of it.

"Senior," Shelby said.

"Ah, well don't be too embarrassed talking to me. I'm only a junior."

Maybe he wasn't annoying the more she looked at him. Her apprehension stayed at bay . . . mostly.

"Gymnastics tryouts?" Sean asked.

"Yeah. You?"

"Me? No, not a gymnast. Track and field."

"Right, the shoes. Makes sense." That gave her another excuse to look down and see his legs. Wait, was she actually checking him out? For real? She hadn't done that in a while.

"From what I just saw, looks like you could do great at hurdles," Sean said with a gleam in his eyes. He was cute-ish, Shelby supposed. "That was quite a leap. Any interest in trying out? They're holding late tryouts tomorrow."

"I sort of just made the gymnastics team. Or, I think I did. Listen, I need to get to the parking lot. My dad will be here soon to get me."

"I can give you a lift if you want. Where do you live?"

Shelby started walking toward the parking lot. "No, thanks, though. Grant is probably already here and waiting."

Sean walked beside her, keeping up. "Grant? I thought you said your dad—"

"Grant is my dad."

"You call him by his first name?"

"Only when he isn't listening to me or I'm mad at him."

"Or when you're trying to scare a guy off?"

Oops.

There was an awkward silence.

"So, the parking lot?" Sean asked.

"Yep," Shelby said, a slight annoyance escaping into her answer. "Look, Sean, it was great to meet you and all but—"

"The parent-student parking lot is the other way." Sean pointed over his shoulder with his thumb. He had a "silly-new-girl" look on his face. He was cute, actually, she decided, if slightly annoying. Forgivable.

"Oh."

"You were headed to the teacher parking lot."

"I'm not used to a school being big enough for two parking lots, I guess."

She turned around and started heading the opposite way. So did Sean.

"It's okay," Sean said. "The high school isn't that big, actually. It's just the way it was built, I guess. Gotta keep the know-it-all parents away from the high-and-mighty teachers, ya know? Where are you from?"

What was it with all the questions today? Was a new student that rare or did she just scream "charity case"?

"East a bit."

"Like, East Coast?"

"Sort of."

Sean frowned playfully and bobbed his head. "Okay, playing mysterious. That's cool, I guess. What brings you to Lamesborough, Texas?"

"Lamesborough?"

Sean harrumphed. "Local slang for Lansborough. You'll catch on."

"Anything else I should know?"

"Oh, I don't know. Everyone knows everything, and everything about everyone. Small town, ya know?"

"What's up with this Chelsea chick?"

"Chelsea Gittrik?"

"I guess."

Sean harrumphed again. "What was it like meeting Her Highness?"

"And her two lap dogs? It was quite the welcome."

"Yeah . . . sorry about that, Sean said, running a hand through his hair. It barely hung low enough to touch his perfectly bushy eyebrows. "See, Chelsea's dad is the mayor of Lansborough, and she thinks that makes her above everyone, as if she were actually the mayor. She rubs just about everyone wrong, especially if she sees you as competition."

"Competition?"

"I heard you did some crazy acrobatics during tryouts and nearly had Coach Anders ask you to marry him."

"What?" She stopped walking. A maintenance worker in an orange shirt with some kind of logo was adjusting a sprinkler head about ten feet away.

"News travels fast. Small town, remember? Everyone and everything. Don't worry, I suspect what she told me came out of jealousy."

Shelby remembered Chelsea's envious stare. "You seem to understand her," she said a little heatedly. Was that a hint of your own jealousy, Shelby? Seriously? She tightened the hoodie's sleeves around her waist.

"Yeah, unfortunately." He smiled, showcasing perfectly straight teeth. Shelby caught a whiff of his cologne in the breeze, and it made her think of cool ocean spray.

"Wait, why was she talking to you? You're not her boyfriend, are you?" *Crap, that's all I need, more reasons for her to hate me.* But, no, Chelsea said her boyfriend's name was Kale, right?

"Uh, no," Sean said. "That would be just so wrong. Hey listen, a few of us are going to hang out tomorrow night. Wanna come with?"

Panic started pulling on her fringes, clawing its way in. "I'm not sure."

"Don't worry, Her Highness won't be there. I don't hang out with my sister."

"Chelsea is your sister?"

"I didn't mention that?" Sean said with a teasing smile.

"Nope. Funny, that."

"I wanted you to give me a fair shot."

They walked for a few moments in silence. Shelby kicked a rock across the grass.

"Soccer now, huh?"

"Your dad's really the mayor?" Shelby asked, ignoring his small jeer.

"Uh huh. Don't hold it against me."

"I don't think I know local politics well enough to hold it against you."

"No one does, it seems," Sean said. "He's won uncontested the last three races."

"Why wouldn't anyone else run?"

Sean shrugged, kicking the same rock she had. "People grumble but don't care enough, I guess. The last contested race was more of a family feud with each side having their dirty laundry aired out in equal fashion. Small town."

"Right, everyone and everything."

They arrived at the parking lot where a few guys in leather jackets surrounded an old Trans Am, some kind of 80's hair metal screaming from the car's speakers. Shelby saw the old familiar Blazer pulling in.

"So, can I call you about tomorrow?" Sean asked. He wasn't nervous at all. That confidence was either endearing or alarming.

"I don't have a phone yet," Shelby said. "Still getting settled."

Sean held up his hands. "Hey, no problem. You don't want to give me your number. It's cool."

"No, Sean, it's not that."

"I'm just teasing you. If you want to come just meet here at eight tomorrow night. It'll be fun."

"How many people? What are you going to do?"

"Just a few friends, guys and girls. As far as what we'll do, probably just go down to the corner of Main and State and watch the stoplight change."

"I, uh . . ."

Sean clapped and laughed a little too loudly. "We're not that small-town, Shelby. You really believed me."

"Did not."

"Yes, you did!"

She did.

"Okay, just kidding with you," Sean said. "We'll probably just hang out, talk, get some ice cream or something. It'll be a cool way for you to meet a few people that aren't the whorey trinity."

Shelby blushed, and the Blazer's horn honked.

"That's not the first time I've heard that term today," Shelby said. "You call your own sister that?"

"No worse than she calls me," Sean said. "Who do you think started that little nickname?" Sean winked. "We're the perfect Lansborough family." This last bit he said with a false smile and mock gusto.

"Your dad?" she asked.

"It was almost his campaign slogan. So, you gonna come?"

"I don't know. Maybe. Thanks for the invite."

"You better go before *Grant* honks again. Eight o'clock tomorrow, right here. See ya then."

Sean turned and jogged off, presumably to his own car. Shelby tried and failed not to notice those calves that bunched up into solid rocks as he ran. Maybe she would go.

Maybe.

As she walked to the Blazer, dodging other students and weaving between parked cars, something changed. A feeling wafted over her, something that made her weak in the knees. The same from before? What's wrong with me today? It was different than her normal anxiety around boys, much different. A calmness seemed to reach out to her, coaxed her into its arms. An Oasis, she again thought. A strange desire welled up inside her, and her lower lip quivered. She felt vulnerable, and yet, safe.

But the feeling wasn't just safety. It was more, so much more. The seeds of longing sprouted within it, a longing of such hopeless intensity that she suddenly felt as if her whole life she had been lost and was now abruptly, permanently, found. Home.

Maybe it scared her because of the warmth that spread through her, all the way to her fingertips and toes, or because of the depth of serenity that threatened to wipe away that deeply rooted anxiety of life. Whatever it was, she knew only this for sure: it scared her.

What scared her just as much was the alien poet that seemingly invaded her brain during these episodes. Not cool.

She threw open the Blazer's door, nearly hurdling into the passenger seat.

Her dad turned to her with a smile. "Hey, Shel. How did—"

"Go, please. Just go."

By the way, I know what you are.

"Dad." She didn't know how to start.

We might have a problem? Some random girl told me she knows what I am? Oh, and by the way, I had a halfway normal conversation with a guy. Alone. Sort of alone.

"What's up, Shelby?"

She could hear the concern is his voice. She could always talk to him. Maybe not about her hair or what celebrity just got dumped, but about real stuff.

"Shel?" he pressed.

"You know how when you're on your period and—"

"Nope," her dad said. "Nope, silence is okay after all."

Shelby smiled.

"Oh," her dad said. "I get it. Your way of telling me to butt out."

"Gymnastics was good," she said. "Sorry, just a weird first day. I slayed the springboard."

Grant's face contorted. "Slayed? You mean 'slew'?"

"Yep, springs and all. You'd have been proud."

Grant raised his eyebrows. "Do tell."

K ale Copeland walked toward the locker room from the football field, streaks of sweat and grass stains alike covering his practice jersey. He held his helmet under his right arm.

"Hey, man, you know my momma said you can come back, right?" Bubba came up hustling to Kale's side. His friend had loosened the laces of his football pads and they jostled freely atop Bubba's girth. "She's making more fried chicken tonight and figuring since the only person who spent more time with their hands on my rump besides her is you, she said to invite you back. Course she was usually beatin' my little butt with her hands."

Kale snickered. "Your butt isn't little, Bubba. I'm surprised the football makes it passed your butt into my hands. You know I almost lose it half the time?"

"Man, shut up," Bubba said, shoving Kale.

"And I'm not going to help your momma spank you, either."

"Man, she ain't tried that in a long time. I'm too quick now."

For a large, very large, young man, Bubba was indeed quick. "I'll give you that," Kale said. "But you're missing those blocks, bro. Anton is spinning right by you."

"You fast, too, Kale. You need help scramblin' is all. Just trying to help you out."

"Uh-huh. Why did your mom invite me back? Aren't you tough enough to feed?"

"She gives me my own pan of chicken, you both split the second. Fair is fair."

The phone in Kale's bag beeped.

"So?" Bubba asked. "Am I telling my momma you comin' or what? Or you too busy with your pom-pom push-ups?"

Kale took out his phone and swiped the screen with his thumb. "I just got a text from my dad. Apparently we're having a new family over for dinner tonight."

"Who's that?"

"No clue."

"Man, don't be breakin' my momma's heart, now. I know she's not a big-wig-money-thug or nothin', and we don't have the fancy place on the hill like you guys, but she still has her pride."

Kale smiled, and he kicked a tall patch of weeds. "All right, I'll come. I think I can show up late for this dinner party."

"Your people do think it's cool to be fashionably late, right?"

"My people?"

"I ain't stutter."

"You're my people, Bubba."

"Darn straight, son, and don't you forget it."

"I might if Anton keeps getting by you in practice."

"Pshhh please, boy. That fool, I gotta help his ego is all."

Kale raised his eyebrows. "How about helping your quarterback?"

"Like I said, you can handle it," Bubba said with a loud slap on Kale's shoulder pads. "As long as you stop daydreaming in the middle of plays."

"Hi, Kale!"

The new voice drew out his name playfully. Both boys looked to the left and saw Chelsea waving and looking like something out of a magazine, flanked by Amanda and Trish. As Chelsea bobbed toward Kale, her bombshell-blonde hair bounced perfectly on her slender shoulders and a syrupy smile plastered her heavily made-up face. Her long eyelashes were so thick with mascara, they could slay mosquitos when she blinked. And blink she did as she approached, long and slow.

I wonder if she uses shoe polish as mascara, Kale mused to himself.

"Now, don't spoil your dinner by having dessert first," Bubba said, eyeing the trio. "Triple delight. Mmm-mmm."

"Shut up," Kale said.

"Better get all the lovin' you can before them scouts take you to some fancy college. How many scholarship offers you got now?" Bubba laughed his raucous guffaw that sounded like welcoming thunder. "Normally I'd say going off to college with a girlfriend already at your hip is like bringing a sack lunch to a gourmet buffet, but mmm this is different."

"Get out of here," Kale said.

"Six o'clock. And remember, you break my momma's heart, I break you."

"I wouldn't dream of it."

Bubba backed into the locker room door, and, while raising his eyebrows at Chelsea, gave Kale a very feminine wave goodbye in his rugged football gear that looked so wrong on so many levels.

"Thanks, that just gave me nightmares for a month," Kale said.

Bubba's laugh echoed in the locker room as he disappeared behind the door.

Kale sighed and turned back toward Chelsea and her disciples.

"Hey, ya'll," he said, purposely not addressing Chelsea directly.

"Sooo, I was thinking," Chelsea started, drawing closer and walking her fingers up his arm, "that tomorrow night you could take me to the Rushing Brook, and, after a romantic dinner, you could ask me an important question." She squeezed his left bicep twice as she said "important question."

"Um, what would that be?" Kale said, trying to swallow his sigh. Amanda and Trish looked conspiratorially at each other and snickered.

Chelsea laughed with forced light-heartedness in its overtones.

"School starts in less than two weeks, Kale, and homecoming is only a month later. We'll need time to prepare and plan the perfect day. Amanda and Trish have already started polling the important people in the school. We're sure to be voted king and queen."

"Oh, uh . . . the Rushing Brook. That's a pretty expensive place, right?"

Chelsea laughed again, that loud, fake laugh. It fit her, Kale thought.

"Don't worry," Chelsea said. "Daddy knows the owner." She tousled his hair, barely able to reach the top of his 6'3" frame. On her tippy toes, she whispered into his ear, "It'll be a good deal. I promise."

"Ya know, that does sound pretty good," he said, gently taking Chelsea's hand off him, which she deftly turned into holding his hand with fingers interlocked. Kale glanced down in embarrassment and had to admit he was impressed in a strange way by how sly she could be.

"But—"

"*But?*" Chelsea said, backing up. The look of warning across her face could have made a tiger think twice. "There's a 'but'?"

As if on cue, Amanda's and Trish's expressions matched Chelsea's.

"No, not really," Kale said, back pedaling. "Just, I'm not sure I'm free tomorrow night. I'll text you, okay?"

"Kale Copeland, is there something you're not telling me? Is there someone *else?*"

She's about to enter banshee mode, he thought. *Careful.*

"Beast mode" was just a little too kind of a description for what happened when Chelsea did not get her way. "Banshee mode" seemed a lot more apt. That's what her brother always called it. Kale had seen it only once, and he never wanted to see it again.

"No, it's not that at all," he said as reassuringly as he could. "It's just, I might have already made plans. For you and me, of course."

Chelsea visibly relaxed, as did her two reflections.

"Oh, I should have known you would have taken the initiative," she said softly. "I like that in a man." She leaned in to him, resting her head on his arm, and sighed contentedly. The wind blew her blonde hair so it tickled his nose.

"Ohmigosh! Trish, do you see this?" Amanda squealed. "Ohmigosh!"

Trish already had her phone out. "Totally Instagramming it. Right. Now! The perfect picture. So, so perfect."

"Wait," Kale said.

"Too late," Trish said, her fingers working her smartphone faster than Kale could blink.

"Oh, look!" Amanda said, scrunching her perfectly waxed eyebrows up to a peak. "Already twenty-three likes!" She brought her hand to her chest. "You're both so perfect."

"Thirty-seven likes," Trish said.

Unbelievable, Kale thought, wanting to shout. *I'm being hijacked by social media paparazzi.*

"Haley Burns commented," Trish said. "'King and queen! Heart, kiss, heart, kiss.'"

"One hundred and nine likes in less than a minute!" Amanda exclaimed. "Oh, you guys!"

Kale realized he had been played. Expertly. He couldn't compete with this.

"Okay, I'll text you about tomorrow, I promise."

He tried to pull away, but Chelsea held on to his arm, looking up at him with dreamy, emerald eyes. They were beautiful, Kale admitted, but shallow. She rose up, just slightly, toward his lips.

"I, uh, really stink," he said. "All the hot water will be gone if I don't get in there." He motioned to the locker room.

"I'm sure a cold shower would do you some good," Chelsea whispered. Looking to Amanda and Trish, she said, "He just wants to save the moment for tomorrow night."

They nodded in unison, faces melted by the apparent tenderness of the moment that Kale seemed to be missing.

By the time Kale extricated himself from the banshee's clutches—without having to kiss her, he proudly reminded himself—the picture on Trish's Instagram account had garnered over 700 likes. It would be many thousands by tomorrow. He was doomed and he knew it. He hadn't even asked her to homecoming. At this point he may not even have to. *Who knew social media controlled your destiny?*

As he stepped out of the shower, drying his chest, Remy Zero's "Save Me" started playing from his phone, the playlist shuffling. The irony made him chuckle darkly, and he turned up the volume as loud as it would go. He loved the song, since he started binge watching seasons of *Smallville*.

After dressing quickly, he grabbed his bag and headed to the parking lot. He wore a pair of faded Levi's—he just couldn't see paying $100 or more for denim and thread that had some designer's name stamped on them—and an American Eagle cream colored shirt.

His new blacked-out Ford Raptor awaited him, gleaming brilliantly in the sun. The upgraded rims added to the truck's already built-in aggressive look. He could have driven just about any car due to the small empire his dad's company had created, but didn't care for the sports car look. Sure, the price tag on a Raptor, fully decked out, could have bought him a Porsche, but he figured he couldn't be faulted by the haters for driving, what was in the end, just an upgraded Ford F150.

Kale stopped mid-stride. Something hit him, not something physical, but something from within. *The same as before . . . but stronger.* His eyes grew wide as he felt a clear burning in his chest. It was not painful, but the intensity was slightly uncomfortable. The burning turned to an urge, and he took short breaths through his mouth. The urge grew, becoming like gravity to his soul. His eyes stung as moisture crept in, but not enough to bring tears.

Primal urges rose in him, those normally only felt when he was not himself, when he was . . . more. But even then, he had never felt them so powerfully. This was different. Greater. More intense. It felt like his soul had just grown, expanded to more than it had been just moments before.

Provide. Shelter. *Protect.*

Those words thundered within him as *feelings*, along with confusion thicker than the blackest night.

Protect what? His heart painfully beat its slow, strong rhythm. He wasn't scared, he realized, just confused. Another part of him was . . . certain? *What is this?*

See, a voice in his mind spoke, and his head snapped up in the direction he felt the voice wanted him to look, toward the parking lot, straight ahead. The voice—deep, almost a desperate growl—guided his eyes. They burned, the same way they burned whenever he became more.

He couldn't shift, not here. He suppressed that part of him, swallowing it. But the urge, the all-compelling force within him—he had to find what it wanted. What *he* wanted, for it was *him,* the part of his soul that had just expanded.

And that image came back to him, playing out in slow motion. A hazy dawn, smoke all around. Trees and embers. And her silhouette, again swallowed by the mist.

People, his fellow students, mingled in the parking lot where the voice had directed him. He still had not moved but scanned intently, trusting he would know what he needed to see when he saw it. His *other* eyes took over, and he sniffed the air instinctively.

Go to her, the urge told him. *Protect.*

The urge within him could not be ignored anymore then the call of an Alpha.

Before he could take a step in that direction, the feeling faded.

No! his mind screamed. *No.*

The urge changed to desperation, to needing, longing, as if to say if he didn't find—*her,* the voice had said?—that he would be lost in the deepest abyss of despair, unable to ever escape.

He ran, dropping the gym bag as he took his first powerful strides forward. It was not that Kale didn't care that others would see him demonstrate speed beyond what could be explained, but that he *couldn't* care in this moment. The urge became fearful, clawing at him from within to move faster, to get to her.

Who? he asked. It didn't matter. Part of him felt like he was dying.

The feeling faded further, and he slowed, a sense of heavy loss coming over him. His legs became iron, anchored by unrelenting hollowness.

It was gone. *She* was gone. As his mind cleared, he wiped the sweat from his brow. A lot of good the shower did him. By degrees, the sadness, nearly as powerful as the urge that had captivated him, left. Something throbbed inside, deep in his chest. It was the new parts of his expanded soul, which now longed to be filled. Or had they always been there? Dormant, waiting for . . . her?

He didn't even know who *her* was, but he needed to find out. More than food, more than oxygen, he needed to find her.

Provide, shelter, protect. The urge spoke quieter now, but still insistently. *Protect.*

Shelby took in the sight of their new home as the Blazer pulled into the driveway. It had only been a few days, and she was still getting used to it. The two-story colonial sported a canary yellow with white pillars and trim. On the siding, much of the paint was cracked and chipped, exposing patches of gray underneath. A wrap-around porch with dilapidated steps bordered the lower level with several segments of the screens missing or torn. Above the porch were the French doors that led into her room from the balcony. A red brick chimney topped off the home. It held a certain charm in that deep-south kind of way.

More than the home, though, Shelby loved the trees and shrubbery. Two giant moss trees guarded the driveway as it met the road, their branches intertwining to form a kind of arch. Other branches sprawled backward to her bedroom windows on the second floor. The shade cast by the trees would cut down the air conditioning bill, or so her father said. White dangling beards of Spanish Moss—teased by a gentle breeze—bespoke more of a whimsical, rather than wise, look.

"So," Grant said as he got out of the car and shut the door, "do you think you made the team? Even though you broke the springboard?"

The first board of the porch creaked under Shelby's foot when they walked up a few steps.

"I think so."

"When do you find out for sure?"

"I made it. Coach Anders said I'm in."

Grant raised his eyebrows. "Right on! That's great!"

Shelby remained a little nonchalant.

"Right?" Grant asked.

"Yeah, sure. It was just different than I expected."

Grant brought the mail in and Shelby started going through it. That had become one of her self-appointed tasks, since Grant often forgot about the little things. Mostly junk from what she could see. She always separated it into two piles: throw-away and bills. There wasn't any other kind of mail they ever received. Today was all throw-away pile. Too early for bills.

"Well, it's a new school, Shel. Not everything is going to be the same. This new team is sure to do a few things different."

"That's not it," Shelby said. She put her gym bag on the kitchen counter.

"Shelby."

"I know, I'll bring it upstairs in a minute. But something happened, Dad."

"Oh?"

Shelby stopped flipping through the mail. Definitely all junk. "I kind of made an enemy. Or three, actually."

Grant smiled. "It's not even the first day of school, Shel. Off to an early start?"

"I guess the mayor's daughter doesn't exactly like new kids." Shelby plopped on the sofa. The leather sighed under her weight, and she imagined a couple pounds of dust flying up from the old piece of furniture. Her dad plopped down next to her. The place came furnished, but she wasn't sure that was really a good thing. The décor made her feel like she was at her grandmother's house, charming or not.

Grant lowered his chin to his chest. "The mayor's daughter. Wow, I've always said you aim high."

"She's the team captain," Shelby huffed.

"The gymnastics team captain?"

Shelby nodded.

Grant wore that look on his face that said he was concerned but also that these kinds of things really didn't matter later in life. Truthfully, it really didn't matter now, but it made Shelby feel a little more normal to have regular high school drama. The shallowness of it grounded her in a way.

"Well, I'm sure she's no match for you. What about friends? Make any of those?"

By the way, I know what you are.

"Um, I think so. Maybe."

"What's her name?"

Before she could answer, her dad added, "Or, is it a *he?*"

"Both."

"A hermaphrodite? I know it's a new generation and all but—"

"No, dad," Shelby said, genuinely laughing, "I made a friend named Sadie and another named Sean."

He was silent for a minute with a confused look on his face. "Which is the boy?"

She slapped his arm. "Stop."

"Well, I can never tell these days. Are they on the team, too?"

"Swearing Sadie is. Hey, what do you think about me trying out for track and field? They have late tryouts tomorrow."

"Swearing Sadie," Grant said out of the side of his mouth.

Shelby shrugged. "Long story. Did the thing about me trying out for track and field not come out of my mouth?"

"Could you do both?"

"Probably not."

"You don't want to do gymnastics anymore?"

Shelby shifted in the couch, wedging herself in the corner, and folded her arms. "I don't know."

"What would you do in track and field?"

Shelby shrugged. "Not sure. Maybe hurdles."

Grant looked knowingly at his daughter, and she hoped she wasn't shrinking under that penetrating stare. Those cold blue eyes of his could always see right through her, and she loved him for that even if she didn't right now.

"So, Sean does track and field."

"Whoops."

"Uh-huh . . ."

Shelby pursed her lips. "It was just an idea. I mean, gymnastics is a very individual kind of sport, right? Even though you're on a 'team' you're still competing with each other. Like golf."

"Sweetheart, golf is not a sport. It's an activity. Like hula-hoop."

"Yeah, yeah."

"Anything you can do while smoking is not a sport."

"So, baseball, then?" Shelby said with a smirk.

"Watch it, kiddo. Not the same thing."

"Why not? Just because you played it growing up?"

"Are you serious about trying out for track and field?"

Shelby leaned forward, and her slightly damp hair covered her face. "I don't know. No, I guess."

"Listen, Shel, don't ever do anything just because . . ."

"Just because of a boy. I know. I'm just not sure the whorey trinity is going to make my life very easy."

Her dad scrunched his face. "Excuse me?"

"Chelsea and her two disciples. That's the mayor's daughter. She's the queen bee around here apparently."

"Wow, I really do not miss high school."

"Sometimes the drama actually helps." But, ugh, three enemies in one day? Nice one, Shelby.

"You'll survive, kiddo. You're tough. It's how I taught you to be, how we've had to be."

"Dad . . ."

"Yeah?"

"My new friend, Sadie." Shelby paused. "I think she might know."

rant stood abruptly. "How? Did something happen?"

"I don't know," Shelby said. "I don't think so, but maybe."

A vein in Grant's neck pulsed, and his hands balled into fists.

"When I did my tryout on the vault," Shelby said, "I felt something. Like, an intense moment or something. I flew really high off the vault, higher than I ever have."

Her dad's fists released. His knuckles had turned purple from squeezing them so tightly. "Is that all?"

"I. Broke. The. Springboard. Remember? In front of everyone."

"Yeah, you 'slayed' it. I remember. And?"

"You really are lost, Grant."

"Shelby!"

"Grant!"

The staring contest lasted for about ten seconds. Her dad blinked.

"What happened then?" her dad asked.

"I landed wrong. It really hurt, and coach had someone call 911 because he was sure I broke something, ya know, like my back. Nothing critical. But then the Chelsea-wench called me fat, and so I jumped up to my feet like nothing had happened and shut her down."

"Were your eyes burning?" her dad asked quietly.

Shelby looked away. "Yes."

"And your voice?"

"I . . . I don't know. I felt a growl inside me, but I don't think it came out."

Her dad looked pensive. "But another werewolf could have heard it, right? Seen it in your eyes? Maybe this isn't as bad as it seemed. Maybe this Sadie girl is like you."

"But … I would have smelled her. I think. Right?"

Grant shrugged with his arms out, palms up.

There were also those that hunted Lycans. Her father had warned her about this, told her what to look out for.

"Maybe she's a hunter and was just being nice to me to get close to me. . . ."

"But, then why tell you she knew what you were? Are you sure she was even talking about . . . you know?"

Shelby wasn't sure, not completely.

The cushions below Shelby angled toward her dad as he sat back down. He took a breath.

"Your friend isn't a hunter, Shel."

"How do you know?"

Grant swallowed, looking intently at his steepled hands. "Because you wouldn't be here right now."

Awesome. Nothing like the "hey, other people *do* want to kill you," vibe to keep things light. But Shelby already knew that all too well.

"Listen," Grant said, changing the subject, "I met with someone today while running errands."

"Someone?"

"An investment manager guy or something."

"We have investments?"

"Actually, we do."

"We do? We have money?"

"Some."

Shelby sat up. "Really? How much?"

Grant wrung his hands and looked like he was considering whether or not to divulge a big secret.

"Dad?"

"Two point three million. Or there about, as of the close of the stock market today."

Shelby thought her eyes widened as far as her mouth opened.

"It's not as much as it seems. Not really," her dad said.

"Where did it all come from? I haven't seen you work more than a middle-income job in like . . . ever."

"Life insurance from your mom," he said. "Some guy sold us a lot, way more than we ever needed. Your mom insisted at the time. The premiums were so high we had to stop paying extra on our mortgage, but she wouldn't be dissuaded. I didn't understand at the time, but . . . well, werewolves can have a high mortality rate, quick healing notwithstanding."

"Did she know . . . know that . . ."

"That she was going to die? No, not at the time. She was just cautious. She took a huge risk in choosing to marry me, but love . . . it's a crazy thing. Makes you do things that seem crazy. Like wanting to try out for track and field."

"Dad! You're ruining the moment!"

"Sorry," he said with a smirk.

"Did you know? What she was when you got married, I mean?"

Grant swallowed. "Yes."

Shelby could not speak, her lips slightly parted as she worked up the courage for the next question. She knew her dad knew more than what he let on. She could feel it sometimes, the way he would say certain things, the way he would *not* say other things. "Are you hiding it from me? How she really died?"

Grant turned to her completely, the leather couch sounding its soft protest as he pivoted. "I have never lied to you, Shel."

"Was it another werewolf? For marrying you?"

"No, Shel, it wasn't. It was cancer, as I've always said."

"But, we heal. Like, superhero-fast. What's the guy with spandex and claws—"

"Wolverine. And you're right, but not with cancer. She told me cancer is very aggressive with werewolves, and no one knows why. Even treatable kinds can be lethal in a matter of weeks, where humans can last years or decades with proper treatment."

"So much for being immortal," Shelby said.

"Nothing is immortal, Shel. Everything can die." Grant turned his head away briefly before looking back to her. She thought she saw the hint of moisture in his eyes. "But, to answer your question, that's where the money came from. The insurance policy paid out after she passed on, and we've been living on the interest ever since. I've always had to use banks and firms out of town just to keep things quiet. Didn't want the local folks to know because . . . well, just because, I guess. But now, I figured we're far enough away from Florida that it won't matter."

"Why are you telling me this now?"

"Because of where we're eating dinner tonight. With whom, more importantly."

"So, the investment guru guy wants to wine and dine us for our money?"

Grant smiled. "It's *our* money, suddenly?"

"Hey, she was my mom."

"And it was definitely you that she was thinking of when we took out the insurance policies. But, no, that's not why we're going to eat dinner with him tonight. I got the distinct impression that he does just fine and doesn't need our account, nor do we really need his investment services."

"But—"

"He's an Alpha."

Shelby froze. "You found a pack?"

Grant nodded once.

"But," Shelby asked, "how did you know where to look? I mean, we just got here. Awfully convenient."

"Elias has a small but growing pack. Your mother taught me what to look for. The signs, mannerisms. Codes."

"Codes?"

"Yes."

"But, you're not a werewolf. Why would they reveal themselves to you?" And then something caught in Shelby's voice, and she wondered what else her dad could have kept from her. Had Nicholas actually bitten him? "You're . . . not one, are you? Dad?"

"No, Shelby. Sometimes, for your sake, I wish I were, but I am not. I swear to you."

Memories of her dad being sick with the flu two years ago came to her and also a serious bout of food poisoning several months ago just as they arrived in Odessa. Shelby, on the other hand, had never been sick that she could remember, not even a cold. Perfect attendance all through school . . . except for the past year.

"So, no disease except cancer can harm me?"

"That I know of, anyway."

"Ebola?"

"Nope."

"Swine flu?"

"Negative."

"Cotard's delusion?"

"What?"

"Zombie disease," Shelby explained. "It's a real thing. People believe they really are dead and spend time in cemeteries, wishing they could be with their own kind. We studied it in biology my sophomore year. . . . or . . . my friends and I looked it up while bored in class, I guess. We're dangerous with our iPhones."

Grant just shook his head.

"Hey," Shelby said, "if werewolves are real—"

"We are not discussing zombies."

"Okay, so dinner with the Alpha?"

"Elias. And his wife, Gennesaret."

"What's up with all the Bible names?"

"I know Elias is from the Bible," Grant said, "but Gennesaret?"

"The place where Jesus healed a bunch of people with diseases and cast out devils and stuff. It's in Luke."

"How do you know that?" Grant asked.

"Kind of started reading it a lot over the past year, searching for answers and stuff."

"So, are there werewolves in the Bible, Shel?"

Shelby raised her hands in an "I don't know" gesture.

"I guess it's fitting, in a way," Grant said. "She's a physician at the local hospital."

"Elias's wife?"

Her father nodded.

"Do you believe in God, Dad?"

Grant was quiet.

"I really want to know," she said. "We've never really gone to church, but we've always had a Bible in the house. I see you reading it sometimes when you don't think I'm watching."

Grant inhaled a large breath and let it escape slowly. "Never was trying to hide that."

"I know . . ."

"Shelby, I have seen so many things, even though my time with the Delta teams was short. Those things would probably make most men question whether or not there is a God. I saw many that did. For me, though, it reinforced it . . . eventually.

"I admit I went through a time wondering how God could allow such atrocity, such degradation in the world. If I described the things I saw, you would be sick. The oppression, the torture . . . I still have nightmares of several missions. And no, I can't talk about it. Won't.

"I guess eventually, though, I came to a clear understanding of something. There is evil. True evil. I know this just as much as I know I'm sitting here with you right now. Knowing that, it eventually came to me that there had to be a counter force to that evil, something that opposed it. Whether that's God or something else, I'm not completely sure, but I'm sure there is something good that opposes all the evil I saw. That goodness resides in us, it's the reason we feel revolted when confronted with evil. That's what I believe, anyway."

Shelby leaned against her dad's arm. Softly, she asked, "Do I have a soul, Dad?"

"Of course you do."

"I mean . . . is what I am . . . evil?"

"Shelby Madison Brooks, you are the daughter of the most kind, caring, beautiful person I have ever known. If she didn't have a soul, then there is no such thing." He headlocked Shelby with his large-muscled arm. "And you, kiddo, are just like her." He kissed her on the head before she could push him off.

"Dad!"

"Go get ready. We need to be there in an hour."

"Our last attempt at joining a pack didn't end well."

Shelby dropped her eyes to her dad's stomach, the side that she knew bore angry scars from Nicholas.

"I know," he said. "I don't know, not for sure, but you need this. There are things that, as much as it pains me to say, I cannot give you. Trust me on how much that hurts, that I have to share my little girl with another family, but I know it is something you will need. Fathers pride themselves on being able to provide everything their family needs, but . . ."

He trailed off.

"How did we escape?" Shelby asked softly.

She saw it on her dad's face. He knew what she meant. Nicholas's pack. She had asked before and always received the same answer from her dad but she hated that she couldn't remember.

She had blacked out just as she'd heard her dad's gun fire. Why? Why had she blacked out? Her vision had shaken, but something . . . she had felt something in her chest, hadn't she? Something had snapped in her head.

"You were hurt bad," Shelby said. "I remember that. There was so much blood. I'm so sorry I brought this on you. I would change it if I could. You know that right?"

Grant swallowed. "Listen, Shel, I don't regret you. I don't regret who you are, nor loving your mother. Never doubt that. You hear me?"

"But—"

"I'm a good shot," Grant said. "That's how we escaped. I hit them enough times to slow them down. May have even killed them. I didn't wait to see. Just scooped you up and ran."

Something rang false in her dad's words, as always when he answered her question about their escape, but she didn't press him. "You know you're my hero, right?"

"Yeah."

"It's cool having a superhero for a dad."

"I'm not a superhero, Shel."

"Yes you are. Don't worry, I won't tell." She winked at him.

"Go on, get ready. We're leaving in forty-five minutes."

As she went upstairs to change, she saw out of the corner of her eye her dad smile in a way that wasn't meant for others to see.

Sherman ducked low in the brush. A black film smeared his face and hands, most of his clothes, masking his scent, even from these creatures of the lowest hell that he and his team stalked. For, surely a demon or Lucifer himself had sired them.

Oh Lord, give me the strength of Sampson, the sword of Your angel in the Garden of Eden. Let my feet move swiftly, as if upon Your chariots of fire.

Puddles on the pavement reflected the amber rays of the waning gibbous moon. Across the street sat the lair of the abominations he hunted. Werewolves, but more advanced. Lycans, blessed with control of their transforming, with the same intelligence as humans, but *not* human. Just on the outskirts of Odessa, Texas, the manor sprawled languidly over roughly two acres. A mixture of black and gray rock, the main house cast itself as almost colonial, but the spires and stone figures on the ledges—some sort of mutated gargoyles— made the atmosphere drift more to the gothic side. A large detached garage, nearly the size of a warehouse and peeking around the side of the lair, sat in the backyard.

Lend me Your scepter, Lord, Your terrible might, that these spawns of Hell might be struck down by Your righteousness.

Beside Sherman, also crouched, his eighteen-year-old boy, Lucas, waited nervously. This was the first mission Sherman let his son join him on. He glanced at Lucas's marred face. The shame of his son's scars was his to bear, for Sherman had suspected what the Brooks girl was but had foolishly allowed Lucas to flush her out. Four other hunters spread themselves out at various points with full tactical loadouts. The M4 rifle slung across Sherman's chest sported a bladed suppressor. After all, even when ammunition ran out, a rifle should still be a weapon of consequence. On his hip, a Sig Sauer P320 with two extra magazines rested with—as Sherman would often swear each of his firearms contained a personality—impatience. He had given Lucas his Glock 17, his most trusted firearm. Its personality was a quiet confidence, something Lucas would benefit from.

The time arrived. Sherman lined up one of the two guards at the front gate in his sights and touched the mic at his throat.

"Execute."

He squeezed the M4's trigger, and an incendiary round struck his target in the chest. The unworthy spawn started to shift to his wolf in reflex, but flames spurted from his center as the incendiary round did its work. To Sherman's right, a grenade shot from a launcher mounted on Chou's M4 and exploded through the manor's main doors. When the smoke cleared, only one piece of debris remained, hanging from a single hinge.

Sherman keyed his throat mic. "Advance."

Nicholas sweated in his sleep. The Alpha of the diminished Odessa pack had found sleep a punishing trial since Shelby Brooks had escaped. She had done something to him. Damaged him. In his dreams, she was there, her dark amber eyes boring into him, stoking the fear she had seeded inside him.

What is she?

But his dreams did not answer. He knew he jerked in his sleep, twisting the damp sheets around him. His mistresses could not comfort him, though he had tried to drown himself in their affections, taking them night after night, sometimes more than one at a time; but even the promised relief from sating his lusts did not last, and his weariness from the constant haunting of Shelby Brooks often turned him to bouts of rage.

Those eyes . . . they burn . . .

He sensed words in those supernatural eyes. Communication.

But she did not shift! What was he seeing then, these eyes? He knew them to be hers, the eyes of her wolf. But he could not believe the communication he felt coming from her wicked glare. *My mind . . . it is just in my head . . . she is not what you think.*

But she was. Nicholas knew it.

Awakened by something, he shot up in bed. He brushed his matted hair from his eyes. There, the sound again. The grogginess cleared with the realization of what he had heard. Gunfire. Then growls. Then screams.

His eyes burned as he shifted.

Sherman and his team strode toward the lair, weapons raised. Green lasers lit up the front of the house, illuminating swirling eddies of lingering smoke. In the windows of the gables, dark figures appeared followed by automatic weapons' fire. Sherman's team responded with discipline and efficiency, lining up the targets and taking two shots. The figures fell. Sherman heard the frenzied voices in the house, people—*no, the hounds of Hell*—coming to life. A shadow darted through the house, barely visible through the windows.

"Dad," Lucas said.

"I saw it," Sherman said. He squeezed his neck mic. "Be advised, the pack has shifted."

Another flurry of darkness darted, this time outside the house, along the side.

"They're out," Sherman said. "Masks. Pop silver smoke."

Two thunks were heard as Chou and Rivera each shot a silver acetylide grenade. Mixed with a gaseous agent, the grenades spewed a mist of the acidic silver salt in a wide radius upon impact, the fumes filling the front yard and foyer in the manor.

"Switching to thermal." Sherman pressed a button on his optical sight, and the world in front of him turned to overexposed splotches of blues, yellows, greens, oranges, and reds. A hunched form sprinted away from the fumes. Sherman fired twice. The wolf grunted but did not go down, disappearing behind the manor.

"Chou, Rivera, clear the house. Decker, Peters, Lucas, on me."

The fire team split up. Sherman took a knee at the southeast corner of the house, and Decker and Peters stacked up behind him. Lucas crouched behind them. Sherman peeked around the corner, M4 raised. No red or orange showed up in his thermal sight.

"Clear. Diamond formation. Lucas, stay against the wall. Everyone watch their vectors."

The unit moved in unison, north along the east side wall. Decker, at the head, ducked below a window and readied himself. Sherman nodded, and Decker popped up, his rifle's laser piercing the glass into the house. A blur of blackness launched through the window. Sherman closed his eyes and turned away in reflex as glass shards rained down upon the men. He heard a shot—Decker's rifle—but only one. It took a split second to open his eyes before Sherman saw the wolf's jaws clenched around Decker's neck and shoulder, the gape of the beast's maw nearly as wide as a torso. Decker screamed as the wolf tore, snarling. Peters and Sherman fired. The wolf's snarls turned to whines as it went limp. Sherman kicked it off his fallen man. Whimpering, the wolf lay on its side as it began to shift back to human form. A young woman, naked, of course, with trails of streaming blood from holes in her side.

Sherman turned to his son. "Lucas."

With shaking hands, Lucas raised his pistol.

"In the head, son," Sherman said. "Right here." He pressed a gloved finger to the center of his forehead.

Lucas swallowed and lined up the head—a human head—in his sights. The woman had nearly shifted completely back to human form, but still had slightly pointed and hairy ears. Delicate features, nonetheless. Furry hands with clawed fingertips moved lethargically to cover her wounds. The amber flecks in her darks eyes, however, had disappeared.

Lord, give him the strength, Sherman prayed. Even though it was his son, and would pain him, Sherman would not hesitate to do what was necessary to protect the clandestine nature of the hunter brotherhood if Lucas proved unworthy. *The Lord's errand is one done in the night, apart from His children's view.*

Lucas fired, and the woman's head jerked back from the impact of the 9mm round.

Sherman simply nodded. "Let's move."

"Wait," Decker wheezed. "Don't leave me like this. It bit me. Don't let me change." Blood poured from his wounds and trickled from his mouth. "I feel it. Already I can feel it."

Sherman pulled his sidearm. "Bless your servant, who has perished in Your service, Lord. Take him unto Yourself." He put two rounds in Decker's chest. The man went still.

"Grab his mags."

Peters retrieved Decker's spare mags from his tactical vest.

"You made me proud just then, son," Sherman said to Lucas, his gloved hand squeezing his son's shoulder. "You feel the calling of the Lord's hunters, now, don't you?"

Lucas shook a bit but sneered as he looked at the dead woman. "I . . ."

"I know what you're thinking, Lucas. Shelby's time will come."

"Yeah, but—"

"It's a wonderful feeling, isn't it? The calling of the Lord."

"Yeah," Lucas said.

"You good?"

Lucas nodded.

He was, Sherman saw.

Good. It's in him after all.

No other enemy contact came as they made their way along the east wall, now in a spearhead formation with Sherman at the point. Just as Sherman's fire team entered the backyard, Chou and Rivera exited the back door onto the portico.

"Clear," Chou reported over the radio.

Sherman nodded. Just ahead of him lay the two story detached garage, and Sherman decided again that it was indeed more of a warehouse. He squeezed his neck mic. "Prepare to breach."

His men took up their positions. Rivera placed a breaching charge on the double doors.

"Set," Rivera said.

A roar—not the bomb—charged the night air and Rivera cried out. The sound of something wet being torn, ended his yell. Sherman spun, rigid. Lucas crouched behind his father. Rivera was gone.

Where are you, beast? Step forth from the shadows of your sin . . .

Suppressed fire sounded from Peters's M4. Sherman pivoted, rifle at the ready. Nothing. His thermal sight revealed only greens and yellows and grays—plants and rocks.

"Peters," Sherman called aloud, breaking protocol. There was no need for stealth any longer. He flipped his tac light on attached to his M4. Three hundred lumens lit up the darkness. His thermal scope had not misled him. Peters was gone. Crimson glistened in the harsh light on the perfectly manicured blades of grass. Something else— Sherman shifted the beam of his light. Half of Peters's buttstock and sling lay on the ground, sheared in half.

"On me," Sherman said.

Chou closed on his position. As Sherman let his light drift across the yard, a pair of yellow orbs cut the darkness. For a moment, fear dared to flicker within him. *Get thee behind me, Satan.* Sherman swallowed the momentary weakness. From his belt, he drew a six-inch K-Bar and rested it under the barrel of his M4. He expected this to get very close and personal. Chou dropped his rifle and drew two ten-inch blades. Three more sets of eyes appeared, followed by low growls.

For God hath not given us the spirit of fear; but of power . . .

"Bring it," Sherman said.

Chou stretched out his forward leg and brought his cimeters into a fighting stance. The wolves tore forward. Sherman fired, taking one between the eyes. It fell with a muted thud. Chou aerialed into the fray, blades whirring. Claws tore across his back, but he spun and impaled the wolf's rear leg with one blade, its back with the other, severing the spine. Two down.

Lucas fired wildly, missing his target. The wolf tackled him, jaws snapping. The boy cried out. Sherman filled the beast with silver rounds just before its jaws found his son's face. The wolf collapsed on Lucas, heaving heavily. The breathing stopped as it returned to human form, the corpse's tongue protruding, fat and swollen. Lucas skittered out from under it, a look of disgust on his face. Sherman and Chou circled the last wolf, the largest. Blood dripped from its fangs. This was Nicholas. The Alpha. The amber of its eyes glowed deeper than the rest.

Chou winced as he rolled his shoulders.

"We need him alive," Sherman said. "He will have answers we need."

Chou nodded. "I know." He blinked erratically, as if trying to stay awake. The man was obviously in great pain from the wounds on his back. Nicholas did not hesitate, clearly sensing the weakness. The Alpha pounced on Chou too fast for Sherman to react. In less than three adrenaline-induced-heartbeats, Nicholas decapitated Chou and flung the head at Sherman. The wolf limped slightly from a new gash in its forward left leg. Chou had not gone quietly.

"Dad?"

Sherman heard his son's airy voice. "Stay behind me. Aim over my shoulder. Be ready to do your duty if needed."

Sherman beheld Nicholas's blasphemous form in his red dot reflex sight. The wolf stood no more than ten feet from him, fangs bared, shoulders hunched, head lowered. Sherman's grip on his K-Bar knife tightened. Slowly, he began lowering his M4 rifle.

"Dad, what are you doing?" Lucas hissed.

"Trust me." *And now, Lord, behold their threatenings: and grant unto Thy servants . . . boldness . . .*

As soon as Sherman's rifle fully lowered, Nicholas pounced. Sherman dropped flat on his back. From a vial secreted in the wristband on his right hand, a short needle emerged. Sherman thrust the tip into the beast with the heel of his hand as the beast flew over him. The vial instantly shot its contents into the wolf. Nicholas shook his head amid a snarl, then collapsed to his side.

Sherman rose and brushed the soil from his backside, nonchalantly. He activated the breaching charge left on the door by Rivera. A short burst of flames and a concussive boom saw the doors open.

"Grab the corpses and haul them inside," Sherman said. "We'll need to burn the bodies when we're done. Fire cleanses." He pointed the tip of his K-Bar at Nicholas. "I'll get that."

Sherman grabbed Nicholas—now in human form—by the hair at the crown of his head and hauled him into the warehouse as if no more than a slab of meat.

Sherman bound Nicholas to a metal chair. He stabbed and twisted the K-Bar blade into the Alpha's thigh. The silver alloy that coated the blade would have prevented the wound from healing if he removed it, but he'd leave it there regardless for now. Nicholas grunted in pain, but did not allow a scream to escape his clenched jaw. Veins bulged at his temples amid sweat-matted hair, and he writhed against his bonds. The steel-twine cables cut deep into his wrists, but Sherman had no pity for the beast.

"Tell me what I need to know," Sherman said in his deep southern drawl.

The warehouse was empty save for the naked corpses at the end of skids of blood. Nicholas's pack. Sherman did not understand why these creatures shifted back to human form when killed. No hunter did. Even the Feral—those who could not shift back to their human form in life—shifted back in death.

Lucas stood next to him.

Nicholas's eyes flashed with amber flecks as he jerked against his bonds.

"Lucas," Sherman said.

Lucas stabbed a syringe into Nicholas's neck and plunged five milligrams of sodium thiopental into the Alpha. The amber slivers died, receding back into the swampy brown of Nicholas's irises.

"Where is she?" Sherman asked.

Nicholas turned his head aside.

Sherman sighed. "Come now. What possible loyalty could you have to her? Didn't Grant steal Moriahna from you? That whelp they spawned should have been yours, isn't that right?"

Nicholas growled.

"Now, now, dog, let's not carry on with your idle threats," Sherman said. "That fine by you?" He ejected the magazine from his Glock. "With all that sodium thiopental running through you, you'll never shift. Funny, in a way, how it's sometimes called 'truth serum'. Keeps you in your true form, after all. Doesn't quite wear off as fast for you as it does for . . . real people, does it? I wonder if that has any, say, symbolic meaning to our setting here." Sherman smiled. "If my boy there gives you another ten milligrams, well . . . you may never shift again. That has to be a bit like being castrated for your kind, isn't that right? Of course, it's really just a form of exorcism. Casting out that demon from you."

Nicholas spat in Sherman's face. The hunter did not pause so much as to wipe the filth away.

"Now these," Sherman said, showing Nicholas the top bullet in his magazine, "are 99.9% silver, hardened by a special forging process hunters have perfected over the centuries. Hollow points, of course, for more damage. We wouldn't want the round to pass right through you, now would we?"

Sherman slapped the magazine into the Glock's mag well. "Now, best I can figure, you're not talking because you don't trust me. Because I need you to trust me, Nicholas, I'm going to need to demonstrate my resolve. Remember, this is only so we can have a relationship of trust."

Sherman pressed the end of the pistol's barrel to Nicholas's left hand, which rested palm down on the armchair. The Alpha squirmed against his steel bindings. A low whistle escaped Sherman's lips.

"Now, I promise, Nicholas, that on the count of three, I'm going to shoot your hand. The damage to your . . . paw will be extensive. You will be maimed for the rest of your life."

"What do you want?" Nicholas seethed. His voice sounded almost like a bark, a staccato rhythm, despite the seething. How appropriate.

"One."

"Wait! I'll tell you what you want to hear. Just ask."

"Two."

"Tell me what you want!"

"Why, Nicholas, I have already told you," the hunter answered condescendingly. "I want you to *trust* me. Three."

Sherman squeezed the trigger. The air cracked with the gunshot. Nicholas howled, and tears streamed from his eyes. The muscles in his neck went taut, drawing deep lines. He writhed desperately in the chair, rocking it back and forth. The hole in the center of his left hand pooled with dark blood. Around the wound's epicenter, the skin turned purple and white.

Nicholas huffed with a cracked voice. "Do you know what we do with hunters?" Nicholas turned his head toward Lucas, a red cluster of burst capillaries spreading across the corner of his right eye. "We devour your entrails right before your—"

Sherman pressed the pistol against Nicholas's wrist, just above the fresh wound. The Alpha instantly stilled.

"Now, Nick—can I call you Nick?—don't go gettin' worked up and all. You'll need your strength, and you won't be shifting." Sherman drew close to Nicholas. "Nick, you trust me, isn't that right?"

Nicholas turned his head to the side, his neck muscles still constricted. "Yes. Yes, I trust you."

"That's good. Makes me feel warm inside that we have achieved this level in our relationship so quickly."

"Me, too," Nicholas said, shaking.

"Whoa, is he panting?" Lucas asked with a sneer.

Sherman pursed his lips almost into a smile. "Yes, son, that's what they do when they've been properly trained. Isn't that right, Nicky boy?"

"Whatever you say," Nicholas answered. "Please, give me something for the pain."

"Well, Nicky, that would be a waste, I'm afraid. Listen, I won't lie to you. You're in for more pain before the end."

Nicholas whimpered. "Please . . ."

"I know, but the more you take it like a man, rather than a dog, the quicker it will be over. You still trust me, right?"

Nicholas started sobbing, tears and mucus spilling over his upper lip. Sherman pressed the pistol down harder.

"I'm going to put a bullet in your wrist. After that, I'm going to place the tip of my barrel against your elbow. At that point, I'll have some questions for you, in which, I know, you will not disappoint."

Sherman fired. Nicholas wailed.

"That's it," Sherman said, as if coaxing the sobbing man. He patted Nicholas on the shoulder. "That's it. Let it out. You're doing fine, just fine."

The wrist had become a mangled mess.

"Hmm, that bleeding *is* going to be a problem," Sherman said, his hand rubbing his chin. "You know where I keep that propane torch in the truck?"

Lucas nodded. "Yeah."

"Wait, wait! I'll talk. I'll tell you." Nicholas took a deep breath. Tears streamed down his eyes. "She's a monster. . . . she's not one of us."

Sherman held up a hand for Lucas to stop.

Nicholas let out an involuntary sob.

"Now, who are we discussing, Nicky?"

"The girl you want. Shelby Brooks." Suddenly Nicholas's demeanor turned cold. Then wild. Blood and saliva seethed from his clenched teeth. He looked Sherman straight in the eye. "She's a monster. A freak!"

"Well, isn't that the kettle calling the pot black," Sherman said. "Still, do tell."

Nicholas whimpered. "The pain. Please."

"Lucas, the torch—"

"Wait!" Nicholas howled. He breathed deeply several more times. "Wait."

"Spit it out, dog!" Lucas said.

"She came to us to join our pack," Nicholas began, panting. "They found us one night a couple months ago. Her father didn't know Tobias was no longer the Alpha. Tobias had promised Grant safety among the pack for his past . . . amends. But I could not allow it! He stole Moriahna from me!"

"Did you know, Nick," Sherman asked, "that she—Moriahna, I mean—was the target of the mission all those years ago? Hmm? See, we've traced the bloodlines for centuries, tracking offspring. Following your own kind's . . . prophecies, as it were. And with the help of modern advances and understandings of genetics, we've been able to make several disturbing projections."

"I don't know what you mean," Nicholas huffed.

"Not important right now. But please, continue, and do skip ahead to the night of the encounter. Our time here is limited. You understand."

"Will you spare me? I can help you."

"The Lord is merciful, Nicky. It's a trait I'm still trying to master, but for now it's still one of my weaknesses. Let us see if you can tip the balances of justice and mercy to your favor." Sherman raised his eyebrows and tapped his watch.

"I wanted revenge," Nicholas said. "It was that simple. Kill Grant. Punish Shelby."

"Punish . . . her, Nicky?"

Lucas wore a haughty grin. Nicholas looked down, as if ashamed.

"Well, it's all right," Sherman said. "I can't say we don't see eye-to-eye on that point."

"I don't know how she did it," Nicholas said. "I . . . she got into my head. She's still there! Pricking my brain. Kicking the inside of my skull. I feel it. Thudding. Pulsing. And when I close my eyes . . . I see . . ."

"What do you see?" Sherman whispered.

Nicholas shook, red saliva dangling from his chin. "The end. I see the end. She is an albatross, the disaster our Mystics have long foreseen."

"You mean the Summer Omega legends," Sherman said.

"She is calamity!" Nicholas shouted.

"What is he talking about?" Lucas asked.

"Lycan legends tell of a time when werewolves will challenge humanity—the children of God—for the world itself. Supposedly, a Summer Omega will be the forerunner of the prophecy coming true. Omegas are rare, but not so scarce that one could say they are anomalies. And, occasionally, a werewolf does manifest late in puberty instead of at eleven or twelve years old . . . blooming in the summer instead of spring, as it were. But a Summer Omega . . . well, I'm sure I've never heard of one in real life. But our own projections and models of the bloodlines—of Moriahna's line—are . . . of interest. The Lycan prophecies on this date back all the way to the early A.D. centuries."

"Calamity will follow her," Nicholas said.

"You sound as if you believe it, Dad," Lucas said.

Sherman saw the questioning squint in his son's eye. "Lycan prophecies have been eerily accurate in the past, son. Remember, the Devil also has power. But we serve the greater light."

"Wouldn't they want that?" Lucas asked. "If they believe that garbage?"

"Not everything in the prophecy is necessarily good for the doggies, son. But who can say? Like most of these things, they're esoteric and require study and the true Spirit to discern."

"Please!" Nicholas said. "Let me help you. I can find her. She must perish."

"So," Sherman said, "instead of killing Grant and taking Shelby for yourself . . ." He again raised his eyebrows.

"They escaped."

"Not good enough, Nicky."

Nicholas swallowed and shut his eyes so tightly that his lids all but disappeared under his severe brow. "She killed the two with me as we charged them. I don't know how to explain it. It built slowly in my head. The visions. The fear. The pain. Vasilis and Booker started whimpering, pawing at their heads. I couldn't move. Paralyzed by pain and fear. Booker clawed at the pavement, rammed his snout into it. Vasilis howled in agony. I felt his agony. It matched my own. They died, bleeding from their ears and eyes. The nose. And I . . . I only survived because I'm an Alpha." Nicholas's bloodshot eyes looked up into Sherman's. "She's not one of us, I'm telling you. She's a vile miscreant."

Sherman smiled. "Yet another thing we agree upon. Now, you mentioned that you could find her." Sherman poked Nicholas's inner elbow with the barrel of his gun. The Alpha stiffened.

"I can track her."

"Leave that to us. For now, I just need to know where she went." He tapped Nicholas's elbow with the gun again, gently this time. "And I know we still trust each other, yes?"

In the end, Sherman was convinced Nicholas told them all he knew. The Alpha managed to keep his elbow intact. The next dose of sodium thiopental from Lucas killed the wolf within him though, ensuring the pathetic man would remain a man. Or whatever his human form had devolved to in his wretched state.

Later, as Sherman turned off the exit that would lead them to Lansborough, he said, "Son, that's one less finger the Devil has upon this world, one less threat to the children of God. You did well."

"We should have killed him," Lucas said.

"No, son. A wretch cursed to wander the land is a worse punishment than death. Remember the wise punishment of God upon Cain, to walk the earth as a cursed creature, hated by all for all time. In time, the Lord may see fit to use ol'Nicky for good."

Sherman saw the pondering upon his son's face.

"Are we going to let Shelby live?" Lucas asked.

Sherman rubbed his hand across his mustache. "No. No we're not, nor her treacherous father. There's no forgiveness for one of our own who spawns one of their kind."

A smile tugged at the corner of Lucas's mouth.

"I'm not sure what I'm more nervous about," Shelby said as the Blazer drove parallel to the property's outer wall. "Meeting an Alpha or entering that house."

The entrance to the Copeland estate rested at the bottom of the only hill in the area. Lansborough made no exception to the famed flat landscape of Texas, so the fact that Copeland Manor was built on a hill with gentle slopes made the majesty even greater. The home presented itself like a small hotel, with grand pillars and stone balconies that ornamented every one of the several gables on the front elevation.

Large trees, all bordering the estate, swayed in the breeze. Oh, a row of willow trees! Shelby loved willows. Somehow they spoke kind reassurance to her. Two flagpoles were set in a single raised cement round base. The taller of the two poles hoisted the American flag, the shorter the Texas flag. Shelby felt suddenly quite underwhelming.

Even if she had worn her best dress—one her mother had left her—she was sure she would still feel out of place here.

"Flaunt it, much?" Shelby said.

"This house doesn't represent his demeanor," Grant said. "You'll see."

She looked at her dad in his dark blue dinner jacket. "I didn't even know you had a sports jacket," she said.

"I spent twenty minutes vacuuming the dust off it."

"Looks a little tight." Shelby winked at him.

"Thanks for noticing. You look wonderful, by the way."

"Just black jeans and my leather jacket."

"Yeah, but they're not your ripped jeans that somehow are all the rage right now," Grant said. "And your hoodie took the night off, I see."

Shelby turned the back of her head to her dad.

"What?" he asked.

"Such a guy," Shelby sighed. "It took me an hour to do this five-strand braid. I think my hands nearly fell off."

"It's beautiful. When did I teach you how to do that?"

Um, hello? YouTube."

"Very country-girl of you. Trying to fit in already? You wearing cowboy boots, too?"

"Nope. Don't push it. The leather jacket offsets the hair."

Grant smiled. "You'll be beautiful no matter what you do. It's just natural."

"I must get that from mom."

Her dad shrugged. "No argument here."

As they pulled up to the main gate, a guard came to the window, and Grant rolled it down. The old Blazer didn't have "power" anything, which Shelby guessed was a good thing, if the EMP that would knock the entire nation back to the eighteenth century ever happened. Yeah, her dad had taught her to think like that. She found it endearing now.

"Evening, sir. Name?" the guard asked. He had a flashlight, black body armor and clothing, an M4 on a two-point sling, and a sidearm at his right hip. A Glock 22, if Shelby guessed it right.

"Grant and Shelby Brooks," her dad answered. "Mr. Copeland is expecting us."

The guard looked at the tablet in his hand, its backlight lighting up his face eerily. He tapped the pad a few times, then said something into his radio. When it squawked back, the guard said, "You're good to go."

Grant said, "Rangers lead the way."

"Heard, understood, and acknowledged," the guard answered.

Grant pulled forward as the gate opened.

"What was all that about?" Shelby asked.

"He was a Ranger."

"How could you tell?"

"I can tell," Grant said. "Lots of us go into private security after we leave the army."

"What's with the heard, understood, and whatever line?"

Grant said, "Rangers used to say 'hooah' a little, the phoneticized initials H U A for heard, understood, and acknowledged; but ever since that *Black Hawk Down* movie, we kind of moved away from it. They just overdid it for us. He was saying it without saying it. See his hardware?"

"M4 carbine, fixed angled front post iron site, keymod rails. Glock 22 at the hip."

"Glock 17," Grant corrected. "But very good. You were close."

"What do you have on you?" She knew her dad always carried something.

"Glock 19. But, that's not going to do us a lot of good if things don't go as planned."

"Do you think—"

"No, I don't. But I'm cautious."

Beautifully designed hedges flanked the private road as they drove up the hill. Yard lights began to glow even though the sun was just starting to set.

"So, this guy is . . . loaded," Shelby said. She took in the exquisite landscape and felt like she had entered an environmental preserve.

"Always have a bullet in the chamber, Shel."

"No, I meant this Copeland guy, not the security guard. He's loaded. Rich."

"Net worth near or at $1 billion."

"That's, like, crazy money, right?"

"To us, you bet."

"Why does he live here, then?" Shelby asked. "Why not some place in the Hamptons? Or even Dallas?"

"His pack," Grant said. "The city packs have a very different view of things, your mother said. Much less accepting and a more rigid hierarchy. They can be more abusive."

"But the big city would be fun for a change, right?"

"We can't risk it," Grant said. "For your sake as well as mine."

They arrived in front of the house, and two valets opened their doors.

"Welcome to Copeland Manor," the one who opened Shelby's door said. "Please enjoy your stay."

Shelby and Grant walked to the front entrance then waited as a servant opened the magnificent double doors that resembled something from a medieval fortress. He motioned them inside.

Her dad put his hand on the small of her back and whisked her inside. Shelby's heels clapped loudly on the marble floor. The floor had a beautiful inlaid design: a shield with two thick red horizontal lines intersected by a diagonal black line. The crest reminded her of the "does not equal" sign from Algebra II, except for the knight's helm at the top, and spanned wider than she was tall. Beyond that, a spiral staircase led up to a loft that looked down upon the entryway.

"Seriously?" Shelby said.

Grant leaned in. "It's the Copeland family crest, I'm sure."

"How many kids do they have? I mean, this place has to have like ten bedrooms."

"Seventeen," answered a kind, deep voice. The man entered from the right. He wore gray slacks and cuff links that had light blue stones in the middle. No tie or jacket. A full head of salt-and-pepper hair was neatly kept in a conservative cut, brushed over to one side.

His smile was quite the opposite of his home/Marriot hotel: welcoming like his voice, not imposing. He stood nearly as tall as Grant but was less impressive physically.

"Mr. Copeland," her father said, walking forward with an extended hand. "So nice of you to have us in your home. Thank you."

Elias took Grant's hand.

He turned his gaze to Shelby. "And this, I presume, is your lovely daughter, of whom we spoke earlier today."

Elias took her hand. "A pleasure."

Then Elias stopped and sniffed the air sharply. "Ah. You won't need that, but I don't blame you for bringing it."

The pistol, Shelby realized. He can smell the gunpowder or the gun lube. Or both. She realized she could as well, the gun powder's slight acrid tincture especially.

Grant looked downcast. "I meant no offense, Mr. Copeland. It's just—"

"No, no, it's fine. I know your previous experience. I take no offense."

Shelby and Grant followed him into a dining room that must have been out of a travel magazine showcasing a castle from France.

Shelby mouthed to her father, "*He's* a werewolf?"

He leaned in close to her. "Not what you were expecting?"

"It's a bit lavish, I admit," Elias said. "We don't use the formal dining hall except on very special occasions."

"Mr. Copeland, you really shouldn't have—" Grant started but Elias interrupted him.

"Elias is just fine. And, yes, we really should have. This is an exciting night. Ah, may I present my wife, Gennesaret."

A beautiful middle-aged woman arose from an equally splendid chair—more of a throne, Shelby thought, with its dark wood and white marble inlays—and came around to greet them. Dark slacks, obviously tailor-made, met a simple sleeveless ivory blouse. An emerald pendant and matching earrings contrasted against her fine ebony hair that showed the faintest signs of silver at her temples. A slender face and naturally rosy lips—some women had all the luck—smiled graciously.

"Welcome," she said to both, her voice quiet and refined. "I hope you enjoy our time together."

"Thank you," Shelby and Grant said in unison.

Grant added, "We're honored to be here."

Gennesaret looked meaningfully at Shelby. Her stare was kind and motherly, but stern. "It is we who are honored to have you here."

Shelby felt a deeper meaning from Gennesaret's words. *What did Dad tell Elias earlier today?* She had no doubt that her "unique standing," as he often called it, came up. Truthfully, she didn't really understand what that meant, and doubted her dad did either. Just because she manifested late? Didn't that make her the runt of the litter?

They approached the table and each place setting was beautifully appointed. Shelby noted the simple elegance, not overboard or gaudy. She ran a finger down the handle of a butter knife, tracing the design of blades of grass etched into the metal. Not silver. Could you imagine the irony? *Pewter*, Shelby thought. *I bet even the silverware is custom made.* Gold rimmed, the china with blue images—flowers and houses and horse-drawn carts—made Shelby squint as she tried to see all the detail.

"From Holland," Gennesaret said. "A client of Elias's owns a shop there."

"Are we missing someone?" Grant asked.

A fifth place setting sat vacant.

"Our son," Elias said. "He had a prior engagement but will be along shortly, I'm sure. Please, let's be seated."

Elias's words *felt* like a command to Shelby, and she found herself *wanting* to obey. An unmistakable charisma attended Elias, that mantle so easily discernible among leaders, power worn lightly but with complete confidence. Presence. There was no other description that came to Shelby's mind as she stared at him. Even that caused her discomfort, and she averted her eyes.

Shelby sat on the far side of the table and she noted that her father took the opposite end of Elias's position. *Always thinking tactically.* She knew her father couldn't help it, and she was definitely grateful for it.

"Now," Elias said, placing an elegant cloth napkin on his lap, "tell us, how have you taken to Lansborough?"

Shelby and Grant each took their turns in talking about their experiences since getting to Lansborough, including today's events at the high school with Chelsea and Sean, though Shelby downplayed those last interactions.

"Ah, the Gittrik kids," Elias said. "You couldn't find a more opposite example of personalities among siblings, could you? Do you know that every election, Mayor Gittrik sends Chelsea over here to tell me they're looking forward to my support? It's not even a request. I used to think it was cute, but well . . . "

Two servers entered the dining hall from doors behind her dad that she thought were part of the wall. So cool! But she saw her dad stiffen slightly when he sensed people behind him.

It's alright, Dad. Was it alright? She did feel moderately relaxed here, bordering on safe.

A wonderful aroma of sautéed vegetables and some kind of meat filled the air. And fresh bread! Shelby's mouth watered. One of the servers set a plate of braised lamb chops, steaming squash, a roll with a perfectly crisped top, and a bowl of some kind of creamy soup before her.

She licked her lips and slyly darted her eyes toward Elias.

"Don't wait on me, Shelby," Elias said. "Dig in."

Not slyly enough, apparently. Why did she feel the need for his approval already? *Runt of the litter, that's why.*

She took her first bite and the lamb seemed to melt in her mouth.

"Wow," she said when she had swallowed. "That is so good."

"Wait until you see what's for dessert," Gennesaret said.

"With all due respect, Mr. and Mrs. Copeland, we aren't here to compare recipes," Grant said.

"We'd lose," Shelby said. "Forgive my dad. He's a little on edge. We both are, I guess."

"Why?" Gennesaret asked.

Grant took the napkin from his lap and wiped the corners of his mouth.

"You mentioned troubles with another pack earlier in my office," Elias said.

Grant stood up. "At the risk of being rude and indecent, let me show you."

He took off his sports coat, untucked his shirt, which exposed his pistol, and lifted the shirt over his head. Shelby watched the Copelands carefully, but they didn't react with the slightest bit of discomfort. Grant turned and exposed his back. From his right shoulder blade, down across his ribs to the front of the right pelvis, streaked four deep purple lines. Scar tissue.

"Who?" Gennesaret asked.

"Pack outside Odessa," Shelby said as her dad put his shirt back on. "My mother's former pack."

"The Alpha's named Nicholas," Grant said. "My wife told me to seek them out if Shelby ever manifested. Had a promise of safe harbor among them. Things changed. The attack was . . . sudden."

"Tobias's pack?" Gennesaret asked quietly, looking to Elias.

"Tobias apparently is no more," Grant said.

"But you survived," Elias said.

"Escaped," Grant corrected. "I killed two of them but Nicholas . . . Shelby shot him at least half a dozen times. I knew he wasn't dead when we ran though, he was too injured to chase us."

Grant was lying. At least, not telling the whole truth. Shelby felt the urge to speak up and correct him, but she resisted. Her dad probably had good cause to be cautious in how much he told. But Shelby again felt that there was more to the story, more than she could remember.

"So, you can shoot," Elias said to Shelby.

She raised her eyes and met his but averted them quickly. "A little."

"Very good to know," Elias said.

"Nicholas is not the leader Tobias was," Gennesaret said.

"You've had dealings with his pack?" Shelby asked.

"Not for some time, Shelby. Not since Tobias was beaten by Nicholas in a challenge. Nicholas is less open to outside pack influence."

"Insecure leaders often are," Elias said. He turned to Shelby. "And you? Were you hurt?"

Shelby shook her head.

Gennesaret said to Grant, "You were extremely lucky you were not bitten."

Grant shrugged. "Still human as far as I can tell."

"Many do not survive the transformation process, the venom in our fangs proving too much. But I somehow believe you would have survived."

"I hope that's not an invitation to try, Mrs. Copeland," Grant said. "I sort of don't mind being just human."

Elias chuckled kindly. "We don't usually go down that road, Grant. Changing humans to werewolves is not our goal. And, as Lycans, we are fully human, too." He turned to Shelby. "And, Shelby, what happened to you during all this? You shifted, I presume?"

"I couldn't," she said, shame in her voice. She knew everyone could hear it. "I wanted to, but . . ."

"Shelby did not manifest until last year," Grant said. "Before we went searching for a pack for her. It was during—well, I'm not sure I'm the one to explain it."

"I was attacked," Shelby said.

"Another werewolf?" Elias asked. "But your father said you were natural born."

Shelby shook her head. "Not that kind of attack. A boy. Someone I went to school with. I thought I liked him and he . . . um . . ."

She put her hands in her lap, balling them into fists. *You're not this weak!*

"He tried to take advantage of you," Gennesaret said. She rose from her chair and came to put an arm around Shelby. She smelled like a field of jasmine in the spring.

"But, that was the first time you manifested?" Elias asked. "You're, what, eighteen now?"

"Almost," Shelby said. "I was sixteen when it happened."

"You poor thing," Gennesaret said, stroking her hair.

"Grant," Elias said, "usually if our children don't manifest at the early stages of puberty, they aren't affected. And, I'm sorry to ask this, but under the circumstances, I feel I must. A Lycan manifesting at the later stages of puberty is atypical, to say the least. Compounding that by the fact that only one parent was a Lycan makes it almost impossible. Are you sure you—"

"I am her father," Grant said firmly.

"I know you care for her deeply, and it's obvious you would do anything to protect her, but are you absolutely positive that you are the biological father?"

"Without any doubt, Elias."

Shelby had to admit it was something that she had wondered about half a dozen times since manifesting, but no more than a few seconds each time.

"You understand," Elias said, "I'm not in any way trying to be rude, but we're dealing with several extremely rare instances here."

"But not impossible instances," Gennesaret said.

Elias and his wife stared at each other for an intense moment before Elias nodded.

"Omega," Elias said to Shelby. "If what you say is true, then you are an Omega."

"It must be," Gennesaret agreed.

Grant nodded. "I am no expert, but I was married to a werewolf, a secret I always kept with complete fidelity. From what I know, I suspected Shelby must be an Omega."

"You thought I was an Omega?" Shelby asked.

"Unique standing, Shel."

"It's why the pack outside Odessa tried to kill your father and take you," Elias said. "They must have known somehow. It makes more sense now."

"No, that was different. It was my wife's former pack, and there was history there that I had foolishly believed might not matter anymore."

"What's so special about an Omega?" Shelby asked.

"They are very sought after," Gennesaret said.

"But why?" Shelby asked.

"Because, young one, Omegas can complete packs. Bring peace and a sense of fulfillment to everyone in the pack. Packs with Omegas often survive longer."

"That also makes them targets by hunters," Grant said. "A way to divide and weaken a pack."

Shelby narrowed her eyes slightly at her father's words. Why would he say something like that? Or even know that? *Well, he was married to a werewolf,* she reasoned. If he had suspected she was an Omega, it made sense why he was always in "super-dad" mode. He had definitely been more chill before she had manifested.

Elias did not respond to Grant but instead leaned back in his chair, staring at nothing while he rubbed his chin, obviously deep in thought. Gennesaret took a small sip of wine from her glass.

"There's a legend," Elias said, "that discusses the completion of a pack, one that has an Omega who blossoms in summer rather than spring. The pack that has such an Omega would experience greater unity and power than otherwise possible and would rise to lead the disparate packs of the earth."

"Okay," Shelby said slowly.

"Yeah, it's just a legend, but many believe it," Elias said. "Many seek that prowess among us. There have been others, packs I mean, who have claimed to have this sought-after Omega but nothing has ever come of it other than strife and death."

Gennesaret looked at Elias. "The Advent?"

"No," Elias said. "Unrelated."

"The Advent?" Grant asked, beating Shelby to the question.

"There's another part of that legend," Gennesaret said. "But it cannot be. They—"

She cut off. "I feel the presence of our son. He is home," she said to Elias.

He nodded. "He just pulled into the garage."

Shelby felt more than heard that nearly imperceptible whoosh of slight air pressure change found when a door is opened.

Immediately, that feeling that had come upon her when leaving the high school earlier came back to her. A warmth in her chest spread throughout her limbs, and things around her appeared brighter, their gleam deeper. A deep exhale escaped her lips, followed by a sharp intake that she held. Faster, her heart beat faster, but not out of fear or anxiety. An ache welled up inside her, one that she didn't know she had been feeling her entire life; a lost, orphaned planet that had finally found its warm, life-giving sun.

Longing. *Belonging*. Security. Home.

Kale drove home from Bubba's house in his Ford Raptor feeling ten pounds heavier. Bubba's mom cooked the best fried chicken in town. Maybe she should open a little place, franchise it eventually if it did well enough. He'd talk to his dad about it. Might be a good little investment, and his dad was always looking for things like that, even though private equity wasn't his forte.

Kale had to admit, that side of the world interested him more and more as he looked to the future. He would eventually need to provide for the pack, in all ways, when his father abdicated. That realization weighed on Kale as he saw what it took to protect and provide for a pack. The overall wellbeing of the wolves was more than just a clandestine presence or protection from outside wolves. It included emotional and financial support as well.

He'd be expected to join the dinner party when he got home. His parents frequently had guests over, whether some important client or, like in this case, someone new in town. Kale could not eat another crumb. He patted his belly. His metabolism was fast as a teenage boy but even more so as a werewolf. Still, he needed a little help to burn through Bubba's momma's chicken.

Hey, there it is, he thought. *Bubba's Chicken. Perfect name for a little chicken joint from the south.*

Kale let the growl inside him, ever present but controlled, rise enough to increase his metabolism and heart rate, but not enough to change him. Learning to control that balance had taken almost two years from the time he first manifested at twelve years old. His eyes stung slightly, like jumping into a pool that had just been chlorinated, as the growl rose a few degrees. It didn't faze him much anymore. After a few minutes, the ball in his stomach lessened significantly, and he didn't feel like he was going to explode anymore.

Bubba's Chicken. He really liked the name and idea. Bubba would never go for it, though. He'd want to keep his mom's cooking a secret, or at least the recipe. Could a patent be obtained for a recipe? If so, wouldn't that make all the ingredients and process public knowledge? Kale had the thought of pitching it on *Shark Tank* only to have the bald guy in the middle, Mr. *Wonderful,* talk to him about how it would be a crime to murder money by investing in this idea, before laughing him out of the room on national TV.

We'll see, Kale thought, determined to follow through on his budding idea a bit later.

His cell phone chirped in the cup holder of the center console, and the screen lit up.

"I'm on my way!" he told the phone as he took it from the cup holder, assuming it was his mother.

It was Chelsea. Crap. He sent his frustration out with a loud sigh through pursed lips.

Hey Kale! it said, followed by a heart and kiss emoji. *Sooo 2mrw night? We staying with my idea or doing something else? Can't wait 2b ur queen!*

The ball in his stomach returned. Why in the world did he put up with her? His natural chivalrous manner was starting to crack, and the other part of him wanted to lash out. Sometimes he wondered which side of him was actually his true self.

He pulled over. What should he say? Maybe just ignore it? That was sure to unleash her banshee mode, and his phone would start blowing up nonstop within ten minutes if he didn't answer. Did the warranty cover fried sim cards due to pervasive abusive texting? He wasn't the only one with two sides. . . . Before he could figure out how to respond, his phone chirped again. It was Trish.

Hey hunk! That pic of u and Chelsea has 2,694 likes! People r reposting it all over Instagram! Emojis of two crowns, a king's and queen's, followed.

Double crap.

Hey Chelsea, he typed, *I'll call you later. Have a thing with my parents.*

He pressed "send," and the phone made a "whoop" noise as the message was delivered.

He should just tell her no, a part of him said, just cut it off cold turkey. But there was nothing to cut off . . . at least in his mind. A couple dates shouldn't automatically latch a ball and chain around his ankle. Geez, they hadn't even held hands. Well, not until this afternoon when she kind of tricked him into it. And there was that awkward semi-kiss she had set up that had somehow made its way onto YouTube. He hadn't even known what was happening at first. Yeah, he'd have to cut it off—their "thing" not his hand—but wanted to at least tell her voice-to-voice, if not in person. A text was not good enough, even for her. He cursed his chivalry, knowing his father would tell him that all girls deserved more than just a text, and got back on the road.

It was 7:06 p.m. when he pulled through the private, side gate entrance and parked in the garage that housed a sizable motorcade. Bruce Wayne would be impressed. Kale opened the door and entered a mud room that led to a butler's pantry, which in turn led to the main kitchen. He pushed open one of the wall-doors and strode into the dining hall.

"Hey, I'm home," he called out, then froze.

Provide. Shelter. Protect. The urges from earlier today slammed into him even more powerfully, and he knew, innately knew, that his life had changed forever. The parts of his soul that had come to life after football practice only a few hours earlier, now ached, a torrent unable to be held back by any emotional dam. A throbbing desire pulsed and flooded through him, and before he knew he had moved, he stood beside the table.

People sat around the table: his father, his mother. A man—a human—he did not know.

And *her.* The girl that kept disappearing into the mist in his mind whenever this feeling came upon him. She looked at him from across the ornate table with deep blue eyes, her narrow face framed beautifully by wavy brunette hair that went to her shoulders and was streaked with blonde. Her face—light almond and as smooth looking as satin—had a dash of mocha colored freckles across her cheeks, so tender, the picture of a desert oasis.

But her scent . . . it was her scent that made him irrevocably hers, whoever she was. It filled him to intoxicating levels, and his knees weakened slightly. Daylight. It was like feeling daylight for the first time, breaking forth in the midst of the bleakest night, thawing the frozen wasteland of his being.

Only a second had passed since he'd entered the room. That ache needed to be satisfied, the thirst of his parched soul quenched. Slowly, he reached forward across the table to touch her. Infinitesimally, she leaned forward in her chair, drawing nearer to him, lips slightly parted.

The human man at the end of the table stood abruptly, a steak knife in one hand. A threat. In the back of his mind, Kale saw the smoke again among the trees, smelled the ashes. Felt the fear of people running from something. Kale inhaled the anger emanating from the man but also smelled concern. Kale's eyes burned.

Her father, he realized, but the threat was real. He had to protect her, had to—

Elias shot to his feet. "Kale. Stand down."

The words tugged at him but not as powerfully as usual. He turned toward the man, *away* from his father, and squared himself. It was like watching from outside his body, not able to control his actions. Instinct. Pure instinct. The knife rose slightly, and the man's free hand went to his hip. Kale felt the rumble of a growl rise in his chest and knew the man had heard it.

"Kale!"

Elias Copeland's voice was thunder, both to Kale's ears and to his mind. The china dishes, elegantly placed in the satin maple hutch behind the table, rattled slightly. He immediately shrank, the power of the Alpha's call impossible to ignore.

Clear your mind! the voice in his head commanded. *Be still!*

His father had used the Call, a power Alphas had over their packs that demanded obedience, a voice that could be sent either audibly or internally, or both. To ignore it would be almost physically impossible, the strength required too great, save for only a few, especially against an Alpha as powerful as Elias.

But the urge! It still surged inside him, swirled like a vortex, pounding its—

"Son," Elias said, now at Kale's side. He felt his father's strong hand on his shoulder. "It's all right." His voice had kinder tones now, fatherly ones, and Kale felt reassured that everything was all right, though his confusion remained as he came to himself.

Elias squeezed Kale's shoulder. "Please, sit. I'll explain."

Shelby saw *him* enter the room, and his presence immediately captivated her. She felt a part of her that was already his, fully, completely, *completed;* another part of her was intrigued but remained free, though she wasn't sure she wanted it to.

It was foolish, this feeling, so rash and unbidden; but it was real, so very real. She could not deny it. Nor, she realized, did she want to. She had always scoffed at all the fairy tales and happily-ever-afters, much preferring the satire of *Shrek* to *Sleeping Beauty*. How many times had she begged her dad to change the DVD from *Snow White* or *Princess Diaries* to *The Lord of the Rings* growing up?

But now, as she stared into his hazel eyes, drowning, she could see them smoldering for . . . her? It wasn't lust, though it was most assuredly desire. It should have scared her, but it didn't. The desire held a purity that shone like a thousand stars in his eyes, a galaxy full of need. And that need, she saw, was for her.

Amber flecks of gold, like pinpricks of light, accented his irises, and they seemed to grow in their radiance, heartbeat by heartbeat. A memory, unwelcomed, came into her mind of Nicholas, how his eyes had flashed with amber before he and others of his pack had attacked and nearly killed her and her father outside Odessa.

The boy must have seen the micro-instant of fear on her face because the stars in his eyes changed, flashing with protective concern. She realized she could almost discern his thoughts through his eyes, like she had known him for centuries.

And then, the strangest thought occurred to her that maybe she had.

Whatever veil had existed that had shielded her from him was being torn from her, ripped away. The world she had once known crumbled, no more than a shadow of memory. For, this boy with the strong presence of a man in front of her had suddenly become her world.

He reached for her and she shuddered at the thought of his touch. Would it be like the feelings that coursed through her, just amplified? Her longing satisfied? Would it be like finally coming home after being a prisoner for a lifetime?

To her left, she saw her father rise from his chair. It was like a passing thought, a dream barely remembered, and she dared not take her eyes from the boy for fear that this vision would disappear, like some cruel joke fate had decided to play on her. Elias was saying something to the boy, but his words were drowned out.

His son, Shelby realized.

They'd mentioned him, but they hadn't mentioned that he would make her fall helplessly, hopelessly in love with him. She knew now why they called it *falling* in love, for the feeling inside her was indeed one of falling, sinking into an unknown abyss. But she was not afraid because she knew he would be there to catch her, to hold her safely from every threat, in his arms.

She yearned to touch him, to take his hand that reached out to her.

"*Kale!*"

The voice exploded in her mind even louder than in her ears. Elias's voice. She immediately looked away and almost got out of her chair, feeling the need to get closer to the ground. The overtone of a growl, not her own, echoed in her mind, and she felt the growl's supernatural ability to command obedience.

Something broke within her at the tension, and she sent forth . . . something. A pulse radiated from her, and she saw the tension lessen, like visible waves dissipating in midair. That was new. She felt Elias look at her with . . . was it gratitude?

"Son, it's all right," he said, placing a hand on Kale's shoulder.

His name is Kale? Shelby remembered what Sadie had said about a Kale: "*. . . if you like that tight chest, broad shoulder, huge biceps-that-you-just-want-to-bite kind of look . . .*"

That Kale?

Yes, definitely that Kale.

But . . . isn't he sorta with Chelsea? What a stupid thought. Her father had his hand on his gun, and her mind wandered to jealous thoughts? Seriously?

"Please, sit," Elias said. "I'll explain."

As Kale slowly sat down at the table, directly across from her, Shelby once again began to drown in the depths of his hazel eyes. This was the kind of drowning from which she did not want to be rescued. What else did he look like? His eyes had been so captivating that she hadn't yet taken the rest of him in, but in some ways it didn't matter. The attraction she felt transcended superficial appearances. As she allowed her focus to widen beyond just his eyes, she saw that physical appearances could be more than skin deep after all.

His brown hair tapered from a thick top, maybe an inch and half long, to a tight cut at the base of his neck, Captain America-like but darker. It was more 1950s than military and definitely worked with his narrow forehead and thick eyebrows. Kale had a short-sleeve t-shirt on, and Shelby had to look at his biceps to see if Sadie was right about them. Oh, she definitely was. And those lashes! Why did men always get natural lashes that women would kill for? Especially when men didn't even care! The unjust irony was an insult to X chromosomes the world over.

Grant still stood, rigid.

"Please, Grant," Elias said.

Grant sat, though Shelby saw a cautious, almost hostile, stare locked on Kale.

"This is Grant Brooks," Elias said to his son, "and his daughter, Shelby. I'll spare you the sanitized introduction of how they've just moved here, us being gracious to have them to dine. That's not true. They sought us out."

"Something potentially lethal . . ." Gennesaret said ". . . and stupid, but noble under the circumstances."

"Hi," Shelby said, reminding herself to blink occasionally.

"Hello," Kale said.

Even his voice melted her? Really? Warm chills—was there such a thing?—rushed over her neck. She had a brief moment of feeling like a complete emotional wimp, but decided if Kale wanted to melt her like soft wax and remold her as his, she wouldn't fight it.

As she took his hand in greeting across the table, his warm, rough one enveloped hers almost completely. The touch of his skin to hers, brief as it was, electrified and quickened her like never before. There was a lot of that going around in the past year of her life, apparently. This, however, was more significant than anything, even more than manifesting as a werewolf; for she somehow knew innately that this boy, Kale, was an answer to a burning question she didn't know she had been asking her whole life. A piece fell into place, one that everyone's soul yearns for in order to be made complete, whole, unified.

Touching him, even in this platonic gesture of shaking hands, ended much too soon, despite lingering many times longer than the social convention normally warranted.

Suddenly, she jerked her hand back and her elbow knocked into her dish, clacking it loudly against the table. Bits of lamb and squash spilled on to the table and the floor. She blushed.

Awesome. Well done, Shelby.

"You don't have a dog, do you?"

Elias chuckled once. "Impressive humor, Shelby."

Oh. Right. The heat of her blush increased on her cheeks. Faux pas, anyone?

Kale looked over to Grant. Shelby saw his steak knife still in hand.

"Sir," Kale said. "I'm sorry. I just . . ." His eyes flicked back to Shelby. "I'm not sure what happened."

Your eyes, Shelby thought. *I'll never be able to escape.*

Kale looked to his father, then mother. "But, he's human."

"I'm right here," Grant said, the soldier in him surfacing. "If you have a question about me or my daughter, you will address me."

Elias raised an eyebrow at Kale, and gestured with his head toward Grant.

"I apologize again," Kale said, turning to Grant. "I obviously walked into a situation I don't understand and—"

"And now you're tripping all over your tail and drooling over my daughter," Grant said. "That about sum it up?"

Grant flashed Shelby a look that simultaneously said, "Don't think I don't see you drooling as well" and "How are you not freaking out right now like you have with every boy since Lucas?"

"I just feel like . . . we've met before," Kale said, turning back to Shelby. "I mean . . . have we?"

Shelby knew what he meant. The feeling was something akin to *déjà vu* but so much stronger.

"No," she said but her mind screamed *yes*. No, it wasn't actually her mind. The voice was different than how a thought sounded. If not her mind, then . . . the feral side of her. Her wolf. And then she recognized that the feelings tearing through her heart and body, beautiful and terrifying, emanated from her wolf. Her human side felt the urges any female would at laying eyes on this gorgeous specimen; but her wolf, from it came the longing, the sense of home, even a degree of familiarity.

Elias stepped in perfectly, obviously a practiced diplomat. "Shelby, perhaps we could start at the beginning, yes? Tell us all how you and your father came to be with us here, perhaps from the attack where you first manifested."

"I . . ." She paused. Did she want to do this? In front of Kale, whom she had just met? In front of Elias and Gennesaret? "I'm not sure I want to."

"Dad," Kale said, "don't make her—"

Elias held up a hand, silencing Kale, his stare locked onto Shelby. She felt the command in that stare and her wolf's desire to obey. She also sensed the trust of Elias within her, within her wolf.

"It was last year." Shelby spoke before the silence went on too long, Grant not deviating from his stony look. She gazed right into Kale's eyes, drawing the courage to speak about it openly for the first time in what felt like forever. "We lived in Tallahassee. There was a boy—"

"Shel—"

"It's okay, dad," she said, looking at Grant. He had finally softened. "Lucas was popular, good-looking, easygoing. Part of that crowd that everyone smirks at but secretly wants to be a part of. When he actually noticed me, I felt like I had somehow arrived." She took a nervous breath. Was she really going to tell this story? "I had crushed on him pretty hard for several months prior, and everyone knew it."

Shelby stopped and took a sip of water, her hand shaking slightly. The water seemed to do nothing for her dry throat. When she spoke again, her voice trembled.

"It was just before junior year started. Lucas asked me out, told me to meet him at Lake Ella for our first date. There's a tree that looks like a deer lying down with huge antlers . . . it was a popular spot for . . ." She looked at her dad. ". . . I should have known. I'm sorry."

"Do not apologize for him," Grant spoke firmly.

She looked to Elias briefly before averting her eyes. She'd never really been in the presence of an Alpha before, not like this. She felt small but not oppressed. Nicholas, she decided, didn't count as an Alpha. Not compared to Elias. Someone looking at Shelby right now might think her to be diminutive in character or inflicted with the shyness of someone long abused. Neither true. Even Kale, this gift to the male species, showed a deference to Elias that was more than the respect of son to father.

But when she looked up at Kale, to once again draw strength from peering into his eyes, she saw a deep, abiding anger flaring, amber flecking his irises. Her story affected him, and she decided to abridge its retelling.

"It was my first time. Shifting, I mean. My only time as well. Lucas had two friends with him, which surprised me because, well, it seemed strange to bring your friends on a date, right? They were there for 'moral support,' he said, but it didn't take long to sense the danger. They held me down while Lucas started to—"

She cut off.

"Sorry," she said.

"Shel—!" Grant said.

But it wasn't an apology for Lucas. She'd told herself she wouldn't say more. And now Kale's eyes watered. Not with sadness but a burning rage. She discerned it easily. His face glowered with a hatred that kind of frightened her. Even Elias, she could *feel* his agitation though much better controlled. Gennesaret radiated concern and regret, a motherly type of feeling that at first she thought was foreign to her but then recalled its familiarity.

The last time she had felt that was before she could walk, from her own mother. She could remember that far back? No, but the feeling of it . . . apparently feelings proved more indelible than actual memories. She couldn't remember what her mother looked like, outside of photographs, but now she realized she knew how she *felt*, at least to a degree.

"When I started to shift, Lucas's two friends freaked. I got free, and they ran. I continued to shift. I didn't know how to stop. My eyes burned, my arms and fingers grew, legs bulged and . . . well, you know it all better than I do. It was the worst pain I've ever felt.

"Lucas fell back, and I slashed out at him before I even knew what I was doing. I didn't know what I was doing, I promise. I didn't mean . . ."

She cut off. Why was she apologizing?

"She arrived home naked, wrapped in a torn sheet with blood on it, and shivering," Grant said, picking up her narrative. "It was not a cold evening, and I know the difference between shaking from a chill and the adrenaline of battle. I didn't know what had happened at first. The only words Shelby spoke were 'Lake Ella,' 'hurt,' and 'Lucas.'

"I jumped in my Blazer and raced to the lake after locking Shelby in the house and calling a neighbor to be with her. Next to the tree Shelby described to you, I found the boy passed out with a gash across his face, down his neck. Did my best to staunch the bleeding as I called an ambulance. If I had known then what I soon after discovered . . . well, I might not have been so inclined to help. When they arrived, the paramedics assumed a wild beast had attacked him."

"That's true," Shelby said, looking at no one. "I scarred him for life."

"That's less than I would have done," Kale said, his husky voice therapy to her soul. Even in the midst of relating the most traumatic experience of her life to practical strangers, she realized how much she wanted Kale. So deeply.

Grant continued, "Lucas was in the hospital for a few days. Shelby was eventually able to tell me enough of what had happened that I knew we had to leave. I had hoped that the time had passed."

"I'm confused," Elias said. "Didn't you know your mother was a Lycan?"

Shelby shook her head. She wished she had, but she didn't blame her dad for withholding that from her. How would that conversation have gone, anyway? Hey, Shelby, you know how your body goes through changes during puberty, well . . .

"Manifesting that late in puberty is very rare," Gennesaret said. "To be an Omega who manifests that late is . . . well, some would say prophetic. Many of our kind can go a whole lifetime without meeting an Omega, never mind a Summer Omega. Every Omega is sought after and protected."

"By all but some," Elias corrected. "There are some packs that would abuse an Omega, taking advantage of her docile nature."

"I'm not docile!" Shelby said. She looked down in self-rebuke from her outburst. "Well, maybe a little."

"Don't mistake docility for weakness, dear," Gennesaret said. "They are really not the same."

"She's right," Elias said.

"Of course, I am, Elias. You don't need to confirm my words, dear."

Whoa. She can talk like that to an Alpha? Gennesaret's words were not spiteful, calmly spoken, but still.

"Of course, *dear*," Elias said. He winked at Shelby, as if knowing her thoughts. Did he? "Go on, Grant."

"Lucas's father came to see me. A man named Sherman, someone I used to know. Once. Seems like a different lifetime."

"Knew him from where?" Genn asked.

Grant hesitated. "The Delta Teams. I didn't know Lucas was his son. I didn't even know he lived near me. He said he was coming for me and my daughter, that he'd been waiting to see if the 'curse' had been passed on from my wife."

"How did he know about your wife?" Elias asked.

Again, Grant hesitated. Shelby felt a ripple of something foreign in the air.

"I don't know," Grant said. "I never told Shelby about her mother until she herself manifested."

"Dad?" Kale said, looking to Elias. "A hunter?"

Elias ran a finger over his upper lip, his eyes distant. "Possibly."

"Right," Grant said. "Let's come to it. I'm Shelby's father. I always will be, and I will always protect and love her. But Moriahna, my wife, made me swear that if Shelby manifested, I would find her a pack. Moriahna impressed it upon me that she would need one, no matter how much I loved her. It's something I can't understand, I'm told."

"How long have you been without a pack?" Elias asked, concern on his face. More, she sensed his concern in the air, somehow. Did she smell it?

"Since it happened when I was sixteen. Almost a year," Shelby said. "You're worried about me going Feral."

Elias nodded.

"I know of the Feral, but why does that happen?" Grant asked.

"We are not sure," Gennesaret said. "Some even choose it."

"But my wife, she was separated from her pack for years. She didn't become Feral."

"She was a mature wolf by the time she left," Gennesaret said. "It's only a threat to newly manifested wolves. Though, older wolves can supposedly choose it also, if they wish."

"Choose it?" Shelby asked. "Why would anyone choose this? To be in wolf form permanently?"

"It's . . . freeing," Kale said. "Right now you fear it. I did when I first manifested. It's natural. But you haven't been able to shift since that night?"

"No. Could have used it. In Odessa." Even she could hear the regret laced with guilt in her voice. "I could have protected you," she said to her dad.

"Not your job, Shel." Grant's square jaw set tightly.

"That's definitely unique," Elias said. "This inability to shift. But perhaps being with a pack can take away whatever blockage exists."

Grant straightened in his chair. "Are you saying you'll accept her into your pack?"

"Yes," Kale said.

Elias fixed his son with a glare and Shelby sensed the soft rebuke in it. "An Omega is valuable," he said. "But that's not why we would accept her. Not solely the reason, anyway."

"Still listening," Grant prompted. Shelby knew her father's military side had had enough discussion and eagerly wanted to come to the point.

"There's a war brewing," Elias said reluctantly.

"War?" Shelby asked.

"The European packs," Elias said. "They are being united under a single head in a movement called the Advent."

"It will move to the U.S. and other parts before long," Gennesaret said. "Already some Advent agents are in parts of South America and Mexico, perhaps Canada as well. They are preparing."

"Genn runs our intelligence side," Elias explained. "She has developed a communication network with many other packs."

"She even has ins with some satellite surveillance contractors," Kale said. "It's really cool!"

So, there *was* a teenage boy inside that masculine body.

"You said preparing," Shelby said. "For what?"

"America, behind Europe, has the largest werewolf population," Elias said. "If the American packs can be united through the Advent with the European packs under a single head, they will be powerful enough."

"For?" Grant asked.

"To take over," Elias said. "To rule."

"Has there never been a united pack with a single ruler?" Grant asked.

"No, you misunderstand," Elias said. "I don't mean to rule the

Lycan species. I mean the world, Mr. Brooks. Humanity."

"What?" Shelby asked. "Why?" War with the humans? She still thought of herself as more human than Lycan.

"Those who believe in the Advent believe we've hunkered in the shadows of humanity, hiding what we are. They want to walk openly in the daylight, in a manner of speaking."

"And those packs that don't join them?" Shelby asked.

Elias inhaled slowly. "That has yet to actually be seen. The Alpha of a pack is challenged by the leader of the Advent, someone who calls himself Alpha Prime. This Alpha Prime has never been defeated, and the pack of the dead Alpha is assimilated into the Advent pack."

"You're worried," Shelby said. It was not a question. She could feel it, not to mention hear it in his voice.

"The most natural entry point for them is through Mexico, into Texas. We would be the front line. Canada as well, but fewer packs are up north to assimilate."

"So you don't agree with the movement," Grant said.

"No," Gennesaret said.

"And you would resist?" Grant asked.

Elias nodded. "We are human *and* wolf, not one or the other. I would resist humans trying to subvert or exterminate werewolves as well."

"Your guards," Grant said. "Not mere hired security, then."

"The illusion of it, at least," Elias said. "As I said, we're preparing."

"Are they . . ."

"Werewolves? Just Ackerman, head of security. He recruited most of the others. Most are former special forces."

"I noticed."

"Wait," Shelby said. "You were telling us why you would allow me into the pack." Did she really want that now, knowing a war was likely coming? *I'm not a warrior or anything.* But her dad had taught her to be, hadn't he? Did he know about the Advent?

"It's related," Elias said.

Gennesaret perked up. "An Omega in full bloom, Shelby, can sense feelings and calm situations."

I already can, Shelby thought, but didn't interrupt her. She thought of the encounter earlier with Chelsea. *Well, when I want to.*

"While those Omega traits are valuable to a pack, the legend of the Summer Omega—an Omega who manifests late—says that she will be able to interpret emotions, to know when someone is lying, for example, and even project emotions to others, causing them to feel what she wants them to."

Shelby found her dad's eyes, which were locked onto something and yet nothing. The distance she saw in them spanned miles.

"Okay," Shelby said. "But—"

"Even see glimpses of the future," Gennesaret finished.

"We don't know if you're *the* Summer Omega," Elias said. "But with a building threat at our door, we'll take whatever advantage we can and having an Omega with us *is* an advantage, regardless of the legend's veracity."

"It is," Gennesaret said confidently.

Elias made a gesture with his hand, flicking it palm up, and pursed his lips. "Perhaps. She could have manifested late simply because she has a human father."

Gennesaret just smiled, her expression clearly saying, "I don't think so."

"You would have to take both of us," Shelby said. "My dad, too."

"Shel—" Grant started but was interrupted.

"Yes," Kale said. He looked directly into Shelby's eyes. Just a few minutes ago, it seemed like Kale was going to try and rip her dad apart . . . or get torn apart by her dad. She wasn't sure which would've happened, but now Kale was open to letting her dad in the pack?

"That's not possible," Elias said. "Not as part of the pack."

"That is my condition," Shelby said, finding enough backbone to look Elias in the eye. "You might be an Alpha, but he is my *dad*." A wave of certainty filled the air. Her firmness on the matter radiated from her. She felt it, and she knew Elias felt it. "He already knows about werewolves and is an ally."

"Security," Grant said. "Make me part of the security detail."

Elias rubbed his hands together, thinking.

"I assure you I could add some steel to the ranks, sharpen a few edges," Grant went on. "If there is a war coming, I'd prefer to be by my daughter's side."

"And he's killed werewolves before!" Shelby said.

Elias raised his eyebrows. "I'm not sure that's a check in the plus column."

"Elias, the girl wishes it," Gennesaret said. "I don't see any harm."

"Kale, you've been relatively quiet other than agreeing with everything Shelby has said," Elias remarked. "Anything constructive you want to add?"

Kale quickly typed something on his phone instead of answering.

"Kale? Should we give you and your phone some privacy?"

"Sorry, just had to break a date tomorrow."

Shelby perked up. *Break a date?*

"Kale," Elias said, somewhat irritated. "Do you have anything else to say on the matter?"

"Just a question," he said, now gazing at Shelby. He half-smiled, and she felt herself start to melt again. "Will you go to homecoming with me?"

The warm evening air rushed past Shelby's face as she rode home from dinner in the Blazer, window down. She felt like she was glowing, and checked the sideview mirror just to be sure she wasn't. *Home Coming with Kale Copeland . . .* Though she didn't glow, her eyes did shine with a gleam of . . . was that contentment? She definitely felt *home* when she thought of Kale. She sighed, happily, and then started preparing herself for the torrent of verbal abuse sure to come from Chelsea. *Yeah, Shelby, you're going to experience Banshee mode.* She still didn't know what that looked like.

She replayed every moment of the dinner, savoring certain moments. *Like when I nearly drowned in the emerald ocean of his eyes.* Then, her stomach groaned, but not from worries about the whorey trinity or the meal.

"Dad, you were hesitant when talking about Lucas's dad. And about mom."

"Old wounds," Grant said.

"Do I know everything? About mom?" Shelby asked.

The obvious pause before his answer gave Shelby more consternation.

"You know enough," he answered.

"Not everything?"

Grant looked out his window then turned to Shelby. "No."

"Why not?"

"Later Shelby."

Shelby shifted in her seat to face her father more fully. "That's not fair. Why not now?" She hated when he did stuff like this. And often when he said "later," he really meant "never."

"Because I said so."

"What am I? Five?"

Grant sighed as they turned into the driveway, more a patch of gravel and dirt than pavement. "Please, Shel, just trust me. Old wounds are painful sometimes."

As they pulled up to the house, the Blazer's headlights swiped across an older blue BMW Z3 with white stripes on the hood parked beneath the large moss tree. Someone was waiting on the porch, sitting on the old steps.

"Sadie?" Shelby asked. She exited the Blazer, the door creaking as she shut it.

The dark red-haired girl sprang up. It was past 8:30, and the sun's last glimmers had just set.

"Hey!" Sadie said.

"Hi," Shelby answered. "Dad, this is Sadie, my friend I met at tryouts today, the one I told you about."

"Aw, how sweet. You told your dad about me."

Shelby saw her dad stiffen a bit but he played it off well. "Hello," he said. "Nice to meet you, Swearing Sadie. Thanks for being a friend to Shelby. Always tough when you move to a new town."

Sadie glared at Shelby. "You called me 'Swearing Sadie' to your dad?" She scoffed and turned to Grant. "*Very* nice to meet you as well." Shelby saw her friend take him in with her eyes in the way only another girl could notice.

"I'll be inside, Shel," Grant said. He smiled politely and nodded at Sadie as he ascended the steps to the front door.

After the door closed, Sadie grabbed Shelby's arm. "I was right. Totally hot."

"Shut up."

"Sooo, how'd it go?"

"Um, how did what go?"

Sadie rolled her eyes. "The meeting with Elias, airhead."

"What? How'd you know about that? Are you spying on me?"

"So it's true what they say about blondes."

"Hey, I only have blonde streaks!" Shelby said.

"I know, that's why I had hopes you'd figure it out. Must've been wrong."

"Okay, no need to get witchy."

Sadie huffed. "Witches never really had much over us, actually. We've been allies on a few things in the past, though."

"Us?"

Sadie looked hard into Shelby's eyes. "Us. I know what you are. You don't have to pretend with me."

Shelby saw Sadie's eyes fleck with gold, almost iridescent in the late evening. She stepped back, astonished but knew she shouldn't have been.

"Okay, you're a . . ." Could Shelby be wrong? Was this a trick to somehow get her to say something she shouldn't?

"Werewolf? Yup. Mom and Dad, too. Little nerd brother isn't . . . yet. He's a year from puberty. Solid waste, he'll make an annoying wolf. Now that we have that out of the way, *finally*, tell me how it went with Elias."

"You're . . . part of his pack?"

"Maybe there's hope for you yet, dark roots and all."

"Right. It went well, I think."

"Oh my gosh, I'm going to have to drag every condemned thing out of you, aren't I?"

"Condemned thing?" Oh, right. Damned thing. "They said I can join the pack," Shelby said, cutting to the chase anyway. "Elias and Gennesaret are extremely nice. Different than what I expected."

"Yay!" Sadie said, doing her little clap dance, the same one she had done at gymnastics tryouts. "And did you meet Kale, or did he skip to go hang out with that she-wench? You should see what's on Instagram right now."

"Yeah, he was there." Shelby tried to say this casually, but by the look on Sadie's face, she'd failed.

"Oh. My. Goodness. You fell for him that fast? Geez, talk about predictable. Did you have to wipe the drool away from your *maw*?"

"He asked me to homecoming."

"Holy feces, what?" Sadie exclaimed, eyes as wide as her mouth.

"I said yes."

"What?" Sadie paced. "Oh, coitus me! Wow, you just dive right in, don't you?"

"Sadie—"

"No, no, don't apologize. This is perfect! Perfect! The whorey trinity won't know what hit them! I *so* cussing love you!"

"Is saying 'cussing' using technical descriptions? Kinda sounds like cheating."

Sadie shrugged. "Lazy sometimes."

"What are you doing?"

Sadie had her phone out, the white light from the screen illuminating her face eerily. "Tweeting."

A small ball of dread germinated in Shelby's stomach. "Sadie, *what* are you tweeting?"

"See for yourself. You can follow me @RedHairBites."

Shelby blinked a few times. "Seriously?"

"I know, clever, right?"

Shelby whipped out her phone and opened her Twitter app. After finding Sadie's handle, she followed her and saw her tweet.

KC chooses new girl over CG for homecoming, ditches banshee.

"So now I'll be even more of a target. Great."

"Relax, you can always just kill Chelsea," Sadie said casually.

Shelby really wasn't sure if Sadie was serious.

"Have you . . . ever . . ."

"A person? Nah. But how much different can it be than a deer or boar?"

"You're a sociopath," Shelby said with a laugh.

"And you're totally infatuated," Sadie said, putting a hand on her hip as she shifted her weight. "I warned you about Kale."

"You just said he was hot."

"Yeah, well, so is your dad, so . . ."

"Oh my gosh, can we not talk about my dad like that?" Shelby said. "And it's not infatuation with Kale, it's so much more."

"Don't get all butt-hurt. And you're obviously an insane chick. Totally coo-coo. I don't mind, don't worry."

"No, I'm not. Well, I might be, but when we touched . . . I mean, it's like the whole world just disappeared, ya know? Like it was just me and him, somewhere else, far away with none of the crap of life, none of the worries, or—"

"When you touched?" Sadie interrupted.

"Shook hands."

"Hold on, you got *that* twitterpated from shaking his hand? Are you that girl who believes she's living a romance novel in real life? That's a real disease, you know."

"Like Cotard's syndrome?"

"Huh?"

"Zombie disease."

"You are the strangest chick I know, Shelby, but I still love you."

"I'm serious," Shelby said, "it's a real thing where people really think they're dead and—"

"Blah blah blah," Sadie said with a mock yawn. "Back to *touching* Kale."

"It was just a handshake."

"Bull feces, but go on."

"It just felt . . . electric. Almost like I was shocked and a part of me woke up, a part I didn't know was sleeping."

Sadie was silent. Even in the low evening light Shelby could see the wonder on her friend's face.

"Sadie."

"Holy feculence," the red-headed girl finally said. "Are you bonded to Kale?"

"What the heck does that mean?"

"You know what I mean."

"No, Sadie, I don't. I'm still new to this werewolf thing, actually. I only manifested last year."

"When you were seventeen?"

"Sixteen."

"Whoa," Sadie put the heel of her left hand to her forehead. "I told you. Strange chick."

"So, bonded?"

Sadie took a deep breath and let it out slowly. "Right. Did you kiss him?"

"What? No, of course not."

"Well, you never bloody know, diving right in like you do. It takes a kiss to meld the bond. Some people say it takes more, but I don't think so."

"You said bloody," Shelby said.

"It's a cuss word in England, not here. But . . . my dad's British, so maybe it is. I'll have to think about that one."

"You watched too much *Sleeping Beauty* as a kid," Shelby said. "My dad made me watch *Saving Private Ryan* to cure me of that fairy-tale garbage. Don't start telling me about true love's first kiss, or I might throw up."

"Were you not the one who just went on about finally waking up, the world going away, just you and him, all gross-like?"

It was true. That evil aliens poet that had taken over her sensible self. "Alright, alright."

"When the world disappeared, were you both in a little snow globe together with a condemned music box tinkling in the background?"

"I said alright, geez. So, a kiss?"

"Believe me, you'll know if you're bonded when you kiss him. Or so say the legends. Probably better to just go and get it over with. When are you seeing him again?"

"I don't know. Soon I hope."

"Didn't Sean ask you to go hang out tomorrow?"

Shelby bit her lip. "Oh yeah, forgot about that. News travels fast."

"Small town."

"Everyone and everything. I heard. You going?"

"Of course. You should just bring Kale," Sadie said, lowering her chin to her chest.

"Yeah, because that wouldn't be weird. 'Why, yes, Shelby, when I invited you I really meant for you to bring another guy along.'"

Sadie blinked slowly, moving her head side to side, as if considering. "Sean's cool, he won't care. Have you seen his calves?"

"Um, yeah, actually, I did notice them."

Sadie licked her lips. "Juicy, right?"

"So, this bonded thing. Are you just messing with me? Is it some kinky thing?"

"I mean, I guess it could be if you wanted it to be." Sadie smiled, glaring at Shelby conspiratorially. "Do you?"

"And you were telling me off for not giving straight answers."

"I wonder if a werewolf can be bonded to a human," Sadie said, glancing to the front door. "Think your dad is still awake?"

"You're really screwed up."

Sadie smiled as her phone toned. "Hey! Look at that! Seventeen retweets and twenty favorites from my Twitter post. You're a rock star already! Oh, and I got twelve new followers. Yes!"

"You're socially murdering me before school even starts," Shelby said.

"Just embrace it. Better to steer into it, Shel."

"Only my dad calls me Shel." She paused. "It's fine, I guess."

"Okay, Shel, so the way you described what you're feeling for Kale could be just a serious case of romance-novelitis or—"

"You made that up—"

"*Or*, it could be that you and Kale could become bonded. That's way different than simply falling in love. When you're bonded with someone, they say you don't have much of a choice. Your wolf doesn't, anyway. Your human side has to choose it still, but if it doesn't your wolf will forever be . . . less."

"Does this happen to all werewolves?"

"Heck no, aren't you listening? It's very rare and only ever happens between Alphas and Omegas." Sadie paused, squinting at Shelby. "You're not . . ."

"Elias and Gennesaret said I might be an Omega."

Sadie nodded and blinked hard once. "That's amazing, actually. Really. I've never met an Omega. I'm not sure anyone in our pack has. Maybe Dakota or Chenoa but they're *really* old. Will you be my bestie?"

"Promise to stop tweeting about me?"

"Nope."

"You're so mean."

"I know. So, besties?"

"Can we call it something that doesn't rhyme with testes?"

Sadie's smile slowly grew until it erupted into a laugh that filled the night. "I love you!"

"Shel," Grant called from a window upstairs.

"I'm pretty tired," Shelby said. "Super long day. Thanks for coming over and for earlier today in the locker room. It's good to have a friend."

As Sadie opened the door to her Z3, Shelby said, "Hey, wait.

Can't you usually smell another werewolf?"

"Duh," Sadie said, resting her arms on the BMW's open car door. The window was down.

"But, I couldn't smell your scent at gymnastics."

"You really are new to this stuff," Sadie said. "I'm a Venatrix."

"Yeah, that cleared everything up. Thanks."

"Don't get snippy with a redhead, Shelby Brooks. A Venatrix is a secret agent werewolf. Used as spies among other packs in ancient times, or something like that."

"Ancient times?" Shelby asked.

"Yeah, I'm not the one for this stuff," Sadie said, as she lowered herself into the seat and started her car. She pressed a button and the convertible top started lowering. "Kale's mom is the resident expert on folklore. You're an Omega. I'm a Venatrix. It basically means my crap don't stink."

Sadie turned on to the narrow winding road and pulled up next to Shelby. "Don't forget to invite Kale. And more importantly," Sadie yelled as she drove away, "to kiss him!"

Shelby felt butterflies in her stomach.

Late into the night, Kale lay in bed, wide awake, with his arm propping up his head. Thoughts that refused to be quieted raced through his mind. His heart throbbed as if he had just finished football practice though he was calmer than he had been in . . . well, a very long time. An understanding resided in him now, something Shelby had caused to open within him, and his life had a new focus—or rather, *a* focus finally.

"Kale?" Elias leaned his head through Kale's opened door. "You still awake?"

"Yeah."

Elias came in and sat at the foot of Kale's bed. Kale didn't feel his dad sit on the edge of the bed, the memory foam mattress living up to its advertising. Kale sat up against the light wood of the bed's headboard. The color reminded him of drift wood found on the beaches of the Gulf Coast.

"So, Shelby, huh?" his dad said.

Were they really going to have a bonding moment talking about girls? Kale shrugged.

"She took my breath away." The words seemed to just come out. Did he really just say that? To his dad?

"I noticed. I think we all did."

"Yeah, her dad didn't seem to look too kindly on that."

"And your reaction to him was dangerous."

Kale exhaled through tight lips. "I know. I feel bad about that. Really, I don't know what happened. I'll apologize again when I see him next."

"Grant's fine. But, those feelings you had . . . you're definitely not a mere boy anymore."

"Seriously, Dad, I don't want to have *that* talk."

Elias smiled. "It's not that kind of talk, trust me. But your wolf, when it wants something, it can be *very* persuasive."

Kale suddenly felt very tired. Or annoyed.

"The normal bodily urges we have toward others we find attractive," Elias went on, "are much harder for us to control when our wolves start adding their own desires."

"We are having *that* talk, then."

"All I'm saying, Kale, is keep in control. If Shelby is an Omega, it will be increasingly hard for you to stay grounded around her."

Kale sat up. "Why?"

"Because, Kale, you are an Alpha. Not yet, but you will be. It runs in your blood. And an Alpha is attracted to an Omega more strongly than mere human emotions can conjure."

Kale pondered this. "Dad, I felt something tonight, but I don't think it's simply thinking that Shelby is hot."

Elias gave his son an appraising look.

"Well," Kale continued, "she is hot. I admit it. But I don't think what I felt was just emotion between an Alpha and an Omega, like you're saying. I mean, I felt it before I even saw her, like as soon as I walked in the house. And not just tonight, I felt it earlier today at school after football practice. Shelby must have been near. It was the strongest sensation, and I can't explain it."

Elias put a hand on Kale's shoulder. "They're called hormones, son."

"No, Dad, that's not it."

"You just told me Shelby is hot. Twice."

"No . . . I mean yes, she is. But the feeling I had, *twice*, was before I ever *saw* her. It only comes when I'm around her. Near her. You know what I mean? It's like that with you and mom, right?"

"Sure, Kale. But I'm not going to have *that* talk with you, remember?" Elias smiled slyly.

Kale realized his father did not know exactly what he was talking about. Was that possible? Kale searched his dad's face. He didn't. Kale could tell by the look in his eyes. The feeling he had around Shelby could not be normal, not simply attraction or even deep love.

"Never mind," he said.

"Listen, Kale, I have to go out for a bit."

"Now? It's almost midnight."

"There's something that requires my attention. It shouldn't be long."

"Alpha stuff?" Kale asked.

"Pack business, yes."

"Should I come?"

"No, not this time. Mom will remain here as well. I just wanted to let you know."

There was some concern in his father's eyes, well-hidden but still there.

"Something's wrong, isn't it? Tell me. Maybe I can help."

"It's nothing you need to be concerned with. Trust me. All will be well."

"It's not problems with another pack, is it? I'm strong. I can help."

"No, it's not that. And I know you're strong. Physically, I'm not sure I know your equal. But strength, Kale, is not always the right tool. We're just going to be observing a few things. We'll be back before morning.

"Oh, and we'd like to introduce Shelby to the rest of the pack in a few days. Think she'll be up for it?"

"I'll ask," Kale said. "Should be cool."

Elias stood to leave.

"Dad," Kale said. "Be careful."

"Always am."

"Who are you taking?"

"Ackerman and James Southeby. A few others. We'll be fine."

Kale heard the small bit of nerves in his dad's voice, cloaked by his usual confidence.

Hill and his team of six hunters walked among the people in downtown Lansborough, dressed in khakis and casual shirts. He tapped the rim of his glasses, and the micro-camera began transmitting the scene before him to Sherman's team offsite.

Of course, the nightlife of downtown Lansborough meant small herds of inebriated people migrating from one bar to the other. Live music blared from one establishment, the Open Barrel, as a bouncer tossed a man to the street. Another man, making threats to the bouncer, tried to help his drunken friend up but ended up losing his balance and joined him on the pavement. The two men laughed, eventually pulled themselves up, and stumbled into Hart's Tavern across the street.

Some of the night owls combed the streets, window shopping as they passed each closed store. The soft sound of cars swooshing by on the freeway about a quarter mile east melded with the din of occasional laughs and the muted scuffle of footsteps by others walking the same street.

Hill felt attracted to the quiet, small-town feel. If only it weren't infected with Lycans.

Their target walked about fifty yards ahead of them. Sherman had sent them to recon the town, to check on Nicholas's intel. Nicholas, as it turned out, had been telling the truth. That intel had cost Sherman his entire team in Odessa, but each hunter knew that sacrifice could be asked of them in the fulfillment of God's work.

The man they followed, James Southeby, if Hill's intel was correct, was an engineer at a local civil engineering company. In fact, Southeby's wife and son were all taken by the curse.

Lead on, cretin. Lead on.

Southeby would lead them to discover more of the pack in Lansborough, if Hill and his team were patient. And cautious. So far, Southeby's nightly strolls had not proved fruitful, appearing no more than a man clearing his head and getting some fresh air. But his route had varied tonight. This had to be it. Hill could feel it.

A handful of teenagers came bursting out of a movie theater, the only one in town. They threw popcorn at each other, and cars that passed by. Hill lost sight of Southeby as the kids blocked his view.

He cursed.

Hill touched a comm unit in his ear. "We can't lose him."

His team picked up their pace, converging on Southeby's last position, pushing through the teenagers.

"Hey, watch it, man!" one of the boys said, obviously showing off for a girl. Some of the teens looked more like college age, now that Hill saw them up close. Hill remembered those carefree days before he had learned the truth about their world and the parasites that had infected it.

His team met at the south corner of the movie theater and looked around. Hill knew their cover would have been blown if someone had been paying attention.

"Down there," one of the team members, Abernathy, said.

Hill pivoted and saw the alley. Yes, there was no other explanation for where Southeby had disappeared to. Subconsciously, Hill felt for the concealed Glock at his hip. His magazine carried nineteen silver rounds, plus one in the chamber.

"This is a trap," Abernathy said.

It did feel that way. But they had exercised extreme caution. Hill didn't believe they could have been discovered, at least not prior to converging—not early enough for Southeby to make plans. The team took a few cautious steps down the alley, but Hill stopped.

Silence. The teenagers' laughs and ruckus had ceased. A chill went up the back of Hill's neck. Facing down the alley, Abernathy looked sidelong at Hill. He slowly lifted his shirt, drew the pistol from his inner-waistband holster and turned his head, looking over his shoulder. Hill's breath froze in his lungs. Five werewolves stood at the mouth of the alley. The moviegoers. Their heads hunched low between their shoulders.

Fool! Hill chided himself.

"Sir," Abernathy said.

Hill gazed back down the alley. At the other end, perhaps fifty feet away, three larger wolves faced them. In the middle of the three stood the largest wolf Hill had ever seen. Black with amber eyes that pierced the alley's darkness, even from this distance. The Alpha. It had to be.

"Elias," Hill whispered. If he could take down Elias Copeland . . . Hill steeled himself.

The Alpha stepped forward. Hill raised his silenced sidearm and cursed himself for letting his team get trapped so easily.

"Johns, Lyons, Russo, take the rear. Abernathy, Murray, on me."

Hill took aim and fired, the suppressed gunfire sounding no louder than a nail gun. The wolves charged. Hill continued to fire but frustratingly could not find his targets in the darkness. The eyes presented the best target, but they darted toward him faster than he could reacquire their position after each recoil. Like demonic duos of fireflies. Behind him, he heard a scream. Then more and the sound of things being torn. Clothing. Skin.

The Alpha sprang onto the stuccoed outside wall of the movie theater and ran several strides sideways. Defying gravity. The slide of Hill's gun locked back, and he reached for his spare mag, but never got a chance to load it. The Alpha landed on him with such force that Hill might have sworn that a train hit him. His glasses sailed from his head, and he felt his collar bones and several ribs break. Just before the Alpha ripped his body apart, he thought of his martyr's award waiting for him on the other side.

Shelby entered the locker room the next morning, hoping to avoid Chelsea and her two disciples. Amazed at the drama that had occurred in the last twenty-four hours and how she somehow stood in the middle of it, Shelby thought it best to avoid deepening any conflict. She didn't want the most popular girl in school as her nemesis, but Sadie had pretty much assured that by her tweet last night. Some friend. Shelby sighed. When she checked this morning, there were over eighty retweets and two hundred favorites. How many "besties" did Sadie have in this "small" town? Chelsea would no doubt be on the warpath.

War paint and all, I'm sure.

Luckily, no one else was in the locker room. Was she late? She stripped down to her leo quickly and stored her clothes in a locker. Just as she turned away, her phone chimed from her shorts' pocket inside her locker and she couldn't resist. She retrieved her phone and saw a text from Kale.

Hey. Miss me?

That stupid girly-grin that always came out when she tried to hide her feelings, spread across her face. She double-checked to make sure she was really alone in the locker room.

U wish, she replied. *Where r u?*

Football practice. My phone is blowing up, he texted. *Did you tell someone we're going to homecoming?*

Just Sadie.

Ugh. Twitter?

Yeah, Shelby texted. *U r pretty popular apparently.*

Well, if the texts I've gotten from Chelsea are any warning, be careful today.

What's she saying?

Typical stuff. I hate you, traitor, spawn of Satan. You know.

Um, wow?

Yeah, just be careful. She can be . . . creative. Full on banshee-mode.

Shelby replied, *Sounds great. Oh, hey, I meant to ask u . . . what r u doing tonight?*

Whatever you are.

Shelby's stupid girly-grin widened. How did she like him this much after one dinner together? After just touching his hand? He had almost tried to kill Grant . . . or was it the other way around? Sadie's words from last night about being bonded came back to her. She still didn't know if she trusted that mystical romance nonsense, but maybe werewolves did have different rules on this stuff.

Sean kinda invited me to this thing. But Sadie said I could just go with u.

Ya, Sean's cool. I know about it. Wasn't sure you wanted to go.

Might b fun.

If you're there it will be.

Do u practice this stuff? Like the perfect things to say and when? R u part of a secret guys' club where u rehearse?

I'll pick you up tonight.

U know where I live?

Ya.

Stalker much?

Concerned citizen.

Uh-huh. C u 2nite.

Yup. Bye. Oh, wait, Dad wants to introduce you to the pack soon. Cool?

Shelby hesitated. Was it okay? She'd have to meet them eventually, right? Still, the thought made her a little nervous.

She responded, *Ya, probs.*

Not a big deal. Trust me. See ya.

K.

Somewhat timidly, Shelby left the locker room and entered the gym. Sadie practiced her floor routine and several other girls waited for their turn. Coach Anders nodded to Shelby.

"Brooks, you need to be on time," he said, looking down at his clipboard. "Do you need a watch?"

"Sorry, coach, I got held up."

"No excuses, Brooks. This team starts on time or you don't start at all. Extra body toning for you today. Fifty push-ups, fifty mountain climbers, five minutes of jump rope. All with a smile or you'll do it again until I'm convinced you're enjoying yourself."

"What, no first warning and a pass?" Shelby asked.

"Oh, this is your warning," Coach Anders said. "Now get to it."

Shelby looked around, surprised she didn't see Chelsea, Amanda, or Trish. That should have been comforting, but wasn't.

She got down and started to knock out the push-ups.

"With a smile, Brooks!" Coach Anders called out. Shelby could hear the forced smile in his tone.

"Seriously?"

"Chandler, am I serious?"

Sadie paused her floor routine. "Absolutely, coach!" She wore a wide smile that was so fake it made Shelby laugh.

"That's the spirit, Brooks!" Anders said.

"You're coming tonight, right?" Sadie asked.

They walked out of the locker room, exiting to the same area where Shelby had met Sean yesterday.

"Yeah, Kale said he'd go," Shelby answered.

"More than just going to Homecoming, I see."

"I don't know. Maybe."

Football players in their practice jerseys rushed past Shelby and Sadie, and Shelby immediately stiffened amid a feeling of falling.

"What?" Sadie asked. "You went pale. You sick?"

"No, I'm fine. Just don't like being around guys sometimes."

"Oookayyy," Sadie said. "That makes no sense. Do tell."

"I know. Some other time."

Then Shelby felt Kale near, and the anxiety turned to that feeling of home and warmth she'd experienced yesterday. She saw him, jogging off to the boys' locker room, his head down. Maybe he wanted to play it cool and not draw attention. But before he entered the locker room, he glanced at her, flashing her a big smile. Shelby waved shyly. Several of his teammates pushed him inside, teasing him as they shoved him.

"Do you see yourself?" Sadie asked. "It's cussing gross."

"I thought you liked the idea of Kale and me."

"Well, yeah, since it undermines the whorey trinity."

"Where were they today?"

"Probably having a cry session together over Kale dumping her for you."

"They weren't going out, just to Homecoming, right?" Shelby wanted to make sure she had the story straight.

"If that," Sadie said. "But Chelsea probably didn't see it that way."

Shelby pursed her lips and crossed her arms. "Kale said she's in 'banshee-mode', whatever that means."

"Yeah, that can be interesting," Sadie said.

"Should I be wearing a gun?"

"Maybe a bazooka. So, your dad . . . he was military?"

"Yup. Army Rangers. Delta Force. Super-secret stuff."

"He ever tell you about it?"

Shelby shrugged. "Not too much. He taught me how to shoot, though."

"Seriously? That's awesome! Can he teach me?"

"Um, maybe."

"Will he have to wrap his arms around me and put his hands over mine to show me proper technique?"

"How demented are you?"

"No one knows," Sadie said airily as she cocked her head to the side, as if in thought. "Okay, so tonight, here at eight. It'll be fun."

"What do you guys do?"

"It's just hanging out, making fun of each other, you know. Just a bunch of donkeys talking cow dung. Nothing serious."

"Okay. Kale is going to pick me up."

"What a gentleman."

"Shut up."

"Bonded," Sadie said, looking off casually. "I'm telling ya."

"Whatever. See you tonight."

Kale's Raptor pulled up in front of Shelby's house just after eight. Shelby waited on the porch steps with her father. The driver door opened, and Kale stepped out of the truck, the rays of sunset glinting off his skin in a way that made Shelby's heart race. She felt a flush on her neck.

"Good evening, Mr. Brooks," he said.

Grant rose to meet Kale and accepted his outstretched hand. "Kale."

"Thanks for letting me take Shelby out tonight."

"You'll be with a group?" Grant asked.

"Dad!" Shelby said. "Don't interrogate him. I invited him."

"Yes, sir. With a group," Kale said, his eyes staying locked on Grant.

"Make sure it stays that way."

Shelby turned bright red. Did he have to be super-protective in front of Kale?

"Come on," Shelby said, pulling Kale away, but Kale stood still.

"My father says your first day with the security team was good. Some of the other guys were impressed with you. Anyway, thought you might like to know."

Grant nodded. "That's generous of Mr. Copeland to say. Now,

Kale, understand, I don't work for you. I don't take to flattery. This is my daughter, and while she is in your care, I expect you to provide for her safety from everyone and anything."

From his tone, Shelby knew he meant "including you, Kale," but didn't need to say it.

"Dad, it's just a bunch of kids hanging out," Shelby said, acting incensed even though she secretly appreciated her dad's concern.

"Sir, I know it was tense between us last night," Kale said. "That was my fault, and I apologize. I will certainly place your daughter's safety above everything, I assure you."

Grant smiled. "See? I knew we could have an understanding." He gripped Kale's shoulder, still smiling, and said, "Have fun, you two. And Kale, not later than 10:30."

Shelby saw Kale wince ever so slightly under her dad's grip.

"Your dad . . . he's—"

"Crazy?" Shelby asked. Kale's truck rode more comfortably than she would have guessed for a massive gas guzzler as they cruised down the road toward the high school.

"Intense. And . . . well, *strong*."

"Yeah, I guess."

"I'm serious," he said. "There aren't too many humans that can make one of us feel pain by a simple grip."

"Sorry. He's really protective."

"It's okay. If I had a daughter that went through what you did—"

"Music?" Shelby said, turning the radio on.

Taylor Swift's "Trouble" came blaring through the speakers.

Shelby laughed. "What other stations are there?"

"It's from my phone. Bluetooth."

Shelby felt her upper lip sneer, just a bit. "*This* is on your phone?"

"What? You don't like Taylor?"

"I guess," Shelby said with a shrug. "This song just makes me think of screaming goats."

"Screaming goats?"

"Yeah, haven't you seen that YouTube video? Where the goats cut in during the chorus?"

Kale shook his head. "Guess not."

"Oh, you haven't lived, Kale Copeland. We'll have to fix that. Pull over, I'll drive."

Kale gave her a look.

"This is important, Kale."

He blew out a breath. "Yes, ma'am."

A few minutes later, when they pulled up to the school, Kale was still laughing in the passenger seat, watching the YouTube clip over and over on his phone.

"Bubba!" he called out. "Hey, come check this out!"

Bubba came to the passenger side and looked utterly bewildered. He flashed a glance at Shelby then back to Kale, who leaned out the passenger window.

"Hey man," Bubba said, "ain't you in the wrong seat?"

"Have you seen this video?" Kale asked.

He pressed replay on the YouTube app.

"Yeah, man, everyone seen that," Bubba said.

"Wait, here's the best part."

The goat screamed perfectly on cue. Kale laughed again, as if it was still his first time.

"The only funny thing I'm seein' is some cute girl driving your ride, homie."

"Oh, right," he said. "Shelby, this is Bubba. Offensive line. Protects me on the field. Sometimes."

"Man, you trippin'. Nobody passes me. Nice to meet you, Shelby. You a minx or something?"

"Um, I . . ." she started, but Bubba went on.

"Because, my boy here ain't never let anyone drive his ride. Not even me." Bubba gave Kale a betrayed look.

"Wait! Wait!" Kale said. "Here it comes again."

The goats screamed. Kale laughed.

"Pshhh whatever, man," Bubba said. "It was funny two years ago."

Sean came up to the driver side. "Hey, Shelby! Glad you came." He opened her door for her, and Kale snapped out of YouTubeopia.

"Sorry, Shelby, I should've got that for you."

"I won't tell my dad."

"Promise?"

"I'll reserve judgment."

"All right," Sean said, waving the others over. There were maybe a dozen altogether. "I think whoever is coming is here. Let's head out."

"Where are we going?" Shelby asked.

"Just outside of town," Sean said. "Bonfire in the desert. You game?"

"Yeah, sure."

Everyone piled into a few cars. Kale switched seats with Shelby, and Bubba slid in the back. A few others jumped in the bed of the truck. Just as they pulled out, Sadie opened the door and hopped in the back with Bubba.

"You want to maybe move over, Bubba Tubba?" she said.

"Darlin', I'm all the way over," Bubba said. "We just gonna hafta get all close like."

"In your condemned dreams," Sadie snapped.

"How'd you know?" Bubba asked. "Got ourselves a minx in the front seat and Morpheus next to me. How we gonna ever survive, Kale?"

"Morpheus?" Kale asked. "Like, from *The Matrix?*"

"Nah, homie, as in the god of dreams. Don't you pay no attention in class?"

Sadie slugged Bubba in the leg, the sound like a tennis racket thwacking a pillow. "There's, like, a copulating foot on your other side, Bubba! Move over!"

"Nah, sweet-thang, the view is better from here. I get car sick if I can't look out the windshield. Know what I'm sayin'?"

Kale started coughing something that sounded a lot like "bull crap."

Sadie looked at Bubba with a glare that Shelby swore was the most predatory expression she'd ever seen, and she'd seen werewolves attack.

"Someday, I just might rip you apart," Sadie whispered.

"Mmm. What a sweet day that will be," Bubba answered with a playful longing in his voice.

Wait, did Bubba know? Was *he* a werewolf? Was this whole town infected with the occult? Sadie, still standing with the door open, must have seen the question in her eyes because she looked at Shelby and muttered, "Oh, please."

"We all in?" Kale asked.

Bubba grinned widely and patted the seat next to him. Sadie rolled her eyes and closed the door, sitting as far away from Bubba as she could—all two inches. They backed out and headed down the road.

"Kale," Bubba said, "you got my girl Beyoncé?"

"For sure," he said, pulling it up on his phone. Soon "Deja Vú" pumped through the speakers.

"Country-pop to hip hop?" Shelby asked. "Anything real on that phone?"

"What?" Kale said. "You don't like Beyoncé's female empowerment?"

"Empowerment?" Sadie scoffed. "Is that what wearing as little as possible means now?"

"Mmm-hmm," Bubba said. "She can get empowered around me anytime she wants."

"All right then, Shelby, you choose," Kale said.

"No, it's fine. I doubt you have anything I like. I'm strange with music, I guess. It's all good. It's your car."

"Not from what I saw earlier," Bubba said. "Shelby, girl, where you pick this loser up from, anyway?"

"I'm still trying to figure that out, actually," she said.

"Hey now," Kale said. "Can't we all just get along?"

Bubba shook his head. "Nah. You do not get to say that, man. You can't quote Rodney King. Nope. Ain't never gonna be Momma's fried chicken for you again."

"Your momma would rather have me over for dinner than you. You know it."

"Maybe I oughtta just bust you in the head."

Kale looked at Shelby. "He hates it when I'm right."

She smiled, her interest piqued. *Time to dig a little.* "Is that a common occurrence?"

"What?" he asked.

"That you're right?"

"Oh, this is gonna be good," Bubba said, settling into the back seat like he was at a movie. "You got some popcorn in here somewhere?"

"I'm only right when I am, I guess," Kale said.

"Oh? How often is that?" Shelby asked. She felt the mischievous smile starting to spread across her lips.

"All the time!" Bubba blurted. "You can't tell this boy nothin'!"

"Good to know," Shelby said with a wicked grin.

"Well, feculence! Can we stop by the store and pick out curtains for you two on the way back?" Sadie asked. "You're all making me sick."

"You say the sweetest thangs," Bubba said, looking dreamily at Sadie.

"I'm kinda feeling sick now," Sadie said.

"Kale let Shelby drive his truck," Bubba said.

Sadie's chronic look of near-grossed-out disappeared, replaced by disbelief. "Shut up!"

"Truth, girl."

"Why is that such a big deal?" Shelby asked.

"Because the only thing Kale loves more than football is this truck," Sadie said. ". . . except I guess, apparently you."

"Dat's more truth right there," Bubba said.

"Damn straight," Sadie said, giving Bubba a fist bump that exploded, then she covered her mouth.

"Little slip, Swearing Sadie?" Shelby teased.

"I don't love this truck more than football," Kale said.

Shelby looked at him as he drove. *What about me?* she almost asked, but stopped herself. Instead, she turned to Bubba and Sadie. "Wait, you two are all buddy-buddy now?"

At the exact same time, Bubba said "More than that," while Sadie said, "So disgusting."

"But you're missing the point," Sadie said. "Kale Copeland let you drive his truck, the T-rex."

"Raptor," Kale corrected.

"Unbelievable," Sadie said. "Still missing the point."

"Momentary lapse of reason," Kale said. "I assure you."

Shelby turned in her seat toward him. "Are you quoting Pink Floyd?"

"Who?"

"You said, 'momentary lapse of reason.' You know, the 1987 album?"

Kale raised his eyes to the rearview mirror. "You know this Pink Floyd guy, Bubba?"

"Nah, homie, but he sounds like he know you, talking lapse of reason and all."

Shelby rolled her eyes, her hopes that Kale knew some good music fading.

They arrived about fifteen minutes later at a turn off and pulled onto a dirt road through a cut section of the barbed wire fence. It didn't seem like there was anything but sagebrush and cacti where there were headed. Two other cars followed. A few hundred feet later they stopped at a large clearing. The place was obviously a popular hangout, with old fire pits and soda cans strewn about. A couple beer bottles, too, but maybe they were just IBC root beer bottles. Some other kids were already there—maybe a dozen—with a bonfire blazing and music pumping. Country, of course. Awesome. Shelby sighed. It was Texas.

This time, Kale did get Shelby's door for her. Sadie made a point of exiting before Bubba could get his bulk out of the truck to even attempt to open her door for her.

"Why's it gotta be like dat?" Bubba called after her.

Shelby broke out her phone and sent her dad a drop pin of their location. She didn't need to because the Find My Friends app was always running in the background, but she did it anyway as a way of connecting to her dad, letting him know she was safe.

"Wow, he makes you do that?" Kale asked.

"No. I just do. Habit."

Kale seemed to understand, and Shelby was a little annoyed by what she perceived to be pity on his face, but she let it go.

The crescent moon rose bright and clear in the cloudless night sky. Shelby met new people and was regaled by stories of the past school year as well as warned of all the teachers to watch out for. Kids sang and danced, kicking up sand around the fire. Shelby had never imagined people in cowboy boots could move so fast. She utterly failed at making s'mores, much to Sadie's delight. The marshmallow dropped from the metal prong to the sand in a gooey mess of blackened, sizzling sugar.

"If you can't even cook a marshmallow, how can I trust you?" she asked.

Shelby still ate the chocolate, of course.

Near 10 p.m., the fire burned low, and the atmosphere mellowed. Kale and Shelby sat together on a blanket, arms resting on their knees, staring into the red coals and yellow flames. What was he thinking about? Did he know about the whole "bonded" thing? Would he try to kiss her? Sadie said maybe the bonding only happened after a kiss. Did she want to him to try?

"It can be so mesmerizing," Kale said. "Fire, I mean."

"You a little pyro, Kale Copeland?"

"Nah."

They were silent for another minute before Kale said, "So, this is kinda strange, right?"

"What?"

"Us."

Us. Was there an *us*? She wanted to tell him all that she had felt, all the emotions that had swum through her since meeting him, how she yearned to never be apart from him; but words failed her. How could she even begin to express how she felt without sounding like a complete psycho? It had only been one day! Just more than twenty-four hours! But, didn't he already know how she felt? She had seen his reaction at dinner last night, sensed his longing for her when they locked stares.

"Shelby," Kale spoke, "I'm trying to figure out how to . . . how to say what I'm feeling. I just can't come up with the right words."

"Me either," she said softly and leaned her head on his shoulder. He smelled so wonderful, like a forest just after the rain.

"I was hoping you could explain it."

"Nope."

"When I met you last night . . . no, even when I just came in the house, before I saw you, I had this rush of . . . just . . . something. It has to have something to do with our . . . other sides."

"I know," she said.

"Come on, help me out here," he said. "I'm floundering."

"You are." She reached up and wrapped her hands around his arm, her head still on his shoulder. Her hands barely made it all the way around his biceps and triceps.

"You don't have to do that," she said.

"I'm just trying to understand this intense feeling you make me feel."

"No, I meant flex for me."

He looked at her, then down at her hands on his arm. "I'm not."

Shelby smiled. "Sure you're not."

Kale looked away for a second then flexed his arm briefly, the muscles going rock hard under her soft touch.

"Not bad," she teased. "My dad could still take you."

Kale laughed. "Yeah, he might be the only human that sort of scares me. So, why are you here? I mean, what brought you here?"

"You and your T-rex truck."

"I'm going to kill Sadie."

"I cussing heard that!" Sadie called from across the fire, maybe fifty feet away.

"You were meant to!" Kale yelled back.

"You'd have to catch me first."

"She's right about that," Kale said to Shelby. "You'd think she'd join track. That redhead is the fastest wolf I know."

Shelby noted that tidbit with interest.

"So, really, why did you and your dad come here?" Kale asked. "There must have been something that drew you here."

We're done discussing the "intense feeling" already? She'd have to work on his focus.

"My mom told my dad what to look for, I guess. Hints and clues, he always says. He doesn't share much more than that."

"You mean like to find a pack?"

"I guess."

"Well, whatever it was, I'm glad you're here," Kale said, resting his cheek on the top of her head.

"Are you always this dramatic?"

"Only when I'm floundering."

"Home," Shelby said and lifted her head from his shoulder.

Kale looked at her, the firelight reflected in his dark eyes.

"That's what it feels like," she said. "The feeling I get when I'm around you, like I've known you for a thousand years but I'm still only just discovering you. Again. Or something. Like I finally belong and . . . wow, I sound really, really stupid. I'm sorry. I'm not a freak, I promise."

"Floundering," Kale teased softly.

"Pathetically," Shelby agreed.

They stared at each other, only a few inches separating them, but those inches suddenly felt like miles. Kale reached his right hand to her cheek, softly caressing it and pulled her toward him. Her breathing became unsteady, the nape of her neck suddenly moist. It was too soon, her mind told her, too fast. She couldn't, not yet. She should be terrified . . . but she wasn't. Not around Kale. There was no logic to her desire as she stared into the eyes of this boy she had only met yesterday. He had a faint scar above his right eye, something she hadn't noticed until the orange glow of the bonfire had hit it just right. In a fleeting thought, she wondered how it had happened. More than that, she wondered how his lips would taste.

Just before the tension in the charged air around them became unbearable, her lips touched his. Everything changed. They were warm and full, firm but inviting, and sent a jolt of warm lightning racing through her body. His scent, musky and male, filled her as she buried her fingers in his hair to draw him closer. She traced another hand delicately down his jawline.

The roughness of his face, the day's growth of whiskers just starting to be noticeable, made her want him even more.

The world around her melted away as everything she thought she knew shattered to pieces and then was rebuilt anew, reforged into something grander, something more graceful and pure. Inhibitions fled as she deepened the kiss. Within her, a connection opened— something supernal—a force, both scalding and biting cold, reached out beyond her soul and found him there, in some distant ether. Kale. Except that wasn't who he was, not his *real* name. He was a part of her and she of him, a bond that extended back past the millennia, to a realm that predated anything she knew, where they had once been one. In this sublime vision of this faraway but somehow familiar ether, she saw that a rupturing had occurred, splitting their . . . what was it even called? Substance? Spirit? Oneness? Whatever it was, whatever had happened eons before to separate them, they had found each other.

Her eyes stung, and she broke the kiss. Sucking her lips into her mouth, she savored the taste as she tried to regain her wits. Her eyes blinked tightly, trying to ward off the sting. It had only been seconds. Kale exhaled heavily. His eyes glowed with amber flecks, and he turned away, fighting the same urge she fought. Oddly, she could *feel* him fighting it and knew that he could feel her doing the same.

"I'm sorry," she said.

"No," he said. "Don't be. I'm not."

"Did you—"

"Yes," he said. "I felt it. I know you. I don't know how but I know that . . . that I . . ."

"Love you."

Kale looked back to her. "Wholly and completely." A love flowed from him that filled her, and she reciprocated, sending it forth to him through the bond that had been forged by their kiss. Not words, more: a depth of emotion springing up from an unknown but bottomless well.

All fear left. Uncertainty, anxiety, doubt, worry. Gone. Only the brilliance of a love she knew to be uniquely theirs remained and it filled her.

"Hey you two, get a room!" Sadie yelled.

Oh. Right. There were still people around. How annoying. "Hey fly honey," Bubba called out to Sadie from the far side of the dying bonfire, "you just jealous. I got enough love to warm even your cold-hearted self. Come on over here, and I'll show you."

"Not gonna happen, Tubba."

"C'mon, now! Why's it gotta be like that?"

Kale took Shelby's hand, interlocking their fingers. His very touch a caress to her heart. Tenderly, he kissed the back of her hand.

"This is like . . . fairy tale stuff," Shelby whispered.

Kale smiled. "That doesn't mean it's not real."

"Obviously, but I still don't believe in it."

"So, it's real, but you don't believe in it. Got it."

"Shut up, Kale Copeland. I'm trying to figure it out."

He kissed her again, only for a second, and as some of the same feelings as before resurfaced, her mind went blank.

"Thanks," she said, "that's really not helping."

"You're complaining?"

She shook her head. Just then, her phone buzzed. "Crap. It's my dad."

"What time is it?" Kale said, looking at his own phone.

"Almost 10:15. I gotta go."

"What did his text say?"

"'Don't make me send out search and rescue.'"

"You sure it didn't say 'search and destroy'?"

Kale speeded down the road, not wanting to get Shelby home late from their first date. That would certainly not do a lot for the trust of her father. Still, the thought of being apart from her now was difficult to process. But that bond between them . . . would he ever feel apart from her completely again? He didn't think so.

Their hands interlocked as he drove, resting on the center console. The truck's engine roared as he pressed down the accelerator and Kale smiled. There wouldn't be anyone on this long desert road. Time to let the Raptor open up a bit.

"Man, we gotta have some tunes, homie. Feel?" Bubba said. "This silence is killin' me."

"What do you want to hear, Shelby?" Kale asked. "Your choice."

"I don't know," she said.

"Someone pick something, sweet Lord above," Bubba said.

"You sound like your mom," Kale said.

"Leave my momma out of it, boy."

"She's putting in adoption papers for me. She tell you? Yeah, letting you go and taking me in."

"Watch, no blocking for you on the field tomorrow. Watch. You gonna go down flat ten times, minimum. I'll let my boy Jarvis know. Watch."

"You love me, Bubba."

Shelby asked, "You have any old Genesis? Before they got all commercial?"

"Who?" Kale, Bubba, and Sadie asked in unison.

"Or early Chicago? When they were still experimental?"

"What language she speakin', Kale?" Bubba asked.

Shelby took Kale's phone and started flipping through it. "Anything embarrassing on here I need to know about?"

"Nah, all my pictures of Bubba's mom got deleted."

"Always playin'. Always got jokes," Bubba said. "Watch. Tomorrow. You'll see."

"Ah, here we go," Shelby said. "Pandora. Let's see . . . Jethro Tull station. Perfect."

"Thick as a Brick" started playing through the Bluetooth connection, and Ian Anderson's melodious flute tones soared. Everyone in the truck looked at Shelby.

"What?" she asked innocently. "You gotta expand beyond Beyoncé and Taylor."

"Eh, your girl human?" Bubba asked.

"Maybe half," Kale said.

Shelby turned to see Sadie in the back seat with a look of "uhhhh" on her face.

"That's cold, man," Bubba said. "You can slap him, Shelby. I'll protect you from him."

"Like you protect me on the field?" Kale asked, catching Bubba's eyes in the rearview mirror. Bubba squinted and pointed ahead of them.

"What the heck is that?" Bubba asked. "In the road."

Kale saw the spike strip too late and plowed right over it. The steering wheel jerked ferociously in his hands, but with an iron grip he steadied it and carefully brought the truck to a stop.

He pulled on the door handle and nearly leaped out of his seat to survey the damage but Sadie beat him to it.

"All four," she said. "Shredded."

Kale ran a hand through his hair. "This was deliberate."

"Really? I thought coming across a strip of tire spikes was completely normal," Sadie said.

Up ahead of them, maybe fifty yards, headlights came to life on the shoulder of the road followed by the sound of an engine. Sadie ducked, going down to one knee.

"Easy," Kale said. "Just wait."

Shelby opened her door.

"No," Kale said. "Stay inside."

He felt her annoyance through the bond, but she stayed in the truck.

The car ahead of them turned onto the road, speeding away. A head leaned out the window, blonde hair whipping wildly in the wind.

"Whooohoooo! Suck it, Kale!"

"Chelsea," Kale growled. "Figures."

"Can I kill her?" Sadie asked. "Please! I can catch her."

"I have no doubt, but no. Let her go."

"You're not the Alpha yet. Hades, I don't have to—"

Kale fixed a sharp glare on her that made her shrink slightly.

"Fine," she said. "Don't get all fecal-faced mad. But if she ends up missing one day . . ."

"We're not that kind of pack, Sadie."

"Maybe we should be."

Kale shook his head and opened the driver door. "Shelby, better call your dad. In the meantime, I'm going to try and figure out a way to talk him out of killing me."

The next day, Shelby woke to the sound of banging. Through a mess of bedhead-hair, she squinted at the clock on her nightstand. The green digits read 7:34. In the A.M.! Disbelieving her clock, she checked her phone. *I hate you,* she thought to her phone when it confirmed the clock's report. More banging. Hammers. Might as well have been a firework show right in her front yard. Her dad was up tinkering—building or destroying something, she couldn't tell. But she only had so many days of her summer left! *And it's Saturday.* Couldn't he wait until at least nine? *Or noon!*

She rolled onto her stomach and pulled the pillow over her head. The fireworks kept right on exploding, rudely piercing her fluffy sound barrier.

"Kill me," she moaned.

Then she heard voices. Was that laughing? Coming from outside the house? This was too much. How dare anyone have any joy before

9:00 A.M.! She stumbled from her bed with her eyes no more than angry slits, fumbled for the lock on her French doors, and stomped, with righteous indignation, onto the balcony that overlooked the front yard.

"Dad! It's Saturday! What the—" Her heart palpitated. Was that Kale? With her *dad?* Swinging a hammer in a sweat-soaked shirt clinging to his body? She blinked the sleep away. It was Kale! His Raptor sat in the dirt driveway with new tires—already?—shaded by the beards of moss hanging from the sprawling trees. Suddenly, she was wide awake, and the rabble of butterflies in her chest warmed her, lighting their own fireworks inside her. She felt lighter.

"Morning, Shel," Grant said, looking up at her.

Kale raised his head, killed her with that smile and single dimple, then turned away quickly.

"So, you decided to repair the porch steps at 7:30? In the *morning?*" Shelby asked. She tried to sound mad, but her words came out sickeningly gleeful. She couldn't help it.

"Kale is repenting for having you home late," her dad said.

"Yep," Kale said, squinting up at her then again quickly averting his eyes. Why was he acting like that? She felt his—was it embarrassment? Yes, but he also felt a thrill of some kind. She'd eventually have to get used to this connection thing between them, whatever it was. Werewolf stuff was so weird.

"Hey, Shel," her dad said, holding a crow bar while Kale busied himself, obviously keeping his eyes from her. "Think you could put some clothes on? Kale here is having a hard time."

What? Oh. Right. She'd slept in a tank top and panties. Black panties. *Trim* black panties. Some might have said *sexy* black panties. Shelby squealed and ran back inside, hands cupping her face, hoping to make the world vanish. Then, she heard Grant laugh. And then Kale!

"I hate you both!" she yelled from her room through the open French doors. But seeing Kale swing a hammer, all hot and sweaty . . . why did all the clichés have to be true? Seriously, *why?* His shoulders seemed broader and waist narrower with his sweaty shirt snuggled all up against his chest and—*stop it!* She pulled on a pair of sweatpants and her hoodie, despite the morning Texas heat, and her feet beat a path downstairs and out the front screen door.

"Kind of overcompensating, Shel?" Grant said.

Shelby folded her arms. "No."

"I kinda liked you the other way," Kale said.

Grant slowly turned his head to Kale, eyebrows nearly high enough to make his forehead disappear. "Watch it."

"Okay, I like you better this way, frumpy and hobo-ish."

"Watch it," Shelby said. Then she couldn't hold back that stupid grin.

"I see there's no winning here," Kale said. He swung the hammer and sunk a nail with one strike. Shelby blinked.

"We're almost done," Grant said.

"Hey, wanna go to the quarry after this?" Kale asked.

"Nah," Grant said. "I've got too much work to do."

"Um . . ." Kale muttered.

"Relax kid," Grant said. "It was a joke."

"The quarry?" Shelby asked.

"Yeah, it's about an hour from here," Kale said. "Water's freezing, but it's fun. You can just wear what you were wearing earlier."

Shelby flushed, but her tankini covered about the same amount as her sleepwear.

When Grant glared at him, Kale held his hands up in surrender. "It was a joke."

Shelby looked at her dad.

"Honestly, guys, I'm not sure," Grant said. "The tire spikes last night have me a little on edge."

"It was that stupid Chelsea girl, Dad. Just a joke."

"A joke that cost me $1,600," Kale said. "I'm definitely not taking her to homecoming. I really am sorry about getting Shelby back late. Our tow truck took forever."

"I didn't mind," Shelby said.

"Yeah, about that," Grant said, pointedly ignoring Shelby's comment, "how'd you get your tires fixed already?"

"Dad has a mechanic on staff," Kale said.

Grant wore an expression of disbelief. "You gotta be kidding me."

"You haven't met Edgar yet?"

"Guess not. So, you two planning revenge on Chelsea? Just remember she is mayor's daughter."

Shelby said, "Yep," at the same time as Kale said, "No."

"We're not?" Shelby asked.

"Nah, better to let her think she's winning."

We. She had said "we're" presumptively and Kale had just went along with it. No hesitation. Like they were already a thing.

But we're more than just a high school "thing," Shelby thought. She did not understand why or how.

"Dad?" Shelby asked. "Can I go? Please?"

Grant shrugged. "Fine with me, I guess. Just have her back by dinner time."

Shelby's felt herself light up. "Really?"

"I'm not all work and no fun. Just ninety-percent."

"Yeah, but 100% awesome."

Grant grinned. "I already said yes. Quit sucking up. Kale," Grant said, looking him in the eye. "By dinner."

"Won't be a problem, sir," Kale said.

"No need for that 'sir' garbage. Just have fun. But not too much."

"Grant!" Shelby hissed.

"Go get ready, kiddo," Grant said. "We've about ten more minutes here."

Shelby's eyes flicked to Kale. She hesitated. "I don't mind waiting." And watching, she wanted to say, but didn't. Kale swung the hammer again, and she bit her bottom lip. She didn't mind the racket anymore either.

Shelby peered over the edge of the gray cliff. The water was only twenty feet down. Really shouldn't be a problem, right?

"Come on!" Kale called from the water below. The ripples from his cannonball still made their way outward across the otherwise glass-like surface of the reservoir.

"How cold is it?" she asked.

Kale splashed water up at her, but it fell short. "Come find out!"

What she wanted to find out was what would happen if she bit into those pecs of his. Just a bit. How did a seventeen-year-old boy resemble a white version of Isaiah Mustafa, that guy from the Old Spice commercials? She wasn't ashamed to say she had looked him up. She thought Kale would give Mustafa a run for his money if he tried out for an Old Spice commercial.

"What kind of deodorant do you use?"

Kale's face scrunched to confusion. "What?"

"Never mind."

"If I have to come up there, I'm going to push you in."

"Promise?"

"Okay, I'm coming up." He started swimming to the edge.

"I got this, Kale." Her toes curled over the lip. She sighed, squeezed her eyes shut, and leaped. The water stung her as she hit and submerged. Shockingly cold! Wasn't this Texas? Shelby broke the surface with a high-pitched scream followed by a shiver-giggle.

"Not bad, right?" Kale said.

"Y-yeah, if you think A-Alaska is n-nice in the w-winter!" Shelby said through chattering teeth.

"Maybe you're cold-blooded."

"What did you call me, Kale Copeland?"

"Um . . . bold-footed?"

She splashed him. "Nice try." The water did feel good now, though she still had goosebumps.

"Let's go again," Kale said, swimming for the rocky, pine-needled beach. "Race ya to the top."

Shelby swam after him. "You're cheating!"

"Am not!"

"You started swimming before you said it was a race." She sounded so childish and giddy, but she didn't care. Even with teeth chattering, she felt so at home in Kale's presence. That didn't mean she would let him win, though. A fierce competitive drive came over her, similar to when she broke the springboard on the first day of gymnastics, and she propelled herself through the water with deep strokes. She hit the beach at almost the same time as Kale and sprinted up the steep incline, pine needles sticking to her feet and bumping against Kale the whole way. She touched the jump-off spot with her foot just ahead of Kale.

"Hah!"

But Kale kept going. "Not the twenty-foot ledge. We just did that!"

Shelby let her eyes followed the ridge line up to the next ledge. It had to be twice as high as this one. "You didn't say which ledge!"

"Can't you read my mind?"

"No!" Wait, could she? "Well, maybe."

Kale stopped at the next ledge. "Okay, what am I thinking?"

She scampered up the incline to him. "I don't think it works like that."

"How's it work, then?" he asked.

"I don't know. It's not mind reading. Or I don't think so."

"It's our wolves," he whispered.

"It is?"

Kale nodded. "You felt it, right? Last night?"

Shelby felt the heat in her cheeks despite her shiver. "When we kissed."

"So, maybe, it only works when we kiss," Kale said with a shy smile. "I'm willing to test that hypothesis."

Her heart stopped. No, it didn't. It was beating a hundred miles a minute, actually. She blinked rapidly. "Okay."

Okay? How lame was that? Just, okay? She hated how Kale could break her down like this, make her sound so illiterate and play fourth grade race-you-to-the-top games. Seriously? Then, he put an arm around her, his hand touching the small of her back and pulling her closer. A streak of apprehension shot through her. She noticed

Kale hesitate as well. His playful demeanor turned quickly to a serious one. She felt that, inside.

"I don't understand what I feel," he said. "This is deeper."

"Than what?" she asked, shaking in his embrace but not from the cold.

His mouth opened, but no words came. Then, "I don't know how to explain this."

"Me either. I'm nervous." She gently pulled free from his hold and sat on the ledge, feet dangling. Kale lowered himself next to her, and she let her head slump to his shoulder.

"When we kissed last night," he said, "I saw things."

"Don't tell me you saw our future together or I might be sick."

"Yeah, you're not that fairy-tale kinda girl. I got that. But I feel like I did see something."

"The past," Shelby whispered.

"Our past," Kale whispered back. "At first I thought it was the future . . . but . . . no. I could tell. There's fire. People are scared. I see you but only from a distance. You always disappear into some kind of fog or haze. Maybe it's the smoke. I mean, I can smell the smoke and almost taste the ashes."

Shelby turned toward him, forehead scrunched. "You see fire, smell smoke, and taste ashes when we kiss? What, am I an ashtray?"

"Um, no, that's not what I mean."

"So far, that's what you've said, though. That's not what it was like for me."

"That really didn't come out right," Kale said. "I don't know. The first time I felt you near, I started seeing things. You. I didn't know it was you at first. It feels just like a memory. The forest, the village. I felt . . . this just incredible need to find you in the memory.

Or whatever it is. To protect you. And I can feel that it's my wolf that is the one remembering." He chuckled. "Yeah, I feel like an idiot saying all this out loud. But you see it, too, right?"

Shelby blinked. "Wow. You're hopeless. Truly, you are the sappiest romantic I've ever met."

"You don't know what I'm talking about," Kale said with obvious sheepishness. He pursed his lips. "I just know that you and I were meant to find each other."

Guys don't talk like this. Stupid prissy girls did. But she definitely had felt that she and Kale had *been* before. Yes, she knew that, but hadn't seen what Kale described.

It was the hormones, Shelby decided. Had to be. People with raging hormones often reported feelings of finding "the one" when someone—anyone—reciprocated or validated their need for intimacy. She had read it in some psychology book. Or maybe it had been on a talk show? Normal relationships were built-up in the minds of those involved to be something more than attraction and compatibility, to be something that was more special. Like destiny or some other romanticized foolish notion.

But, did that apply to Lycans? She seriously doubted a study existed on the hormonal and mental effect of intimacy with werewolves. She giggled as a breeze brushed over her, leaving chills on her arms in its wake.

"What?" Kale asked.

"Nothing."

"Don't keep secrets from me, or I'm bound to think you're laughing at me."

"Oh, there's plenty to laugh at about you, Kale Copeland."

He nudged her head up from his shoulder and looked at her with those fathomless hazel eyes. "Do tell."

"Well, for one, you drive a freaking monster truck but listen to hip hop."

"Yeah?"

"Not even you are dense enough to not see that contradiction."

"It's not a monster truck."

"Close enough."

"Wait, did you just call me dense?"

She glanced at his arms. Dense. Her stomach fluttered again. "Um."

"Sadie says you're a strange chick. The music you listen to makes me think you're from a different era."

"Aren't we?" she asked, more to herself. That kiss had somehow opened her mind to things that felt eternal. Beyond this world at least. And Kale said he'd seen glimpses of memories. *I feel them but don't see what he does. Totally unfair.*

"I'm not sure you're strange, Shelby Brooks, but you are deep," Kale said.

Huh. Deep. Was that a good thing? Her brain had certainly become more poetic around Kale. Did that happen with all people when they were drowning in hormones? Or just werewolves? "Well, let me know how *deep* that water is, will you?" She shoved him from the ledge, and all the way down, he flailed his arms as if rolling up old car windows. She smiled when he hit the water, and then came up. "So? Deep?"

"You know you better jump before I get back up there!" he yelled from below.

She stood and jumped, also rolling up the windows on her way down.

Kale skipped down the curved staircase the next morning, running his hand along the dark smooth wooden rail. He caught the scent of breakfast—toast with melting butter and freshly squeezed orange juice—the scent of juice from concentrate had a much more pungent tang—coming from the kitchen. And sausage. That made both sides of him salivate.

He hit the bottom floor, feeling like a giddy fifth grader, and his shoes squeaked. If he was in his wolf, he was sure his tail would be wagging. Rays of the early morning sun raked across the marble-inlays in the wood flooring that formed the Copeland crest. It was a tremendously good day! He just felt *awesome*, like any clouds in his life had been permanently swept away by a warm breeze. That breeze, he knew, was named Shelby Brooks.

He was going to be late to football practice if he didn't hurry. Afterwards, he planned to take Shelby out mini golfing. So cliché, but he didn't care. She had made fun of him for suggesting it, but she still said yes. As long as he was next to her, they could be basket weaving and he'd be content. But, he'd *really* rather not have to resort to crafts to be around Shelby. She definitely didn't strike him as that kind of girl anyway.

As he passed his father's study just before entering the kitchen, Kale stopped. He leaned back and poked his head over the study's threshold and saw his father and Bubba standing around the large oak desk, the one with gnarled knots he had hidden under when playing hide and seek as a kid with his dad. Of course, having a dad that was a werewolf and could smell you no matter where you hid was just not fair. He hadn't known that about his dad at the time, of course. He supposed he'd torture his children some day by the same methods.

Wait, when did I start thinking about having kids?

Elias and Bubba looked up from the papers they were staring down at with apparent scrutiny. His dad, wearing jeans and a golf shirt, had his brow furrowed.

"Bubba?" Kale said. "What are you doing here?"

"Came to pick you up for practice, but your dad asked me to come early so we could look over my business plan," Bubba answered. "You forget it's my turn to drive?"

Kale took a couple steps back, squaring himself with the study's entry, and felt his upper lip raise in confusion. "What business plan?"

"Deshawn asked if I would look over his numbers and projections," Elias explained. "I must say," he said, turning his head to Bubba and tapping one of the pages on the desk with a finger, "I'm fairly impressed."

Kale walked up to the desk, and saw one stack of papers titled

"Executive Summary," and several spreadsheets arrayed across the desk, complete with graphs and charts. "What is all this?" He asked.

"What's it look like?" Bubba asked. "I'm getting ready to launch a business based on Momma's chicken recipe. Even got a sample menu." Bubba held up a laminated menu, complete with graphic design, a logo, and prices.

Kale took the menu. "Man, Bubba, this is . . ."

"Shocking? What, you thought I was just your token fat black friend around for comic relief?"

"I was going to agree with Dad and say impressive."

"Check out my retained earnings projections at year five," Bubba said, pointing to a spreadsheet.

"I do think those are a little aggressive, Deshawn," Elias said. "I think you need to adjust things based on a variable cost model. Costs don't stay fixed."

"So, like, what . . . three percent a year?"

"For your lease payment, that's probably good, but—"

Bubba shook his head and his torso jiggled a bit under his shirt. "Nah, Mr. C., I'm going to own the real estate. See, people think this is a business about chicken. But it's really about the real estate."

Elias smiled. "You read Ray Kroc's book?"

"Who?"

"The founder of McDonald's," Kale said absently, still focusing on the menu. "When did you do all this?"

"Over the past year or so. You know you were just our guinea pig, testing out different recipes, right?"

Kale smiled awkwardly. "I've been thinking about how to franchise your mom's recipe. I had no idea you . . ." Kale trailed off. "What's this?" he asked, pointing to the logo at the top of the menu. "SuperFly Chicken?"

"That means "the best chicken" for the white folks in the room.""

Elias chuckled and Kale shook his head. "Yeah, I know," Kale said. "It's . . . not the right name."

"What do you mean?"

"You gotta go with 'Bubba's Chicken,'" Kale said. "That's what I always thought it would be called."

Bubba crossed his arms over his chest. "You mean, when you were thinking of my business, you also thought you'd be kind enough to name it for me?"

"I . . . um . . ."

"Yeah, go ahead and think about that for a bit. Epic friend fail, right there."

"Regardless of the name, Deshawn," Elias said. "I think you've got something promising here. You should think about taking Mr. Goff's business class this year."

"I tested out of it last year, Mr. C. Got bored in the first week, feel?"

"I didn't know that," Kale said. "I'm taking it this year. I heard it can be brutal."

"There's a lot about me you don't know."

"Right, like why you let Jarvis get by you sometimes at practice." Kale put the menu back on the desk.

"Ain't no one get past me if I don't want them to." Bubba gave Kale a meaningful look.

Elias gathered up the papers. "When you're ready to look for funding, come talk to me again. I can probably point you in the right direction."

"No offense, Mr. C., but I won't take your money. Gotta earn my own way, know what I'm saying?"

Elias smiled. "I do. Now, Kale, unless you want to do more pom-pom push-ups, you boys better get going."

Bubba chuckled. "That was something."

Kale groaned. "Does everyone know about that?"

"Kale!" he heard his mother call from the kitchen. "You're going to be late and have to do more—"

"Yeah, I know," he called back, craning his head into the hallway. He looked at Bubba. "Alright, let's go. But, I'm telling you, 'Bubba's Chicken' is the right name."

"Mm hmm. Got my life all planned, huh?"

Kale just laughed. "C'mon, let's go."

They walked toward the front door. "Thanks, Mr. C.!" Bubba called over his shoulder. "Hey," he whispered to Kale, "you seeing your minx later?"

"Shelby? Yeah, why?"

"I heard she and Sadie are all like best friends and stuff all of a sudden."

"Sadie has dozens of best friends," Kale said.

" Yeah, well," Bubba said, rubbing his jaw, "think Shelby could put a good word in for me with Sadie?"

Kale coughed. "That is something that's not going to happen."

"Man, why's everyone so cold?"

"Trust me, bro," Kale said, slapping Bubba on the shoulder as the front door closed behind them, "Sadie's just . . . not right for you."

21

S helby changed into her leo next to Sadie in the locker room. Over the past week, Shelby had been doing her best to avoid Chelsea and her disciples, since Kale had asked her to homecoming. But, of course, with Chelsea being the captain of the gymnastics team, that proved impossible. The texts the banshee—a most apropos description, Shelby had decided—sent her unrelentingly were enough to make anyone hire a personal bodyguard. Where did Chelsea come up with such colorful metaphors, describing what she was going to do to Shelby? So far, though, besides laying out the tire spikes, Chelsea had been all bark and no bite.

Shelby's text alert chimed.

"Chelsea again?" Sadie asked.

"No, Trish," Shelby answered through a sigh.

"Same difference. What's it say?"

Shelby gave the phone to Sadie and slammed her locker shut. "I still don't know how they got my number."

Sadie read the text and raised an eyebrow. "She's threatening to shun you on Instagram and Snapchat unless you tell Kale to take Chelsea to homecoming. That's it? Really? Is she Amish or something? Un-copulating-believable. Wait, do Amish people have Snapchat?"

"I guess some people actually think social media matters that much," Shelby said. "Come on, we're going to be late, and I don't want to do more push-ups with a smile plastered to my face. Hey! What are you doing?"

Sadie pulled away, holding Shelby's phone up high while working her thumbs furiously. "Nothing."

"Sadie!"

"I'm just helping you out, girl."

"Give it back!"

"Nope."

Shelby reached around Sadie, trying to pry the phone from Sadie's grip and nearly tripped over the bench that split the row of lockers.

"Condemn it, I'm almost done!" Sadie grunted, fighting Shelby's grip. "Anyone ever tell you you're deceptively strong?"

Sadie let go. Shelby stared in horror at her Instagram account. A meme of Trish in her leotard with a white beard, black hat, and a long white unbuttoned cotton shirt—stereotypical Amish garb— glared back at her. The caption read, "Shunning Shelby Brooks since 2016." Shelby's—Sadie's—comment below the picture read, "How'd I get so lucky?" followed by three cry-laughing emojis.

"That doesn't sound like something I would post," Shelby said.

"You're welcome. Twitter and Facebook, too."

"I hate you."

Sadie closed her locker. "No, you don't."

"You know this could count as cyberbullying, right?"

"She's the one that sent you that feculence about shunning you."

Shelby rolled her eyes. "I don't really care about that small stuff. I should just get a flip phone."

"So, the pack meeting is tonight, huh?" Sadie asked. "Excited?"

Shelby groaned. "I guess."

"Got your Cub Scout uniform all picked out and ironed?"

Shelby pursed her lips. "What?"

"Ya know. Pack meeting? What my nerd brother goes to? He's ten now and the proud rank of Wolf Cub." Sadie waggled her eyebrows. "Get it? Wolf Cub?"

"You're not serious," Shelby said.

"Better believe it. You don't have any brothers. I forgot. He's got the neckerchief and everything. You can borrow it for tonight if you want."

Shelby crossed her arms. "Let me guess, Mrs. Copeland is the 'den mother.' And wolf cubs are eight, by the way."

Sadie laughed. "So you *do* know about Cub Scouts! I hadn't thought about a den mother. Awesome. And, yeah, I know wolf cubs are normally eight but my brother's a slacker.

"But you should be excited. Another excuse to see Kale, right? As if seeing each other all day every day for the past week hasn't been enough. The way you two gawk at each other. Seriously." Sadie mimed throwing up.

"He's at least starting to listen to some decent music. Gotta train them early."

"He's placating you. Trust me. You know he still bumps Beyoncé when you're not around, right? As scarce as those times are."

Shelby shrugged. "Small progress is still progress. Not like I own him."

"Uh, ya, you kinda do."

"Don't start on the bonding thing again," Shelby mumbled.

"Hey, what's wrong?" Sadie asked.

"I don't know. I just . . ."

"You can't tell me you don't like him anymore. Moving on that fast?"

Shelby's heart skipped a beat. "No. No, of course I . . . like him." Such an incomplete description, so lacking. *Like* him? Shelby was head-over-heels for Kale Copeland, so far beyond "liking" him. But still . . .

"I kissed him at the bonfire—"

"Yeah, we all saw that lovely showing of PDA."

"What?"

"Public display of affection?" Sadie said. "Holy Hades, girl, you better be careful when school starts next week. They'll suspend you for that stuff, even though the whorey trinity seems to get away with it just fine."

"I haven't kissed him since."

Sadie lowered her chin. "Because . . ."

Shelby had wondered the same thing. What did that mean? Shouldn't she be having the opposite problem, of not being able to keep her hands off him? But, Kale also seemed hesitant . . . not to be around her—she could tell he wanted to be with her as much as she did him—but to kiss again.

"I think I'm scared."

Sadie sat on the bench. They were definitely late now. Push-ups-with-a-smile it would be.

"Sit," Sadie said.

"We're late."

"Condemn it, Shel, sit."

Shelby sat.

"Look, I don't know what happened before you got here, but something did. Every time a group of guys passes us, you shrink away. I mean, your face turns pale. Except for Kale, of course."

"And Bubba," Shelby said.

"Bubba Tubba doesn't count."

"He makes me laugh."

Sadie scrunched her face up and sighed through her nose. "I guess he's good for something occasionally. So, what happened?"

What happened? How could she even begin to explain?

"Oh, don't you look at me like I wouldn't understand," Sadie said.

So, Shelby told her. Everything. Lucas. His friends. Her first shifting and not being able to shift since. Her shame. By the end of it, Sadie's eyes glistened, not with pity but anger. Shelby could tell from the amber flecks that glowed in her irises.

"Want me to kill him?" Sadie said. "I so will."

Shelby actually laughed, a pitiful choked sound.

"So," Sadie went on, "this is why you're scared to kiss Kale again? I mean, if you need a proxy to stand in with Kale . . ."

Shelby laughed again. It felt good. "Actually, no, it's not why." Shelby paused. Was it? "When Kale and I kissed, I felt things. Sensed things."

"His tongue?"

"I'm not answering that."

"Uh-huh. Go on."

"You talked about this bonding thing. Explain it to me."

Sadie brought a knee up to her chest. "You know I was kidding about you guys, right? I mean, bonding *is* a real thing for us, but it's really rare, and I don't know much about it. I'm seventeen, remember? And how have we not discussed this over the past week? I only come over to see your dad every night."

Shelby gasped. "No! You're only pretending to be there to see me?"

"Well, can't a girl have more than one purpose?"

"I guess I've just had a hard time making these feelings fit inside me. Like, finding the right place for them. It makes it hard to talk about. Something . . . changed when we kissed." How could she explain this without sounding like a complete dork?

"Haven't we been over this?" Sadie asked. "Romance-novelitis?"

Shelby ignored her friend's comment. "I saw him."

"You didn't close your eyes? You really are a strange chick."

"It felt . . . it felt like our past or something. Like we had met before. Like, we *were* before. I mostly just feel things but Kale says he sees things when we kiss or sometimes when he's just around me."

"Yeah, he's imagining you naked."

Shelby put her head in her hands. "I don't know what I'm saying. It's like I feel that we've had a past together and he sees it."

"Wait, you don't 'see' what Kale sees when you kiss?"

"Not exactly."

"That's sexist."

Shelby looked up. "What?"

"The universe is sexist. Why does the guy get to see copulating visions of your past but not you?"

"We're not making love in his visions, Sadie."

"You know what I mean. Don't take my literal swearing literally. And why not?"

Shelby felt the heat of her blushing cheeks. "From what he says, it's not a good thing. He's scared in the visions. There's fire and smoke and a village with scared people."

Sadie lowered her chin to her chest. "I knew it. You're both getting high when you make out."

"No, we're not. And we haven't made out. It was just that one kiss."

"Chill out, girl. I know you're not doing drugs. What would be the point?"

"Huh?"

"Seriously? You don't know?"

Shelby shook her head. "Know what?"

"Drugs don't affect us. Well, barely, anyway. At a party last year, I downed a twelve pack of Budweiser before I felt the slightest tingle in my fingers."

"You drank a twelve pack?"

"Oh ya. Shotgunned that crap." Sadie mimed opening a beer can over her mouth, then made guzzling sounds.

"You're insane. A twelve pack?"

Sadie made an indignant face. "Don't try to tell me you've never drank."

"Nope. Never."

"Not even a small sip? Once?"

"Nope. It smells like carbonated urine. Why would I want to drink it?"

Sadie's eyes looked up as if in thought. "Yeah, it kinda does. Condemn it. Thanks for ruining that for me."

Through the door that led from the locker room to the gymnasium, Shelby heard Coach Anders's muffled voice as he bellowed at someone to point their toes.

"So, Mrs. Copeland said something about a Summer Omega at dinner last week."

Sadie rolled her eyes. "Yeah, she's full of those legends. I think she really believes them."

"She thinks I'm an Omega. Actually, I think I am, too. And I did manifest late."

"Maybe you just hit puberty last year?" Sadie asked. "Were your boobs just ant bites before last year?"

"Sadie!"

"Just theorizing. Don't get your pantyhose in a pretzel."

"*Anyway*, back to me and Kale. It scared me. The kiss, I mean. It was totally amazing to kiss him, but . . . this was more than a kiss. It was like a portal opened."

"Let me guess. A portal to your heart?"

"I didn't say that.

"Well, holy dung, Shelby, it's not like you're hard to read."

Shelby sighed. "Maybe you were right, Sadie. Maybe this is like being bonded or whatever."

Someone burst into the locker room from the gymnasium. The door slammed against the wall, and it echoed with indignation.

"Here it comes," Sadie whispered.

"What?"

The clopping footsteps made Shelby think whoever was stomping their way had platypus feet. They stopped at their aisle of lockers. Shelby blew out a pent-up breath through pursed lips.

"There you little tramps are!"

Chelsea Gittrik. Perfect. Her sweaty hair was all in a bun. Somehow, her makeup still held its place. And now that Shelby looked, Chelsea did have very flat feet.

Sadie stood and folded her arms. "Thought you were shunning us."

Trish and Amanda came storming up behind Chelsea, also in their leos. Trish's face flushed with embarrassment or rage, Shelby couldn't tell. *Likely both.*

"Oh, look, the whole whorey trinity is here. How sweet," Sadie said with the most syrupy voice she could manage.

"What. Is. This?" Chelsea hissed, holding up her phone. The Amish meme of Trish blared in all its political incorrectness. That was fast.

Shelby stood and decided it was better to defuse the situation. "Trish, I'm sorry, it was just a bit of fun. Thought you would laugh a little."

Trish's eyes widened and her mouth opened in what could only be disbelief. Chelsea's eyes, however, seemed to darken. "My dad is going to see the principal about this! You could get expelled for it. It's still bullying. Trish is very hurt."

Trish blinked twice, appearing lost, then caught herself and buried her head into Amanda's shoulder. Amanda, on cue, softly rubbed Trish's back.

"You see?" Chelsea almost barked. "She's crushed. Well done, tramps."

"Ohhhh," Sadie mocked, "daddy's going to make it all better, is he? Well, I bet Shelby's dad can beat up your dad. Oh, and he's hotter, too."

"Sadie!" Shelby said from the side of her mouth.

"I know you're not allowed to say it," Sadie whispered. "He's your dad. It's okay, I'll say it for you."

Chelsea made that disgusted gasp noise then looked to Amanda with feigned disbelief. "Is . . . the redhead mocking me? Like, how is she even speaking? To *me?*"

"Oh, I'm sorry," Sadie said, "did you think we were going to kiss your posterior?"

"My what?"

"Big word for a—" Trish whispered, but Chelsea waved her hand to cut her off.

"I knowwww!"

Trish backed away, sucking in her lips.

"Well," Chelsea huffed, "it is rather perfect, isn't it?" She rubbed her rear.

Sadie made a show of looking at Chelsea's butt, then pursed her lips. "Not as nice as Amanda's, but I think Shelby has us all beat. She did snag Kale for homecoming within five minutes of meeting him. Kind of freakin' amazing, huh?"

Amanda shook her head, as if the parent of a child who would never learn.

Chelsea's own facial expression turned condescending and pitying. "Listen, girls, I know it's fun to play make-believe and dress-up—"

"—you're in a leo, too, your eminence—"

"—but make no mistake. This is real. You're declaring war. And this"—Chelsea's index finger trembled as she squealed—"is not a war you can win." Chelsea drew nearer, her face so close to Shelby's that her perfume made Shelby's eyes water. "Kale is mine. I promise you that."

"Hey, Chels," Sadie asked, "has Shelby ever told you about her first kiss with Kale? It's really a great story, but it will take about an hour to get through. Lots of steamy details. Wanna have a seat and hear all about it?"

"Erghhhh!" Chelsea shrieked, her hands turning to claws as she looked up at the ceiling. She swooped out with her disciples in tow back to the gym.

"So, you like my butt?" Shelby asked.

"Grow up," Sadie said. "Ready for push-ups?"

Shelby smirked. "Thought you'd never ask. Oh, and Sadie?"

"Yeah?"

"Will you make a pinewood derby car with me for tonight's pack meeting?"

"I'm nervous, Dad," Shelby said.

"So am I," Grant answered.

They pulled through the gate to Copeland Manor, the security guards there giving Grant a friendly nod.

"You like working here?" Shelby asked. "It's not weird?"

"It'll keep me around you as you get older. That's all I care about."

"Dad?"

"Yeah?"

"You . . . ever thought about dating?" Shelby felt heat rise to her cheeks. Her dad looked stunned by the question.

"Thought about it, I guess." They pulled to a stop in the circular driveway. Shelby counted eight, no, nine cars. She recognized Sadie's—an older model BMW Z3. It kind of even looked like a small wolf copping an attitude.

"Ever done more than think about it?" Shelby asked.

"What?"

"Dating? Hello?"

"I was hoping we were done with that line of questioning."

"My hands are sweaty," Shelby said.

"Relax, kiddo," Grant teased, "it's not that crazy of a topic."

"No, I'm feeling things."

"You just told me you were nervous about meeting the pack."

Shelby sat in the old Blazer, not moving. Then, as she opened her car door, more feelings started to invade her. Anxiety. Concern. Nervousness. Excitement.

"They aren't my feelings."

Grant turned his head toward her, cocking it so that his cheek nearly rested on his shoulder.

"Don't make your sarcastic pouty face at me, Grant," Shelby said.

"Whose feelings are they? *Kale's*?"

"You're so immature."

Grant chuckled. "Ok, for real, tell me."

"No."

"Shel."

"I think . . . I think I'm feeling the emotions of the pack." She took note of the cars again. "There's gotta be like thirty people in there."

"Not just people. Lycans. I'm the one who probably needs to be nervous."

Shelby paused. "You are. I sense it."

"C'mon, Shel, even if you are an Omega, or even this Summer Omega that Gennesaret believes you might be, I'm not a Lycan. You can't sense my feelings."

"But you are my father." She paused again, then smiled shyly. "And you are nervous."

"I'm not going to like having an Omega for a daughter, am I?" Shelby punched his arm.

Grant feigned a wince. "Who taught you to throw a punch?"

"The same guy who taught me how to shoot." Shelby's mind flashed unbidden to the only time she'd had to shoot someone to protect herself. "What happened . . . the night we escaped Nicholas's pack? I know there's more than what you've told me."

"Shel . . . "

"I need to know. Please."

Grant nodded his head slowly, as if making a heavy decision. "You killed the two that charged with Nicholas at the end."

"How?"

She saw her dad's Adam's apple rise and fall as he swallowed. "It was brutal, Shelby. You don't need to know the details."

"Yes, I do. Please. Did I shift?"

Grant shook his head. "No. But you did do *something* that I can't explain. You screamed. I fired my gun and hit one of them, but they kept coming. You screamed again, longer this time. It . . . frightened me. It was . . . savage."

Shelby covered her mouth with her hand. "Don't stop," she whispered.

"The wolves halted. Your eyes glowed a deep yellow. Your whole body shook. The air around you vibrated. Shimmered . . . like heat waves in a desert. I saw the power of whatever it was radiate from you. And your skin . . . it looked like it was cracking with a red glow beneath. It made me think of lava tearing open the earth."

Shelby closed her eyes and tried so hard not to let her lower jaw quiver. She failed.

"They howled. Nicholas and the other two," Grant said. "Clawed at the air, at the ground and their heads. They jerked like they were being stabbed. Their cries were . . . I pitied them. The two that flanked Nicholas died. Blood streamed from them. Nicholas twitched on the ground, whimpering. He shifted back to his human form, probably subconsciously. And then, you collapsed."

"I'm a monster," Shelby said. She was. What other explanation was there? She could kill . . . with her mind. She didn't even have to be awake, apparently. Though that bothered her, did she really regret killing those wolves?

"No," Grant said. "No, you are nothing of the kind."

Shelby was shaking. "How can you say that?"

"Because I know you. And I knew your mother. You are both the most beautiful people I have ever known. You hear me, Shelby Madison Brooks? Ever."

"Why can't I remember?" she asked, her voice quavering. It wasn't fair to demand that of her father. She knew it.

"Shel, I don't know. I hate saying that. I hate not knowing what happened that night. But please believe me that I didn't tell you in order to spare you from it."

"I don't regret it," she said, slowly shaking her head. "I don't regret killing them. I should, though, right?" She wiped a single tear from her eye. Only a monster could kill without regret.

"This pack, the Copelands, are the best shot we have at unraveling what you're going through. They're different than most packs. And I don't just mean that because there's that boy you're interested in."

Shelby felt the smile tug at her lips. Grant muttered something.

"How do you know they're different?" Shelby asked.

"I have come across many in my time."

"Because of mom?"

"Come on, kiddo. Let's go. They're all waiting."

"How do I . . . *join* the pack?"

Grant opened his door. "It's simple. You take a bite out of each pack member—their leg or arm—then howl in unison—"

"Shut up!" She punched her dad again in the arm. Grant didn't flinch. Wait . . . was he serious?

"That's really a decent punch. You make me proud."

In the grand hall of Copeland Manor—how many square feet was this *house* again?—Shelby stared at the group in front of her. They were all werewolves, of course. She could smell it. Odd how that scent had become so familiar—comforting—lately.

The room seemed to glow with ambient light despite being evening. The chandeliers hung so high from the elevated ceilings that you could not see them unless you looked up. Thick candles atop exquisitely gaudy sconces softened the room's glow. In the far corner, Shelby could see glimpses of a grand hearth with a roaring fire between the pack members.

Sadie waved at her. What was she wearing around her neck? Sadie turned around. Yeah, she was wearing the Cub Scout Wolf Cub neckerchief. Unbelievable.

And then there was Kale, standing there between his mom and dad, broad shouldered with that amazing, stupid, heart-melting, life-giving, worth-dying-for smile on his godlike-gorgeous face. Shelby felt weak in her knees, and her heart fluttered. Literally, she felt it *flutter.* Like something out of those romance books she always saw Sadie reading.

Kale came up and hugged Shelby. "Welcome to the pack."

She hugged him back. "Is that it?"

He smiled sheepishly. Damn him. *But don't stop.*

"No, not quite," he whispered in her ear. He could keep doing that as well for all she cared.

"Shelby," Elias said, and she felt his words in her chest as well as heard them. He wore more casual dress tonight: a pair of jeans with a Polo quarter-zip pullover. His sleeves were pulled up halfway on his forearms. "I am proud to introduce my pack to you."

Elias motioned to each person one by one, introducing them. And as he did, only mentioning their names briefly before moving to the next, Shelby felt them become a piece of her heart. Not replacing anything therein, but her heart expanded to accept them. She felt pieces of who they were as she locked eyes with each, seeing flashes of their lives and souls.

The Southebys. James and Belinda. Their son, Tyler. James, fifty, the son of military parents. His father died in a helicopter training accident. Not a natural born Lycan. Survived an attack from one of the Feral at seventeen. Fierce but reckless. Belinda, forty-five, daughter of a long line of Lycans. Shy, a bit entitled, but kind. Not one to cross. Tyler, thirteen, manifested just last year. His grades in school have suffered since then. He largely withdrew from social life after manifesting but does not feel alone.

The Chandlers. Paul and Sophie. Their daughter, Sadie. Paul, forty-four, from England. Son of potato farmers. Also the victim of an attack while saving his fiancé, Sophie, an American exchange student in London. Both were bitten. Both survived. They killed the

Lycan who attacked them, someone from another pack. No one except Elias knows, not even Sadie. They hate the movie, *American Werewolf in London.* Sophie, forty-two, and loves muscle cars. Rebuilt a '68 GTO once. Wrecked it trying to outrun a train. Sadie, feisty but sensitive. Hides her uncertainty behind insults. Believes she will struggle to find happiness because she is not sure happiness is real, but if it is, she is sure Airheads candy is the path. Shelby started. *She loves romance novels! Really?* She hides them, as if embarrassed by them, but hopes they are somehow a metaphor for life having a happy ending. Avoids Nicholas Sparks books. And she's a venatrix, which does, indeed, mean she can mask her scent. *And change the color of her coat? Whoa!* Shelby would have to see that. Natural born.

Jerod Ackerman. Goes simply by "Ackerman." Twenty-seven but already balding. Head of security for the Copelands. Elias trusts him implicitly, and Ackerman values that trust. Never married. Considers it a distraction of his duty to the pack. Hard man. Sees the world in black and white. Natural born but abandoned. Manifested in an orphanage in Arizona and escaped. That had not turned out well. Found by Elias, who had read about the incident in the news. Luckily, the news reports varied wildly and were written off as an animal attack. Ackerman was presumed dead.

The Kenzies. Ryland and Miranda. Their children, Tommy and Karina. Ryland, thirty-nine, owns a general contracting business. Small projects mostly but has a custom home up for an award. Natural born. Miranda, forty, an interior designer and works with Ryland. She is also up for an award for her work in the same custom home. She doesn't care if they win or not. Natural born. Tommy, plays on the football team with Kale. Sophomore. Holds back because he is afraid he will hurt someone. *Yes!* is his favorite band.

Shelby noted that with interest. Natural born. Karina, freshman. Manifested at eleven. Cried for days. Hates being a werewolf and believes she's damned to hell. Despite this, she is fascinated with the Lycan history and legends. Spends a lot of time with Gennesaret.

Jonas Abbot. Twenty-one years old. Largest of the pack. Loves UFC and is constantly hungry. Loud, boisterous, loves to know things others do not, but he doesn't gloat. It's a quiet pride. Bullied as a kid but thinks he's overcome it. He hasn't. Loyal when it serves him or when he feels compelled. Natural born.

The Riverwinds. Dakota and Chenoa. Dakota, four hundred and sixty-three years old. Shelby started. Yes, her insight was correct, but Dakota did not look more than thirty. Pack elder. *But not the Alpha?* Shelby wondered. Son of a famous Cahuilla chief. Survived an attack when he was twenty-three. Quiet, unassuming. Accepts his existence as a blessing from Menily, the moon goddess. *And he's blind, but sees so much,* Shelby thought with amazement. He might be blind, but his wolf was not, and he uses his wolf eyes to see the world unless he's in public so he doesn't draw attention. *No wonder his eyes are amber now.* His stare felt warm to her. Fascinating. Chenoa, three hundred and eleven years old. Descendent of Dakota. Natural born. Fought in the French and Indian war against the British. Speaks French fluently. Has killed more than anyone else in the pack. Has recently written a screenplay about her people's struggles in California. Feels uneasy around . . . her. Shelby. *Why?*

The Binghams. Ben and Anna. Their children, Rachel and John. Ben, forty-one, valedictorian at Penn State. Owns a business consulting firm and often works with Elias's investment firm, Copeland Capital Management. Voluntarily became a Lycan at twenty-four after Anna, his new wife, revealed herself to him against her Alpha's wishes. He loves fried green tomatoes with loads of black pepper. Anna, natural born and also forty-one, secretly married Ben behind her Alpha's back. Because of love, she granted Ben's wish to convert him. She never wanted anything more than a small home off a windy country road with flower pots on the window sills. She has seen more strife than she cares to admit and struggles to find meaning. Reads the Bible often, but tends to pick out verses that focus on hell and damnation rather than hope and peace. Knows Gennesaret tries to keep her from spending time with Karina Kenzie. Loves the show *Hell On Wheels*.

John, nineteen, just graduated from Lansborough High, a year late because of his . . . hormones. Also loves *Hell On Wheels*. Good looking and apparently knows it. Teases but secretly admires his sister. Natural born. Rachel, sixteen, number one in her class at Lansborough High. Got moved to a prep academy for her eighth-grade year but ran away in protest. Manifested while still on the run. Lived on trains for two months on her own. Hunters found her but didn't kill her. They intended to experiment on her but then her father and Dakota found her. The hunters did not survive. She made up her eighth-grade year in six weeks. Natural born.

The McKinneys. Joe and Abigail. Their son, Anson. Joe, sixty-four, and Abigail, fifty-nine, both natural born, lead a small congregation as ordained ministers in a non-denominational Christian church. That proved almost as shocking to Shelby as Dakota and Chenoa's age. Really? Werewolf preachers? But this was Texas, so why not? Shelby discerned, though, that they truly believed. Wait, did the Bible talk about Lycans in some mysterious code? Joe, despite being in his sixties, secretly loved early punk rock bands like the Ramones, Less Than Jake, and Bad Religion—when he thought punk rock was still "respectable." Shelby would have to look into those. Anson, thirty-nine, guitarist. Long black hair to the shoulders. Still living in the days of yesterday with his music, stubbornly refusing to give up on his dream of complete rock-stardom. Howls at a full moon if for nothing else than to keep Hollywood's stereotypes of werewolves alive, and to create rumors of wolves in the deserts among the locals. Natural Born.

The Kaplans. Emily, Austin, and Will. Triplets. Twenty-five. Natural born. Parents dead. Hunters. Shelby cringed. Austin and Will were identical in appearance, except for that cleft chin that Austin has beneath his short-cropped beard. Growing up, Austin and Will switched girlfriends occasionally. The girls never knew. Shelby blushed. Emily. Selfish because she feels she must be to get anything in life. Nothing has come easy for her, and despite having two brothers, she often feels alone. Shoots archery professionally. *Wait, really?* Has won several national competitions but thinks the Olympics are a joke and so refuses to try out. And loves to bow hunt, but not because she's skilled at it . . . because she fears letting her wolf out. Hard to tame.

The Copelands. Elias and Gennesaret. Elias, one hundred and twelve. Shelby's heart leaped in surprise, though she shouldn't be as surprised by now. Emigrated from Scotland in 1933 when he was thirty during the Great Depression to try and find work under Roosevelt's New Deal plan. *But no Scottish accent,* Shelby noted. Too bad. She always loved Irish and Scottish accents. Returned to Great Britain seven years later to join in the war against Hitler. While tracking a German squad in France with a small British platoon of twenty soldiers, the German squad shifted and attacked. Eight wolves. Elias's platoon was killed. He survived, though he harbors a modicum of shame for that. *He thinks he should have died with his fellow soldiers.* Somehow, Shelby understood that feeling. She glanced sidelong at her dad. Maybe Army Ranger genes were genetic.

Gennesaret. Eighty-six, but looked like a young forty. *Guess werewolf women can have children . . . forever?* She would have been sixty-nine when she had Kale. Natural born. Gennesaret, beyond her appearance of a refined and cultured wife, was vicious. And she had two PhDs, one in Experimental Psychology and the other in International Relations, on top of her medical degree. *Okay, so she is cultured,* not just a front. Her concern for the pack is genuine, and she sees love as the reason for life. She tries to radiate that to all she meets, except those who threaten her pack. Again, vicious. Feels guilty for the death of the Kaplans' parents, for missing the warning signs of hunters tracking them. And loves exploring libraries throughout the world and visiting ancient tribes and towns to collect legends and stories of Lycan lore.

Shelby's eyes moved cautiously to Kale, but she stared at his chest, refusing to meet his gaze. Her heart speeded up and her palms turned sweaty. What would she see? Was he actually like fifty years old? She swallowed then lifted her gaze to meet Kale's and immediately went weak in the knees. Again.

Kale Copeland. Seventeen. Feels pressure to one day lead in his father's steps, but knows that is far away. Loves people, his friends, even those he doesn't know well. A gentleman, loathe to hurt other people's feelings. Cheats on math sometimes, though. He's thinking about ways to franchise Bubba's mother's chicken recipe. *Really?* Yes, really, though he and Bubba are arguing about the name.

And, in a way that baffles him, he is completely, hopelessly, in love with her. Shelby felt the room—those in it—change as her feelings intensified. *They are responding to my emotions? Do they even know why their feelings have changed?*

Kale does not see Shelby as his girlfriend, but as his soulmate. And yes, normally that would make Shelby die from cheese overload, but not now. Not with him. Looking into Kale was like looking into herself. *Can you see into me like I can see into you, Kale?*

Mundane things came to her: he hates spinach but liked Popeye as a kid; he loves football, but not the NFL, only college; Texas A&M would be his choice to play for; he really never does let anyone else drive his truck. For some stupid girly-reason, that made her smile. He's afraid to kiss her again, just as she is, but really really wants to, just as she does. Inside, Kale smoldered for her. She felt adrenaline rush through her suddenly, running through her veins like fire, cleansing and purifying, and leaving desire in its wake.

"Shelby." Elias's voice saved her from drowning in her thoughts of Kale. *But I don't want to be saved . . .*

"You're projecting," Elias said with a sheepish smile.

"What?" she asked.

"We all feel your . . . emotions. Omegas can project them, make others feel what they feel, especially their own pack."

"I mean, condemn it girl, you got it *bad*," Sadie quipped. "I'm starting to find Kale irresistible. Can I have him when you're done?"

Heat rose on Shelby's cheeks and the back of her neck, and her eyes went so wide she thought they might pop out of her head. *Oh . . . um . . . where do I go to die?* she cried inwardly.

"I don't feel anything," Grant said.

And thank goodness for that! She was already mortally embarrassed without having to have her dad sense her mushy-blubbery-dreaming of Kale. Why was she less embarrassed to have her feelings known by mostly strangers than her own dad? *Because he's my dad!*

Elias chuckled kindly at Grant's comment, and Kale looked at his shoes with a smile. Was he acting . . . shy? Kale came off as anything but shy around others except for her . . . but he was. She saw that now. Much of his portrayal of confidence hid insecurities about himself. Heaven knows girls want their men strong and sure, but this small insight made Shelby love him even more.

"Shelby?" Elias again.

Right. "Sorry," she said. "I . . . don't know what I'm doing, really. Why is this happening so suddenly." And then a terrifying thought hit her. "Have you . . . always been able to feel my emotions?" Her eyes shot to Kale's quickly then back to Elias's. "Before tonight?"

"No," Elias said. "Your wolf feels safe among us. Can't you feel it?"

A knot in her chest had seemed to release, but she had taken that to simply be relief. Perhaps it was her wolf's relief.

"This projection thing is just new to me," she said.

But it wasn't, was it? She had projected before. Flashes came to her now of that night with Nicholas's pack on the streets of a new neighborhood just outside Odessa. Newly laid pavement. Streetlights with no power. Her dad bleeding from fierce wounds but still placing himself between her and three approaching wolves. Grant's earlier confession seemed to breach whatever had kept the memories from her as bits of repressed memory seeped through the fissures. But they were not her memories . . . they were her wolf's.

Her wolf had projected something into the other wolves' minds. Emotion. Beliefs. Fear great enough to cause the mind to fracture. Her wolf had pushed deeper with the projection, forcing it into them with merciless abandon. They died—two of them—horribly. Nicholas survived but would never be the same. *What . . . are you?*

She felt her, the wolf inside her, timid, refusing to come out. *Or am I the one refusing to let her out?*

Shelby noticed the demeanor of those around her change. They looked and felt confused.

"Is that because of me?"

Elias's smile was sad this time. "You'll learn to control it. Having an Omega as part of the pack is an honor for us."

She felt Elias's sincerity. "Am I part of the pack? Do I have to do something?"

"You have," Elias said.

She had? What had she done? "So, I don't have to . . . eat your flesh or something? Drink your blood?"

A few soft chuckles filled the room. Shelby flushed.

"Actually," Sadie blurted, "you have to dance naked with each one of us as Dakota beats on his war drum. And then you—"

Elias snapped his head toward Sadie, and she immediately fell silent. Whoa, Shelby felt the rebuke in Elias's stare through Sadie, sensed her friend cower slightly.

It's okay. Calm. The feelings flowed from Shelby to Sadie and Elias. They both mellowed, and Shelby realized Elias could have a little temper beneath his collected demeanor. Or maybe that was just Sadie's effect on him. Regardless, the Alpha raised an eyebrow now at Shelby.

"Impressive."

"You feel it, don't you?" Gennesaret asked. "The pull toward us, the call of Elias as your Alpha."

"Yes," Shelby answered.

"Your wolf has chosen us; more specifically, chosen Elias as your Alpha. And, in turn, he has accepted you."

"So, really, that's it?" Grant asked, sounding a bit skeptical.

"There's always the dancing thing," Sadie chirped.

"It may sound simple," Gennesaret said, "and I suppose it is. That doesn't mean that it is insignificant, however."

Shelby did feel the connection to the pack. And, as an Omega, she had seen into their souls. Kinship. The bond knitted itself so quickly, an immediate love and concern for those around her. Yes, kinship was the right word. She squinted as something dawned on her from the connections made with the pack as they were introduced. "You are all so young." She flickered her eyes to Dakota and Chenoa. "Most of you. Even you, Mr. and Mrs. Copeland."

Gennesaret said, "By Lycan standards, that's true. Dakota and Chenoa are more middle-aged compared to how long we can live. But, being a werewolf comes with certain elements that often times truncate our lifespans."

"Cancer," Shelby said, and she longed for her mother with a solemn yearning.

Gennesaret nodded. "Particularly ravaging upon us, true. But other forces are often at play. We are not always predators, dear. Now, if you will end your projecting, we'd love to get to the party."

"Party?"

"Of course. We can't have our closest friends and family around with a new member of the pack and not celebrate."

Shelby bit her bottom lip. "How do I . . . stop? I don't even know how I started."

"Ask her," Gennesaret said.

Ask who? Shelby thought. But she knew, and for the first time, she tried to communicate with what lay within her.

Hello, she thought. It would have been a whisper had she spoken the word aloud. In response, she saw in her mind a set of deep amber-almost-orange eyes, each looking like a lantern moon eclipsed by a passing meteoroid that got trapped in its light. Shelby thought her breath would come out as visible vapor if she exhaled. The room's temperature seemed to cool considerably. She shivered. Despite Shelby's own hesitation, she felt her wolf's bashfulness.

"It's okay," she whispered. "You can go back to rest."

The lantern moon eyes seemed to droop a bit.

Rest, Shelby thought, more firmly. Her wolf obeyed, and the vision in her mind of those wonderful, beautiful, deep eyes vanished. This time, Shelby didn't *feel* the relief of those around her, but heard it in their collective sigh.

"I . . . I'm sorry," she said to the group.

Dakota smiled gently. Shelby liked him. Chenoa did not smile. *What did I do to you?* Shelby wondered.

"Genn," Elias said, "perhaps you and Shelby can spend some time in the upper backyard together."

The upper *backyard? How many people have more than one backyard? And at different elevations?*

"Of course," Gennesaret said, smiling at Shelby.

As if on cue, the doors to the hall opened, and a string quartet began playing as they entered. Servers with food also swooped in, and the pack turned lively. Shelby spun to follow Gennesaret out. Grant quickly stepped to her side.

"There's no way you're leaving me here in the middle of this den all alone," he said.

The "upper" backyard sprawled as long as a football field before gently sloping down to another field that could have passed for a small golf course. Shrubs and trees rimmed the entire property with lights shining up from the ground, illuminating Shelby's surroundings with a soft yellow glow. Small insects swarmed above the manicured grass in their seemingly erratic patterns. At various points, Shelby caught glimpses of people walking in pairs along the perimeter and across the lawns. Security guards.

"Now, Shelby," Gennesaret said, "let us see that wolf of yours."

"I don't know how," Shelby said. "It's only happened once, and I really don't remember most of it."

Gennesaret nodded. "With Lucas."

Shelby turned her gaze down to the lawn. "Yes." She felt her father stiffen slightly. Her Omega senses seemed to apply to the pack and to her father, at least to a point.

"Elias wanted to come out here with you and command your wolf to reveal itself, but I convinced him to let me try a gentler approach. You see, a Summer Omega, if this is what you are, is said to be more independent. I believe your wolf must be coaxed out rather than commanded."

Shelby breathed out a long exhale as her stomach fluttered with butterflies. "Okay, I'll try."

"This may not be a good idea," Grant said.

"Why not?" Gennesaret asked.

"I kill people," Shelby said flatly. "Werewolves."

Grant grimaced. "Our run-in with Nicholas's pack did not go as planned."

"I remember your recounting of it last week at our dinner," Gennesaret said. "Is there something more? I don't recall details of you shifting, Shelby."

"I . . . I didn't," she admitted. "I just killed them, somehow."

"She didn't shift," Grant said. "She did something else."

"Yes?" Gennesaret asked, intently.

Shelby adjusted her weight. "It was with my mind, I think. Or my wolf's mind. She . . . this sounds so stupid."

"No, please, explain."

Shelby told her, revealing the glimpses of memories that had broken through along with her father's details from his point of view. "It was like I was inside them," she explained, "like I could . . . make them see or feel whatever I wanted them to. I made them fear me— or my wolf made them fear her—and believe they were being crushed by something they couldn't see or escape. I felt their fear at the time—I remember that now—and I . . . I *liked* it. I wanted them to die but to know the fear they had caused me first."

Shame. And a bit of guilt. Those emotions prickled across her face and swarmed in her chest. "I didn't know what I was doing."

"It wasn't you, Shel," Grant said.

"Your father is right," Gennesaret said. "An Omega can project her feelings upon other Lycans, it is true, but her wolf has the same ability. It is a symbiotic magic. You each feed off each other. But a Summer Omega is said to have a much greater degree of this ability. Obviously, you can use it as a weapon."

"You keep saying things like that," Shelby said. "Like all of this is written somewhere."

Gennesaret nodded. "It is. And some of it is verbal lore as well."

"Where? Where is this written?"

"Among our people," said a new voice.

Shelby turned to see Chenoa and Dakota approaching. Dakota's long braid shimmered in the ambient glow of the property's perimeter lights, almost appearing to be liquid. His wolf eyes glowed a dim amber. Chenoa's lips still held that grim line. Did the woman even know how to smile?

"And elsewhere," Chenoa continued. "But if you are a Summer Omega, as the Luna believes, it is nothing but an ill wind for the earth."

"Luna?" Grant asked.

"What the Cahuilla call the mother of a pack," Gennesaret said. "Me."

"It is foretold," Chenoa said, "that when the one who is born into the late hour and blossoms late in the season rises in the world, she will carry the desert winds upon her lips and the fire upon her feet. The Summer Omega is a messenger that opens the way for destruction. The season of dead things always follows summer."

"Change," Dakota said, his voice kind and slow. "The actual word is 'change,' not destruction. It also says that she will use the fires of wrath to flood the earth with tears of mercy."

These two were at odds with each other, Shelby saw. No, felt. They interpreted their people's prophecies differently. Chenoa did not speak again but Shelby felt her agitation with Dakota.

"Elsewhere, throughout the world, there are legends and myths about a Summer Omega wherever Lycan lore and stories exist," Gennesaret said. "Each of them are different to varying degrees. In remote villages of the Carpathian Mountains in Romania, where the people strive to maintain a mediaeval lifestyle, the legends say that a 'late birthed' *vârcolac,* a term that originally meant something closer to 'werewolf' but now refers more to 'vampire,' will essentially eat those that approach God because of their unworthiness. Or because of envy. The legends differ from village to village. They all agree, however, that this *vârcolac* will open the eyes of the world and burn them out."

"Um, awesome?" Shelby said. "I don't think I like this."

"Just stories, Shel," Grant said.

"The oldest monastery in the world, St. Anthony's in Egypt, has written accounts of werewolves collected from all over the Mediterranean and parts of the Middle East. In nearly every case, each has some reference to 'one who is last and least' that will cleanse the world."

"Or burn the world," Chenoa broke in.

Gennesaret smiled. "Fire can be cleansing."

"Or a tool for destruction."

"That, I think, is entirely up to Shelby."

Shelby felt their eyes upon her.

Grant let out a soft laugh. "Right."

"You were there, Mr. Brooks," Gennesaret said. "Were you not? Can you explain what happened to Nicholas and his pack?"

That caught him short. He shook his head.

"Let her out," Gennesaret said. "*Bring* her out."

Shelby licked her lips and reached within to where she knew her wolf resided. Slumbered, really. Those lantern moon eyes opened. Shelby flinched. *You're there. I feel you.* The wolf didn't answer. How would she even answer? Thoughts? Words? Feelings? *Thank you for saving me. Us.* Shelby said inwardly, *I . . . want to know you. Will you come out?*

In her mind's eye, Shelby saw more of her wolf. A light blue, almost gray, narrow snout, drew sleek lines that sloped up beneath her eyes, then continued on to graceful ears that lay nearly flat against her head. *You're beautiful,* Shelby thought.

"Many times our wolves are a reflection of our innermost traits," Gennesaret said, almost as if she heard Shelby's thoughts. "Our beliefs, prejudices, mannerisms, viewpoints, and so on. But they are indeed independent of us in many ways as well."

"I . . . always thought that my wolf was just a part of *me*," Shelby admitted.

Gennesaret smiled. "No, they are indeed separate from us. Distinct creatures."

"But how—"

"We don't know."

"Some do," Dakota said. "Menily has blessed us with a portion of her spirit."

"Some see it as a blessing of the Moon Spirit," Chenoa said. She looked at Dakota. "Others not."

"We don't really know," Gennesaret said. "Will she manifest?"

The wolf inside Shelby retreated so that Shelby only saw the eyes again. "I don't think so."

Gennesaret looked disappointed. "Perhaps now is not right."

"It is best," Chenoa said.

Shelby felt heat rise in her. Anger. Of course she carried around the guilt for what she had done to Lucas, no matter that he deserved it, and now what she had done to two of Nicholas's pack. *They had deserved it, too.* But to have another person tell her it was best she didn't manifest? That her wolf remain within. Hiding. Dormant. And that she was part of some kind of prophesied destruction? Well, screw that. And screw Chenoa for that matter. Who was she to dictate Shelby's future and what she was?

Shelby turned to Chenoa, and the old woman, who did not look old, flinched. So did Dakota beside her.

Why do you hate me? Shelby thought. *I am not what you think. I am not something out of the Book of Revelations or your people's legends. What I am will not be determined by myths. How dare you tell me my path!*

"Shelby," Gennesaret whispered. "Shelby, dear, stop."

Shelby blinked. Her eyes burned but so did her skin. Her jaw felt sore, not just from clenching it under Chenoa's judging glare. And Chenoa . . . a single tear streamed down her cheek. Then blood from her nose.

"I . . . I'm sorry."

"Look, child," Dakota said, pointing at her hands.

Shelby raised them. On the backs of her hands, dark coarse hair waved in the gentle breeze. Her nails had darkened a couple shades and extended perhaps an inch. Her fingers pulsed beneath her nails. She turned her hands over and touched her palms. The skin was raised, thick and padded . . . almost like paws. With a tentative tongue, she tested her teeth. The molars felt flat and smooth, but her cuspids pricked her tongue. She tasted blood.

Grant put his arm around her, and his touch, even through her clothes, felt like fire on her skin. "It's okay. Let it retreat. Let it go."

Shelby sucked in a nervous breath. "Dad?"

"It's okay, baby girl."

She *felt* the hairs on her hands retreat back into her skin, the pulsing beneath her nails fade. Kale was there suddenly. And Elias. Others followed them. From her dad's hold, she jumped into Kale's arms. She felt his strong arms around her, comforting in a way that no one else's arms could ever be. She buried her head in his hard chest, trying to disappear.

"What happened?" Kale asked.

"Just hold me," she whispered.

"We felt something," Elias said. "We all did."

"She was projecting again," Gennesaret said. "She didn't know what she was doing. And she partial-shifted."

"That's not possible. Not for one so young."

Even with her head buried in Kale's chest, Shelby could hear Elias's disbelief and imagined his face looking likewise.

"She is the Summer Omega," Dakota said. "Menily has touched her."

"She attacked Chenoa," Gennesaret said. "She didn't mean to."

"I'm sorry," Shelby mumbled. "I'm a monster." A soft hand touched her arm. Chenoa's.

"I am fine, young one."

Shelby managed to extricate her tear-ridden face from Kale's chest.

"And you," Chenoa continued, "are stronger than I perceived. Perhaps you can control what is within you."

"But you doubt it," Shelby said.

Chenoa's face remained stoic. "I do."

"I didn't mean to hurt you."

A faint line of red smeared Chenoa's upper lip where she had wiped away the trickle of blood.

Chenoa nodded and walked back to the manor.

"She is a new desert rock," Dakota said, as if that explained everything, and then he left also.

"Shel, let's go," Grant said. "This was a mistake. I'm sorry for allowing it to progress this fast."

"No," she said. "I just need to be with Kale for a minute. Please."

Her dad recoiled inside slightly, feeling as if he had been stung. She felt it. Even *his* emotions she could sense, but not project hers upon him? She couldn't sense other humans' emotions, though. Or she didn't think she could. Perhaps the connection of father and daughter allowed some of her Omega abilities to work between them. The hurt left just as quickly as Grant had felt it. She sensed him sweep it aside.

"Alright," he said, and walked back toward the house.

Shelby heard more footsteps on the grass as the others left. Soon, it was just her and Kale under the starry night.

"Maybe I'm not supposed to be with a pack," Shelby whispered. "I should be alone."

"That's nonsense, Shelby," Kale said. "And you would go Feral if you were alone."

"Maybe that's better. I could have killed her."

"Yeah, but, most might've thanked you for that," he said with an uneven smile. Even his fake smiles warmed her chest.

She punched his arm. "Were you flexing again?"

"What?"

"Never mind."

She looked into his eyes, wanting to escape into whatever world they would bring her to. "Will you leave with me? Just us?"

"Yes."

"Yes?"

"If that's what you wanted to do, then yes. But I don't think it is."

Shelby huffed. "It's not. Not really."

Kale leaned closer, just slightly. Shelby didn't know what Heaven smelled like, but if it wasn't Kale's scent, she wasn't interested. She felt lightning in her fingers and toes as he drew closer. "What do you want?" he asked.

No, don't do that. Her breathing shortened. Her heart raced. She wanted to scream for him to pull back. What could she do to him if she weren't careful?

"Kale," she whispered. "I'm scared."

"Yeah, but what do you *want?*"

"I . . ."

He drew even closer and his chest pressed against hers. *Can he feel my heart thudding against my rib cage?* What would she sense this time if they kissed? If they . . . oh, his lips looked so succulent! He ran a finger along her jawline, and she trembled beneath his touch.

"I . . . just . . ."

"Me, too," he whispered.

She grabbed a fistful of his shirt and pulled him the rest of the way to her lips, nearly lunging for him. That lightning in her fingers and toes erupted in a brilliant explosion in her mind. A thin layer of sweat broke out on the small of her back, and she felt it tingle. She tingled all over, actually. Running her fingers through his thick hair, she pulled him still closer and kissed him long and slow. She jumped into him, wrapping her legs around his waist, and she felt his strong hands catch her, running up and down her back. She lifted her chin, and he kissed her neck; she groaned softly. No, it was a growl, right next to Kale's ear. He clutched her hard when she did that, and she nibbled his ear, then trailed kisses down his neck as he continued to kiss hers.

When their lips found each other again, Shelby dug her nails into Kale's back so deep, she was afraid she might make him bleed. But she couldn't get close enough to him as their kiss deepened, and she felt herself trembling with fear and delight and wonder and awe and—

Kale pulled back.

"You don't have to do that to me," he said softly, nuzzling her nose fondly with his.

"What?"

"You're projecting."

Her cheeks burned. "I am?"

He smiled. "Oh, yeah. Definitely. I already feel what you want me to feel, Shelby Brooks. You don't have to convince me with your secret Omega magic tricks."

"I didn't know—"

"Shut up, Shelby," he said, and kissed her again as he raised her chin, and Shelby thought the world had indeed disappeared as she melted into Kale's embrace completely.

"I'll never let anyone hurt you again," he whispered. "I promise."

Why had he said that? Lucas. She was projecting her anxiety rooted deep within about Lucas.

"He's far from here," Kale said.

"I forget about him when I'm with you."

"Not completely."

No, obviously not. Those scars were deep.

Kale ran his hand through her hair and cupped the back of her head. He looked intently into her eyes.

"I love you."

He loved her? Crap, what did she say to that? It had only been a week! But the simple truth of her feelings could not be denied.

"I love you," she whispered back. "I always have, but I don't understand how. It's like . . . rediscovering you."

Kale's smile was so wide it looked like it nearly touched his ears. The perimeter lights lit half his face, the moonlight the other half, though more dimly. "Are you quoting Journey to me?"

"Wait, you know Journey?"

"'Two strangers learn to fall in love again—I get the joy of rediscovering you . . .'"

"Oh. My. Gosh. First, Kale Copeland, don't quit your day job. You're no Steve Perry."

"Ouch."

"Second, you cannot know that song. It's not by Maroon 7—"

"—5—"

"—Or Taylor Swift or Bibber—"

"—Beiber—"

"—Or Sam Smith—"

"Shel," Kale said, putting a hand over her mouth. "'Faithfully' is like the ultimate 80's sappy love song. Everyone knows it. Anson can rip it on the piano."

"No. That's 'Total Eclipse of the Heart' by Bonnie Tyler. Don't you know anything?"

"Have you seen the literal music video version of that song?"

"The what?" Shelby asked.

"Oh, Shelby Brooks, you have not lived."

Kale took her by the hand, interlocking his fingers with hers, and pulled her back toward the house. "We have to YouTube it."

"Hey! I'm not finished with you!" she complained.

"This is important," he said, obviously mocking her for when she showed him the goat video of Taylor Swift. "You can kiss my lips off later."

"And your neck? And earlobes?"

"You're into the lobes, huh?"

"Just yours." Shelby heard herself talking and realized how she sounded. "Sadie's right, I've somehow caught romance-novelitis. I need to watch *Hacksaw Ridge* when I get home." But that had a romance story in it as well. *Crap.*

"What are you mumbling?"

"You know I can make you kiss me, right?"

"Mm-hmm," Kale mumbled.

She projected what she wanted. *Exactly* how she wanted him to kiss her. Kale stopped cold next to one of the two small servant-quarter houses on the property. He turned toward her. "So, you know that's not just to me, right? Everyone else can feel it when you do that."

She ripped her hand free of his and covered her face. "Crap. Holy feculence."

"Sadie's really worn off on you."

"Shut up."

And then he was there again. Close to her, his warmth so intoxicating. She blinked rapidly, trying to focus her vision, but his presence so undid her!

"I hate you," she mumbled.

"I see I don't need to project anything to make you want me." Kale pulled her to the side of the small house and pushed her up against the brick wall. He pinned her hands above her head and her heart speeded up for the thousandth time tonight. She giggled as he tenderly kissed the underside of her wrists, then the inside of her elbow.

"Still hate me?" he asked.

"More than ever," she said breathlessly and reached for his mouth with hers. He pulled back just out of reach, then moved in half the distance between them. She reached further, vying for his sweet kiss, those full lips, but again he pulled away.

"Okay, now you're just being a jerk," she said.

He moved in, more slowly this time. Shelby didn't take the bait. She shook her head. "I don't trust you."

"Yes you do."

She did, so completely that it scared her. He released her arms from his hold, and she found her hands running across his broad shoulders again, clutching and digging for him, unable to stop herself. Tenderly, cautiously, he let her lips find his, and she felt him tremble this time. She smiled, breaking their kiss and loving the feel of his scruff around his lips as she pulled back. "What's wrong, Kale? I scare you?"

"You have no idea."

She let herself become lost in his kiss once again.

"Hey," Lucas said, sitting down next to her with his maple body acoustic guitar slung over his shoulder. "You're Shelby, right?"

Shelby nodded, her lips parted slightly. He had the cutest crooked smile and golden curls of hair with dark roots. It was open mic at The Warehouse, a club that occasionally shut down its bar during the day to let high school kids come and perform. A constant rain had been doing its best to ruin the last days of her summer before 11th grade, but now it seemed romantic somehow. The soft patter of it on the street and the roof, the guy with a guitar next to her . . .

"Yeah, hi," she finally said.

He looked down with a smile that was too cute and disarming.

"You playing?" Lucas asked, motioning toward the stage. A guy and girl were singing a duet, the guy with a guitar and the girl slapping a tambourine on her leg on the second and fourth beats of every measure.

"No," Shelby said, "just here to hang out and listen, really."

"That's cool."

A silence descended that made Shelby feel a little awkward.

Without any other preamble, Lucas said, "You want to hang out sometime?"

Shelby's heart skipped a beat. Was she making this up in her head? She felt her neck flash hot for a second.

"Um, yeah, sure," she said, trying to sound casual but failing.

"Cool, cool. What about tonight? The rain is finally supposed to let up, and we could walk around Lake Ella or something. You free?"

Was she *free*? Currently, yes, but she was definitely considering handing the key to her heart to him. How long had she been trying to get him to notice her? At least three months, and she thought there was no way when summer hit that he would ask her out. There was an advantage to school being in session, easily seeing those you wanted to be seen by every day. She had made every effort during the summer to put herself near him if she could, without being a stalker. Okay, maybe she had sort of crossed the "stalker" line a few times.

She looked down, and a piece of her wavy, sandy blonde hair fell in front of her face. Lucas reached forward and moved it behind her ear. His hand gently touched her jawline as he pulled back a little too slowly.

"Yeah, I'm free," Shelby said.

"Sweet. Meet you there around 7:30-ish?"

"Okay. Where, exactly?"

"You know the antler tree?"

"Yes."

The small crowd of about thirty or so started clapping when the guitar-tambourine duo ended their song.

"Okay, cool. Listen, I'm up next. Stay and listen, and then I'll see you later tonight?"

He wanted her to stay and listen specifically to him? That was the only reason she was there but decided to play it cool.

"Promise not to mess up, and I'll stay."

"Ha! Won't let you down!"

Holy crap, was she his groupie already? There were other girls who cheered a little too enthusiastically when he got on stage. Annoyance akin to jealousy brewed within her. How stupid girls could be, she thought, trying not to categorize herself there just yet.

Lucas sat on a stool and adjusted the mic. "Nights in White Satin" by the Moody Blues started ringing out, that rich E minor chord filling the club. Lucas's voice wasn't whole-toned like Justin Hayward's, but the raspy, more nasally tone definitely worked. It came out as a surfer's version of the classic song.

He was good. And she realized that she just might be in trouble, her crush turning into something a little deeper. Stupid weak girl stuff. She clapped at the end, promising herself she wasn't going to go swooning all over him like a few of the other girls. Forcing herself to leave before he came to find her was hard, but she wasn't going to play that easy to get.

The oak tree did look like a large buck, lying down with its head turned up and looking to the right, its antlers the sprawling branches. Sort of. Whatever. The rain had let up, but the smell of it still hung in the air, the smell of things freshly cleaned. Lake Ella's shoreline was perhaps fifty feet away, its water smooth and seeming to swell at the edges from all the rain. Shelby looked at her phone. 7:35 p.m.

She heard Lucas's voice laughing and talking to someone. Was he on the phone? Lucas was coming around some brush, but she couldn't see him yet. As he came into view, she was leaning on the tree, but stood upright when she saw two friends with him. Dave and Ryan. She had English with Ryan but didn't know him well.

Lucas gave her a raised chin nod and said, "Shelby. What's up?"

"Hey." She looked at Dave and Ryan with a bit of a weird glance. Dave wore a Jacksonville Jaguars hoodie.

"Oh, don't mind them," Lucas said. "They kinda hang out with me all the time. Moral support, you know?"

"You need moral support?" Shelby asked, trying to keep her smile unconcerned.

"Hey, you ran off after my performance. Was it that bad?"

"It was great, actually," Shelby said. "I just had to run and do some stuff. You've got a great voice."

"Thanks," he said in way that told her he was used to hearing that. "Ya know I dedicated that song to you."

"Really?" Shelby said. "Because I don't recall hearing you do that."

"It was in my head."

"How special."

Lucas chuckled. "Yeah, I know."

"So . . ."

"Is it weird that Dave and Ryan are here?"

"Um, no, I guess. I just thought, ya know, it was just going to be us. I scare you or something?"

"Ha!" Lucas said. "Not at all. I figured we could just have our own version of a night in white satin, though."

Shelby felt a warning in the air, something inside her starting to emerge. She kept her tone calm and playful, not wanting to be a freak or anything. "Okay . . . what do you mean?"

"You like me, right?" Lucas said.

"This is kinda weird, Lucas."

"I like you, Shelby. I hope you don't make this harder than it needs to be."

Dave took out a white sheet from under his Jaguar hoodie.

"Um, what's that for?" Shelby asked, not caring if she seemed concerned now. Something stirred in her chest.

Dave unfurled the sheet and laid it on the ground.

"We having a picnic?" Shelby asked, tensing.

"Kind of." Lucas smiled. It was different this time, not the lovable, cute grin he usually wore.

"Okay, well, this was fun, but I think I'm going to go now." She reached into her back pocket to grab her phone, feeling the need to reach out to her dad. Lucas snatched it away from her and threw it in the lake.

"Hey!" Shelby yelled.

"You won't be needing that," Lucas said. "We have our own." He took out his phone. "You don't mind if we record this, right? It's always good for later."

Move, her mind told her. *Get out!* The instinct to run came just as she realized what was really happening.

Ryan moved behind her and grabbed her before she could escape.

"Get off!" she yelled. "What are you doing?"

She struggled, stomping on his feet, twisting her torso, but Ryan was too strong. He was on the wrestling team she remembered in dismay. Reaching up and clawing behind her head, she blindly searched for Ryan's face. He moved his head out of the way of her scratching hand, and she slammed her head backwards, catching him in the face.

"You little—"

"Aw, she got you, huh?" Lucas said.

"It's gonna be a black eye, you slut!" Ryan said.

Lucas gave Ryan a look of feigned worry. "You gonna live, Ryan? Need to go home to see Mommy first?"

"Shut up, Lucas! You said it was my turn this time," Ryan said, still holding her firmly.

"Oh, I think there's enough for each of us with this one," Lucas said. "But I got first dibs."

Lucas punched Shelby in the stomach. All the air jettisoned from her lungs, leaving her gasping in shock and pain as she squinted her eyes, the first of her tears starting to fall.

"That'll take some of the fight out of her," Lucas said. "Let's get on with it."

Dave grabbed her legs and lifted her off the ground, Ryan still holding her arms. They put her face down on the sheet, and Ryan knelt on her shoulders, pinning her.

"Stop! Get off me!" Shelby screamed into the sheet, still trying to get her breath back. Her cries sounded little more than muffled.

"Shut her up!" Lucas said.

Dave shoved a sock in her mouth, and Shelby's eyes watered as she felt a length of rope pulling tight against her cheeks and being tied at the base of her skull. She screamed into the gag. She felt Dave kneel down on her hips while Lucas tugged on her white-denim shorts, reaching under her and undoing the front snap. He tore them free despite Shelby's frantic kicking.

Terror. It was the absolute terror of this nightmare that let it loose from its cage. Her eyes started to sting, burning like someone held a blowtorch to them. She wanted to claw them out, but Ryan was too heavy to free her arms. Her back cracked next, and her skin felt too tight, like wearing clothes three sizes too small. It was tearing, wasn't it? That's what she was feeling? What were they doing to her? All her bones ached, not like a feverish ache; something deeper, in their core.

"You really don't need to fight," Lucas said. "You remember Mindy Hannon? She ended up really appreciating what we did for her. I see it every time she looks at me now."

They've done this before, Shelby realized, and the horror inside her redoubled as did the physical pain.

"And Cara Thompson?" Lucas went on. Shelby remembered Cara. She hadn't seen her since 9th grade.

Dave snickered. "Man, that one was sweet, bro!"

"She kinda took it wrong," Lucas said. "Changed schools. I mean, really? Kind of an overreaction, right?"

"Just trying to help little girls grow up," Ryan agreed.

"The best might have been Veronica. I mean, she still hangs out with us. See, Shelby, that's what I mean. Gratitude. You'll understand soon."

"Man, those legs are hairy, bro" Dave said. "You sure you want that?"

"Whoa," she heard Lucas say. "Look! What the Hell?"

It spread over her body—a feeling of being stabbed in a thousand places at once. She tasted blood in her mouth. Had they hit her? Her skin split along her spine, and she screamed. But it didn't come out as a scream, rather as a bloodcurdling howl.

"Holy—" Dave started to yell but was cut off as Shelby's hips rose violently, throwing him off her. Ryan cursed in surprise as he flew from her shoulders, falling hard into the tree. She smelled them both, each a distinct scent, heard their hearts pounding.

"It's a freaking monster, bro!" Dave cried.

She heard Dave and Ryan running away, their steps awkward, stumbling desperately.

Shelby came to her knees, the pain still ripping through her. She looked down and saw her hands changing, morphing. Claws jutted forward from her fingertips as her fingers grew closer together, becoming stubbier with pads where fingerprints had been. Her legs bent unnaturally and her knees buckled, the joints snapping inward and popping sickeningly. Again, the howl-scream came out.

"My dad was right."

Lucas's voice. He was still there. His dad was right?

"You're a demon."

She whirled around, alacrity in her limbs like never before, her back hunched, and she felt . . . hair? . . . stand up on her withers. Strength. Endurance. Lethality. A growl rumbled in her chest, the growl of a predator facing its prey.

Lucas stood but stumbled and fell, tripped up by a tree root. He hit his back hard but immediately tried to roll over and get up again. There was a fear on his face that she hadn't known could exist, one that must have only been worn by those who knew they faced death.

But she was not death. No matter what they had tried to do, what they did do, she could not kill despite the wolf within her aching to tear him apart. In an empowering yet terrifying moment, she realized she actually could.

She lashed out with her right paw, a shimmering dark blue coat covering her arm. It flew through the air and caught Lucas in the face, her claws tearing his cheek as she dragged her paw down to the side of his neck. Lucas wailed as the smell of wet iron scented the air.

Shelby shot up in her bed, her sheets dripping with sweat and heart thudding. She took a loud breath, as if she had been underwater too long, starving for oxygen.

"Oh my gosh," she said, no more than a whisper. "It's just a dream, just a dream . . ."

She reached for the lamp on her nightstand and switched it on. The yellow incandescent glow filled her room. She swung her legs off her bed, then put her head in her hands, resting her elbows on her knees. Her lavender tank top was damp at her back as were the roots of her hair.

"It's okay," she told herself, rocking slightly. "You're okay."

Embarrassed even though no one was with her, she checked her boxers. Slightly damp, the faint smell of urine. Deeper embarrassment. If her nightmares weren't so terrifying, she might have believed something to be wrong with her, wetting herself as a seventeen-year-old. She gave herself a pass on that, grateful this was the first occurrence in the past three months. That had to be a good sign.

A note sat on her nightstand under the lamp, her dad's handwriting scribbled on it. She looked at the digital clock. Its green glow read 11:14 p.m.

Had to run out and get some milk for the morning. Be back soon.

"Of course we're out of milk," she said and put the note down. "What else is new?"

I need to start doing the grocery shopping, she thought. You know, like a responsible adult. Late night grocery runs were always part of their life. Heaven knew Grant would never grow up enough to actually plan ahead on the little things. Like food.

Her heart still raced as the nightmare's echoes lingered in her mind. Thoughts of Kale pushed her anxiety aside. Their kiss last night after meeting the rest of the pack … she had lost herself in that moment. How could she feel so deeply for this boy whom she had only known for days?

Not days, she reminded herself, but ages. Eternities.

That made no sense. Her mind spun as her brain tried to quantify what her heart and soul seemed to already know. How could her logical brain understand the language of love that was eons old?

She'd had to practically pry herself from Kale's side when it was time to go last night, her heart aching to not leave him, to remain in his presence evermore and her lips begging for his just once more. They had actually tingled when she said good-bye. Through the bond—that enigmatic but wonderful bridge between them—she had felt his longing to remain with her as well, as if being separated from her would be the trial of his life and—

"You're hopeless, Shelby," she told herself aloud. "Get a grip. He's just a boy."

She felt something inside her stir in disapproval at the lie. You miss him, too, don't you? she said to her wolf. Shelby felt her wolf's longing as well, but more for Kale's wolf. Huh. That stirring within her produced a new feeling. How would she ever manage two sets of hormones? Do you have periods and stuff to deal with, too? Shelby closed her eyes. Don't answer that, she told her wolf, but, of course, there was never an answer.

Werewolf stuff was freaking weird sometimes, she decided. Imagine that. How about some normal stuff, like what would she wear to homecoming? It was still about six weeks away, but she already fretted about it. There. See? Normal girl stuff.

Shelby stood up and went to her bathroom. The fluorescent light above the mirror made her squint as it fluttered to life. Why did these kinds of lights always seem to make that annoying hum sound? She splashed some water on her face and grabbed the hand towel, patting herself dry. In addition to new boxers, she'd have to change her tank top. Werewolf or not, her sweat stank. Really stank.

Crap, probably my sheets, too.

She went to her dresser and found a new shirt and boxers. Sheets . . . did they have extra sheets yet? Grant really needed to get married again at some point. He had the protector/provider thing down cold but the homemaking thing? Yeah, he'd never figure that out.

She walked into the hallway to see about sheets in the closet. The old floor creaked. Feeling her way along in the dark, her fingers traipsing over the old textured wallpaper, she found the closet doorknob and stopped. One more creak from the floor sounded. Had it come after she had already stopped walking? Maybe it was just a floorboard flexing back into place as she stepped off it. But it had sounded farther away than she would have expected if it were from her steps.

Still. Perfect stillness. She stood at the hallway closet listening intently. Only the faint sound of breathing found her ears. Perhaps this would have been calming to her if she had not been holding her own breath.

Chills slithered up her back, down her arms.

"Dad?" she whispered.

She looked down the hall to his bedroom. Dull moonlight spilled through the open door. He slept with the door closed. Always. He still wasn't back from the store.

The wrongness in the air grew so thick she almost thought she could see different shades of black in the night.

When she was a little girl, she would go downstairs to get a drink of water at night. Sneak some fruit snacks, too. Sometimes, that feeling that made her think she wasn't alone, that someone was with her in the dark, played upon her mind. She'd run back up the stairs, the heebie-jeebies tickling her back, knowing that if she turned around the boogieman would be there, at her heels, snarling and reaching for her. Her blanket was her force field, that magical barrier that could protect her from everything sinister.

Maybe it was that engrained childhood reaction that made her run to her room instead of down the stairs to safety, the belief that her blanket would send the shivers of fear away like always. But in her room, a monster did indeed await, one with a scar across his face and neck, standing on the opposite side of her bed. She'd never make it to her bed in time to make the nightmare dissipate, never be able to close her eyes fast enough to protect her from the horrific vision illuminated by the lamp on her nightstand.

"Hey," Lucas said. "Remember me?"

The floor creaked behind her and a hand reached across her face, covering her mouth. She screamed into the beefy palm and Lucas smiled. She felt the prick of the syringe in her neck before her knees went weak and everything faded to black.

K ale awoke, startled. He sat up and ran a clammy hand through damp hair. His heart raced, and his stomach ran hollow. He didn't remember any dream . . . what had shaken him so? He checked his phone. 11:31 p.m. He had only been asleep for half an hour or so. On the lock screen, he saw a preview of what would no doubt prove to be a tirade from Chelsea. Thankfully, his eyes were too blurry to make anything out. He tried to rub them clear but ignored the text, and put the phone face down on his nightstand.

Shelby. His thoughts turned toward her. Of course they would. *That first kiss . . .* Well, every kiss, every time he was around her changed him a little more. Something new had started growing within him when their lips had first touched a little over a week ago at the bonfire, something that had let him see through time, through different planes. But it had actually started before that, on the football field the first day of tryouts, when he was introduced to pom-pom pushups.

You're such an idiot.

Kale had never thought of himself as overly spiritual or religious, but something *had* touched him when he and Shelby first kissed. His dad would tell him those were the hormones talking again.

Kale stood, rising a bit shakily from his bed. He was glad Bubba wasn't here to make fun of him. But Kale did feel wobbly, unsteady. Or was it that he felt unsure? But of what?

He walked into the hall, down to his parents' room. He always liked the feel of the contours in the thick Brazilian cherry planks that made up the wood flooring under his bare feet. When he arrived at his parents' room, he peered through the slight crack between the door and frame. His father's form lay next to his mother's.

"Kale? What's wrong?"

Elias never slept deeply. Sneaking out to be with friends had never worked out well for Kale. He nudged the door open a few more inches.

"I don't know. I woke up and feel . . . strange."

Elias sat up as Gennesaret stirred. "You look . . . agitated."

"I . . . think I had a bad dream."

"Of what?"

Kale rubbed his eyes. "I can't remember."

Elias stood. "Kale, we always remember our dreams. If you can't remember it, then it wasn't a dream."

Gennesaret sat up. "What's wrong?"

"He's had a dream he can't remember," Elias said.

"Then it wasn't a dream."

"That's what I told him."

Kale rubbed the back of his neck. "I'm sorry to wake you. It's nothing. I'll go back to—"

Kale grunted and doubled over, falling to his knees. Pain lanced through his stomach, up the right side of his chest, like being stabbed from the inside. He felt veins thumping in his temples, a dull throbbing that made him shut his eyes.

His father knelt at his side, a strong arm around his shoulder. "What is it?"

Elias's words sounded distant, muted, as if Kale were underwater.

"Kale? Sweetheart?" The concern in his mother's voice grounded him, allowing him to regain a semblance of focus.

And then, he smelled it . . . a familiar scent. *Her* scent. Shelby. Within the degrees of her normally intoxicating aroma, he sensed a certain emotion.

"Something's happened," Kale said through the pain, still doubled over. He held his abdomen and rocked on his knees. "She's afraid. I can smell it."

Elias and Gennesaret spoke softly, words Kale could not make out but he still heard the concern in their tones.

"Kale," Elias said, "did something happen between you and Shelby last night?"

He took deep breaths, trying to tamp down the pain in his chest. "We just kissed." More deep breaths. The pain slowly ebbed.

"First time?" his mother asked.

"No, that was a week ago at the bonfire. But it happened even before that, even when I'm just around her."

"What do you mean, Kale," Elias asked.

He shook his head, grimacing. The lancing pain dulled more,

receding. "It was like . . . like I saw something open. I don't know."

"Go on," his mother said. "Tell me."

Kale sat on his haunches, his head against the heels of his palms, finally breathing more normally. "It's stupid. Maybe Dad's right, and it's just hormones or whatever."

"Tell me anyway."

Kale took a resigned breath. "Like I said, we kissed. That's it, I promise. But . . . in my mind . . . I don't know, it was like I knew her, ya know? Like I had always known her but somehow forgot her. And then, it felt like we were once the same, part of the same . . . stuff. Elements. Wow, this sounds really dumb out loud."

Kale looked up at his mother. She stared intently at Elias.

"What?" Kale asked. "Come on, you guys are scaring me."

"Son, your mother believes in the legend of the Summer Omega," Elias said. "It is said that if an Alpha bonds with a Summer Omega, their connection will be as if they were of one body. Some legends go so far as to say that Alphas and Summer Omegas that are able to bond *were* one, somehow, before this world."

Kale's mind snapped clear. "Yes, that. I felt that."

Elias glanced sidelong at Gennesaret. "It's really just a legend, Kale. Mom's interest in information can delve beyond intel and into mythology."

"Your father's lack of belief in the legend does not invalidate its truth," Gennesaret said. "Now, tell me what you felt and saw that woke you just now."

"I felt fear, but I knew it wasn't mine. It was Shelby's. I could tell by the scent." He shook his head and squinted. "I didn't see much. Whatever it was, it was murky. Not foggy, but like . . ." He paused. "I think I tasted something. Like cloth. Or sheets. Yeah, it was like seeing through sheets."

Elias put a firm hand on Kale's shoulder. "Like a blindfold or a hood, maybe?"

A chill went up Kale's neck. "Yes." He swallowed hard. "Why would you think that?"

Elias sighed heavily. "A group of hunters entered our territory several days ago. We thought we had tracked them all."

Hunters? Here? "That's where you went the other night?"

Elias's phone rang. "That will be Grant," he said as he stood to take the call. "Grant, it's Elias. Yes, we know. We're on our way." Elias hung up. "Genn, get to the control center. We'll need everyone called up. Protocols are already in place."

"I know. I built them, remember?"

Elias smiled a tight smile. "Of course."

Kale leaped up and sprang down the hall to his room.

"Kale?" Gennesaret called after him, then her voice faded to mumbles as his mind focused on Shelby. His eyes started to burn. He threw his jeans on, then shoes, grabbed a t-shirt, and shot out the back door. His Raptor roared to life, and his tires screeched as he slammed the gas pedal down. Flood lights around the compound lit up, and security guards scrambled to alert positions. Kale speeded through the main entrance, barely waiting for the gate to fully open.

Hunters have her. You were supposed to protect her! The shame he felt was only surpassed by the anger he breathed. Something cankered within him, a feeling so deep and raw. Hatred. Loathing. His eyes burned, hands tightened, bones ached. *No.* He shook his head. *Not now.* The shifting ceased, retreating, but not completely. He kept it near the surface. He would need his wolf tonight. A deep growl rumbled in his chest, begging for escape.

Something landed in the bed of his truck with a loud thud. Kale glanced in his rearview mirror, catching sight of a familiar form. He locked gazes with his father. But Elias was not merely his father in this moment, but the Alpha, the protector of his pack. Kale saw the glowing yellow breaking forth in his eyes, the indignation surfacing for the violation of one of his own, rage that Kale was sure also brimmed in his eyes. Elias nodded at his son, and Kale pushed the accelerator down, taking the winding small-town roads at reckless speeds. But his wolf aided him, increased his reflexes and anticipation.

Forgive me, Shelby. We're coming.

Grant ran his fingers over Shelby's sheets. Damp. He sniffed them. Sweat. A faint whiff of urine.

A nightmare again.

He crumpled the sheets in his fist. He had always felt like a failure for not having the answer to his daughter's hauntings. Worse, he knew that the hunters targeting Shelby were, in part, due to him. And not just because he dared to love a Lycan, and she him, but because of his former allegiances.

He found the note he had left for Shelby on her nightstand. *Foolish.* In a new town, he had thought they were shielded enough from those who might seek them, certainly since they had just arrived and inserted Shelby into a pack. Surely she would have been safe. But, of course, that had exposed a weakness. He had become complacent.

Then he saw something else. A piece of paper under Shelby's pillow. Even before he snatched it up, he could see the handwriting on it. A note.

"If only you had completed your mission. You brought this on yourself."

A coldness swirled in Grant's chest. The mission, that one last mission. Nearly two decades ago. Sherman.

You let your guard down. And now he has her.

He stood, letting his training take over. The abductors had destroyed his weapons cache—or the one he meant for them to find. His serious gear lay entombed under the front porch steps, buried beneath the ground. He sprinted down the stairs two at a time and nearly took the screen door off as he exited the house. Grant tore the new steps free with a crowbar in less than a minute, adrenaline fueling him. Scraping the soil with the clawed end of the crowbar, he outlined the concrete box, then smacked the center of it. On the second whack, it cracked. He continued pummeling the concrete until the top was only chunks of debris.

"Anyone ever tell you that's, like, so crazy hot?"

Grant turned mid-swing to see Sadie behind him.

"Oh, please don't stop on my account," she said.

"They took her," Grant said, and swung again.

"I know. Elias put out a warning. He's called the pack to the manor."

"So, what are you doing here, Sadie?"

"Duh, Shelby's my cussing best friend."

Grant turned, wiping salty sweat from his face. "Sadie, you just met her. That kinda sounds insane. Or sad."

"Yeah, well, that female whelp Chelsea hates her so that makes Shelby my bestie."

Grant felt his face make an incredulous expression. "What?"

"Not important. I'm going with you."

Grant reached down into the concrete box and grabbed a black duffel bag. From it, he pulled out a tactical vest and shoved M4 magazines into the pouches. He felt the vest for the flashlights and found them already in place. Next, he pulled out his M4 carbine and slammed in a mag, charged the weapon, and then double checked the safety. He raised it to his shoulder, checked the ACOG reflex optics. All good.

"No you're not." He slapped his Glock 17 with extended magazine into the holster at his right hip. Running his thumb over the flat of the blade of his Fallen Oak Forge Sovereign knife—the final piece of his kit—he felt the stamped acorn there. It was the signature mark of the forger. This blade had tasted Lycan blood many times. Tonight, it would seek a different flavor. He slammed it home in the horizontal kydex sheath at his back. "Go to the manor, if that's what Elias ordered. There may be other threats to the pack we can't yet see."

"Can I just watch you? Like, forever?"

"You're not coming, Sadie."

"That's bull feces."

Grant turned, fully equipped. "Sadie—"

Where Sadie had been, stood a werewolf, smaller than most Grant had encountered—than he had killed. Flecks of brindle spotted the white-based coat in a beautiful pattern. Beside the wolf sat the clothing Sadie had been wearing, torn.

Grant's heart stuttered, and he felt cold sweat on his neck. Even having been married to a werewolf and having one for a daughter did not stop the split second of fear from trampling his stomach. He tightened the grip on his rifle.

"I'm sorry, Sadie. You're still not coming."

A car approached. Kale's truck, from the sound of it. The tires skidded to a halt in the driveway, and the headlights lit up the trees at the edge of the house. Grant turned to face the truck square on as Elias and Kale hopped out.

"How did you know?" Grant bellowed at Elias. He knew he sounded accusatory but didn't care. "You said you knew Shelby had been taken when I called. How?"

Elias glanced sidelong at Kale. "It's complicated. We don't have time to explain. Gennesaret is setting up aerial support as we speak."

"Aerial?" Grant asked.

"Drones, Mr. Brooks," Kale said. "They will help us search. But I think I can get us close without them for now."

"How?"

"It's a feeling. Something that Shelby and I have. It's how I knew she was in trouble. She's scared, wherever she is. We have to go."

"This is no time for relying on Lycan magic, boy." Grant stepped closer to Elias. "You knew there were hunters here."

Elias did not flinch. "Yes."

"Why didn't you tell me?"

"We thought we had them under control. I had people watching them. I'm sorry, Grant. We're going to get her back. I promise."

"You don't understand," Grant said. "You don't know these hunters. These aren't some glorified weekend warrior club members."

"We're going to get her back. Now, let's go."

"What about that?" Grant motioned toward Sadie with his head, not breaking eye contact with Elias.

"She's not coming," Elias said. "We need to protect the manor as well."

"I know. I told her that. She doesn't seem to care."

Elias smiled wanly. "Yes, well, she *is* a redhead." He turned his look to Sadie, still in her wolf. Grant sensed something occurring in the silence between Elias and Sadie, between Alpha and a member of his pack. After nearly a minute, Sadie's tail lowered, and she looked away. Then she darted off in the direction the truck had come from.

"She's headed to the manor," Elias said. "Take Kale's truck."

Kale tossed Grant the keys. "We'll go on ahead. You'll be able to keep up with us. Genn will be in contact, tracking our position."

"Won't we all be faster to go in the truck?"

Kale shook his head. "No." He stripped down to his boxers, throwing his clothes off recklessly, and shifted. Grant stepped back as Kale Copeland became something else, something grander. Paws as large as Grant's hands pressed upon the moist earthen ground, imprinting heavily. No matter how many times he had seen Moriahna shift, the process still took Grant aback. Kale's face elongated into a snout, teeth lengthening to fangs. His eyes changed, morphing to a dark golden color that bespoke a rage that Grant knew many Lycans struggled to control when in their wolf form.

Kale lowered his head, a constant deep, barely audible rumble seeming to emanate from him. He dashed off, the night cloaking him.

"He feels her, but more keenly when in his wolf," Elias said, answering the question that must have been upon Grant's face. "I can't actually explain it. It's more than just 'Lycan magic.'"

"Still sounds like fairy-tale stuff, Elias," Grant said. "This is my little girl we're talking about, not Snow White."

Elias squared up to Grant. The man was impressive in his

stature, the image of a business man long departed. "She is your daughter, Grant. But she is also one of mine. I don't mean this as any slight to your role as her father, but I also feel a protective urge as her Alpha in a way that you cannot. Please trust that." He paused. "And as for the fairy-tale stuff . . . well, you did marry a werewolf, right?"

"Yes. And no happily-ever-after happened for her." Grant felt his lip twitch, the beginning of a sneer he tried to hide.

"I know, but the longer we stand here the more the danger for Shelby. Let's go."

Elias took off after his son, shifting into his wolf mid-stride. Grant clenched his fist, trying to calm his nerves. Jumping into the truck, he started the engine. He took two slow and deep breaths then slammed the accelerator down. Gravel churned up in his wake as he skidded onto the road.

Shelby awoke slowly. Her head felt heavy. Sluggishly, she moved her jaw, sucked back the drool hanging from her numb lower lip. The weight that pulled her head down, as if a sand bag hung from her forehead, gradually lessened. Her eyelids fluttered. They failed to open, but splotches of dull light filtered through.

The slow draw of her arm to her forehead stopped short for some reason. She had a languid swallow despite her dry mouth . . . where was she? A dream, a feeling . . . something teased her mind at the fringes. Gingerly, she drew in a deep breath through her nose and winced at the soreness in the center of her chest.

Again, her eyes fluttered, and this time she caught glimpses of her surroundings. She was upright. Sitting. Her feet, though somewhat numb, were cold. Bare. With a slight tingle. Smooth, cold ground. Concrete.

Her eyelids drooped, but Shelby swayed her head upright and somehow convinced it to stay put. Something rattled. A dull clanking. Her eyes obeyed this time as she forced them open.

Shelby sat in a chair in a large room. The floor was indeed concrete with pitted holes, and chunks of the floor—those she at first mistook as rats in the pale, dim light—lay scattered about randomly. A solitary window high above the metal rafters ushered in that pale light, almost silver in color.

Anxiety started to grind at her heart, a ball of ice forming in her stomach. She raised her hand to part the hair in front of her face, and again her arm stopped short. The dull rattle . . . she squinted as she saw a chain with a thick cuff around her wrist. Both wrists. In reflex, she yanked against the chains, whining slightly as her lower lip tightened.

"Hello?"

She tried to move her legs, but something secured them to the chair. Her feet definitely tingled. Loss of circulation.

Shelby whimpered.

She was in her boxers and tank top, the clothes she had slept in, the . . . she remembered. Her dad, gone out for milk. The nightmare that had woken her.

No . . .

Lucas, in her room.

In my room.

Not part of the nightmare.

Frantically now, she tugged at the chains, kicked her feet, felt duct tape crease and pull at her skin. From a dark corner, a figure took shape among the shadows. A man wearing tactical gear and a thick mustache approached.

Shelby clenched her jaw, sticking her chin forward slightly. A small measure of defiance, but something.

The man spoke. "And I looked, and behold a pale horse: and his name that sat on him was Death, and Hell followed with him. And power was given unto them . . . to kill with sword, and with hunger, and with death, and with the *beasts* of the earth."

"Revelations," Shelby said quietly.

The man smiled slowly. "Yes, Miss Brooks. I see you know your Bible. I'm sorry for the uh . . ." He spread his arms, palms up and made a show of looking around. "Accommodations. Best we could do on short notice, I'm afraid."

"Who are you? What do you want with me?"

Shelby hated the strain and fear in her timbre.

"As for the first part, my name is Sherman. As for the second, oh, we'll come to that, Miss Brooks, because you are special . . . isn't that right?

"Let me re-introduce someone. I realize this will be uncomfortable, and his behavior at your first meeting was . . . well, it was deplorable. As his father, I must apologize on his behalf. Heaven knows he never will. Stubborn and such. See, I needed to know for sure if you were . . . well, you know. One of them. But, truth be told, I didn't expect him to act in such a manner, though it was effective in determining your . . . condition. High stress situations often reveal our true selves, don't you think?

"We know about your mother, of course. In fact, she was on our target list. Low hanging fruit, as it were. Living outside a pack, on her own, with a human." Sherman licked his lips. "Easy. But then, we found out she was pregnant. Was it a human child? Or a whelp of a dog? We couldn't be sure, and one thing hunters have always sworn by Heaven was to protect humankind."

Sherman pulled a chair near Shelby and sat on it backwards, facing her with his forearms propped loosely on the backrest. He leaned in close, reeking of grime and sweat, and Shelby tried in vain to recoil.

"So," Sherman said, "prudence demanded we wait until you—" he stabbed a beefy finger into her sternum—"were born. We couldn't break our vow, of course, even if that meant sparing your . . . oh, how to put it . . . *unhallowed* mother. For a time."

Shelby felt her eyes sting at the mention of her mother. Sherman squinted.

"Interesting. My intelligence says you can't shift. Or haven't since . . . well, why dig up the past?"

Shelby stoked her anger, gathered it into her center, her core, trying to force out the fear to clear a path for her wolf. She had felt something there, in her core, something not her own but warm and comforting.

"Kale," she whispered through a shudder.

"I'm sorry, Miss Brooks, I didn't catch that," Sherman said.

It failed. The stinging in her eyes retreated as doubt and fear washed over her anger. It was shame, the feeling that rose within her, as her wolf skulked away, retreating to its hiding place deep within her.

"No, I thought not," Sherman said, obviously seeing the amber in her eyes die. "But as I said, I have someone to re-introduce you to."

A figure, only slightly smaller than the man in front of her, stepped from the same shadow that Sherman had emerged from, carrying a pistol in one hand. Shelby knew that outline—it had haunted her for over a year almost every time she closed her eyes—

even the very gait—carefree and cocky—with which he walked. She wanted to turn away but forced herself not to, but the tremble in her lower lip, that she couldn't control.

How had she ever found him attractive? How had she not seen the arrogance? The snideness? The cruelty that so plainly now gleamed in his eye? Perhaps the scars on his face she had left him helped clear the earlier facade, bringing out his true nature.

Lucas came close. He ran the back of his finger down her face and pushed a lock of hair behind her ear. Bile rose in her throat at his touch.

Sherman stood. "I'm going to let you two . . . talk on your own."

Suddenly, Shelby didn't want Sherman to leave, not to abandon her alone with this monster in human skin.

"I'm sure you two have a lot to discuss," Sherman said.

A bolt of defiance shot through Shelby, and she felt her wolf nose forward within her slightly. She didn't shy away from Lucas's next touch as he stroked her jawline.

"I missed you," he whispered.

"My dad and Kale are going to tear your limbs from your body. They will find me."

Lucas sneered. "I certainly hope they do. We have plans for your traitorous daddy."

Shelby squinted at him, not understanding.

"He never told you?" Lucas asked. He looked at his father, then back to Shelby.

Sherman folded his arms. "See, Miss Brooks, Daddy—Grant— was once one of us. A hunter. Imagine the irony of him taking up with an enemy she-wolf and spawning . . . well, you."

A hunter? My dad? "You're lying," Shelby said.

"No, Miss Brooks, I wish I were," Sherman said. Shelby thought she saw a hint of regret in Sherman's eyes, but mostly anticipation. He shook his head. "I wish I were."

"When your daddy comes," Lucas said, bringing his face to within an inch of Shelby's ear, "I'm going to make him watch a replay of our date, but with a very different ending."

"No, Lucas," Sherman said, "you'll not be debasing yourself in any such manner again. The Lord's will must be carried forth honorably."

Shelby felt her wolf retreat inside again. But that bolt of defiance still remained. She snapped her teeth at Lucas, barely missing his ear. He stumbled back and nearly tripped over himself, eyes bulging.

Shelby couldn't help but chuckle, trying to cover the dread that boiled inside her.

She felt something cold flow through her veins. They must have put her to sleep again. Now, she awoke to a chill spreading down her arm, across her chest, down her legs. She had no illusions or confusion about her whereabouts this time as the grogginess lifted. Something sharp left her arm.

"A syringe . . ." Her voice barely registered as a whisper. Were they bringing her out of her sleep with another drug?

"There." Sherman's voice. "I honestly didn't think we'd need it, but Lucas . . . well, his first experience left him wary. And then you snapping at him? You understand."

"What did you do?" Shelby asked, her words slurred.

"Sodium thiopental, of course," Sherman said. His voice, ironically chipper, grated against her. "It prevents your kind from shifting."

"But—"

"I know, you can't shift. But as I said, Lucas . . ."

"I scare him." Shelby heard the dark satisfaction beneath her lazy timbre. Her tongue felt thick and dry.

"Hell, sweet thing, you scare *me*. Your whole fallen race does."

Shelby felt the smile creep across her face. "Good." She cracked an eyelid. As her vision focused, she saw others around her, all decked out in tactical gear like Sherman. Lucas was still there, a look of smugness on his face. Yes, he thought he *owned* her.

Shelby forced herself to focus on the newcomers, moving her eyes from one to the other, struggling to see through her drowsiness.

"Reinforcements," Sherman explained. "Roberts and his men are here on special assignment from a unit in Arizona."

Shelby actually felt a ray of hope break forth in her chest. "Only five?"

Sherman's expression turned deprecating. "Oh no, child. These you see here are part of a larger force, of course. They are here to see that other pieces of the plan are . . ." Sherman paused, as if thinking of the right word. "*Executed.*"

Shelby shivered, whether because she was cold or because of the drugs, she couldn't tell.

"Roberts," Sherman said, "they're narrowing in. Maybe ten minutes, maybe less. Start heading to the manor."

They? Who, they? Shelby thought. Her lip trembled. "My dad?"

Sherman turned back to Shelby. "Miss Brooks, it's time for my men and I to take our positions, so I'm afraid I'll need to cut our visit short. Please don't think me rude, but the Lord's errand must be accomplished."

"I . . . don't understand," she said groggily.

"I explained this, Miss Brooks. We have hunted your kind ever since your appearance on earth, first recorded over 1800 years ago. Of course, most of us believe you've been around much longer than that."

Shelby worked her mouth as she tried to clear her brain fog. "Appearance?"

Sherman pursed his lips. "Bad choice of words. Arrival is more accurate. Now, Miss Brooks, I really must go."

ennesaret peered over René's shoulders as he worked the controls for the drones combing the city. Eight 20" monitors, each portraying an image from one of the eight drones, covered the wall. Each drone was equipped with hi-definition cameras that included night and thermal vision, not to mention the highly illegal but effective after-market addition: an automatic modified FN PS90 complete with a silencer that delivered armor-piercing 5.7mm rounds.

The command center buzzed with the quiet hum of servers and their liquid cooling systems. On the adjacent wall, more monitors displayed images of the outside of Copeland Manor, switching between images and angles every few seconds.

René's left hand danced over a keyboard as his right hand gently maneuvered a control stick. Each drone had autonomous capability, but a human could take over at anytime.

"Where are they now?" Gennesaret asked.

René pointed to one of the monitors. "I have Kale and Mr. Copeland here. Right along Weber Ave. The other seven drones are searching the city in grids."

"They're heading north of town?"

"Seems so," René said as he stroked a command into the keyboard. A red border illuminated a screen on the top row, second in from the left, signaling human control had been toggled to the drone whose image filled that screen.

"What's in that direction?"

A hybrid topographic and satellite map popped up on one of the screens on the adjacent wall.

"Looks like some small oil operations," René said. "A few industrial parks."

That was it. Gennesaret could feel it. "Redirect all drones to Elias's position."

"Are you sure?" René asked.

"Do it."

"Redirecting now."

Gennesaret's phone rang. "Grant?"

"I'm in Kale's truck," Grant said. She could feel the tension in his voice. "Kale and Elias are . . . somewhere off the side of the road. I only catch glimpses of them."

"We're tracking you with a drone and the rest are being redeployed to your heading. I'm sending a few drones ahead of your vector, but Grant, do you know where you're headed?"

"No, I'm just following Kale. Elias said something I didn't understand, about Kale being able to track Shelby."

Gennesaret fell silent for a moment.

"Mrs. Copeland?"

"I'm sorry. You can call me Genn, Grant. I would trust Kale's promptings."

"I'd personally settle for a little more solid intel than twitterpated emotions, Genn."

"I realize you're upset. But please, trust me on this."

She heard Grant sigh. "Elias said the same thing."

Genn leaned closer to the screen that showed Kale's Raptor. "Grant, how fast are you going?"

"About 80 miles per hour. I'd go faster, but I don't know where I'm going, and I don't want to lose track of Elias and Kale."

"Are you saying that they are sprinting alongside you, matching your speed?"

"We're actually moving up to 85 now. Or Kale is. I don't see Elias. Now 90. Finally!"

"Grant, that is . . . unheard of," Genn said, tense.

"What?"

"Running at those speeds even for our kind. Kale . . . I doubt he can sustain it, strong as he is."

"He better. And he better be right about tracking her."

"We'll get her back, Grant. I promise you."

"Yeah. Your husband also said that."

The line went dead. Genn closed her eyes and rubbed the bridge of her nose.

"Mrs. Copeland," René said. "The Chandlers have arrived. The other families are not far behind."

"Thank you."

A moment later, Sadie burst into the control room. "What in the sanguineous underworld is going on?"

"First, dear," Genn said, "this isn't England. It's not a curse to say 'bloody.'"

"Oh. Really? Yes!"

"Second, you will find fresh clothes in the west guest room. I'm sure you know the way."

Sadie looked down and seemed to just now realize she was naked, but did not blush. "Right. I kinda stripped in front of Grant."

"I'm sure." Genn raised an eyebrow at Sadie.

"Fine, I'm *bloody* going."

Paul and Sophie, her parents, entered just as Sadie left.

"Did she just say 'bloody'?" Paul asked.

Genn nodded.

"I'm British," Paul said. "It's a curse in our house."

Genn breathed in deeply.

"Paul," Sophie said.

"Sorry."

Sadie stepped back into the room in sweats and a t-shirt that said "Yellowcard" on it. "Now, will someone please tell me what the underworld is happening, for SWAC's sake?"

"SWAC?" Sophie asked.

"Solid Waste of the Anal Crevice," Paul explained. "An acronym for S-H-I—"

"I got it," Sophie said, holding up her hand.

"It's not a curse, at least."

"No, no, it's actually sort of cute," Sophie said with a smile.

Sadie's red ponytail swayed as she shook her head in frustration. "I'm going to kill someone."

"Kale, Elias, and Grant are in pursuit of Shelby now. With the help of the drones, René has narrowed her possible location down to three buildings in an industrial park. We should have her location in another minute or two."

"Why are they after Shelby?" Sadie asked. "It might be the whorey trinity."

"These are hunters, Sadie. This is not some high school game."

"Do you remember high school, Mrs. Copeland? It's pretty vicious."

Ignoring that remark, Genn said, "From what we can tell, this is personal. It sounds like some kind of vendetta perhaps between the Brooks and these hunters."

The look on Sadie's face told Genn she wasn't buying it. "Our intelligence does point to a potentially larger operation," she admitted.

"To what end?" Paul asked.

"Uncertain. We'll discuss what we know when the rest of the pack arrives."

An alarm beeped on one of René's monitors.

"What is it?" Genn asked.

"We have a breach in the south entrance," René said.

"The kitchen?" she asked.

René entered a command on the keyboard, and one of the pictures on a monitor switched to the kitchen. Now Sadie leaned in, squinting, her mouth agape. The fridge door was open with a large black man in a New England Patriots jersey bent over, peering in at the food and energetically shaking his butt to some unheard rhythm. Genn saw Sadie's lip raise in what could only be disbelief. Or disgust. No, it was definitely both.

"Mother copulating SWAC!" Sadie whispered hoarsely. "Is that . . . Bubba?"

Gennesaret sighed. "René, obviously a 300-pound person strolling into our kitchen and casually fixing a meal during high alert is problem, yes?"

René turned a deep shade of purple. "Yes, Mrs. Copeland. I'm on it."

"No," Sadie said. "I've got this."

"**B**ubba!"

Bubba jerked his head, banging it on a shelf of the fridge. He stepped back with half a dozen eggs cradled in his arms, a bag of bell peppers hanging from a finger, tubs of butter and sour cream held in place by his chin, and a package each of bacon and shredded cheese hanging from his teeth.

"What. Are. You. Doing?" Sadie hissed.

Bubba smiled stupidly. "Heyyy, sweet thang." He still held the packages of bacon and shredded cheese between his teeth, so his words were somewhat muffled. "I was just making me an omelet. You want one?"

An egg fell from his arm and splattered on the floor. Bubba's face turned as serious as it could currently look. He sucked in a sharp breath.

"That's gonna have to be yours on account of you scarin' me."

"How did you get in here?"

He said with a shrug, "That door right there," and another egg fell. "Oh. That one's my bad."

"Bubba! Focus!"

"You know how there's always mad gobs of private poh poh everywhere here?"

Sadie glared at him.

"Well," Bubba said. "There ain't tonight. It's like total freedom out there, ya feel?" He sidled cautiously to the nearest countertop and released the bacon and cheese from his . . . maw. "And where Kale at? Mofo won't answer his phone. Mama done made a fine dish of fried chicken and he didn't come over." Bubba raised his eyebrows. "Mmm-hmm. She pissed, feel? I even wore my new Vince Wilfork jersey to irritate him." Bubba half turned, showing the name "Wilfork" along with a large "75" printed on the back of the jersey. "Kale hates the Patriots, but Wilfork does hard work on that defensive line. Straight respect."

"Didn't he get traded to the Texans?" Sadie asked.

Bubba smiled in wonder. "You know that? I really think I love you, Swearing Sadie."

Sadie heard footsteps behind her and glanced over her shoulder. Gennesaret with Ackerman and another security personnel.

"Deshawn, did you say there are no security guards outside?" Gennesaret asked.

"I ain't stutter, Mrs. C.," Bubba said. "Just rolled right in. You know how strange it is for a black man *not* to be stopped and questioned by white men with guns? And don't you worry about them eggs down there. Sweet thang's gonna clean that. Her fault."

Gennesaret turned to Ackerman. "Have all teams check in immediately."

Ackerman touched the mic at his throat and spoke softly.

"I know y'all trippin' 'cause this a rich man house/castle, but y'all startin' to make me have goosebumps," Bubba said. "Where you keep the frying pan, Mrs. C.?"

"I'm not reaching any of the team leaders, ma'am," Ackerman reported.

Sadie felt the chill in Gennesaret's words when she spoke next. "Send out the distress signal. We are under attack. Crash the house."

Ackerman and the other guard sprang into action, barking orders over their radios. Only the internal security forces knew whom— what—they protected. The house lights went out, and a dim red glow illuminated the meeting of the walls and ceiling.

"Say what?" Bubba said. "Y'all hosting a rave now? Mm. Gotta call some of the homies."

"Shut up, Bubba," Sadie snapped.

"Daaaamn, girl. Always so harsh. But don't you worry. I know you can't help it with all that fiery hair and all. Mm. I forgive you."

"The signal's out," Gennesaret said. "The other families will hasten their arrival. Until then, we're on our own."

"I'ma start shootin' straight bricks of fecal matter—that was for you, Sadie—if someone don't start explaining exactly what's goin' on!" Bubba said, his voice cracking.

Sadie cocked her head to the side. "Bubba, that was actually sort of sweet."

"Thanks, sweet thang."

"Deshawn, it would be best if you hid yourself in one of the panic rooms," Genn said.

"Panic . . . rooms? I didn't know y'all had those. Kinda . . . scary, right?"

"Please," Genn said, motioning with her arms to the opening that led out of the kitchen, "this way."

Headlights pierced the red darkness through a window.

"Two cars," Ackerman said. "Coming up through the main gate. Looks like the Kenzies and the Southebys." Ackerman cursed. "What are they doing? They should be approaching in stealth!"

Just as he finished speaking, a trail of smoke streaked toward the Southeby's SUV followed by an explosion. Angry balls of orange and yellow tore through the night. Sadie stiffened, too shocked to even flinch.

"Holy—"

Automatic weapons fire cut off the rest of Bubba's curse. Muzzle flashes sparked like firecrackers in the night. Now Sadie ducked, but could not tear her eyes away from the burning wreckage. And then, from that wreckage darted three forms: wolves aflame, sprinting directly toward the muzzle flashes. They only made it a few strides before falling lifeless, smoldering on the immaculately manicured front lawn. Sadie's stomach turned.

James. Belinda. She nearly retched as she thought of their thirteen-year-old son. *Tyler.*

During the distraction of the Southebys' desperate dash, the Kenzies bolted from their bullet-riddled car, making a beeline directly for the house, their black coats almost impossible to make out against the night. Sadie heard the security system admit the Kenzies entrance through the fortified front doors, followed by gunfire much closer.

That's coming from inside the house.

"It's cover fire from our forces," Genn said, obviously seeing Sadie's concern.

"Did I just see panthers come out of that car?" Bubba asked. "When'd they start being allowed to drive?"

Genn turned to Ackerman. "How many do we have?"

"I have nine men here. I sent eight to back up Mr. Copeland."

"Recall them," Genn said. "Elias and Kale will be fine."

Ackerman looked hesitant. "Yes, ma'am."

"So," Sadie said, "we have nine two-leggers, seven wolves—depending on the conditions of the Kenzies—and that." She pointed at Bubba. The rest of the eggs fell to the floor. Bubba seemed frozen. Or numb. Or just stupid.

"You say, wolves?"

"No," Ackerman said. "We have eight wolves." Copeland Manor's head of security shifted into a slinking black wolf whose posture bespoke a lethal agility.

Bubba screamed and dropped the rest of the food in his arms.

Locked in a panic room, Bubba thought it looked more like a padded squash court. Or a cell in a mental institution.

"That's right," he mumbled. "Lock the black man up. That's what you get for your best friend being a white boy, son."

He didn't really feel that way, of course, he was just scared. From what he had seen, he was glad for the panic room. Wolves were driving cars and burning and being shot by . . . by who? "Bad guys, man. Real bad guys." But Sadie and Mrs. C. seemed unsurprised, or at least to have some idea of what was going on.

He rubbed a hand over his short hair. "Wish I had gotten to make that omelet."

Thankfully, several days' worth of food sat on pallets in one corner, a small kitchen—a single burner, small fridge, sink, and microwave—right next to it. He should eat. Food calmed his nerves. That was probably why he was always so easygoing.

"Never hungry, never grumpy."

He tore open a box and found macaroni and cheese, ramen, freeze dried fruit, cans of chicken, beef, and tuna. And rice. Lots of rice. He grabbed two cans of chicken, two packages of ramen, jalapeño cheese spread, and three bags of chili-cheese Fritos.

He locked his eyes on the single burner, focusing hard, then blinked. He heard the small release of gas from the port beneath the burner. Perfect. He blinked again. The ignition mechanism sparked and the gas caught, flowering to a low blue flame. Bubba immediately felt better with the stove prepped.

On one wall, three monitors rotated camera views throughout the property, each monitor's picture in a grainy green.

"Night vision. Dope."

He saw men clad in black moving in on the manor from multiple angles. More than two dozen, he guessed, though he didn't take the time to count them out.

"Now that ain't dope."

This called for desperate measures. He grabbed another pack of ramen. And then, next to the small kitchen area, he noticed a peculiar lever, the kind in a Frankenstein movie that, when thrown, connected all the circuits and shot crazy amounts of electricity through the monster, bringing it to life.

"Release?" he said, reading the label on the side of the lever with a down arrow. "Release what?"

Sadie shifted. Her heart raced as she retreated into a shadowy pocket. Dim red light glowed along the ceilings and walls. *I can't believe this is happening,* she thought. She had dreamed of a day when she would fight—really fight. For true love, of course—if such a thing existed. That—the desire to fight—wasn't only her wolf instinct, according to her parents, for Sadie had *always* been feisty and scrappy about everything in life. Everything was a challenge. Everything was a wrong that needed to righted through a good pounding. But she had always thought when the time came to fight, it would be against a rival pack. Those brawls rarely proved lethal, except for an Alpha occasionally.

But hunters . . .

She had only ever heard legends of them. Normally, humans would never drive fear into the heart of a Lycan; but the aura around the legends of hunters did just that. Her chest heaved with adrenaline as she tried to calm her breathing. Then came that scent of musky sweat and iron, the smell of a human. A tincture of fear also lanced the air as the scent grew stronger. Was that her fear or the hunter's?

The man turned the corner. Sadie sank deeper into her shadowy recess but bared her fangs instinctively. Dressed in all black, he pressed a tactical rifle against his shoulder. Some kind of optical gear covered most of his face, but Sadie could still see that his black face paint glistened with his sweat.

He's afraid . . .

Afraid or not, he didn't look human. The optical gear Sadie recognized as those night vision thingies. Her nerd brother got a free pair with the collector's edition of the newest Call of Duty game. This pocket of shadow would do her no good if he turned her way. Which, of course, he would.

The hunter stepped cautiously but deliberately. Yes, confidence. She saw it in his walk. Arrogance, even. The fear she smelled must be her own. *Typical,* she chided herself. She let the rage build inside her, let it push aside her hesitation, her doubt. Her shoulders hunched, her rear legs bent, muscles coiling in anticipation. Just as the hunter turned his head toward her, Sadie sprang.

The sound of muted gunfire ripped the air as she hit the hunter. He did not crumple to the ground under her weight as she imagined he would.

SWAC, he's strong!

A fist that felt forged of iron grabbed her skin as she snapped her jaws at his face, once, twice, vying for the taste of his flesh. But her attacks fell just short as the hunter held her at bay. A cold sweat broke out along her spine as she saw the dull red glint of the knife. She caught his wrist in her mouth as the knife swung toward her, and the man screamed. Sadie sank her teeth through his clothing, into his flesh. Deeper. Oh, the taste of salty warmth! Something primal awakened in her as the first droplets of blood touched her taste buds. She yanked her head, teeth still clenched, with strength born of innate survival instincts, and heard a pop as the man screamed louder. Somehow—no doubt his own survival instincts kicking in— the man punched her again and again with his free hand with surprising speed. The blows made Sadie flinch but she did not let go. The whites of his eyes in stark contrast against his black face paint, she saw the terror now in his eyes, almost pleading. The punching stopped. *Where did his other hand go?* She heard the pistol come free from the holster too late. Pressure pushed against her side and she knew it was the cold barrel of the gun.

She tensed.

"Drop it, mofo."

Sadie thought for a fraction of a second that the words were meant for her, but she knew that voice.

Bubba?

She felt the pressure at her side fade followed by the dull clank of metal hitting the marble floor. Sadie did not hesitate. She wrenched the hunter's wrist savagely. As the knife fell free finally, she released her grip on the ruined limb and looked up at Bubba. He flinched. He was kneeling by the hunter, pressing something against his head.

"Nice freakish big doggie," Bubba said. "I just saved your life. You know that, right?"

What was in his hand? A magic marker? Seriously? Bubba was holding a magic marker to the hunter's temple to save her?

Her look, even in her wolf form, must have expressed her disbelief, because Bubba said, "What? It worked, didn't it?"

Pick up the gun! Sadie screamed in her mind. *Pick it up, Tubba!* But of course, Bubba did not have the mental link of the pack.

The hunter's eyes flashed, and Sadie could see he sensed something amiss. He pivoted and slammed a fist into Bubba's solar plexus. Bubba's eyes went wide as his scream was cut short, all the wind fleeing his lungs. The hunter lunged for the gun, but Sadie pounced, all human thought leaving her as she let her wolf take over. It was long moments later when she realized her jaws had clamped around the hunter's neck, the taste of his hot blood washing over her tongue. Several strong arterial pumps shot the blood from his mortal wound into her mouth, then sporadic pumps, then weaker pumps. Then nothing.

Nothing.

Sadie Chandler just took her first life. No remorse. No guilt. Just a quiet relief swelling inside her.

Bubba found his breath and began to scream. For a large man, Bubba could really hit that high register quite nicely. Good thing there were no windows in this part of the manor. Sadie winced, then shifted but remained crouched.

"Bubba! Shut up!"

The abrupt silence shocked Sadie. Screeching goblin to nada? Just like that? Bubba blinked so rapidly she thought he might actually take flight. The boy did actually have enviable eye lashes.

"Hey, girl," Bubba said hesitantly. "You know you're naked, right?"

"I was naked before I shifted, too, genius."

Bubba's face contorted. "Yeah, but that was hairy naked." He whistled a low note. "This right here ain't hairy naked. No siree."

Gunfire sounded in other parts of the house.

"Why did you leave the panic room?" Sadie asked.

"I saw you gettin' crept up on, ninja style. Ya know, had to come save your naked self, feel?"

And save her he had.

"How did you get out?" she asked.

"See, as I was making my ramen spread, jailhouse style, I got to thinkin' that a panic room ain't no cell, right? It's to protect them on the inside. Figured there had to be a release button. Found it. Saw you in danger. Came running and . . . aw, man! My ramen! It's still cooking!" Bubba sighed. "Ain't no good now, boy. You went and ruined that." He shook his head.

"We have to move," Sadie said. "Grab his gun and stay close. I really wish you had stayed in the panic room. I don't have time to watch out for you right now."

"Who watchin' out for who?"

"Pick. Up. That. Cussing. Gun."

"Aight, Swearing Sadie, aight."

Sadie shifted and felt her confidence rekindle. She knew what she was about now, had tasted the blood of a hunter. *They can be killed.* The rank odor of sweat and fear permeated the air and she honed in on her next target: a scent that wafted from below the banister of the upstairs lobby. She was focused now, ready to—

"You know, when this is all over, maybe momma will invite you over for chicken," Bubba said. "Kale is on her bad side now on account of him missin' dinner tonight. Momma holds grudges."

Sadie growled.

"Shutting up," Bubba said.

K ale crouched low beside the warehouse, sniffing the air. Above, he heard the soft whir of several drones. He was grateful for the backup.

She was close. Shelby. He would probably find her before the drones did if he quieted his mind. Fury. It sweltered like a shapeless torrent within him. He needed to give it shape. Focus.

Kale? Elias said into his son's mind.

We're close, he answered through that same mental link.

Three warehouses, each two stories, sprawled out in view in front of him. His gaze turned to each one, his frustration increasing every second, waiting for some kind of affirmation of Shelby's exact location. He was still new at this bonded thing, if that's what it actually was.

That first kiss sealed us somehow . . .

How suddenly she had come into his life, so unbidden, so unexpected, but so welcome.

To his left, he spied Grant sidling along an adjacent warehouse, stopping at the corner. He moved extremely stealthily, for a human.

Better let him know I'm here.

Before Kale could take a step forward, Grant snapped his head and fixed his eyes on Kale's. It startled him for a brief moment.

How did he . . .

Grant ran to Kale's position with impressive speed and silence. Elias joined them from behind a stack of barrels and shifted back to human form. Grant did not seem phased by Elias's nakedness.

Well, he was married to a werewolf, Kale told himself. *He would know what to expect.*

Grant touched a comm unit at his ear. "Gennesaret says it's that warehouse, sixty feet northwest. The drones are in position to assist."

"Good," Elias whispered. "We should have the element of surprise."

Grant looked confused. "Oh, they know we're here. Kale tripped their early detection system about three minutes ago. You didn't notice?"

I what? Kale thought to his father. He supposed he would have looked abashed had he not been in his wolf.

"They won't be expecting our aerial support, regardless," Elias said.

Grant nodded. "Let's move."

Elias shifted back into his wolf, standing nearly as tall as Grant's shoulders. If it weren't for the amber eyes, Grant might have lost sight of Elias against the black of the night. As quietly as possible, they moved toward the target warehouse. His mother was correct;

this was the right building. Kale felt it pulsing in him. And he felt Shelby's fear. She had awakened recently. He could tell even that through their bond. She knew they were coming for her, and this . . . why didn't Kale sense her relief if she knew they were coming?

She knows it's a trap, Elias said.

And we know it's a trap. Isn't there a better way?

Elias growled in Kale's mind. *Best thing to do when you know there's a trap is to spring the trap.*

That made no sense to Kale, but he advanced on the warehouse all the same. A warning jolted through him, almost a voice, a thought invading his mind.

Shelby?

Back! Go back!

Grant had reached the warehouse and crouched at the left side of a dirty window, peeking through the window with an optic of some kind. Elias positioned himself on the right side of the window. A drone swooped low and lined itself up with the glass.

Father! Wait! Kale shouted through their link.

Grant broke the glass with his buttstock and tossed two grenades through the window. A bright flash followed by a massive boom shook Kale's chest. He sensed Shelby's reaction to the flash and concussion grenades, then, their connection went mute. The drone entered the opening followed by another. Green lasers began sweeping the dark interior of the warehouse, the drones seeking targets.

Kale dashed to Grant just as he was about to jump through the window and blocked his entrance.

"Get out of my way, Kale!"

He shifted. "Shelby says not to enter."

"You have got to be crazy. I'm getting my girl."

Kale grabbed Grant by the arm. "You'll put her in danger if you do."

Grant's glare turned murderous. "You don't know that."

"I do. I feel it."

Elias moved closer, still in his wolf. *Are you sure, son?*

"Yes, I'm sure," he answered aloud. He felt the muted connection with Shelby resurfacing as the flash bang's effects wore off her.

Grant seemed to intuit the silent half of the conversation. Then he put his hand to his ear, obviously receiving a transmission. "René says the drones report the area is clear except for a single person in the center. It appears to be Shelby. She's alive."

"I know," Kale said. "I still feel her, though she's groggy."

Just as Grant was about to respond, the drones flew back out the broken window and kept going. The other six above the warehouse suddenly retreated as well, leaving them without aerial support. Elias shifted.

"What's happening?" he demanded. "Why did they leave?"

Kale's stomach dropped as he saw his father's ghostly pallor.

"The manor is under attack," Grant reported, still touching the comm unit in his ear.

"What?" Kale hissed.

Elias looked hard at Grant, and Kale sensed the ambivalence in his father. "I'm sorry," Elias finally said and shifted. Kale literally felt the terror in his father's footsteps as he tore through the industrial park in the direction they had arrived. But Kale also sensed the righteous fury coursing through his father's mind, frantic though it was.

"Go," Grant said. "It's your family. I've got this. Go."

Anguish split Kale's soul. With a pained voice, he said, "I can't. I can't leave Shelby. She is my family." He paused. "You are now, too."

Grant's sigh seemed to express all his frustration. "Your mother is at the house, Kale."

"I . . . I know."

Flood lights from above illuminated the night and shone directly on Kale and Grant. Kale immediately shifted. Grant raised his M4 to his shoulder. The lights came from the rooftops of nearby warehouses. They were surrounded from an elevated position.

Grant dropped to one knee, bringing his rifle to his shoulder. He shifted his aim from one light to the other, searching for any distinguishable form. His pulse thudded loudly in his ears.

"For this cause shall a man leave father and mother, and shall cleave to his wife," a voice said. "Touching, really. Except she's not actually your wife, is she, Kale Copeland, son of Elias?"

Grant adjusted his aim toward the sound of the voice. It came from the roof of a building to his right. "Let the kid go, Sherman. He's not part of this."

"Oh, but the Lord's justice extends itself upon all the spawn of Satan," Sherman said. "Pity He warned you not to enter. This would have been over by now."

"Pressure sensors," Grant said, almost to himself. He glanced at Kale. His shoulders hunched, and his lips peeled back revealing menacing fangs. Grant could still only make out inky shadows on the warehouse rooftops. He tried not to stare directly into the floodlights.

"Yes, of course," Sherman said. "Imagine the irony of a Lycan saving a former hunter, and that of his Lycan daughter. I remember our joint missions, Grant. You were . . . ruthless. Truly on the Lord's errand."

Grant saw Kale pull away from him slightly. The air around Grant shifted. He felt it charge with confusion and accusation from Kale.

"Kale, yes, I was a hunter. But I am not now. He's trying to get inside your head. Don't let him."

"Hard to trust a man who has hunted your kind, isn't it?" Sherman said, his voice mockingly sympathetic. "Who do you trust? Him? Your feelings? The feelings you feel for young Miss Brooks? Who says Grant isn't part of this whole thing?"

Kale took another step back. He growled, but not at Sherman. Grant pivoted, switching his M4 to his left hand, aiming it at Kale while simultaneously drawing his Glock and pointing it at his best estimation of Sherman's position.

"Your daddy took Shelby in," Sherman continued, "and now look, Grant has you here all alone with us. How was it that we so easily grabbed Shelby in the first place? Maybe he just let us waltz in there and take her, hmm?"

"Kale," Grant whispered. "It's not what he says. I would never do anything to put her in harm's way."

"Perhaps she isn't in harm's way at all," Sherman said. "It wouldn't be the first time a Lycan turned on their own kind and helped us. Tell me, Kale, did Grant here ever tell you how he met Shelby's mother?"

Grant fired his Glock, taking out one of the flood lights, and rolled forward, knowing return fire would come immediately. He was right. Gun shots rang out. He fired then moved, fired then moved. Holstering his sidearm, he brought his M4 to bear and shot out the other lights, then moved again, taking refuge behind a jersey wall. He did not see Kale. Bullets slammed into the concrete, the sound of their ricochets whistling around him. He tossed a flashbang onto one of the warehouse rooftops, then hunkered behind his barrier. Men cried out. Grant rose, his night vision monocle activated, and sighted three men. He squeezed his trigger three times, and each of his targets fell still.

"Grant? You still there?"

It took him a second to realize the voice came from the comm unit in his ear.

"René?"

"Good," René said. "I kept one drone behind, about 100 yards south of you."

"How did the drones not pick these guys up?" Grant shouted over the gunfire. "They were on the rooftops!"

"They're wearing some kind of thermal camouflage, something that hides their body heat. That's my best guess. I can pick them out manually now that I know what to look for."

"Well stop explaining and get to work!"

Kale darted from Grant's side at the first report of gunfire, taking shelter behind a corner. His mind spun with Sherman's words. More gunfire, and men atop a warehouse grunted then fell still.

Whatever Grant is, he's killing hunters.

That would have to be good enough for the time being. Kale felt

Shelby's awareness sharpen as the gunfire increased. She was terrified. Bullets impacted the ground just inches from him. The vibrations of their thuds were jolting.

Keep moving!

He launched himself onto a stack of pallets and then leapt over fifteen feet to the top of a warehouse. Surprised men—four of them—pivoted at the sound of his landing, the metal roof being anything but silent under Kale's weight. He did not hesitate. Pouncing upon one, he sunk his fangs into the man, his jaws spreading from the man's shoulder to his chest. Kale ripped the flesh free, and the man's screams died in gurgles.

Heat shot up his left leg, and Kale barked savagely. *So that's what it's like getting shot.* Just registering the taste of human blood on his tongue, he thought, *And this is what it is to kill.* It shocked him how easy it had come, and he knew his work had just begun. Leg stinging, he turned and leaped at the man who shot him. The whites of the man's eyes went wider as he fired wildly, trying to overcome his fear and find his target.

Kale tore him apart, leaving him mortally wounded, and slammed into the next hunter, somewhat smaller than his comrades. The hunter fell, scrambling to draw a knife from a sheath at his belt, but it clattered on the metal roof as the hunter toppled off the edge. Kale heard the man grunt as he hit the ground over twenty feet below.

No, not a knife, Kale thought. A red light pulsed at one end of the rectangular device, dimly illuminating a button. A trigger. Kale had never seen a detonator before, but he knew this was exactly that. The last hunter dove for it.

No! Kale launched at the man, but he grabbed the detonator before Kale reached him. Kale, however, caught the man's wrist and sunk his fangs just barely into his flesh.

The man froze. "It won't matter. I'll press that button before you can—"

Kale bit down with all his strength. The hunter screamed as his hand came free and pulled his mangled limb to his stomach, bending over. He staggered back, retreating from Kale's slow advance.

"I die a martyr for the cause of righteousness," he said, voice quavering. "The sword of justice will see to your end soon enough."

He died in silence as Kale ended him swiftly. The same thought, how easy it came to kill, flashed in his mind, and he found that it bothered him, no matter his motives. In the severed hand still lay the detonator. He shifted to human form and pried the device free, then toggled a switch to the "disarm" setting. Was it really that simple?

He stood and spied Grant taking cover behind a jersey wall, trading fire with a group of hunters atop another warehouse. He was pinned.

"Grant! I disarmed the bomb." Kale held up the detonator. "Should be safe to enter."

"Kale!" Grant yelled. "Get down!"

The bullet tore through Kale's chest, entering his left side at the ribs and exiting through his right pectoral. He stumbled, the burning so intense he could not even cry out. Kale tumbled from the edge of the roof. His vision blackened before he hit the ground.

Grant saw Kale disappear from the roof of the adjacent warehouse. Sniper. Grant quickly calculated the vector of the shot. *Has to be*

around 800-1,000 meters out. From inside the warehouse, he heard a tormented scream rise above the din of gunfire. Shelby. The pain in that wail sounded inhuman.

Grant fired his M4 as he stood, covering his move to the edge of the warehouse that held Shelby. Hunters returned fire, and he flattened against the wall. A new pitch of gunfire, faster and higher, rang out. The drone. Grant peeked around the corner. Above the hunters who had him pinned from the roof of another warehouse, the drone fired devastating 5.7mm rounds in fully-automatic bursts. Men let out truncated grunts as they died.

"Grant," René said into the comm unit. "They're coming."

Grant swiveled his head, moving his rifle from one vector to the other. "From where?"

"For me," René said. "They'll breach the control room any second."

"Get out, René!"

"It's too late. Switching all drones back to autonomous flight. Good luck."

Grant heard a loud crash through his earpiece. "René!"

Tinny gunfire erupted in his ear, then silence. "René!"

No answer. Grant pulled the comm unit from his ear, and the wire hung loosely over his shoulder.

Another wail from the warehouse.

Grant's chest hurt from hearing his daughter in such agony. The drone jerked violently followed by the sound of the shot that had struck it. The sniper again. Spinning out of control, the drone bounced off a building and crashed to the ground.

"Your air support is gone," Sherman said, his disembodied voice still coming from the same roof as before. "That beast your daughter was so sweet on is dead. You're alone, Grant."

"So are you."

"Not so," Sherman said. "They that be with us are more than they that be with them."

"Ya know, I always hated your misuse of scripture to justify what you did."

"What *we* did, Grant. What we did. Or have you forgotten?"

"It's just you and me, Sherman. Come down, and we'll settle this."

"Oh, it's not just us, Grant."

The sniper. Grant cursed.

"Yeah, I thought you might feel that way," Sherman said.

"I can evade your sniper."

"Right. There's that. But why? We can talk this out, can't we?"

Grant realized Sherman's delay tactic a split second too late. The soft scuffle of a footstep sounded behind him, and he spun, M4 raised, just as Lucas pulled the trigger of his pistol. The bullet tore into Grant's left hip, and he jerked from its momentum but issued nothing more than a surprised grunt. In the fleeting moments it took him to bring his rifle back to bear, Lucas was gone. More bullets struck the ground from his opposite side, barely missing him. He flattened himself against the wall again.

"He's fast, isn't he?" Sherman asked. "Proud of that boy. He's overcome quite a bit, you know. Your girl, leaving him like she did and all."

Grant staggered. From a pocket in his vest, he tore open a packet of QuikClot and dumped it on his wound. He grimaced as the powder hit the bullet hole. A glancing blow, thankfully.

"Yeah, but he's a bad shot," Grant called back. "You taught him, I take it."

"Well, he is nervous, I'll give you that."

"Dad! Dad!" Shelby cried.

"Sounds like she's really upset, Grant," Sherman said. "Best see if you can comfort her, don't you think?"

Grant again peeked around the corner. A round slammed into the metal just an inch from his eye, and he pulled back. Then, praying the sniper was using a bolt action and needed to chamber another round, he dashed from his cover and jumped through the window he, Kale, and Elias had breached earlier. He landed and rolled, then came up to a one-knee position, swinging his gun from corner to corner. His hip smarted like nothing else.

In the middle of the dark warehouse sat an empty chair and broken chains.

Shelby felt the burning in her chest, like someone had stabbed her with a white hot blade. She screamed. The pain ceased suddenly, and her connection to Kale—that lifeline that had been forged when they first kissed—snapped. She fell, still bound to the chair. Her heart, her soul . . . Again she wailed, and her wolf wailed with her. She sensed her rage, the depth of loss that matched her own. Shelby's eyes burned as salty tears sprang from them, and she jerked the chains that bound her to the chair. Again, she pulled on her restraints. The metal cuffs bit into her arms as she yanked yet again, harder.

"Kale!"

She grunted on her next pull.

Kale! Memories swam before her as if a lifetime's worth. *Her insides fluttering with a comforting warmth when she'd felt him near on her first day at gymnastics tryouts; the drowning depths of his hazel eyes at the dinner table; first touching him, his rough but kind hands . . .* She pulled the chains harder, and her wrists started to bleed. *Please, Kale . . .*

The first time she made him laugh—that joyful, large laugh—when showing him the goat music video on YouTube; the bonfire, that fateful kiss that had opened something within her, that something that now shriveled and wilted; him helping her dad repair the porch steps; the quarry's shockingly cold water, pushing Kale from the ledge . . .

This time, her grunt sounded more like a growl. And the chains . . . had they flexed at her last pull? She felt her wolf, saw her lantern-moon glowering eyes, saw the pain in them. *Pain for Kale's wolf,* Shelby realized. But Shelby also saw the hesitation. How? How could her wolf be hesitant now? No, it was . . . weariness, not hesitation. Sluggishness.

The drug. Sodium thiopental. What had Sherman said it did? Her chest ached, physically and emotionally for that connection to her love, the man she had only known for just over a week and yet had always known in some way she could not explain. They had taken that from her. From *them.* Something pulsed in her, beneath her skin.

Sharing her music with him; feeling his solid, steady heartbeat as she laid her head on his strong chest; him holding her the night of the pack meeting, of him kissing her against the servant-quarters, making the whole world feel safe and complete . . .

She ripped her arms forward savagely, not caring for the pain or damage it would do to her. As the metal bit into her skin more deeply, she heard something creak. She turned. The plates bolted to the floor to which the chains were attached now bulged higher in the center. They had given.

"Come on, girl," she said aloud but speaking to her wolf. "I don't know how to do this! I need you. Please! Fight through it."

Her wolf emerged further in her mind, and Shelby saw that beautiful bluish-gray, svelte muzzle again. The struggle . . . her wolf struggled against the drugs in her system. The pulsing beneath her skin intensified and turned to a burn.

Muted gunfire outside. Bullets pierced the warehouse walls, sounding like fishing weights rattling on a metal trashcan lid. Shelby flinched as one struck the ground next to her then ricocheted away.

"Please!" Shelby begged. She felt her eyes stinging as if hot needles pricked them. Then, the vision of the wolf inside her mind changed. An older wolf took its place, the face black with beautiful white and gray flecks around the short muzzle, and the eyes a deep glow of amber. Half of the wolf's face morphed to a beautiful woman with thick dark hair and piercing green eyes. Eyes, just like Shelby's.

Shelby froze. And, in that moment, she knew her wolf saw the vision as well. The *memory*.

A tear trickled down Shelby's left cheek, and her breath caught as a sob choked in her throat. "M . . . Mom?"

The woman smiled. Such longing and relief all at once filled Shelby. Was this real? She knew it was, just as she knew that she and Kale had belonged to each other before their lives had begun on this earth. She knew the regal woman she now beheld was her mother, and that she saw that her mother had also been an Omega. How she discerned that eluded her, but Shelby knew it. Felt it.

"Mom, how—"

A gunshot. Much closer this time. Just outside the warehouse. A grunt that sounded familiar. The face of her mother—Moriahna— paled with what could only be trepidation, and she turned toward the sound of the gunshot.

"Dad!" Shelby screamed. "Dad! Dad! Dad!" Her voice went hoarse as she writhed.

Moriahna whirled her head back to face Shelby, her eyes sparking with deep orange pinpoints, like angry stars on a moonless night. *Release her,* Moriahna said.

Shelby's voice broke. "I don't know how!" She screamed in utter frustration and fear and anxiety and doubt.

You must, her mother said.

Shelby jerked on her chains again, but they did not budge. Her arms shook with pain and rage. "Help me!"

Her wolf longed for her mother, the same way Shelby ached for her. The vision of the black lupine face with snowy streaks filled her mind again. So beautiful and graceful. In her mind, Shelby's wolf howled a solemn tone, and emerged from that haven that had concealed her within Shelby's heart for too long.

"No more," Shelby said in whisper. "No. More."

You must become that which you were born to be, my daughter. Moriahna's voice danced in Shelby's mind like an echo, beckoning and commanding. *You must awaken.*

With a final scream, Shelby Brooks released her anguish, her fear, her hopes and dreams, her love and hate, her strength and weakness. Her *being.* In that terrible but supernal scream—a declaration that became a howl—she cried a name she had once known but that had been buried deep in ages of memory. And with that name, she called forth her wolf.

The shackles that bound her came free.

Lucas found the naked body of Kale Copeland. He shook with revulsion at being so close to a Lycan, dead or not. He bit the inside of his cheek so hard it bled. There . . . the pain. Just enough to charge his courage.

The son of the Alpha lay still on a stack of pallets and empty oil drums. He had broken through at least one pallet from his fall.

"Not so tough with a bullet through you, huh doggie?"

Although . . . the cursed Lycan had killed three hunters before being taken down by their sniper. That, Lucas had to admit, was somewhat impressive. And, the detonator. Where had that fallen? It would be near impossible in the dark to find it. He looked up. It could still be on the warehouse's roof.

"Lucas!" someone whispered.

He turned to see his dad against the wall of the adjacent warehouse, ducking below the window Shelby's dad had just jumped through.

Yeah, I made you bleed.

"The pup is dead," Sherman said.

The sniper, a man named Frowly, hustled up next to Sherman. "Nice shooting," Sherman said. His eyes returned to Lucas. "It's time to finish this."

Lucas looked back at Kale's body. A dark gleam of red liquid streamed from his chest. Lucas smiled. Maybe he could learn to be a sniper with the hunters. The ability to meet out pain and death stealthily, to watch prey from afar and know that he controlled whether they lived or died . . . yes, that appealed very nicely.

From a pocket, Lucas withdrew a silver self-injecting vial of sodium thiopental and popped the cap, revealing a short syringe. Twenty milliliters ought to be plenty. Kale *was* probably dead, but Sherman always said it was tough to kill these bastards. Best to be certain. Even if Kale was still alive and somehow survived, the death of his wolf would leave him as little more than an invalid. Just a husk of a man. Lucas had inklings of how that might feel. He advanced toward Kale's still form, silver vial raised.

Grant moved to the empty chair. Chains lay on the cement floor, several links twisted and torn, as if no more than a soda can. At the end of the chain rested a shattered metal cuff. The moonlight's dull glint provided little illumination, but his eyes adjusted quickly. A catwalk ran above his head and bordered the inside perimeter of the warehouse. Machinery lay randomly scattered throughout. Grant hunkered down behind a forklift.

"Shel?" he whispered. "Shelby."

Footsteps sounded outside. Sherman and Lucas, or so he thought. He blinked sweat from his eyes and winced at the pain in his hip.

"Shelby!"

Grant heard a soft noise from the corner, a low rumble. A growl, he realized. Switching his optic to its thermal setting, he swept his M4 toward the sound. In a darkened corner, a deep red object filled the scope. The shape of a large wolf.

Grant lowered his rifle. Two golden eyes stared back at him, hanging like disembodied orbs in the darkness. Despite the lupine influence in their appearance, Grant recognized them, for he saw the unmistakable similarity to Moriahna's eyes.

"Shelby . . ." He held his hand out to her. "It's okay."

A canister hit the ground and skidded while dispensing smoke. Grant ducked back down below the forklift and slammed a new magazine into his rifle, then stuffed the old one in his tactical vest. The smoke, he knew that smell. Silver acetylide.

"Shel, get out!"

Grant heard the patter of fast-paced steps ascending metal stairs that led to the second floor of the warehouse. The gas was heavy and probably wouldn't rise higher than eight feet. Hopefully.

"Come on, Grant," Sherman called. "Bring her out. Show me you've still got those hunter instincts in you. Show me you still have a righteous heart."

Red lasers pierced the haze around him, and his eyes watered. Sherman was inside with others. Grant detected three lasers. Lucas and someone else. Maybe more. He moved silently from his cover, rifle at his shoulder. Through his thermal optic, he saw a splotchy bluish-purple image that looked like the outline of arms holding a rifle. He fired. The object did not react.

"Anti-thermal camouflage," Sherman said.

"Good," Grant said. "I prefer it the old-fashioned way." He lowered his M4 and drew his Glock with his right hand and knife with his left, the one stamped with the small acorn.

Kale's finger twitched. His eyelids fluttered. As they slowly opened, only the dimmest light entered. The pain in his chest seared him as he tried to roll off the pallets that had broken his fall, and he breathed short, sharp breaths. He slid more than rolled, and fell onto a pile of metal barrels on their sides. Things moved in his chest. Bones. Or bullet shrapnel. He couldn't be sure.

The two things missing as he awoke were the sounds of gunfire. And Shelby. He could not feel her. Their link . . . he didn't sense it. He groaned as he pushed his naked body onto all fours. Blood and mud crusted his torso. It hurt to breathe.

He could feel his body attempting to heal, and it had to a degree; silver shrapnel must still be inside him. Yes, he felt the burning, pulsing most fiercely at his joints. As he tried to take a deep breath, he wheezed. Pierced lung, probably collapsed. Not like he had any medical training, but that felt correct.

Through shaky vision, he saw the warehouse with the broken window, heard faint sounds coming from within it. He thought he had disarmed the bomb right as he was shot. If sounds were coming from inside the warehouse, he must have. Cautiously, he rose and swore as a new torrent of pain rippled through him. He tried to suck in a deep breath but could not. Oxygen, he needed more, but the pain . . .

His vision shook as he stepped toward the warehouse, the same way videos of someone running with a GoPro looked. The ground seemed to bounce, and a wave of dizziness came over him. *Shelby.*

Things inside were wrong. Broken. His brain wasn't working right. *Shift!* But his wolf, where was his wolf? That place where it resided felt hollow, only a speck of the presence that usually filled it remained. *What is this?*

He took another step toward the warehouse and kicked something. His vision still unstable, he peered down and saw a silver metal vial. He picked it up and squinted at one end. Was that a needle? *A syringe.*

Despite his sluggish mind and injured body, Kale understood. Yes, he could feel some kind of poison coursing through him, something attacking his wolf. Silver shrapnel plus the poison. He couldn't heal. Couldn't shift. He fell to his knees on the gravel and dirt.

"I can't feel you," he whispered, speaking to his wolf, but realizing he also meant Shelby. Then, he fell face first to the ground and watched the world spin before his eyes languidly closed.

Far below the surface of his consciousness, he felt something within him thrum.

S helby, fully in her wolf, lurked on the catwalk above the hazy bank of gas below her. Even the trace amount she had inhaled while darting up the stairs had stung her nose and eyes. Beams of red cut through the acidic smoke, searching. Wispy curls rose and wafted against a stack of pallets, almost seeming to caress it.

Movement in the haze. A low rumble stirred in her chest. They were closing in on her dad.

Shelby?

She knew that voice. *Elias? I'm here.*

You shifted, he said to her mind through the pack link.

Yes. Where are you? You're scared. I can feel it.

The manor is under attack. I'm almost there.

How . . . can I speak with you from this distance?

Alphas and Omegas have unique connections, so I'm told. Apparently true. You're the first Omega we've had in the pack.

Then she heard and felt others in her mind, though she could not speak with them from so far away. Gennesaret. Sadie. Dakota and Chenoa. The others of the pack. She felt their concern, their fear. Their rage. *The Southebys? I can't sense them.*

Shelby felt Elias's grief, and she responded reflexively to counter it, sending him reassurance.

They are dead, Elias said.

Kale . . . ?

Their severed link flailed in her heart like a torn sail in a storm, its moorings snapped. Elias struggled to keep himself from despair. Yes, she could feel it brimming inside him.

I . . . do not feel him, he said. *But nor did I feel him die like I did the Southebys.*

Below, another swirl of smoke caught Shelby's attention, faster than the first. The smoke parted for brief moments. She saw her dad, his knife at another man's throat, a quick pull of his arm. The other man jerked, but her dad's hand over his mouth muffled his surprised yell. Shelby smelled the fear, the scent of fresh blood. She salivated. No, her wolf salivated.

"Found your sniper," Grant said.

"You were always good."

Shelby growled louder at hearing Sherman's voice.

"Uh-oh, sounds like someone's awake," Sherman said.

No, she was not awake. She was dying. The rage inside her wailed more, like the death throes of her heart, not the focused power she needed it to be. *Kale, please.* She reached out for him through her wolf, using the same link through which she had first felt their life together from a different time. Their bond. A tendril vibrated through that link, so soft that she dared not even hope. A pulse. Such a weak and slow, yet wonderful thrumming. *Kale.*

Shelby smelled something different. The air around her carried a familiar scent. Her hackles raised in warning. *Lucas.* She whirled. He was there, gun raised. Shelby did not hesitate. She dodged just as he fired then sprang forward. She heard the snarls coming from her, heard the viciousness in her bark. Lucas cried out as she collided with him, and they both rolled. That scarred face of his—she had done that. And she no longer felt guilt. He came to his feet at the same time she did. She bared her fangs, tasting the air rife with his fear but also something else. Lucas was aroused. He *liked* the pain, the death. She smelled his need to dominate and hurt others.

His gun lay roughly six feet from him. Shelby growled a warning then leaned toward it.

"Oh don't worry, I've got what you need," he said with a sadistic grin. "I promise to finish this time."

Lucas dove for the weapon. Someone stepped on the gun before he reached it and punched him viciously, sending Lucas spinning. Shelby stared in wonder.

Kale! she screamed through their link, but it bounced back to her. The link was too thin. She still couldn't feel him. But he was there! Standing right before her.

Oh. And naked. So there was that.

He stumbled, nearly falling to a knee. Then she saw the blood, how he shook as he struggled to remain on his feet. Why wasn't he in his wolf? And further, how had he made it through the smoke below up to her? It should have burned him severely.

"Fire escape," Kale said, as if knowing her thoughts. He looked at her with those deep hazel eyes that usually radiated such strength. But now, Shelby only saw pain in them. "You're beautiful," he said. "I've never seen a blue coat before."

Blue? Was her coat blue?

Kale smiled sadly, then coughed. It sounded like a wheeze and Shelby began to sense the gravity of his injuries.

Lucas recovered and wiped blood from his mouth. "How'd you like that cocktail I gave you? Honestly, thought you were dead, but ya know, had to be cautious. You can't feel it, can you? Your wolf? That's because *I* killed it. Looks like you're not too far from joining it."

Kale's balance failed him, and he stumbled to a knee, striking the metal plank of the catwalk hard.

What was Lucas saying? Kale's wolf . . . was dead? Shelby pushed her mind into that thrumming she had felt earlier that she identified as him, his wolf. So faint. Fading.

Shelby came up next to Kale, and he leaned on her.

"I can't heal," he whispered. "Can't . . . shift."

"That's because I killed you!" Lucas hissed. "*Me.* I did that! I put that dog in you down!"

Shelby raised her glowering eyes to the boy that brought such pain to her and, now, to the man she loved. Kale slumped, and Shelby felt his full weight lean into her. His body went limp. Pain wrenched Shelby's heart, and she howled.

"That's right, you pathetic whelp. Cry. Whine!"

Lucas dove again for the gun during Shelby's distraction, but she reacted with the ferocity of her lupine side. Her claws raked his leg, tearing through his pants. He yelled out but grabbed the gun and fired wildly. Shelby ducked. Something burned against her rib cage. *Glancing hit.* The pain focused her, and she leaped again for Lucas. Her jaws found his neck, but she hesitated. Lucas froze.

"Don't kill me. Please."

She wanted to. How many had he hurt? Shamed? Broken? How many more would he in the future? And Kale, Lucas had done something to him, perhaps killed him. But could *she* kill? She had before. Nicholas's pack. *But that wasn't me.* It had been, though. Conscious or not, she and her wolf made up her whole being.

"Shelby, please," Lucas said.

She felt his neck muscles constrict beneath her fangs. Forgiveness . . . could she be that strong? A flash, a dull glint of light came toward her side followed by sharp pain. The knife took her in the shoulder. She whimpered and pulled away. Lucas laughed.

She thought she heard her dad calling out to her from some distance, but the burning and pulsing within her drowned him out. Dim though it was in the warehouse, Shelby's vision turned amber, and the edges shook, though Lucas remained perfectly in focus. Fury drove her forward. She knocked into Lucas, clawing at his chest, tearing him open. Rather than hesitation, this time his screams brought out more savageness as Shelby sensed wounded prey. She tore through clothing and flesh, ignoring his desperate pounding on her, his pleas, another stab to her shoulder that barely missed her neck. When her jaws found his throat again, she sunk her teeth in deep, savoring the salty thickness of the blood.

And Lucas went still.

The silver haze thinned. Grant heard Lucas's scream stop short. A thudding sounded from the corner staircase. Grant spun. The sound of something being dragged . . . He squinted. Through the thinning smoke, Grant saw a wolf—Shelby—hauling something by her teeth. A body trailing a bloody mess.

"No!" Sherman cried out, a tortured sound.

Grant caught sight of him breaking from cover, sprinting toward Shelby. Sherman raised a pistol and fired recklessly. Shelby tried to scamper to safety but Grant heard several whimpers as rounds struck his daughter.

Grant sheathed his knife in one swift motion and brought his free hand to steady his aim. He fired, and missed. New sweat broke out on his spine and the nape of his neck. He took aim again at Sherman, at his ear, and squeezed the trigger. Sherman ducked, as if anticipating the shot. Of course he had been. Grant fired repeatedly, but the hunter was deft in his evasion. Grant's slide locked back, his magazine emptied. Shelby limped, fear in her amber eyes as Sherman approached with furious intent. He threw his spent pistol aside and drew a knife. She barked savagely but the hunter did not seem impressed.

"You killed him!" Sherman cried.

Grant charged his former friend. The pain in his hip made him do a fast hobble more than a run. He threw the pistol aside and just as the hunter reached Shelby and his dead son, tackled him. A lightning barrage of fists and elbows hit Grant in the stomach and head. A sharp elbow to his temple sent him spinning, followed by a merciless kick to his wounded hip. He actually felt tears spring to his eyes, and he cried out amid the white hot pain. Shelby, wounded and bleeding, attacked, but Grant could see her timidity, brought on by her own wounds. A blade emerged from the toe of Sherman's boot, and he kicked Shelby full in the ribs. She howled. Grant's chest ached from the sound of his daughter's agony. But Shelby, despite her wounds, launched herself again and when Sherman attempted a second kick, caught his leg with her fangs. He pounded Shelby's head with a hammer fist and she flinched but did not release. Sherman gasped as Shelby's clutched teeth dug deeper, and Grant knew bones broke beneath her bite.

Grant intercepted Sherman's next blow to Shelby's head, landing his own volley of attacks that stunned Sherman and sent him reeling backward, free of Shelby's fangs. Blood flowed from his nose.

"Ah, I think you went and broke it," Sherman said. He spat blood and limped tenderly on his right leg, blood flowing over his boot and onto the ground. "But the righteous must suffer all manner of pain and evil for the world's sake, just as our Master did." He retrieved a silver tube from his tactical vest, popped the cap on one end, revealing a needle, and slammed it into his thigh. "That'll take care of your infected saliva in my blood, Miss Brooks."

Grant heaved a breath. He knew at least one rib was broken. Shelby slunk back, behind her dad, also limping badly.

"Oh, now, he can't save you, darling," Sherman said. "Look, he can barely stand. Besides, I owe you." Sherman pointed to Lucas's body. "For my boy. Twice now." The hunter smiled a bloody grin. "Tell me, Miss Brooks, did your father ever tell you how he met your mother?"

Shelby's ears perked up. What was Sherman saying? Of course she knew the story: they met after one of his missions when he was on leave and got married shortly after that. But as the often-repeated story played in her mind, she sensed a fraying at the edges. Something rang false. Her wolf could sense it. She felt her blood pulsing in her ears and wounds. At least two silver rounds were still in her, preventing her from healing. The entry points pulsed with agony.

"Enough, Sherman," Grant said. "We'll finish this. You and me."

"Oh, she'll want to hear this. See, Miss Brooks—can you hear me in there? I always wondered if you can still comprehend language in that satanic form—your daddy here, before he betrayed us and the Lord's errand, was sent to kill your dear mother."

What? Shelby growled.

"It's true, I promise you," Sherman continued. "Our projections of the bloodlines led us to see that eventually through Moriahna's line would be born the harbinger of death your own Mystics tell of."

Shelby stepped back from her father. Chenoa's words came back to her. *The Summer Omega is a messenger that opens the way for destruction.*

"It might seem odd, naturally, that a hunter would place any stock in Lycan nonsense, but we have to admit that your Mystics have been strikingly accurate, to our dismay."

"The Summer Omega legends are just stories," Grant sneered. "You've used them to justify murder."

"Murder? No, Grant, you know just as well as I do. This isn't murder. This is extermination of that which threatens the Children of God. It is the work of righteousness. Even something as vile as *cancer* can do His work at times."

Shelby took another step back. Her wounds ached and her mind spun, and her wolf retreated at the revelations. Her own father had been sent to kill her mother? Could that be true? This was Sherman who was talking . . . but . . . Shelby began to shift back to herself.

"Oh see, now that's heartbreaking," Sherman said, looking at Shelby. "They only do that when they're near death. You know that, Grant. She must be close to bleeding out. Still, I see what Lucas always saw in her. She is a beauty. Poor thing."

"Dad?" Shelby whispered. She hugged the ground, pressing her breasts on the cold floor, feeling somewhat foolish for even trying to hide her nudity. "Is it true?"

Grant glanced over his shoulder. She could only make out the side of his face, but even in the darkness, she could see the truth on it. Shelby's heart lurched. In a pained voice, she asked, "Was it you? Was the cancer a lie?" Her voice growled now. "Did you kill her?" Her emotions made her logic run afoul. She could feel them tinkering with her perceptions of reality. Or maybe that was what happened when you were dying.

"No," Grant said in husky tones. He turned more toward her. "I loved your mother more than anything, Shel. Yes, I was a hunter. Yes, I've killed Lycans. Yes, she was my mission. Once." He swallowed. "But things changed. We fell in love, and she forgave me. I can't understand how she did that, but she did. And you, Shel, you are the evidence of that love."

"She's evidence of their blasphemous Mystics being correct," Sherman interrupted. "Nothing more, Grant. You see that now. Don't you? She is the manifestation of the Summer Omega prophecy. *And you know what that means!* You know what the world will become! She must die!"

"Dad?" Shelby felt herself slipping. But she sensed something else in Sherman's words, her Omega senses tingling even as they diminished. *Even something as vile as cancer . . .* "He's lying about mom. How she died."

"Shelby, hold on, kiddo," Grant said with choked emotion.

She saw him turn back toward Sherman. "He's lying," Shelby rasped.

"What is she saying?" Grant asked his old comrade, still squared off, standing between Shelby and Sherman. She saw her dad stagger slightly.

Had the floor ceased to be cold? Or was she just going numb? *Kale . . . come back to me.*

"Oh, I was hoping we wouldn't have to get to this part," Sherman said. "Best to let bygones be bygones."

"You seem awfully fond of stirring up the past," Grant said. "What about Moriahna's death aren't you telling me?"

Sherman rolled his eyes. How could he be so callous and flippant? His son lay there, not five feet away, dead.

"Fine, fine," Sherman said. "I killed her."

Grant shook his head. "I was there in the hospital with her, from diagnosis through treatment to the end. It was cancer."

"Yes, of course, you're right. But how did she develop cancer?"

Shelby barely heard the conversation, drifting in and out. *Please, Kale.* Her father had hunted her mother. To kill her. She pulled herself farther away, sliding on the hard floor.

"It just happened!" Grant shouted. "There's no explanation for these things."

"Aflatoxin," Sherman said. "Large doses of it, of course. Well, not as large as it would take to infect a human. Doesn't take much for cancer to take hold in them, you know. You can't appreciate how difficult it was to obtain the right compound, the costs we incurred. It took over a year to figure out how to get it into that vixen you betrayed us for, but eventually we did. Too late, I'm afraid to say, because she still birthed that whelp of yours. Is she still alive back there?"

"You're lying," Grant said between clenched teeth.

"He's not lying," Shelby moaned. And again she dragged herself farther away. The emotional pain rivaled her physical pain, and she had to withdraw from her dad. His presence seemed to inflame her wounds suddenly. *He was a hunter. Like Sherman.* As she retreated, she felt more and more numb. Slipping. Fading. That was okay, though, wasn't it? Would she be with Kale if she just let go? But still, she felt that faint thrum. He still fought, tenuous though his strength seemed. Shelby wished she had his will to live, but after Sherman's words . . .

She closed her eyes.

Fury boiled in Grant, the air brittle with tension. Questions burdened his mind, but doubt did not. He knew Sherman had spoken the truth. He heard the truth in his words, backed by Shelby's declaration.

"He's not lying."

Her voice sounded farther away. Weaker. Worse, it sounded slightly accusatory . . . toward him. But the fury that raged in him . . .

"You killed her," he said in a dangerous, low tone.

"Yes." Sherman smiled as if humbly accepting a compliment.

Slowly but deliberately, Grant reached behind himself and withdrew the dark blade from the sheath at his back. He brought it in front of him.

Sherman seemed to accept what would happen next. No words came to Grant's mind, just the pure focus of a warrior facing an enemy. Sherman brought his own blade to bear.

Grant lunged and slashed, retreated quickly as Sherman countered. They circled, Grant's hip stinging with every step. The QuikClot had failed by now, and he felt warmth trickling down his thigh. Sherman lunged toward Grant's neck. Grant sidestepped the attack and grabbed Sherman's arm, pulling with the momentum of his enemy's thrust. Sherman came forward unbalanced, and Grant's knee struck his chest. Sherman jumped up slightly as the knee landed, but Grant could tell he still had done damage. The hunter rolled to the side and then found his feet. He cradled his ribs with one arm, held the knife with the other.

Grant stepped forward, slashing and pressing his advantage. Sherman blocked his arc, blade to blade, then rotated his hand so his knife slid down Grant's and ran across the back of Grant's hand. Fresh blood hit the floor, but Grant ignored the new burst of pain and grabbed Sherman's wrist with his free hand.

With a grip of iron, Grant twisted Sherman's arm behind his back, his knife still clutched in his hand. As Grant forced the arm up higher, he heard something pop, and Sherman dropped the knife. With a quick leg sweep, Grant forced Sherman face-first to the ground. Even with a dislocated shoulder, Sherman proved strong, but Grant knelt on his spine and pressed his knee down hard enough to make Sherman stop resisting. He grabbed the man by the hair and pulled his head back.

"You were always the strongest," Sherman croaked. "It had to be done. You know it did."

"What I know is that you murdered my wife, allowed your vile son to rape young girls, and kidnapped my daughter with the intent to kill her. You speak of righteousness. As so, in righteousness, I claim your life."

"Wait, the prophecies, you've only read—"

Grant thrust his blade through the back of Sherman's neck, with such force the tip bit into the concrete, pinning Sherman to the ground.

All turned quiet.

Elias sprinted with all his energy toward the manor. He felt his pack in full battle, desperately fighting for their lives, for each other. *And you are not there!* he roared, internally scolding himself.

Above him, he heard the whir of the drones, also at full throttle. He had caught up to them, and now he passed them, pushing himself harder. His muscles ached in protest, but he ignored the pain, demanding all the endurance they could provide.

His home came into view. Smoke seemed to hang accusingly in the air, as if to blame him for what had happened in his absence. The sting of that accusation lanced his chest, adding to the hollowness he felt at the loss of Kale. *They have taken my son from me!*

Others of his pack had died. The Southebys. Anna Bingham. Will Kaplan.

A soft glow of orange shimmered as Elias drew closer, still sprinting. A car in flames. Sounds of automatic weapons fire sent new streaks of anger through Elias. The acrid scent of spent gunpowder and smoke. A small explosion. He was close enough now to know that it came from within his home.

He leaped over the perimeter wall of his property, discarding all concerns for stealth, and howled a commanding tone, deep and resonant. He landed in the midst of a copse at the north end of the front yard. Five hunters that had been advancing on the house turned to him. Excellent. Elias salivated.

The hunters fired their guns, and Elias darted for the cover of a tree, then another. In the darkness, he hunched low and prowled beneath the shrubs. The hunters fired at the first tree, obviously thinking him to still be there, still advancing. Elias launched himself from his crouched concealment and pounced on the closest enemy, dispatching him before he could scream, then the next. This one did scream as Elias bit through his Kevlar vest, tearing a piece of the man's torso free. The other three turned in surprise and fired wildly. Elias sprinted to the next tree and sheltered behind it until he heard the slides of their guns lock back. He took them quickly.

Above him, he heard the drones arrive followed by their higher-pitched guns firing. The autonomous targeting system had taken over. Several other hunters were taken down by the drones. Elias turned swiftly, sensing the approach of Dakota and Chenoa. Their snouts were stained with a dark crimson.

Several have fallen, Dakota said through the pack-link.

I know, Elias said.

And the girl? Chenoa asked.

Her father and Kale are seeing to her.

Dakota averted his gaze. *I do not feel your son.*

Elias did not answer but sprinted toward the house. Dakota and Chenoa raced after him.

Sadie's paws trod lightly on the marble floor on the lower level of the manor. Bubba, beside her, held a pistol. She wasn't sure he knew what to do with it. The emergency lighting flickered red sporadically, leaving them in darkness mostly. But if they were going to move stealthily, Bubba needed to stop breathing through his mouth. It was like a small avalanche with each breath. She wondered what his snoring must be like. Did his mom take sedatives so she could sleep through it? Or maybe she made him sleep outside?

Two red dots danced on the floor in front of her, then one jumped to her and the other to Bubba. Lasers. Sadie bit Bubba's shirt and tugged hard just as the gunfire erupted. Bubba screamed. Holy SWAC did he have a pair of lungs! The muzzle flashes from the two hunters' guns betrayed their positions and Sadie charged, too swiftly for them to target her, though a trail of bullets struck behind her as she leaped upon one hunter and took him by the throat. The other drew a pistol when his rifle ran dry, but something flew into him before he could raise it. A deep snarl rose from a dark shape that the flickering red light revealed to be Elias. The hunter twitched with the Alpha's jaws around his throat.

Gunfire sounded from other parts of the house. And Bubba screamed again.

What is he doing here? Elias roared into Sadie's mind.

Sadie craned her head to see Bubba, his side pressed against the wall, one leg raised as if shielding his stomach, and his arms covering his head. One wide staring eye peeked out from the crook of his arm. What the . . . dozens of bullet holes pockmarked the wall around Bubba, as if outlining his body perfectly.

"Aw, *hell* no!" he cried. "They put a hole in my Wilfork jersey. Look at that! Right there!" He fingered a hole near his belly. "Hell. Naw!"

Long story, Sadie said to Elias. *He saved me with a magic marker, though.* Sadie felt Elias's flustered attitude. Dakota and Chenoa strode up next to the Alpha.

"I'm so hangry," Bubba said. "That's right. Hungry and angry." He sighed, leaning his hand against the wall, apparently for balance. He shook his head. "Mostly hungry."

Where is Gennesaret? Elias demanded.

I'm here, she said through the pack-link, coming around the corner. The McKinneys and Emily and Austin Kaplan, as well as Sadie's parents, followed Gennesaret.

Where is Shelby? Sadie asked. *And Kale?*

We have to clear the manor, Elias said. *This is our den. We have been invaded. This is our priority right now. Let's focus.*

Sadie heard the strain in Elias's voice, even through the pack-link. He was suppressing pain.

Gennesaret shifted to her human form. "Deshawn, I thought we had you safely stowed away in the panic room."

"Yeah, about that. See, I was making some ramen and uh . . . um, are all y'all always naked when you do that?"

"Please Deshawn, focus."

A gunshot rang out, closer. Upstairs. Sadie saw Bubba flinch but smile when a snarl answered the gunshot followed by a scream.

"That's Ackerman," Gennesaret said. "He's fine. The hunter is not."

"Yes, ma'am," Bubba said. "So, like I was sayin', my girl Sadie here got herself in a hot spot, and I had to rescue her. That's all, ya feel? Just doin' what needs doin' is all."

Sadie felt Gennesaret's inquisitive gaze and averted her eyes.

"I see," Gennesaret said. "It seems we'll have to have a talk once this is all over, won't we?"

"Yes, Mrs. Copeland," Bubba said meekly.

Something tugged at Shelby's consciousness. She knew she was dying. And, she found she didn't care. Kale's thrumming had ceased, either that or she was too weak to feel it anymore. Pressure, she did feel pressure, a sensation that she knew should have brought pain, but she had drifted beyond that.

She just wanted to let go. Strength had found her when she needed it, but her wounds, the silver, the truth of her father . . . she was mortal and could only take so much.

Something stirred in her ears, daring to take her from her drifting. There, again. Were those words? A voice?

"Shelby!"

Pain like a white hot fire sliced up her side. She wanted to scream, but her lips did not obey her instinct. And again, in her arm, the same pain. Her mind came closer to the surface, and she felt something pulled from her. Strength began to surge through her now.

Healing. Mental awareness. She reached the surface in her mind and sucked in a large, painful breath as her eyes snapped open.

"It's okay, Shel."

Her dad's voice. He came into focus, too slowly, but she saw the knife in his hand and recoiled. He dropped it.

"Had to pull the rounds out," he said. "The one in your arm was deep. You're healing now, though. Anyone ever tell you you're tough?"

Shelby's eyes flickered to where Sherman lay. "He killed Mom."

"He's gone," Grant said.

"I saw her. When I shifted. She . . . helped me."

Her dad went still. "How did she look?"

No disbelief. No patronizing words. Her dad's simple acceptance of her statement at face value steadied her. "Beautiful," she said.

"I brought you your clothes," he said, "for all the good they will do. They're pretty much shredded."

She took them anyway. And then she remembered. "Kale!"

Grant sucked in a breath. "He got shot. I saw him fall."

Shelby touched her chest above her heart. "He's on the catwalk!"

"What?"

"He's up there. Came in through the fire escape."

"But . . ." Grant sputtered.

"We have to get to him." But she knew, even now, she was probably too late. What could she possibly do? "They did something to him. He couldn't heal or shift."

Grant groaned. "Sodium thiopental."

"They used it on me," Shelby said.

"But you still shifted," Grant said. "How?"

She *had* shifted. Somehow that momentous event felt lost in the midst of this tragedy. "I think Mom did something. I'm not really sure what happened." Her mother had helped, but that was not the full answer. No, Shelby had called forth her wolf by the use of a name. What name? Why could she not remember? It had been just minutes ago, hadn't it? She felt that memory stolen from her. Erased.

"I . . . I don't know."

She started to get up but stopped abruptly. Healing or not, the pain was real. Holy hell was it real. She quickly dressed as best she could in the torn rags of her clothes, wincing with every move and not shy at all in front of her dad. With what they had just been through, such a petty thing as modesty was the furthest thing from her mind.

"What he said about Mom," Shelby began, but could not finish.

Her dad swallowed hard. He hadn't known what Sherman had done. Truly, he hadn't. That comforted her, but the revelation that he had been sent to kill her own mother . . . how to process that. She couldn't. Not now.

"I had to get him away from Kale," Shelby whispered. "Lucas. I . . ." Her eyes darted to the mangled mess of Lucas's corpse. "I couldn't leave him next to Kale. It just felt . . . blasphemous. Like his presence was killing Kale." She suddenly felt small in the wake of all that had happened. "I shouldn't have left him. How could I have left him alone?" That was what felt blasphemous, she decided. Her lip quivered. "Is he really dead, Dad?"

Grant still wore the face of a hardened warrior, but his eyes swam with grief. "Let's go get him," came his husky reply.

Shelby knelt over Kale's body. As if to preserve his dignity, a stack of wooden crates cast shadows that cloaked his privates, though the dim moonlight that peeked through the windows gave little enough illumination. Grant's flashlight made Shelby blink when he flipped it on. The sudden light seemed harsh against Kale's body, an irreverent interruption to the desperate scene.

Shelby recoiled. Crusted blood covered the chest of this man she loved. Streams of crimson ran down to his hips from two wounds. Her lip quivered more and she dry heaved a sob.

"Hey," Grant said. "You need to stomach this if we're going to save him."

"Isn't he . . ."

Grant felt Kale's neck. "If he's got a pulse it's too weak for me to find. But his wounds are still bleeding. That's a good sign, though the flow is slow."

Shelby nodded. "Okay," she said, as if speaking would summon the bravery needed. It did help. Even though her lip still trembled.

Her dad tore open a packet of QuikClot and dumped it on the entry wound and then the exit wound on Kale's right breast. The exit wound looked like a geyser had burst through his skin. Shelby reached forward to touch him, as if to comfort him, but her hand shook.

"He's lucky it was a smaller sniper round. Probably a .260. A .338 la pua or .50 cal might have torn him in half."

Lucky? This was lucky?

"What do we do?" she asked.

"He's not healing on his own," Grant said. "Or not fast enough. He needs to shift."

"But he's unconscious!" Tears brimmed in Shelby's eyes. "And he has that stuff in him. Lucas injected him with it."

Grant lifted her chin. "Shel, you have to do it."

"Do what?" She started to cry. "I don't know what to do!"

"You do. You shifted despite the drug. You can help him shift. Somehow, you can enter other werewolves' minds. I've seen you do it."

"No." She shook her head defiantly. "I kill them when I do that. I can't control it."

Grant heaved a heavy breath, wincing from his own wounds. "He's already dead if you don't try, Shel."

Such cruel words; not because of how Grant spoke them, but because of their truth. She gritted her teeth, so mad at her disobedient tears that spilled liberally, so mad at herself for allowing this to happen, for bringing this upon Kale, upon his family. She felt the loss of others in the pack and reeled for them, their deaths feeling like candles extinguished from her soul forever. It was the blessing and the curse of an Omega, to love the pack so completely and so fully, so immediately.

And the man before her, dying, had struggled with his last bits of energy to come for her. To save her. The price others had paid for her pulled on her neck like a millstone. She leaned over Kale's body, heaving with an anguished sob. She beat her fist on his chest with the next sob.

"Try, Shelby," Grant whispered. "Just try."

Shelby shut her eyes, squeezing them dry. Searching for and finding those lantern-moon eyes in her mind did not take long. "I need you. Please." And yet, she felt her wolf's uncertainty. *I don't know what you do, but please, I need you to try.*

From the den of her mind, Shelby saw her wolf come forth. Sights, sounds, and scents all became sharper. Even the dried blood on Kale's chest seemed to glisten, and she smelled the iron in the air. As she laid her hand on him, she felt the contours of his cooling skin more keenly, like the smooth sand of a desert at night. He had always appeared so strong to her. Invincible, even. Then her vision started to wobble at the edges, as if something tore at it. But the focus of her eyes, locked on to Kale, remained steady and constant.

"Shel, your eyes are changing," Grant said.

She felt the amber flecks scorching her irises, felt the growl building within her and, suddenly, saw Kale's wolf—its eyes—peering back at her in her mind. They were not amber, not the bright vividness she might have expected, but a pale, sickly jaundiced color.

Shelby felt the wolf's fear and helplessness. It was dying, and had given into despair, believing no deliverance would come. She reassured Kale's wolf, trying to comfort it, to give it hope, but she could not mask her own sense of hopelessness and she knew Kale's wolf felt it through her facade.

Again, that overwhelming feeling of familiarity came upon Shelby, a recognition that she knew Kale. "He said it was you," she whispered to Kale's wolf. "That it is you, our wolves, that carry the memory he speaks of. Show me."

Through that tendril of a link, Shelby felt the weakening of Kale's wolf. It struggled to rise to Shelby's request . . . because, she saw, it loved her and her wolf with a timeless love. It summoned the energy and into Shelby's mind flashed a panoramic scene.

A forest. Fire. Smoke and ashes. A village with screams. *Her* village. *Her* people's screams. Wolves darted through the forest, attacking men with swords, the same men that had brought death and terror to her people. Yes, the wolves fought as her people fled, yet again, into the forest to escape the persecution. So many invaders had come this time.

Nothing made sense. She tasted the acrid air, saw the orange embers floating like drunken fireflies, but where was she?

A wolf nuzzled her side. In this waking dream, Shelby was not surprised to see her companion. The royal blue coat shimmered like the deepest ocean, and her wolf's eyes shone like two beacons hovering over the gray clouds of a storm. Yes, the coloring of her snout did resemble the bluish-gray of angry storm clouds. Children ran past her, seeking refuge among the trees as their homes burned. *This has happened many times,* she somehow recalled.

The vision changed, and she saw herself kneeling with frantic grief over a young boy, her wolf still at her side. She wore a simple shift, a crude nightgown, with ties at the V over her sternum that barely revealed her cleavage. Streaks of crimson stained the shift. The boy held a wound at his side, trying to stop a river of flowing blood. Kale knelt beside her—but not Kale. That was not his name in the vision, but his name did not come to her. Nor, she realized, was the dream version of herself named Shelby. The boy coughed, and her attention turned back to him.

"Can you save our son?" the man she knew as Kale asked. Daeglan. The dream Kale's name was Daeglan.

Could she save their son? Why would Daeglan ask her that? But he wasn't asking her, he was asking her wolf.

"You're showing me what I need to see," Shelby said to Kale's wolf. The vision became hazy, but the weakened wolf mustered what seemed the last dregs of his strength, and the picture refocused.

In the vision, a large black wolf was at Daeglan's side. Beside the boy—*my son?*—a gray and black wolf with a lighter gray shade at the paws lay curled up beside him. They were the Sköllaer, those who had communion with the Immortal Wolves in the ancient lands of

Alsvoira and protected the *Isluxua*. The invaders had never found the ancient tome with the secrets of their existence, but had come dangerously close this time.

But . . . this is not on this earth, Shelby thought as more of the vision—both things seen and unseen—unfolded to her.

"Can you save Mareus?" Daeglan asked.

Shelby's wolf sniffed at Mareus's wound, and the boy's wolf whined softly.

"I'm going to kill those people," Daeglan said, desperate words born of grief. He beat a clenched fist on his leg. "I swear it."

They had fled from the invaders again, but their son had been run down by a barbarian's sword before his wolf could take the man out.

The amber eyes of Shelby's wolf glowed. Mareus moaned fitfully, and his wound sizzled as Shelby's wolf hovered over him, using her magic to heal the wound. A sheen of sweat shimmered on the boy's face.

"It will take more than she can give," the dream version of Shelby said, referring to her blue wolf. "She sealed the wound, but he's still bleeding inside. The most she can do is give him the comfort of an Omega."

"Mother," Mareus said. The frailty in his voice stung her heart.

"I'm here," the dream Shelby said, taking her son's hand.

"I don't want to die."

"You have to do something," Daeglan said. "Please, Eira."

Eira. The name of her wolf. *How could I have forgotten?* She had screamed that name when calling forth her wolf, but . . . *why did you take that memory from me?*

"Please, Thyra," Daelgan said. "Your wolf has to be able to do more."

Thyra? Shelby remembered her own name then.

"He wants me to go with him," Mareus said.

"Who does, son?" Thyra asked.

"Viersin."

Thyra looked at Mareus's wolf.

"He says he can heal me if I go with him," Mareus said.

"Go where?" Daeglan asked.

Eira growled, locking her stare on Viersin. Something came into Thyra's mind as she knelt by her son, something Eira had tried to hide from her, that all the wolves had hid from their chosen humans.

"Inside him," Shelby whispered, watching the panoramic scene before her.

"Viersin can heal our son if he lets him," Thyra said. She looked accusingly at Eira, and the she-wolf turned aside. "It's true, isn't it?"

"Eira is the only one who can heal," Daeglan said.

"A human, yes," Thyra said, still looking at Eira as she received more insight. "But all wolves can heal themselves with the same magic Eira uses to heal us." Thyra put a hand over her mouth. "No."

Knowing Thyra's thoughts—her own long stowed memories—Shelby understood what Eira communicated to her.

"He would have to join with Viersin," Thyra said. "Let his mind flow into the wolf's. They would . . . become one."

"Then do it!" Daeglan shouted.

"Wait," Thyra said. "There are consequences. This is why they did not ever share this knowledge with us. It . . . it costs them their sovereignty to allow the union."

Daeglan's wolf growled now. "It's true," Daeglan said. Shelby saw the dream version of Kale understanding, apparently receiving reluctant confirmation from his wolf. "Our son would be changed forever."

"Ascension," Thyra whispered, discerning the mind of her wolf. "They seek ascension."

"What does that mean?" Daeglan asked.

Mareus coughed.

"He is weak," Daeglan said. He looked at Thyra. "He is going to die."

But they would lose their son if Viersin healed him anyway, wouldn't they? At least his body? She swallowed. "It is better that he live in the form of an Immortal Wolf than die." She looked at Viersin. "Very well."

Daeglan's wolf growled at Viersin as did Eira. And suddenly, watching this vision, Shelby understood that Thyra misunderstood what Eira had shown her.

"Wait!" Shelby screamed just as Viersin bit Mareus's arm, even knowing the dream versions of herself and Kale could not hear her. The boy yelped.

"What have you done?" Daeglan shouted, rising to his feet.

Mareus convulsed on the ground, writhing, and foaming at the mouth. The broken skin on his arm festered, oozing a thick yellow pus. Viersin's eyes weakened after the bite, and he stepped away from his human. As the wolf lay on his side, he pawed at the ground, then went still.

"Viersin is dead," Thyra said. She looked to Eira with eyes wide. "What is happening?"

Mareus continued to writhe. Then, a scream, a sound so tormented that Shelby's heart twisted. His arms shot out from his sides, then jutted violently at unnatural angles. His shoulders twitched followed by his elbows. Snaps and pops sounded as Mareus's fingers contorted. But it was his eyes that Shelby focused on. She saw them change, saw streaks of amber like lightning stain the irises until they glowed a burnt orange. Mareus's face elongated from his nose, jutting toward the sky he stared up at. Even though it was a memory, Shelby smelled the telling odor of acidic citrus.

Thyra turned away, but Daeglan did not, and Shelby saw his face go gaunt as his son shifted to the form of a wolf. A fierce wind whipped the cloak around Daeglan's shoulders, but he stood firm, stoically watching the scene before him. The boy's scream turned to a howl, then he fell quiet. Thyra looked back at the sudden silence, tense. Mareus had become the mirror image of his wolf. So riveted on the change that had come over Mareus, Shelby had momentarily forgotten about Viersin. She looked beside the altered body of Mareus, but the boy's Immortal Wolf had vanished. Or was it Mareus that had vanished?

No, neither has vanished, Shelby realized. *They have joined.*

"Look!" Thyra said, pointing to the wolf's side where a purple bulge throbbed just below the ribs. It was the same location of the wound that Mareus had sustained from the invader's sword. The throbbing . . . internal bleeding. But the swelling lessened; the wound's angry scar tissue, from Eira's superficial healing, lightened. In seconds, it looked days old, then weeks. In less than two minutes, the wound completely faded. The form of Viersin changed, disappearing into the form of Mareus.

"Shelby! Shelby!"

The vision vanished from before her. "Shelby!" Grant said again.

She blinked her eyes then looked at her dad.

"I've been saying your name for thirty seconds," Grant said "What happened?"

Thirty seconds? Had it been only thirty seconds? Lifetimes

seemed to have passed by. She flung her head to the left, hard, shaking the grogginess from her. "I know how to save him."

"All ears, kiddo."

"I have to make him shift. His wolf is dying."

"That's what I was saying. How are you going to do that?"

Right. There was that little issue. "I have to use its name."

"It has a name?" Grant asked.

"All our wolves do."

Her dad raised his eyebrows. Huh, that surprised him. For a moment, Shelby thought that perhaps only she was ignorant of this.

We hold them sacred. To allow others this knowledge is to potentially grant them control over us.

That was a new voice in Shelby's head. She knew it to be her wolf's. *Eira?*

Time is fleeting.

I . . . I don't understand what was shown to me.

Viersin gave up his sovereignty to save your son. Eventually, all the immortal wolves of Alsvoira did so for the love of their humans.

If you love your humans, Shelby asked, *why do you shield your names?*

Love and trust are different. We have . . . seen the frailty of humanity before.

Shelby wanted to ask more, so much more. For starters, where *was* this Alsvoira? But Kale, the man she had loved for eons, was dying.

You will need to send him strength, Eira said. *It is incredibly arduous to force a shift when our human does not will it.*

Shelby understood. She had feared Eira, feared what lay within her. And twice, at least partially, Eira had manifested to save Shelby. *I will it now,* Shelby said to her wolf. *I need your power.*

The ache started in the center of her core and radiated outward in rippled pulses. It was only moments, the change occurring so quickly now, so naturally.

"Well, I wasn't expecting to see you again," Grant said, stepping back from his daughter.

Shelby, fully in her wolf, stood over Kale, still connected to him through their thinning bond. She and Eira sent him strength and endurance through the symbiotic magic of an Omega, calling upon Kale's wolf to rise. But the wolf was sluggish, fighting and losing against the sodium thiopental coursing through Kale's veins.

Skotha!

The name jolted Kale's wolf. Its pale, slit eyes, drooping with defeat, opened slightly wider. Shelby sent more strength, so much she feared their tenuous bond might rupture.

Skotha! Shift!

Shelby growled, staring at Kale's closed eyes and into Skotha's with her mind's.

I will not lose him, Skotha! Not after what I have learned. Not after just finding him again. You will fight and shift!

Eira spoke. *If he does not shift, I cannot help heal him. His body is too close to death. Skotha must manifest.*

Shelby's strength slackened, having sent so much of herself to Kale and Skotha. She trembled as adrenaline shot through her, fighting against her own weariness.

You. Must. Shift. Skotha. Shelby panted. *Please.*

Do not plead, Eira said. *Command him.*

Command him? A future Alpha? She was just an Omega. How could she command him?

Because you are the Summer Omega, Eira said.

Chenoa's grim words came back to Shelby. "It is foretold, that when the one who is born into the late hour and blossoms late in the season rises in the world, she will carry the desert winds upon her lips and the fire upon her feet. The Summer Omega is a messenger that opens the way for destruction . . ."

Shelby's soul shrank as if covered by acid. Had she not brought destruction? Upon the pack? Her dad? Her vision darkened as she stared at Kale's still form. *Upon you.*

". . . The season of dead things always follows summer."

Then Dakota's words surfaced in her mind: "It also says that she will use the fires of wrath to flood the earth with tears of mercy." But that was contradictory. *Fire would evaporate tears, even those of mercy.* Something caught in her mind as she wrestled with the meanings. *Evaporate . . .*

Gennesaret's words: "Fire can be cleansing . . ."

Shelby's eyes burned hotter, and she stoked that fire, letting it build until she saw the glow of them reflecting off Kale's body. In her mind, she joined with Eira and bore into Skotha's eyes, holding them with her focused intent, sending forth that fire. Kale's body began to shake. Skotha's eyes tried to look away, but Shelby growled, maintaining her hold over Kale's wolf. She saw the poison in him and Kale, in their blood, saw it draining away Skotha's life. Shelby attacked it, scourging Kale's veins with her fire, evaporating it then blowing the clouds of it from him.

. . . She will carry the desert winds upon her lips . . .

Tears streaked from her amber eyes onto Kale's lips.

. . . With tears of mercy . . .

And then, the change began. Subtle enough, but there. *Yes, thank you, Skotha.* Shelby scraped the bottom of her reserves for anything extra she could send and felt Eira doing the same. Kale manifested, and the large black form of Skotha came forth. The wound on his left rib cage sealed, and the one on the right side of his chest steamed as it excreted tiny slivers of silver shrapnel, then sealed. Skotha stirred.

Thank you, Eira, Shelby said.

I must rest, Thyra.

Thyra. Shelby smiled at the use of her ancient name.

Shelby shifted back to her human form.

Grant cleared his throat. "I, uh, think your clothes are completely ruined now."

Kale's wolf twitched, then groaned. Shelby laughed through an exhalation. He shifted, and that gorgeous color returned to his face as his human form re-emerged. His hazel eyes opened, pinpricks of amber lingering in the irises, and she saw them flutter before focusing on her.

"Hey," he said, his voice sounding like he had swallowed sand. "I had the craziest dream."

Shelby wiped a tear away and hugged him. "I know."

"You do?" Kale asked. "Was I talking in my sleep?"

"Not exactly."

He did not hug her back but just lay there on the catwalk, seeming to concentrate on breathing. "Oh. Don't you think the name 'Bubba's Chicken' is a cool name for a franchise?"

Shelby started to laugh and cry at the same time. "I love you, Kale Copeland." Then she kissed him, letting her tears stream down her nose and onto his face. He *did* kiss her back.

"So, I know this is a unique moment in your lives," Grant said, "but I'm really not ready to see you and my daughter kissing while naked. Or even clothed."

Kale sat up with a grimace, looking down. "I'm naked?" Then he looked to Shelby and quickly turned his eyes aside. "Uh, yep, we're both naked." He glanced at Grant. "In front of your dad."

Shelby felt a weight drop in her heart. She reached out and grabbed Kale's shoulder, digging into it. "Kale," she rasped.

"What is it, Shel?" Grant asked.

Kale turned toward her.

"Eyes up, Kale," Grant grunted.

Shelby swallowed hard. "The manor . . . so many have died . . ."

Kale's look hardened. "Who, Shelby?"

She felt his dread through the bond.

Elias led the pack through the manor, clearing each wing, room by room. With the help of the drones and security forces on the outside, the pack focused on the threats within the manor. There proved to be few left. He felt pride in them, banding together as they had during his absence, confronting the threat. But nineteen-year-old John Bingham took a silver round to the head in one of the corridors near the control room, where René lay dead. John's sister, Rachel, lay down next to his body and would not be moved. Their mother, Anna, had also fallen. Most in the pack sustained minor wounds. Ackerman and Jonas Abbot each took rounds but survived.

In the end, nine security personnel had died along with six members of the pack. Not including the hunters that died at the industrial park, Elias counted twenty-six hunter corpses on the manor grounds.

"We will have to move quickly," he said. Most of the pack shifted back to their human forms and retrieved their clothing.

"Yes," Gennesaret said. "The police will be arriving shortly."

"Have all the files been created?"

"Yes, dear, of course."

In order to explain any kind of attack that Copeland Manor might suffer, Elias and Gennesaret had contingency plans ready to implement at a moment's notice: an international client of Copeland Enterprises, who had made investments through shell corporations, had been using Copeland to launder money. Copeland discovered the breach and had been just about to alert the authorities when the client became aware of Copeland's discovery. A team of private military contractors had been hired by the client to put a stop to Copeland's plans to reveal the crime. Fortunately, Copeland's security forces had been enough to repel that attack. Files, trade blotters, and records had been preloaded into Copeland Enterprises's servers. The story would hold up.

"Ackerman," Elias said. "I'll leave things with you for the cleanup."

"Yes, sir."

Elias held a hand out to his wife. "Genn, let's go see our son."

"He is not dead," Gennesaret said. "I feel him as only a mother can." And then Gennesaret smiled. "And Shelby shifted. I am proud of her."

Elias nodded.

"She did?" Sadie squealed. "Really?"

"Did you not feel her reassurance and comfort during the battle?" Gennesaret asked. "I think she radiates it subconsciously."

"Whoa," Sadie said. "That's what that was?" She looked at Bubba. "I actually thought I felt confident because you were with me, Deshawn."

Bubba looked stunned, whether because of the use of his real name or her unexpected civility, Elias could not tell. Bubba smiled widely.

"Really?"

Sadie's eyebrows pitched. "No."

"Cold. Just cold."

"You know Bubba Tubba, we don't let humans know our secret and live."

Bubba swallowed. "I ain't gonna tell."

"Nothing for it," Sadie said. "I'm going to have to turn you."

"What's that? What you mean, girl?"

Sadie lowered her chin, her red hair falling around her face, staring at Bubba from beneath her eyebrows, and took a single step toward the large man with a low growl coming from her chest. He flinched and moved back, stumbling and falling on his butt.

Sadie laughed. "You'd just become a panda bear if I turned you."

"Hey, they're cute right?" Bubba said, laughing with obvious relief.

"Deshawn," Gennesaret said, "we will have that discussion I mentioned earlier."

"The one you talked about when you were naked?"

"We'll also discuss maturity."

Bubba's smile disappeared. "Yes, ma'am. Should I invite my momma?"

"Most assuredly not," Gennesaret said with a soft smile. "Do not leave until Elias and I return."

It was then that a hunter, lying slumped in a corner and presumed dead, weakly raised a pistol. Elias saw the motion in his peripheral vision but did not register the danger until he heard the shot. But Gennesaret had seen the action and put herself in front of her husband. The silver bullet struck her back. Gennesaret fell forward into Elias, and he caught her.

"Genn?" Elias felt his throat constrict.

Her eyes blinked wide. Her mouth gasped for breath.

Elias held her, kneeling to the floor as her legs weakened.

"Genn!" Elias roared, calling her name as her husband and as her Alpha.

Her eyelids fluttered, responding to his call. She found her voice. "I'm okay." She actually smiled with what Elias knew to be nervous relief.

He patted her back, gently, searching for the wound he knew was there. He found it, and felt the warm wetness. The wound was right at the top of her back, right at the spinal cord. His fingers came away bloody.

"You're not okay," he said. "You've been shot in the spine."

"It's just shock," she said, blinking. "It was just a graze."

Elias shook his head, the muscles in his forehead contracted with worry. "No, I saw—"

"Bloody Hades," Sadie said with hoarse amazement. Elias looked up and saw Sadie pointing. The bullet, its tip flattened, hung in the air, spinning.

"I'm sorry, Mrs. C.," Bubba said with a strained voice. "I couldn't catch it fast enough. Hope I got it before it did too much damage."

Sadie turned with utter astonishment to Bubba. Deep lines of concentration formed in his forehead, collecting streams of sweat before it spilled over down his cheeks. His eyes were locked on to the bullet.

"What?" he said, obviously feeling all stares on him, but not breaking his focus. "Y'all ain't never seen *The Matrix*?"

"Deshawn," Gennesaret said, a bit breathless. "You're a PK."

"What's that? A player killer?"

"Psychokinetic."

The hunter, obviously also stunned, raised his pistol again. Before he could pull the trigger, the bullet zipped through the air and struck him in the forehead. His arm fell limp and the gun clattered on to the ground.

"I don't know where y'all get off calling me psycho," Bubba said, wiping the sweat from his face. "Y'all get naked and turn into dogs."

Gennesaret, still a little shaky, stood. Elias helped her up and felt her back, gingerly. He did indeed discover her wound to be superficial. It had already started healing. He exhaled deep relief as he raised his head, eyes to the ceiling. "Thank you," he whispered.

"I'm right here, Mr. C."

Elias chuckled. "Deshawn, how long have you known?"

"About y'all? Not until tonight. I thought I was the only freak in town. I'm starting to wonder if I should call animal protection."

"No, about your abilities."

Bubba shrugged. "Ever since my balls dropped and I got fat."

Gennesaret grimaced. "Yes, we're definitely going to have that talk still." Then, she hugged Bubba and held the embrace for several long seconds. "Thank you."

"Seriously, people, my stomach is rumbling. You know how much of my metabolism it takes to deflect and stop bullets."

"The hallway," Sadie said softly. Her eyes took in Bubba, looking him up and down, her mouth slightly opened. "Where . . . did you go?"

Bubba patted his torso and stomach. His Wilfork jersey suddenly appeared three sizes too big. Pulling up the front of his shirt, he knocked a fist against rock hard abs. "Like I said, people, I need to refuel. Takes a lot out of me." His stomach grumbled loudly. Elias saw Sadie blinking rapidly.

"So," she said, more breathlessly than she would have probably liked. "You're a PK?"

Bubba shrugged broad and square shoulders. "Guess so."

Sadie blinked again. "OMG. That's . . . so freaking hot."

EPILOGUE

Mareus leaped off the bow of the sleek speed boat just before its hull met the Gulf Coast beach, and scanned the vacant shoreline. The familiar sting came as he called upon his wolf's—Viersin's—eyes to give him greater sight. He curled his toes as his bare feet sank into the wet sand.

So this is what Texas feels like.

In truth, it was the first time he had ever been to this hemisphere in his centuries of life. Odd, that, but he supposed he felt rooted to the land now called Europe, where he had arrived after fleeing Alsvoira. He had failed to see the Advent to fruition on that world. He would not fail here.

Even past midnight he could still feel the thick humidity in the air. It was like holding a warm cloth over his mouth as he breathed.

Ascension is near. Yes, that higher communion between humans and werewolves could now happen. In one arm, he clutched the *Isluxua,* now freed from its magical preservation capsule. The ancient book held the secrets of the Immortal Wolves, though translating the ancient language, even with Viersin's help, had progressed frustratingly slowly.

Still, so much has been revealed . . . He gently rubbed—caressed—the edges of the *Isluxua's* brittle pages.

Athena, his daughter, landed next to him on the beach in her seductive human form, followed by Otto. The former German Alpha stood a little too close to her. Tepid waves washed over their ankles, and Mareus felt the sand get pulled away beneath his feet by the undertow. Two other speed boats, each ferrying six Lycans in human form, anchored on the beach.

"Why did we come here, my Alpha Prime?" Otto asked. "We should have joined the rest of the pack invading through Canada."

"I feel them," Mareus said. "My . . . parents."

"Daeglan and Thyra?" Athena asked.

"After a manner."

"Will Skotha and Eira have forgotten Alsvoira, as you had, Father?" Athena asked.

It was true. Mareus had forgotten his home world as he journeyed here through the crystal portal of Alsvoira. The portal had enshrouded his mind in some kind of veil, stealing his memories. Viersin, his wolf, had not forgotten, but had slumbered for centuries before awakening within him. That also seemed a repercussion of the crystal portal's usage. For ages, he had been a rogue, a freak that could not die. No family. No understanding of who he was, of his *birthright*. Oh, grand were the revelations that flooded him when Viersin had awakened! As was the violence.

Mareus felt the longing in his daughter to see where her father had come from, the world of the Immortal Wolves. She would never see it, of course. He had left it no more than a smoldering rock in vengeance.

"No," Mareus said. "Skotha and Eira will not have forgotten.

They have been in a type of discarnate hibernation, waiting for their humans to be reborn. And . . ." Mareus paused. "They have found each other. Their bond beckons to me as their son."

Daeglan and Thyra had perished long ago, killed by hunters on Earth shortly after their Immortal Wolves had awakened. Their control had been . . . weak. Though reborn, they were not *really* his parents any longer.

"But their bond is not yet as it once was. It is young. Fragile, still."

Athena smiled wickedly. "Bonds can be broken."

ACKNOWLEDGMENTS

Many people are a critical part of any story's creation. To each of these, we extend heartfelt thanks. To our beta readers, who helped us shape the story and avoid some pot holes. To Rachel, whose eagle eyes caught even the most minor of typos. To Renee, for anxiously demanding (sometimes under threat of violence) more of the story as it unfolded. To Deranged Doctor Design, for a killer cover. To Kate Reading, for bringing the story to life magnificently in audio form. To September C. Fawkes, editor extraordinaire, for her deep insights into the characters, the plot, and the execution of excellent storytelling. To the folks at Audible Studios, for taking a chance on a new adventure in a new genre for us as authors.

ABOUT THE AUTHORS

JK Cooper is a husband and wife writing team. They write paranormal romance and romantic urban fantasy. After nearly two decades of marriage and four children, they have plenty to write about. When not writing about werewolves and the end of the world, they enjoy spending time with their family, traveling, reading, making fun of social media, and outdoor power sports (and watching Glimore Girls reruns … well, K does). They live in Utah with their four daughters and two massive Akitas.

JK Cooper loves hearing from their readers! For updates, sneak peeks, and werewolf sightings, join our newsletter! Sign up here:
https://authorjkcooper.com/newsletter
Facebook: facebook.com/authorJKCooper/
Twitter: @authorJKCooper

Want to follow some of the characters in
The Summer Omega Series on Twitter?

Shelby Brooks @SummerOmega
Sadie Chandler @redhairbites
Bubba @Bubba_Tubba